WAR LORD

BERNARD CORNWELL

War Lord

HarperCollins*Publishers*

HarperCollins*Publishers*
1 London Bridge Street
London SE1 9GF

www.harpercollins.co.uk

HarperCollins*Publishers*
1st Floor, Watermarque Building, Ringsend Road
Dublin 4, Ireland

This paperback edition 2021
1

First published in Great Britain by HarperCollins*Publishers* 2020

A catalogue record for this book
is available from the British Library

ISBN: 978-0-00-818398-1 (b-format)
ISBN: 978-0-00-818399-8 (a-format)

This novel is entirely a work of fiction.
The names, characters and incidents portrayed in it, while
at times based on historical figures, are the work of the author's imagination.

Set in Meridien by Palimpsest Book Production Limited,
Falkirk, Stirlingshire

Printed and bound in Great Britain by
CPI Group (UK) Ltd, Croydon, CR0 4YY

MIX
Paper from
responsible sources
FSC C007454

This book is produced from independently certified FSC™ paper
to ensure responsible forest management.

For more information visit: www.harpercollins.co.uk/green

War Lord
is for Alexander Dreymon

CONTENTS

PLACE NAMES

The spelling of place names in Anglo-Saxon England was an uncertain business, with no consistency and no agreement even about the name itself. Thus London was variously rendered as Lundonia, Lundenberg, Lundenne, Lundene, Lundenwic, Lundenceaster and Lundres. Doubtless some readers will prefer other versions of the names listed below, but I have usually employed whichever spelling is cited in either the *Oxford Dictionary of English Place-Names* or the *Cambridge Dictionary of English Place-Names* for the years nearest or contained within Alfred's reign, AD 871–899, but even that solution is not foolproof. Hayling Island, in 956, was written as both Heilincigae and Hæglingaiggæ. Nor have I been consistent myself; I have preferred the modern form Northumbria to Norðhymbralond to avoid the suggestion that the boundaries of the ancient kingdom coincide with those of the modern county. So this list of places mentioned in the book is, like the spellings themselves, capricious.

Bebbanburg	Bamburgh, Northumberland
Brynstæþ	Brimstage, Cheshire
Burgham	Eamont Bridge, Cumbria
Cair Ligualid	Carlisle, Cumbria
Ceaster	Chester, Cheshire
Dacore	Dacre, Cumbria
Dingesmere	Wallasey Pool, Cheshire
Dun Eidyn	Edinburgh, Scotland
Dunholm	Durham, County Durham
Eamotum	River Eamont

Eoferwic	York, Yorkshire
Farnea Islands	Farne Islands, Northumberland
Foirthe	River Forth
Heahburh	Whitley Castle, Cumbria
Hedene	River Eden
Hlymrekr	Limerick, Ireland
Jorvik	Norse name for York
Lauther	River Lowther
Legeceasterscir	Cheshire
Lindcolne	Lincoln, Lincolnshire
Lindisfarena	Lindisfarne Island, Northumbria
Lundene	London
Mærse	The Mersey
Mameceaster	Manchester
Mön	Isle of Man
Orkneyjar	Orkney Islands
Rammesburi	Ramsbury, Wiltshire
Ribbel	River Ribble
Scipton	Skipton, Yorkshire
Snæland	Iceland
Snotengaham	Nottingham, Nottinghamshire
Sumorsæte	Somerset
Strath Clota	Strathclyde
Suðreyjar	Hebrides
Temes	River Thames
Tesa	River Tees
Tinan	River Tyne
Tuede	River Tweed
Wiltunscir	Wiltshire
Wir	River Wyre
Wirhealum	The Wirral, Cheshire

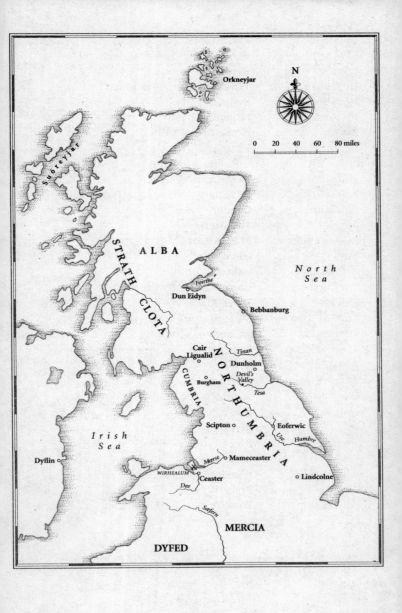

PART ONE

The Broken Oath

ONE

Chain mail is hot in summer, even when covered with a pale linen shift. The metal is heavy and heats relentlessly. Beneath the mail is a leather liner, and that is hot too, and the sun that morning was furnace hot. My horse was irritable, tormented by flies. There was hardly any wind across the hills that crouched under the midday sun. Aldwyn, my servant, carried my spear and my iron-bound shield that was painted with the wolf's head of Bebbanburg. Serpent-Breath, my sword, hung on my left side, her hilt almost too hot to touch. My helmet, with its silver wolf's head crest, was on the saddle's pommel. The helmet would encase my whole head, was lined with leather, and had cheek-pieces that laced over my mouth so all an enemy would see were my eyes framed in battle-steel. They would not see the sweat or the scars of a lifetime of war.

They would see the wolf's head, the gold about my neck, and the thick arm rings won in battle. They would know me, and the bravest of them, or the stupidest, would want to kill me for the renown my death would bring. Which is why I had brought eighty-three men to the hill, because to kill me they would have to deal with my warriors too. We were the warriors of Bebbanburg, the savage wolf pack of the north. And one priest.

The priest, mounted on one of my stallions, wore no mail nor carried a weapon. He was half my age, yet already showed grey at his temples. He had a long face, clean-shaven, with shrewd eyes. He wore a long black robe and had a golden cross hanging from his neck. 'Aren't you hot in that dress?' I growled at him.

'Uncomfortably,' he said. We spoke in Danish, his native language and the tongue of my childhood.

'Why,' I asked, 'am I always fighting for the wrong side?'

He smiled at that. 'Even you can't escape fate, Lord Uhtred. You must do God's work whether you wish it or not.'

I bit back an angry retort and just stared into the wide treeless valley where the sun glared off pale rocks and shivered silver from a small stream. Sheep grazed high on the eastern hillside. The shepherd had seen us and was trying to move his flock south away from us, but his two dogs were hot, tired and thirsty and they panicked the sheep rather than herded them. The shepherd had nothing to fear from us, but he saw riders on the hill and saw sunlight glinting from weapons and so he feared. Deep in the valley the Roman road, now little more than a track of beaten earth edged with half-buried and overgrown stones, ran straight as a spear-haft beside the stream before bending west just beneath the hill where we waited. A hawk circled above the road's bend, the still wings tilting to the warm air. The far southern horizon shimmered.

And from the shimmer one of my scouts appeared, galloping hard, and that meant only one thing. The enemy was coming.

I took my men and the one priest back so we were behind the skyline. I pulled Serpent-Breath a hand's breadth from her scabbard, then let her rest again. Aldwyn offered me

4

the shield, but I shook my head. 'Wait till we see them,' I told him. I gave him my helmet to hold, dismounted, and walked with Finan and my son to the crest where we lay staring southwards. 'It all feels wrong,' I said.

'It's fate,' Finan answered, 'and fate is a bitch.' We lay in the long grass watching the dust kicked up from the road by the scout's stallion. 'He should have ridden along the road's edge,' Finan said, 'no dust there.'

The scout, who I recognised now as Oswi, swerved off the road and began the long climb to the hilltop where we lay.

'You're sure about the dragon?' I asked.

'Can't miss a big beast like that,' Finan said, 'the creature came from the north, so it did.'

'And the star fell from north to south,' my son said, reaching under his chest to touch his cross. My son is a Christian.

The dust in the valley died away. The enemy was coming, except I was not sure who my enemy was, only that this day I must fight the king coming from the south. And that felt all wrong, because the star and the dragon had said that evil would come from the north.

We look for omens. Even Christians search the world for such signs. We watch the flight of birds, fear the fall of a branch, look for the wind's pattern on water, draw breath at a vixen's cry, and touch our amulets when a harp string snaps, but omens are hard to read unless the gods decide to make their message plain. And three nights before, in Bebbanburg, the gods had sent a message that could not have been clearer.

That evil would come from the north.

The dragon had flown in the night sky above Bebbanburg. I did not see it, but Finan did and I trust Finan. It was vast, he said, with a skin like hammered silver, eyes like burning coals, and with wings wide enough to hide the stars. Each beat of those monstrous wings made the sea shiver like a burst of wind on a calm day. It had turned its head towards Bebbanburg, and Finan thought fire was about to be spewed across the whole fortress, but then the great slow wings beat once more, the sea shuddered far beneath, and the dragon flew on southwards.

'And a star fell last night,' Father Cuthbert said, 'Mehrasa saw it.' Father Cuthbert, Bebbanburg's priest, was blind and married to Mehrasa, an exotic dark-skinned girl we had rescued from a slave-trader in Lundene many years before. I call her a girl out of habit, but of course she was middle-aged now. We grow old, I thought.

'The star fell from the north towards the south,' Father Cuthbert said.

'And the dragon came from the north,' Finan added.

I said nothing. Benedetta leaned on my shoulder. She too said nothing, but her hand tightened on mine.

'Signs and wonders,' Father Cuthbert said, 'something dire will happen.' He crossed himself.

It was an early summer evening. We were sitting outside Bebbanburg's hall where swallows flew around the eaves and where the long waves rolled incessantly against the beach beneath the eastern ramparts. The waves give us rhythm, I thought, an endless sound that rises and falls. I had been born to that sound and soon I must die. I touched my hammer amulet and prayed that I would die to the sound of Bebbanburg's waves and to the cry of her gulls.

'Something dire,' Father Cuthbert repeated, 'and it will come from the north.'

Or maybe the dragon and the falling star were omens of my death? I touched the hammer again. I can still ride a horse, heft a shield, and wield a sword, but at day's end the aches in my joints tell me I am old. 'The worst thing about death,' I broke my silence, 'is not knowing what happens next.'

No one spoke for a while, then Benedetta squeezed my hand again. 'You are a fool,' she said fondly.

'Always has been,' Finan put in.

'You can watch what happens from Valhalla perhaps?' Father Cuthbert suggested. As a Christian priest he was not supposed to believe in Valhalla, but he had long learned to indulge me. He smiled. 'Or join the church of Rome, lord?' he said mischievously. 'I assure you that from heaven you can watch earth!'

'In all your efforts to convert me,' I said, 'I never heard you say there was ale in heaven.'

'I forgot to mention that?' he asked, still smiling.

'There will be wine in heaven,' Benedetta said, 'good wine from Italy.'

That provoked silence. None of us much liked wine. 'I hear King Hywel has gone to Italy,' my son said after the pause, 'or perhaps he's just thinking of going?'

'To Rome?' Finan asked.

'So they say.'

'I would like to go to Rome,' Father Cuthbert said wistfully.

'There is nothing in Rome,' Benedetta said scornfully. 'It is ruins and rats.'

'And the Holy Father,' Cuthbert said gently.

Again no one spoke. Hywel, whom I liked, was King of Dyfed and if he thought it was safe to travel to Rome then there had to be peace between his Welshmen and the Saxons of Mercia, so no trouble there. But the dragon had not come from the south, nor from the west, it had come from the north. 'The Scots,' I said.

'Too busy fighting the Norsemen,' Finan said brusquely.

'And raiding Cumbria,' my son said bitterly.

'And Constantine is old,' Father Cuthbert added.

'We're all old,' I said.

'And Constantine would rather build monasteries than make war,' Cuthbert went on.

7

I doubted that was true. Constantine was King of Scotland. I enjoyed meeting him, he was a wise and elegant man, but I did not trust him. No Northumbrian trusts the Scots, just as no Scot trusts the Northumbrians. 'It will never end,' I said wanly.

'What?' Benedetta asked.

'War. Trouble.'

'When we are all Christians . . .' Father Cuthbert began.

'Ha!' I said curtly.

'But the dragon and the star do not lie,' he went on. 'The trouble will come from the north. The prophet has told us so in the scriptures! "*Quia malum ego adduco ab aquilone et contritionem magnam.*"' He paused, hoping one of us would ask him to translate.

'I will bring evil from the north,' Benedetta disappointed him, 'and much destroying.'

'Much destruction!' Father Cuthbert said ominously. 'Evil will come from the north! It is written!'

And next morning the evil came.

From the south.

The ship came from the south. There was hardly a breath of wind, the sea was lazy, its small waves collapsing exhausted on Bebbanburg's long beach. The approaching ship, its prow crested with a cross, left a widening ripple that was touched with glittering gold by the early morning sun. She was being rowed, her oars rising and falling in a slow, weary rhythm. 'Poor bastards must have been rowing all night,' Berg said. He commanded the morning's guards posted on Bebbanburg's ramparts.

'Forty oars,' I said, more to make conversation than to tell Berg what he could plainly see for himself.

'And coming here.'

'From where, though?'

Berg shrugged. 'What's happening today?' he asked.

8

It was my turn to shrug. What would happen was what always happened. Cauldrons would be lit to boil clothes clean, salt would evaporate in the pans north of the fortress, men would practise with shields, swords and spears, horses exercised, fish would be smoked, water drawn from the deep wells, and ale brewed in the fortress kitchens. 'I plan to do nothing,' I said, 'but you can take two men and remind Olaf Einerson that he owes me rent. A lot of rent.'

'His wife's ill, lord.'

'He said that last winter.'

'And he lost half his flock to Scotsmen.'

'More likely he sold them,' I said sourly. 'No one else has complained of Scottish raiders this spring.' Olaf Einerson had inherited his tenancy from his father, who had never failed to deliver fleeces or silver as rent. Olaf, the son, was a big and capable man whose ambitions, it seemed to me, went beyond raising hardy sheep on the high hills. 'On second thoughts,' I said, 'take fifteen men and scare the shit out of the bastard. I don't trust him.'

The ship was close enough now that I could see three men sitting just forward of the stern platform. One was a priest, or at least he was wearing a long black robe and it was he who stood and waved up at our ramparts. I did not wave back. 'Whoever they are,' I told Berg, 'bring them to the hall. They can watch me drink ale. And wait before you smack some sense into Olaf.'

'Wait, lord?'

'Let's see what news they're bringing first,' I said, nodding at the ship that was now turning towards the narrow entrance of Bebbanburg's harbour. The ship carried no cargo that I could see, and her oarsmen looked bone weary, suggesting that she brought urgent news. 'She's from Æthelstan,' I guessed.

'Æthelstan?' Berg asked.

9

'She's not a Northumbrian ship, is she?' I asked. Northumbrian ships had narrower prows, while southern shipwrights preferred a broad bow. Besides, this ship displayed the cross which few Northumbrian ships carried. 'And who uses priests to carry messages?'

'King Æthelstan.'

I watched the ship turn into the entrance channel, then led Berg off the ramparts. 'Look after his oarsmen. Send them food and ale, and bring the damn priest to the hall.'

I climbed to the hall where two servants were attacking cobwebs with long willow switches tied with bundles of feathers. Benedetta was watching to make sure every last spider was driven from the fortress. 'We have visitors,' I told her, 'so your war against spiders must wait.'

'I am not at war,' she insisted, 'I like spiders. But not in my home. Who are the visitors?'

'I'm guessing they're messengers from Æthelstan.'

'Then we must greet them properly!' She clapped her hands and ordered benches to be brought. 'And bring the throne from the platform,' she commanded.

'It's not a throne,' I said, 'just a fancy bench.'

'*Ouff!*' she said. It was a noise Benedetta made whenever I exasperated her. It made me smile, which only irritated her more. 'It is a throne,' she insisted, 'and you are King of Bebbanburg.'

'Lord,' I corrected her.

'You are as much a king as that fool Guthfrith,' she made the sign to ward off evil, 'or Owain, or anyone else.' It was an old argument and I let it drop.

'And have the girls bring ale,' I said, 'and some food. Preferably not stale.'

'And you should wear the dark robe. I fetch it.'

Benedetta was from Italy, snatched as a child from her home by slavers, then traded across Christendom until she

10

reached Wessex. I had freed her and now she was the Lady of Bebbanburg, though not my wife. 'My grandmother,' she had told me more than once, and always making the sign of the cross as she spoke, 'told me I should never marry. I would be cursed! I have been cursed enough in life. Now I am happy! Why should I risk a grandmother's curse? My grandmother was never wrong!'

I grumpily allowed her to drape the costly black robe over my shoulders, refused to wear the bronze-gilt circlet that had belonged to my father, and then, with Benedetta beside me, I waited for the priest.

And it was an old friend who came from the sunlight into the dusty shadows of Bebbanburg's great hall. It was Father Oda, now Bishop of Rammesburi, who walked tall and elegant, his long black robe hemmed with dark red cloth. He was escorted by a pair of West Saxon warriors who politely gave my steward their swords before following Oda towards me. 'Anyone would think,' the bishop said as he came closer, 'that you were a king!'

'He is,' Benedetta insisted.

'And anyone would think,' I said, 'that you were a bishop.'

He smiled. 'By the grace of God, Lord Uhtred, I am.'

'By the grace of Æthelstan,' I said, then stood and greeted him with an embrace. 'Do I congratulate you?'

'If you like. I think I am the first Dane to be a bishop in Englaland.'

'Is that what you call it now?'

'It's easier than saying I am the first Danish bishop in Wessex, Mercia and East Anglia.' He bowed to Benedetta. 'It is good to see you again, my lady.'

'And to see you, my lord bishop,' she said, offering him a curtsey.

'Ah! So rumour is wrong! Courtesy does live in Bebbanburg!' He grinned at me, pleased with his jest and I smiled back. Oda, Bishop of Rammesburi! The only surprising thing about that appointment was that Oda was a Dane, son of pagan immigrants who had invaded East Anglia in the service of Ubba, whom I had killed. And now the Danish son of pagan parents was a bishop in Saxon Englaland! Not that he did not deserve it. Oda was a subtle, clever man who, as far as I knew, was as honest as the day is long.

There was a pause because Finan had seen Oda arrive and now came to greet him. Oda had been with us when we defended Lundene's Crepelgate, a fight that had put Æthelstan on the throne. I might be no Christian and no lover of Christianity, but it is hard to dislike a man who has shared a desperate battle at your side. 'Ah, wine,' Oda greeted a servant, then turned to Benedetta, 'no doubt blessed by the Italian sun?'

'More likely pissed on by Frankish peasants,' I said.

'His charms don't grow less, do they, my lady?' Oda said, sitting. Then he looked at me and touched the heavy gold cross hanging at his breast. 'I bring news, Lord Uhtred.' His tone was suddenly wary.

'I supposed as much.'

'Which you won't like.' Oda kept his eyes on me.

'Which I won't like,' I echoed, and waited.

'King Æthelstan,' he said calmly, still looking at me, 'is in Northumbria. He entered Eoferwic three days ago.' He paused, as if expecting me to protest, but I said nothing. 'And King Guthfrith,' Oda went on, 'misunderstood our coming and has fled.'

'Misunderstood,' I said.

'Indeed.'

'And he fled from you and Æthelstan? Just the two of you?'

'Of course not,' Oda said, still calm, 'we were escorted by over two thousand men.'

I had fought enough, I wanted to stay at Bebbanburg, I

wanted to hear the long sea break on the beach and the wind sigh around the hall's gable. I knew I had few years left, but the gods had been kind. My son was a man and would inherit wide lands, I could still ride and hunt, and I had Benedetta. True she had a temper like a weasel on heat, but she was loving and loyal, had a brightness that lit Bebbanburg's grey skies, and I loved her. 'Two thousand men,' I said flatly, 'yet still he needs me?'

'He requests your help, lord, yes.'

'He can't manage the invasion on his own?' I was getting angrier.

'It's not an invasion, lord,' Oda said calmly, 'just a royal visitation. A courtesy between kings.'

He could call it what he liked, but it was still an invasion.

And I was angry.

I was furious because Æthelstan had once sworn an oath that he would never invade Northumbria while I lived. Yet now he was in Eoferwic with an army, and I had eighty-three men waiting behind the crest of a hill not far south of Bebbanburg to do his bidding. I had wanted to refuse Oda, I had wanted to tell him to take his damned ship back to Eoferwic and spit in Æthelstan's face. I felt betrayed. I gave Æthelstan his throne, yet since that far-off day when I had fought at the Crepelgate he had ignored me, and that did not upset me. I am a Northumbrian and live far from Æthelstan's land, and all I wanted was to be left in peace. Yet deep inside I knew there could not be peace. When I was born, Saxon Britain was divided into four countries; Wessex, Mercia, East Anglia and my own Northumbria. King Alfred, Æthelstan's grandfather, had dreamed of uniting them into one country he called Englaland, and that dream was coming true. King Æthelstan ruled over Wessex, Mercia and East Anglia, and only Northumbria remained, and Æthelstan had sworn to me that he would not snatch that land while I lived, yet now he was in my country with an army, and he was pleading for my help. Again. And deep down I knew that Northumbria was doomed, that either Æthelstan would take my country or Constantine would add it to his lands, and my loyalty was to those who spoke my language, the Saxon tongue we call Ænglisc, and that was why I had led eighty-three warriors from Bebbanburg to ambush King Guthfrith of Northumbria who had fled from Æthelstan's invasion. The sun burned high and bright, the day was still.

Oswi, on a sweat-whitened horse, brought news of Guthfrith's approach. 'Soon, lord,' he said.

'How many?'

'A hundred and fourteen. Some prisoners too.'

'Prisoners?' Bishop Oda, who had insisted on accompanying us, asked sharply. 'We were only expecting one captive.'

'They've got some women, lord,' Oswi still spoke to me. 'They're driving them like sheep.'

'The women are on foot?' I asked.

'Some of the men too, lord. And a lot of the horses are limping. They've ridden fast!' He took a leather flask from Roric, swilled out his mouth with ale, spat into the grass, and took another swig. 'They look as if they've been travelling all night.'

'And so they might have,' I said, 'to have got this far so quickly.'

'They're worn out now,' Oswi said happily.

Bishop Oda had brought me his news from Eoferwic and his ship had made the journey in two days despite the fitful winds, but the men approaching on the long straight road had fled the city on horseback. I reckoned to take a week to ride from Bebbanburg to Eoferwic, though admittedly that was slow and allowed me long nights in friendly halls. I had once ridden it in four days, but never in heat like this

14

early summer. The fugitives from Eoferwic had fled fast and they had ridden fast, but Bishop Oda's oarsmen had easily overtaken them and now the weary horses were bringing them into our ambush.

'It is not an ambush,' Bishop Oda insisted when I used the word. 'We are merely here to persuade King Guthfrith to return to Eoferwic. And King Æthelstan requests your presence in Eoferwic too.'

'Mine?' I said curtly.

'Indeed. And he also requires you to gain the release of Guthfrith's captive.'

'Captives,' I corrected him.

'Indeed,' Oda said dismissively. 'But Guthfrith must be returned to Eoferwic. He simply needs reassurance that King Æthelstan comes in friendship.'

'With over two thousand men? All in mail, all armed?'

'King Æthelstan likes to travel in style,' Oda responded loftily.

Æthelstan might describe his visit to Eoferwic as a friendly visitation, but there had still been fighting in the city because in truth it had been a conquest, a lightning fast invasion and, reluctant as I was to give Æthelstan any credit, I had to admire what he had achieved. Oda had told me how Æthelstan had brought an army of over two thousand men across the Mercian border, then led them at a relentless pace northwards, abandoning any man or horse that faltered or weakened. They pounded the road, reaching Eoferwic while their presence in Northumbria was still an unconfirmed rumour. The city's southern gate was opened by West Saxon warriors who had infiltrated Eoferwic pretending to be merchants, and Æthelstan's army had flooded into the streets. 'There was some fighting on the bridge,' Oda had told me, 'but by the grace of God the pagans were defeated and the survivors fled.'

Those survivors were led by Guthfrith, and Æthelstan had sent Bishop Oda with a demand that I bar the northern roads and so keep Guthfrith from escaping into Scotland. Which is why I waited on the hillside under the burning sun. Finan, my son and I were prone on the crest, staring southwards, while Bishop Oda was crouched behind us. 'And why,' I asked him sourly, 'shouldn't Guthfrith escape to Scotland?'

Oda sighed at my stupidity. 'Because it gives Constantine a reason to invade Northumbria. He'll simply claim he's restoring the rightful king to his throne.'

'Constantine is Christian,' I said, 'why would he fight for a pagan king?'

Oda sighed again, his eyes on the far distance where the road vanished in the heat. 'King Constantine,' he said, 'would sacrifice his own daughters to Baal if it increased the size of his realm.'

'Who's Baal?' Finan asked.

'A heathen god,' Oda said dismissively, 'and how long do you think Constantine would tolerate Guthfrith? He'll put him back on his throne, marry him to one of his daughters, then have him quietly strangled, and the Scots will own Northumbria. So no, Guthfrith must not reach Scotland.'

'There,' Finan said, and in the far distance a group of horsemen appeared on the road. I could just see them, a blur of horses and men in the summer haze. 'They're tired right enough,' Finan said.

'We want Guthfrith alive,' Oda warned me, 'and back in Eoferwic.'

'You told me,' I grumbled, 'and I still don't know why.'

'Because King Æthelstan demands it, that's why.'

'Guthfrith is a piece of raddled shit,' I said. 'It would be better to kill him.'

'King Æthelstan demands that you keep him alive. Pray do so.'

16

'And I'm supposed to obey his orders? He's not my king.'

Oda gave me a stern look. 'He is *Monarchus Totius Brittaniae.*' I just stared at him until he offered a translation. 'He is the monarch of all Britain.'

'Is that what he calls himself now?' I asked.

'It is,' Oda said.

I snorted at that. Æthelstan had been calling himself the King of the Saxons and Angles ever since he had been crowned, and he did have some claim to that title, but ruler of all Britain? 'I imagine King Constantine and King Hywel might disagree?' I suggested sourly.

'I'm sure they will,' Oda said calmly, 'but nevertheless King Æthelstan wishes you to prevent Guthfrith from reaching Scotland, and to release his captive unharmed.'

'Captives.'

'Captive.'

'You don't care about the women?' I asked.

'I pray for them, of course. But I pray for peace even more.'

'Peace?' I asked angrily. 'Invading Northumbria brings peace?'

Oda looked pained. 'Britain is unsettled, lord. The Norsemen threaten, the Scots are restless, and King Æthelstan fears a war is coming. And he fears it will be a war more terrible than any we have known. He yearns to avert that slaughter and to that end, lord, he begs you to rescue the captive and send Guthfrith safely home.'

I did not understand why sending Guthfrith home would make peace, but I remembered the dragon flying above Bebbanburg's ramparts and its grim message of war. I looked at Finan, who shrugged as if to say he no more understood than I did, but we had best try to do Æthelstan's bidding. Down in the valley I could see the approaching men more clearly, and see the women captives walking at the rear of the long column of horses. 'So what do we do?' Finan asked.

'We ride down there,' I said, easing my way back from the crest, 'we smile politely, and tell the stupid bastard that he's our prisoner.'

'Guest,' Bishop Oda said.

Roric helped me into the saddle and Aldwyn gave me the silver-crested helmet. The leather liner was uncomfortably hot. I buckled it under my chin, but left the cheek-pieces unlaced, then took my wolf's-head shield from Aldwyn. 'No spear yet,' I told him, 'and if there's any fighting, you stay out of trouble.'

'He used to say that to me,' Roric said, grinning.

'Which is why you're alive,' I growled. Roric had been my servant before Aldwyn, but was now old enough to stand in the shield wall.

'There'll be no fighting,' Bishop Oda said sternly.

'It's Guthfrith,' I said, 'he's a fool, and he fights before he thinks, but I'll do my best to keep the beef-witted idiot alive. Let's go!'

I led my men westwards, always staying out of Guthfrith's sight. When I had last seen him he had been perhaps a half mile from the bend in the road and travelling painfully slowly. We went fast, our horses fresher than his, then turned down the hill and threaded through the pine trees, splashed through the hurrying stream and so reached the road. There we formed a line of two ranks so that when the approaching fugitives appeared they would see two rows of mailed horsemen with bright shields and sun-glinting spearheads. We waited.

I did not like Guthfrith and he did not like me. He had spent three years trying to make me swear an oath of loyalty, and for three years I had refused. Twice he had sent warriors to Bebbanburg, and twice I had kept the Skull Gate barred, daring Guthfrith's spearmen to assault the fortress, and twice they had ridden away.

Now, in the hot sun, his spearmen were on my land again, only this time they were led by Guthfrith himself, and Guthfrith had to be bitter. He believed his kingdom was being stolen, and in a moment he would see my men, see my wolf's head badge on their shields, and he not only disliked me, but would realise he outnumbered me. Bishop Oda might piously hope there would be no fighting, but a cornered Guthfrith would be like a polecat in a sack; maddened and vicious.

And he had hostages.

Not just the women, though they had to be rescued, but Guthfrith, cunning as he was, had snatched Archbishop Hrothweard from his cathedral in Eoferwic. 'During the Mass!' Oda had told me in horrified tones. 'During the Mass! Armed men in the cathedral!'

I wondered whether Guthfrith would dare harm the archbishop. Doing so would make him the enemy of every Christian ruler in Britain, though perhaps Constantine would swallow his anger long enough to put Guthfrith back on Northumbria's throne. A dead archbishop would be a small price to pay for a larger Scotland.

Then they appeared. The first horsemen turning towards us at the bend in the road. They saw us and stopped, and gradually the following warriors joined them. 'We'll go to them,' Oda said.

'We won't,' I said.

'But—'

'You want a slaughter?' I snarled.

'But—' the bishop tried again.

'I go,' I said impulsively.

'You—'

'I go alone.' I gave my shield back to Aldwyn and swung down from the saddle.

'I should come with you,' Oda said.

'And give him two priests as hostages? A bishop as well as an archbishop? He'd like that.'

Oda looked towards Guthfrith's men who were slowly arranging themselves into a line that overlapped ours. At least a score of them were on foot, their horses too lamed to be mounted. All were pulling on helmets and hefting shields that showed Guthfrith's symbol of a long-tusked boar. 'Invite him to come and talk to me,' Oda said, 'promise him he'll be safe.'

I ignored that, looking at Finan instead. 'I'll try to meet Guthfrith halfway,' I told him. 'If he brings men, send me the same number.'

'I'll come,' Finan said, grinning.

'No, you stay here. If trouble starts you'll know when to come, and when you do, come fast.'

He nodded, understanding me. Finan and I had fought together for so long that I rarely needed to explain what I planned. He grinned. 'I'll come like the wind.'

'Lord Uhtred—' Oda began.

'I'll do my best to keep Guthfrith alive,' I interrupted him, 'and the hostages too.'

I was not sure I could succeed in that, but I was certain that if we all rode forward until we were within shouting distance of Guthfrith's men then there would almost certainly be a fight, or else blades would be held at the hostages' throats. Guthfrith was a fool, but a proud fool, and I knew he would refuse a demand that he give up his prisoners and meekly agree to return to Eoferwic. He must refuse because to agree would be to lose face in front of his warriors.

And those warriors were Norsemen, proud Norsemen who believed they were the most feared warriors in all the known world. They outnumbered us and they saw a chance for slaughter and plunder. Many were young, they wanted reputation, they wanted their arms ringed with gold and silver, they wanted their names to be spoken with terror. They wanted to kill me, to take my arm rings, my weapons, my land.

So I walked towards them alone, stopping a little more than halfway between my men and Guthfrith's tired warriors, who were then about a long bowshot away. I waited, and when Guthfrith made no move, I sat on a fallen Roman milestone, pulled off my helmet, and watched the sheep on the far hill crest, then looked up to admire the hawk balancing on the small wind. The bird was circling, so no message from the gods in that.

I had come alone because I wanted Guthfrith alone, or at most with only two or three companions. I was sure he was ready for a fight, but he knew his men were tired and his horses blown, and I reckoned that even a fool like Guthfrith would probably explore the chances of avoiding a fight if he could win this confrontation without sacrificing a dozen or more of his warriors. Besides, he had hostages and doubtless thought he could use them to force me into a humiliating retreat.

And still Guthfrith made no move. He had to be puzzled. He saw that I was alone and apparently unafraid, but a man does not become a king without some measure of cunning, and he was wondering where the trap lay. I decided to let him believe there was no trap and so I stood, kicked at some of the half buried stones in the old road, shrugged, and started walking away.

That prompted him to spur forward. I heard the hooves, turned back, pulled on my helmet, and waited again.

He brought three men. Two were warriors, one of whom was leading a small horse that carried Archbishop Hrothweard who was still dressed in the brightly embroidered robes that Christian priests wear in their churches. He looked unhurt, though tired, his face burned by the sun and his white hair tangled.

I also heard the hooves behind me and glanced back to see that Finan had sent Berg and my son. 'Stay behind me,' I called to them. They had seen that Guthfrith and his two men had drawn swords and they too now pulled their long blades from their scabbards. Berg was behind and to my right, facing the man who held Hrothweard's horse. My son was to my left, confronting the other warrior.

'What—' my son began to ask.

'Say nothing!' I said.

Guthfrith curbed his stallion just two or three paces from me. His plump face, framed by the steel of his helmet, glistened with sweat. His brother, the one-eyed Sigtryggr, had been a handsome man, but Guthfrith had drunk too much ale and eaten too much rich food so that he now sat heavy in the saddle. He had small, suspicious eyes, a flattened nose, and a long, plaited beard that hung down his elaborate mail. His horse had silver trappings, his helmet had a raven's black wing on its crown, and his sword was now held at Hrothweard's throat. 'Lord Archbishop,' I said in greeting.

'Lord Uht—' Hrothweard began, then stopped abruptly as Guthfrith pressed the blade's edge against his gullet.

'Address me first,' Guthfrith growled at me. 'I am your king.'

I looked at him and frowned. 'Remind me of your name?' I said, and heard my son chuckle.

'You want this priest dead?' Guthfrith asked angrily. The pressure of his sword was forcing Hrothweard to lean back in his saddle. His frightened eyes watching me over the grey blade.

'Not particularly,' I said carelessly, 'I like him well enough.'

'Well enough to beg for his life?'

I pretended to think about that question, then nodded. 'I'll beg for his life if you swear to release him, yes.'

Guthfrith sneered at that. 'There will be a price,' he said. I noticed how awkward Guthfrith looked. Hrothweard was

22

on his left, and Guthfrith was holding the sword with his right hand.

'There's always a price,' I said, taking a small step to my left, thus forcing Guthfrith to half turn his head away from Hrothweard. The sword wavered. 'King Æthelstan,' I said, 'merely wishes to speak with you. He promises you both your life and your kingdom.'

'Æthelstan,' Guthfrith said, 'is shit from a swine's arsehole. He wants Northumbria.'

He was right, of course, at least about what Æthelstan wanted. 'Æthelstan,' I said, 'keeps his promises.' Yet in truth Æthelstan had betrayed me, he had broken his promise, yet here I was; doing just what he wanted.

'He promised,' Guthfrith said, 'not to invade Northumbria while you lived, yet he's here!'

'He came to talk with you, nothing else.'

'Maybe I should kill you. Maybe the little turd would like that.'

'You can try,' I said. My son's horse stirred behind me, a hoof clicking against one of the road's broken stones.

Guthfrith edged his horse towards me and swept the sword over and down so the blade was in front of me. 'You have never sworn me an oath of loyalty, Lord Uhtred,' he said, 'yet I am your king.'

'True,' I said.

'Then on your knees, Jarl Uhtred,' he said, sneering at the word 'jarl', 'and give me your sworn oath.'

'And if I don't?'

'Then you will feed Boar Tusk.' I assumed Boar Tusk was the name of his sword that was now close to my face. I could see the nicks in the sharpened edges, could feel the heat of the steel on my cheek, and was dazzled by the sun reflecting brilliant from the vague whorls in the hammered steel. 'Down!' Guthfrith commanded, jerking the blade.

23

I looked up into his small dark and suspicious eyes. 'I shall demand the archbishop's life in exchange for the oath,' I said, 'and the lives of the other hostages.'

'You can demand nothing,' he snarled, 'nothing!' He prodded the sword hard, grating its tip on my mail until it lodged in one of the links, forcing me back a half pace. 'You will be my sworn man,' he said, 'and you will get only what I choose to give. Now down on your knees!' He prodded again, harder.

There was a gasp of astonishment from my son as I knelt meekly and lowered my head. Guthfrith chuckled and held his sword's tip close to my face. 'Kiss the blade,' he said, 'and say the words.'

'Lord King,' I said humbly, and paused. My left hand found a stone about the size of a fist.

'Louder!' Guthfrith snarled.

'Lord King,' I said again, 'I swear by Odin . . .' and with that I brought the stone up and smashed it into the stallion's mouth. I hit the snaffle, crushing the silver decoration, but the blow must have hurt because the horse reared and whinnied. Guthfrith's sword vanished from my sight. 'Now!' I bellowed, though neither my son nor Berg needed the encouragement. Guthfrith was struggling to stay in the saddle of his rearing horse. I stood, cursing the pain in my knees, and seized his sword arm. My son was to my left, keeping that man distracted by thrusting a sword at his belly. I hauled on Guthfrith, pulled again, was jerked to my right by the stallion, but Guthfrith fell at last, crashing down onto the road and I wrenched his sword free, dropped on his belly with my knees, and held Boar Tusk's blade at his straggling beard. 'You'll only get one oath from me, you miserable slime-toad,' I snarled, 'and that's a promise to kill you.'

He lurched up and I forced the sword down hard, which stilled him.

And behind me Finan was charging. My men's spears were lowered, the blades glittering in the harsh sun. Guthfrith's men had been much slower to react, but now they were coming too.

And once again I was not certain I was fighting for the right side.

TWO

Was it the wrong side?

I had no liking for Guthfrith. He was a drunken bully, a fool, and in the short time he had been King of Northumbria he had only succeeded in shrinking its borders. Now, on the hard road, he grunted something and I pressed the sword to silence him.

My son had pierced his enemy through the belly. He had ripped the sword free, turned his horse, then swung the blade back onto the man's neck. It was brutal, it was quick, and it was well done. The man swayed, his horse swerved, and he fell with a thump into the weeds beside the road. His body jerked as the blood stained the dust.

Guthfrith lurched again and I rammed the sword-blade harder, crushing his beard against his throat. 'You're a guest on my land,' I told him, 'so behave yourself.'

Berg had freed Hrothweard. The man holding the arch-bishop's horse had released his grip on the reins, then tried to turn and flee. That was fatal, especially against a man as skilled and fierce as Berg, a Norseman himself. Now the man was writhing on the ground and his horse was trotting away alongside Guthfrith's bloody-mouthed stallion. 'To me, Berg!'

I bellowed. Guthfrith tried to speak and flapped a hand at me. 'Move again,' I told him, 'and I'll cut your fat throat.' He stayed still.

Finan, as he had promised, was coming like the wind, the horses leaving a plume of dust from the dry ground. Our horses were far less tired than Guthfrith's stallions and so Finan had reached me sooner. 'Stop!' I bellowed at Finan over the thunder of hooves. 'Stop! All of you! Stop!' I had to stand and hold my hands wide to make them understand, and Guthfrith tried to haul me down so I smacked his helmet with the flat of Boar's Tusk. He tried to seize the blade and I jerked it back and saw blood start from his hand. 'Idiot,' I snarled and thumped him with the blade again. 'Gerbruht!' I shouted. 'Gerbruht! Come here!'

My men had stopped in a cloud of dust. Gerbruht, a hugely strong Frisian, kicked his stallion towards me and slid from the saddle. 'Lord?'

'Hold him upright,' I said. 'He's a king, but you can hammer the bastard senseless if he struggles.'

Guthfrith's men had been much slower to understand what was happening, but they had finally responded by spurring forward and now saw Gerbruht holding their king upright with a sword-blade at his neck. They slowed and stopped.

Guthfrith did not struggle, just spat at me, which made Gerbruht increase the sword's pressure. 'Keep him alive,' I said reluctantly.

I had captured a king, a king who had wasted his kingdom, robbed his people, and let their enemies ride hard and savage across his western lands. Now King Æthelstan was in Eoferwic, and King Æthelstan was a just king, a stern king, but he was only king because I had fought for him at Lundene's Crepelgate. I had once thought of Æthelstan as a son. I had protected him from powerful

27

enemies, taught him the skills of a warrior, and watched him grow. Yet he had betrayed me. He had sworn never to invade Northumbria while I lived, yet he was here, in Northumbria, with an army.

I am a Northumbrian. My country is the wind-flogged coast and the rain-darkened hills and the gaunt high rocks of the north. From the lush farmlands around Eoferwic to the high pastures where folk scratch a living from thin soil, from the harsh waters where men fish to the bleak moors and deep forests where we hunt the deer, it is a land my ancestors conquered. They settled it, built strong homesteads and fortresses, and then they defended it. We are Saxons and Danes, Norsemen and Angles, and we are Northumbrians.

Yet a little country in a big land has a small future. I knew that. To our north was Constantine's Alba, which we called Scotland, and Constantine feared the Saxons to our south. The Saxons and the Scots were both Christians, and Christians tell us that their god is love, and we must love one another and turn the other cheek, but when land is at stake those beliefs fly away and swords are drawn. Constantine ruled Alba, and Æthelstan ruled Wessex, Mercia and East Anglia, and both wanted Northumbria. 'Northumbria speaks our tongue,' Æthelstan had told me once, 'the tongue of our folk, and they must be part of one country, the country that speaks Ænglisc!'

That was the dream of King Alfred. Back when the Danes seemed to have conquered all of Britain, and when Alfred was a fugitive in the marshes of Sumorsæte, that dream had been as feeble as a dying rushlight. Yet we had fought, we had won, and now King Alfred's grandson ruled all the land of Englaland except my land, Northumbria.

'Fight for me,' a voice said.

I turned and saw it was Guthfrith who had spoken. 'You could have fought at Eoferwic,' I said, 'but you ran away.'

28

He hated me, yet I saw the shudder cross his face as he forced himself to speak calmly. 'You're a pagan, a Northumbrian. You want the Christians to win?'

'No.'

'Then fight for me! My men, your men, and Egil Skallagrimmrson will bring his men!'

'And we'll still be outnumbered six to one,' I said curtly.

'And if we're behind the walls of Bebbanburg?' Guthfrith pleaded. 'What will that matter? Constantine will help us!'

'Then he'll take your kingdom,' I said.

'He promised not to!' he blurted desperately.

I paused. 'Promised?' I asked, but he said nothing. Guthfrith had doubtless spoken in despair and spoken more than he had meant to say, and now regretted it. So Constantine had sent envoys to Eoferwic? And Guthfrith had received them? I wanted to draw Wasp-Sting, my short-sword, and ram it into his belly, but Archbishop Hrothweard was at my side and Bishop Oda had dismounted and now stood beside him.

'Lord King,' Bishop Oda bowed to Guthfrith, 'I am sent with brotherly greetings from King Æthelstan.' Oda looked at Gerbruht. 'Release him, man, release him!'

Guthfrith just stared at Oda as if he could not believe what was happening, while Gerbruht looked at me for confirmation. I nodded reluctantly.

'Lord Uhtred will return your sword, lord King.' Oda spoke reassuringly, as if to a frightened child. 'Please, Lord Uhtred?'

This was madness! Holding Guthfrith as hostage was my only chance of avoiding a slaughter. His men still had drawn swords or levelled spears and they outnumbered us. Guthfrith held out his hand, still bleeding. 'Give it to me!' he demanded. I did not move.

'His sword, lord,' Oda said.

'You want him to fight?' I asked angrily.

'There will be no violence,' Oda spoke to Guthfrith, who paused, then gave an abrupt nod. 'Please return the king's sword, Lord Uhtred,' Oda said very formally. I hesitated. 'Please, lord,' Oda said.

'Stand still,' I snarled at Guthfrith. I ignored his bloody outstretched hand and stood close to him. I was taller by a head, which he did not like, and he flinched when I took hold of his gold-decorated scabbard. He probably thought I was about to steal it, but instead I slid Boar's Tusk through the scabbard's fleece-lined throat, then stepped back and drew Serpent-Breath. Guthfrith put a hand to his sword's hilt, but I twitched Serpent-Breath and he went still.

'King Æthelstan,' Oda said, still calm, 'beseeches a meeting with you, lord King, and he vouches for both your life and your kingdom.'

'Much as Constantine did, no doubt,' I put in.

Oda ignored that. 'There is much to discuss, lord King.'

'This!' Guthfrith snapped, gesturing at me, then at my men. 'Discuss this!'

'A misunderstanding,' Oda said, 'nothing more. A regrettable misunderstanding.'

Archbishop Hrothweard had said nothing, just looked frightened, but now he nodded eagerly. 'King Æthelstan's word can be trusted, lord King.'

'Please,' Bishop Oda looked at me, 'there's no need for a drawn sword, Lord Uhtred. We meet as friends!'

And a woman screamed.

I could not see the hostages, they were hidden by Guthfrith's men, but Finan must have seen something because he spurred his stallion forward, shouting at Guthfrith's men to let him through, but some young fool lifted a spear and urged his horse at Finan. Finan's sword, Soul-Stealer, swept the spear aside, lunged into the man's chest, pierced mail, but seemed to glance off a rib. The young rider leaned back in his saddle, his nerveless hand letting go of the spear, and Finan burst past him, swung Soul-Stealer back onto the man's neck and there was a bellowing of rage, men were turning horses to pursue Finan, which only provoked my men to follow the Irishman. It happened in an eye-blink. One moment the two sides were calm, though wary, then the scream brought a tumult of hooves, bright blades and angry shouts.

Guthfrith was faster than I expected. He shoved Oda hard, making the bishop stagger against Hrothweard, then stumbled away, shouting at his men to bring him a horse. He was heavily built, hot and tired, and I caught him easily, kicked the back of one knee and he sprawled onto the road. He swung an arm at me just as one of his men spurred hard towards us. The man lowered his spear, leaned from the saddle, and Guthfrith swung again, this time trying to hit me with a stone, but his wild swing only knocked the spear shaft aside. The butt of the spear hit me on the arm so hard that I almost dropped Serpent-Breath. Guthfrith was trying to draw his own sword, then Gerbruht barged past me and kicked the scabbard so fiercely that it wrenched the sword's hilt from Guthfrith's hand. The horseman had turned. His piebald stallion was sweat-whitened, its hooves skewing gravel and earth, the man wrenched the reins, his mouth open and his eyes wide beneath the grey helmet's rim. He was young, shouting, though I heard nothing. He spurred savagely, but the horse reared instead, towering above me. The young man had been trying to move his spear from his right to his left hand, but now let the weapon fall and gripped the saddle's high pommel as the horse flailed. Then he half fell backwards as I rammed Serpent-Breath up his thigh, ripping mail, cloth and flesh from his knee to his groin, the blade only wrenched free as his horse bolted, pounding up

31

the road to where my men had pierced Guthfrith's troops like a swine-horn splitting a shield wall.

'Stop it!' Oda shouted, 'stop it!'

Gerbruht had seized Guthfrith and dragged him to his feet. The king had managed to retrieve his fallen sword, but I smacked his arm aside and held Serpent-Breath's bloodied blade across his throat. 'Enough,' I bellowed at the horsemen, loud enough to hurt my throat. 'Enough!'

Guthfrith tried to stab my foot with his blade, but I tightened my own on his gullet. He whimpered and I drew the edge of Serpent-Breath a finger's width across his neck. 'Drop the sword, you bastard,' I whispered.

He dropped it. 'You're choking me,' he croaked.

'Good,' I said, but released the blade's pressure slightly.

A horseman with Guthfrith's boar on his shield spurred towards us. He held a spear low, the blade pointing at me, but then he saw Guthfrith, saw my sword, and he curbed his horse just paces away. He kept the spear pointed at me and I saw his eyes flicking between mine and Guthfrith's scared gaze. He was judging whether a lunge could pierce my shoulder before my sword cut the king's throat. 'Don't be a fool, boy,' I said, but that just seemed to enrage him. He stared at me, raised the spear-blade slightly and I heard the stallion panting, saw the wide whites of its eyes, then suddenly the rider's back arched, his head went back and a second spear-blade appeared.

That second blade came from behind and shattered the boy's spine. It slid through his guts and made a bulge in his mail coat before bursting through the iron links and thumping into the high pommel. Berg had thrust the spear and let go of it as the boy whimpered and gripped the spear-haft that now pinned him to his saddle. Berg drew his sword and wheeled his horse to face the other horsemen, but the fight was already dying. Berg looked at me. 'There's no fight in the bastards, lord!' He edged his horse close to the dying boy and slashed his sword hard down to shear the spear-haft, and the rider, freed now from the saddle, fell.

There had been fight in them, but not much. They had been tired, and Finan's assault had been so fast and so savage that most had tried to avoid battle, and the few that had welcomed it or had been forced to it had suffered. Finan was coming back now, his mail coat drenched with blood. 'Off your horses! Weapons down!' he was shouting at Guthfrith's men, then turned in the saddle to threaten one fool who hesitated to obey. 'On the ground, you miserable turd! Throw your sword on the ground!' The sword fell. Enemies often lost their courage when Finan was in a killing mood.

I kicked Guthfrith's sword well away from him, then let him go. 'You can talk to the royal bastard now,' I told Oda.

Oda hesitated because Finan had spurred close to us. The Irishman nodded at me. 'Young Immar took a nasty cut to the shoulder, but otherwise? We're unhurt, lord. Can't say as much for this bastard.' He tossed something at Guthfrith. 'That's one of your beasts, lord King,' Finan snarled and I saw he had thrown down a severed head that now rolled clumsily towards Guthfrith's feet where it came to a bloody standstill. 'He thought he'd take a child away,' Finan explained to me, 'for his amusement. But the women and bairns are safe now. Your son's guarding them.'

'And you, lord King, are also safe,' Oda said, offering Guthfrith a bow, 'and eager to meet King Æthelstan, I'm sure.' He spoke as if nothing untoward had happened, as if there wasn't a bloody head on the stones or a young man writhing with a shattered spear through his belly. 'The king is eager to meet you!' Oda spoke cheerfully. 'He looks forward to it!'

Guthfrith said nothing. He was trembling, though whether with rage or fear I could not tell. I picked up his sword and tossed it to Gerbruht. 'He won't need that for a while,' I said, which made Guthfrith scowl.

'We must go to Eoferwic, lord King,' Oda went on.

'Praise God,' Hrothweard muttered.

'We have a ship,' Oda said brightly. 'We can be in Eoferwic in two days, three perhaps?'

'Jorvik,' Guthfrith growled, giving Eoferwic its Danish name. 'To Jorvik indeed.'

I had spotted Boldar Gunnarson among the defeated horsemen. He was an older man, grey-bearded, with a missing eye and a leg mangled by a Saxon spear thrust. He had been one of Sigtryggr's most trusted men, a warrior of experience and sense, and I was surprised that he had sworn allegiance to Guthfrith. 'What choice did I have, lord?' he asked when I summoned him. 'I'm old, my family is in Jorvik, where would I go?'

'But to serve Guthfrith?'

Boldar shrugged. 'He's not his brother,' he allowed. Guthfrith's brother had been Sigtryggr, my son-in-law, and a man I had liked and trusted.

'You could have come to me when Sigtryggr died.'

'I thought of that, lord, but Jorvik is home.'

'Then go back there,' I said, 'and take Guthfrith's men with you.'

He nodded, 'I will.'

'And there'll be no trouble, Boldar!' I warned him. 'Leave my villagers alone! If I hear a whisper of theft or rape I'll do the same to your family.'

He flinched at that, but nodded again. 'There'll be no trouble, lord,' he paused, 'but the wounded? Dead?'

'Bury your dead or leave them for the crows. I don't care. And take your wounded with you.'

'Take them where?' Guthfrith demanded. He was remembering he was a king and recovering his arrogance. He pushed me aside to confront Boldar. 'Where?'

'Home!' I turned on him angrily, pushing him in turn. 'Boldar takes your men home, and there'll be no trouble!'

'My men stay with me!' Guthfrith insisted.

'You're going by ship, you miserable turd,' I stepped closer, forcing him to retreat further, 'and there's no room on board. You can take four men. No more than four!'

'Surely—' Oda began, but I interrupted him.

'He takes four!'

He took four.

We went back to Bebbanburg with Guthfrith, his four warriors, and with Archbishop Hrothweard who rode next to Oda. My son escorted the women south, waiting until Boldar and his men were safely gone. The ship that had brought Oda to Bebbanburg would carry him, the archbishop and the captive king south to Eoferwic. 'King Æthelstan also wishes to see you, lord,' Oda reminded me before they sailed.

'He knows where I live.'

'He would like you to come to Eoferwic.'

'I stay here,' I growled.

'He commands you, lord,' Oda said quietly. I said nothing and, when the silence had lasted long enough, Oda shrugged. 'As you wish, lord.'

Next day we watched Oda's ship row from the harbour. The wind was a chilly north-easterly, which filled the sail. I saw the oars brought inboard and the water seethe along her flanks and widen white behind as she passed the Farnea Islands. I watched her till she vanished in a squall of rain far to the south.

'So we're not going to Eoferwic?' Finan asked.

'We're staying here,' I insisted.

Æthelstan, whom I had nurtured as a boy and helped to the throne, now called himself the *Monarchus Totius Brittaniae*, so he could damn well sort out Britain by himself.

I was staying at Bebbanburg.

Two days later I sat with Finan and Benedetta in the morning sunlight. The hot weather of a few days before had given way to an unseasonal cold. Benedetta tucked some windblown strands of hair beneath her cap and shivered. 'Is this summer?'

'Better than the last two days,' Finan said. The chill northeast wind that had driven Oda's ship southwards had brought a sullen stubborn rain that had made me fear for the harvest, but that rain had gone and the sun shone weakly, and if the wind backed, I reckoned, the warmth would return.

'Oda should be in Eoferwic by now,' I said.

'And how long before Æthelstan sends a summons to you?' Finan asked, amused.

'It's probably on its way already.'

'And you go?' Benedetta asked.

'If he asks nicely? Perhaps.'

'Or perhaps not,' Finan added.

We were watching my younger men practise their swordcraft. Berg was teaching them. 'Roric's useless,' I growled.

'He's learning.'

'And look at Immar! Couldn't fight a slug!'

'His arm is still healing.'

'And Aldwyn! He looks like he's cutting hay.'

'He's still a boy, he'll learn.'

I leaned down and scratched the coarse hair of one of my wolfhounds. 'And Roric's getting fat.'

'He's humping one of the dairy girls,' Finan said. 'The fat one. I suspect she brings him butter.'

I grunted. 'Suspect?'

'Cream too,' Finan went on. 'I'll have her watched.'

'And have her whipped if she's stealing.'

'Him too?'

'Of course.' I yawned. 'Who won the eating contest last night?'

Finan grinned. 'Who do you think?'

'Gerbruht?'

'Eats like an ox.'

'Good man, though.'

'He is,' Finan said, 'and he won the farting contest too.'

'*Ouff!*' Benedetta grimaced.

'It amuses them,' I insisted. I had heard the laughter in the hall from the seaward ramparts where I had been watching the moon's long reflection on the sea and thinking about Æthelstan. Wondering why he was in Eoferwic. Wondering how many years or months I had before none of it mattered to me any longer.

'They're easily amused,' Finan said.

'There's a ship,' I pointed northwards.

'Saw it ten minutes ago,' Finan said. He had the eyesight of a hawk. 'And not a cargo ship either.'

He was right. The approaching vessel was long, low and lean, a ship made for war, not trade. Her hull was dark and her sail was almost black. 'She's the *Trianaid*,' I said. The name meant Trinity.

'You know her?' Finan sounded surprised.

'Scottish ship. We saw her at Dumnoc a few years ago.'

'Evil comes from the north,' Benedetta said balefully, 'the star and the dragon! They do not lie!'

'It's only one ship,' I said, to calm her.

'And coming here,' Finan added. The ship, under sail, was close to Lindisfarena and turning her cross-decorated prow towards Bebbanburg's harbour channel. 'Silly bugger will go aground if he's not careful.'

But the *Trianaid*'s helmsman knew his business and the ship skirted the sandbanks, dropped her sail, and rowed into the channel where we lost sight of her. I waited for the sentries on the northern ramparts to bring me news. One ship could not pose a danger. At most the *Trianaid* could carry sixty or seventy men, but still my son roused resting warriors and sent them to the walls. Berg broke off his practice and led men to retrieve most of Bebbanburg's horses that had been put to pasture just outside the village. Some of the villagers, fearing that the dark ship's arrival presaged a short, savage raid, were driving livestock towards the Skull Gate.

Vidarr Leifson brought me news. 'Scots, lord,' he said. 'They hailed us. They're moored in the harbour now and waiting.'

'Waiting for what?'

'They say they want to talk to you, lord.'

'Are they flying a standard?'

'A red hand holding a cross, lord.'

'Domnall!' I said, surprised.

'Haven't seen that bastard in a good while,' Finan commented. Domnall was one of Constantine's war leaders and a formidable warrior. 'Do we let him in?'

'Him and six men,' I said, 'but no more than six. We'll meet him in the hall.'

It was a half hour or more before Domnall climbed to Bebbanburg's great hall. His men, all but the six who kept him company, stayed on their ship. Plainly they were under orders not to provoke me because none even tried to come ashore, and Domnall even went so far as to voluntarily surrender his sword at the door of the hall, and instructed his men to do the same. 'I know you're terrified of me, Lord Uhtred,' Domnall bellowed as my steward took the blades, 'but we come in peace!'

'When the Scots talk of peace, Lord Domnall,' I said, 'I lock up my daughters.'

He paused, nodded curtly, and when he spoke again his voice was sympathetic. 'You had a daughter, I know, and I'm sorry for her, lord. She was a brave woman.'

'She was,' I said. My daughter had died defending Eoferwic against Norsemen. 'And your daughters?' I asked. 'They're all well?'

'They're well,' he said, striding down the hall towards the blazing fire we had revived in the big central hearth. 'All four married now and squeezing out babies like good sows. Dear Lord above,' he held his hands to the flames, 'but it's a raw day.'

'It is.'

'King Constantine sends his greetings,' he said casually and then, more enthusiastically, 'is that ale?'

'The last time you drank my ale you said it reminded you of horse piss.'

'It probably will again, but what's a thirsty man to do?' He saw Benedetta sitting beside me and bowed to her. 'My sympathy, lady.'

'Sympathy?' she asked.

'Because you live with me,' I explained, then waved Domnall to the other side of the table where benches could seat all his men.

Domnall was looking about the hall. The high roof was held by great beams and rafters, the lower walls were now dressed stone, and the rush-covered floor was made from wide pine planks. I had spent a fortune on the fortress and it showed. 'It's a grand place, Lord Uhtred,' Domnall said, 'it would be a pity to lose it.'

'I'll try not to.'

He chuckled at that, then swung his great legs across a bench. He was a huge man, and one I was devoutly glad never to have faced in battle. I liked him. His companions, all but for a whey-faced priest, were similarly impressive, no doubt chosen to intimidate us by their appearance, but chief of them, and sitting on Domnall's right, was another huge man. He looked to be around forty years old, had a lined and scarred face burned dark by the sun against which his hair, worn long, was a startling white. He stared at me with undisguised hostility, yet what was strangest about him were the two amulets hanging above his polished mail coat. He wore a silver cross and, next to it, a silver hammer. Christian and pagan.

Domnall pulled an ale jug towards himself, then gestured that the priest should sit on his left. 'Don't worry yourself, father,' he told the priest, 'Lord Uhtred might be a pagan, but he's not such a bad fellow. Father Coluim,' Domnall was talking to me now, 'is trusted by King Constantine.'

'Then you're welcome, father,' I said.

'Peace be on this hall,' Coluim said in a strong voice that conveyed a deal more confidence than his nervous appearance suggested.

'High walls, a strong garrison and good men keep it peaceful, father,' I suggested.

'And good allies,' Domnall said, reaching for the ale jug again.

'And good allies,' I echoed him. Behind the Scots a log fell, spewing sparks.

Domnall poured himself ale. 'And at this time Lord Uhtred,' he went on, 'you have no allies.' He spoke quietly and again sounded sympathetic.

'No allies?' I asked. I could think of nothing else to say.

'Who is your friend? King Constantine holds you in high regard, but he's no ally to Northumbria.'

'True.'

He was leaning forward, looking into my eyes with an intense gaze, and speaking so quietly that men at the ends of the benches had to strain to hear. 'Mercia used to be your best friend,' he went on, 'but she died.'

I nodded. When Æthelflaed, Alfred's daughter, had ruled Mercia she had indeed been an ally. A lover too. I said nothing.

'Hywel of Dyfed admires you,' Domnall continued remorselessly, 'but Wales is a long way off. And why would Hywel march to your help?'

'I know no reason why he should,' I allowed.

'Or why would any Welsh king help you?' He paused, expecting an answer, but again I said nothing. 'And the Norse of Cumbria hate you,' Domnall went on. He was talking of Northumbria's wild western lands beyond the hills. 'You defeated them too often.'

'But not often enough,' I growled.

'They breed like mice. Kill one and a dozen more come at you. And your own King Guthfrith dislikes you. He wouldn't lift a drunken hand to help you.'

'He hates me,' I answered, 'ever since I held a sword to his throat two days ago.' That plainly surprised Domnall who had yet to hear of Guthfrith's flight from Eoferwic. 'He was on his way to you, I suspect,' I went on blandly.

'And you stopped him?' Domnall asked cautiously.

I decided not to reveal I had heard of the Scottish envoys' meeting with Guthfrith, so I shrugged. 'His men had raped some of the women in my villages. I didn't like that.'

'You killed him?'

'I gave him a choice. Fight me or go home. He went home.'

'So Guthfrith is no ally of yours.' Domnall was intrigued by the tale, but sensed he would get nothing more by questioning me about it. 'So who is your ally? Æthelstan?'

I gave him an answer he did not expect. 'Owain of Strath Clota is your king's enemy,' I said, 'and I daresay he would welcome an ally. Not that he needs one. How long have you been trying to defeat him?'

And then it was Domnall's turn to surprise me. He turned to the man on his right, the grim-looking warrior with the long bone-white hair who had the cross and the hammer hanging at his chest. 'This is Dyfnwal,' Domnall said, still speaking softly, 'brother to Owain.'

I must have shown my astonishment because the hard-faced Dyfnwal responded with a mocking look. 'Dyfnwal,' I repeated the name clumsily. It was a Welsh name because Strath Clota was a Welsh kingdom, formed by the Britons who had been pushed northwards by the Saxon invasion. Most Britons, of course, had gone to Wales, but some had found a refuge on the western coast of Alba where their small kingdom had been strengthened by Norsemen seeking land.

'Owain of Strath Clota has made peace with us, formed an alliance with us,' Domnall said, 'so King Constantine has no enemies north of Bebbanburg. Owain is with us, so is Gibhleachán of the Islands. So who will be your ally, Lord Uhtred?'

'Egil Skallagrimmrson,' I said. It was a fatuous response, and I knew it. Egil was a friend, a Norseman, and a great warrior, but he had few men, just enough to man two ships. I had given him land north of Bebbanburg along the southern bank of the Tuede, which was the border between Northumbria and Constantine's Alba.

'Egil might have a hundred warriors?' Domnall suggested, almost sounding sorry for me. 'A hundred and fifty, perhaps? And they're all rare fighters, but Egil's not an ally to strike fear into a whole nation.'

'Yet I dare say you sailed well clear of his coast on your way here?'

'We did,' Domnall admitted. 'We sailed a good way offshore. No need to prod a wasps' nest unnecessarily.'

'What am I? A dung beetle?'

42

Domnall smiled at that. 'You're a great warrior with no strong allies,' he said, 'or do you think of Æthelstan as a friend?' He paused, as if judging his next words before they were spoken. 'A friend who breaks his oaths.'

And this meeting, I thought, was no different to Guthfrith talking with Constantine's envoys. I had been angered when I learned of that, yet here I was, entertaining Domnall in my fortress. Æthelstan, I knew, would hear of this conversation. I was sure there were men in Bebbanburg who were paid to report to him, or else his spies in Constantine's employment would make sure he heard. Which meant he must hear what I wanted him to hear. 'King Æthelstan,' I said harshly, 'has broken no oaths.'

'No?' Domnall enquired gently.

'None,' I said sharply.

Domnall leaned away from me and took a long pull of his ale. He cuffed his mouth and beard with his sleeve, then nodded at the small priest next to him. 'Father Coluim?'

'A little more than a month ago,' the priest said in his surprisingly deep voice, 'on the feast day of Saint Christina, virgin and martyr,' he paused to make the sign of the cross, 'in the great church at Wintanceaster, the Archbishop of Contwaraburg preached a sermon before King Æthelstan. And in that sermon the archbishop urged, most strongly, that oaths taken with pagans are not binding to Christians. He said, indeed, that it is a Christian's pious duty to break any such oaths.'

I hesitated a heartbeat, then, 'King Æthelstan is not responsible for the rubbish a priest vomits.'

Father Coluim was unmoved by my rudeness. 'And that same day,' he went on calmly, 'the king rewarded the archbishop by giving into his keeping the lance of Charlemagne that Hugh, ruler of the Franks, had given to him.'

I felt a chill. I had men and women in Wintanceaster who sent me news, but none had mentioned that sermon, but then the oaths that Æthelstan and I had exchanged were supposed to be secret.

'The very same lance,' the priest continued, 'with which a Roman soldier pierced the side of our Lord.' Father Coluim again paused to cross himself. 'And the very next day, on the holy day of Saint James the Apostle,' another pause, another sign of the cross, 'the archbishop preached from the book of Deuteronomy, castigating the pagan places, and laying upon the king the most Christian duty of eradicating them from his land and from among his people.'

'Castigating,' I said, repeating the unfamiliar word.

'And as a reward,' Coluim was looking into my eyes as he spoke, 'the king gave into the archbishop's keeping the sword of Charlemagne which has a sliver of the true cross enshrined in its hilt.'

There was silence, all but for the crackle of the fire and the sigh of the wind and the long waves beating on the shore.

'It is strange, is it not?' Domnall broke the silence. He was gazing up into the rafters. 'That King Æthelstan has never married?'

'I'm sure he will,' I said, though I was far from sure.

'And he wears his hair in ringlets,' Domnall said, smiling at me now, 'tangled with gold thread.'

'It's a fashion,' I said dismissively.

'A strange fashion for a king, surely?'

'A warrior king,' I retorted. 'I have seen him fight.'

Domnall nodded, as if to suggest that Æthelstan's choice of hair decoration was of small importance. He cut himself some cheese, but did not eat it. 'You were his teacher, yes?'

'Protector.'

'A warrior king,' he said carefully, 'has no need of a

44

protector, nor of a teacher. He just wants,' he paused, searching for a word, 'advisers?'

'No king lacks for advice,' I said.

'But they usually only want the advice that agrees with them. An adviser who opposes his monarch will not long stay an adviser.' He smiled. 'This is good cheese!'

'Goat cheese.'

'If you can spare some, lord, my king would appreciate the gift. He is fond of cheese.'

'I shall order it readied,' I said.

'You're generous,' Domnall smiled again, 'and it seems that your warrior king has found an adviser who agrees with him.'

'He has Wulfhelm,' I said scornfully. Wulfhelm was the new Archbishop of Contwaraburg and had the reputation of being a fiery preacher. I did not know the man.

'I am certain King Æthelstan listens to his priests. He is famed for his piety, is he not?'

'As was his grandfather.'

'Yet King Alfred did not have a Norseman as his chief adviser,' Domnall hesitated, 'or should I say companion?'

'Should you?'

'They hunt together, they kneel together in church, they eat at the same table.'

'You mean Ingilmundr.'

'You've met him?'

'Briefly.'

'A young and handsome man, I hear?'

'He's young,' I said.

'And King Æthelstan has other,' he paused, 'advisers. Ealdred of Mærlebeorg offers advice when Ingilmundr is away.' I said nothing. I had heard of Ealdred, a young warrior who had made a reputation fighting against the southern Welsh kingdoms. 'But Ingilmundr seems to be the chief,'

45

another pause, 'adviser. You know that the king has generously given him much land in Wirhealum?'

'I do know that,' I said. Ingilmundr was a Norse chieftain who had fled Ireland with his followers and had taken land on Wirhealum, a wide strip of land between the seaward reaches of the Dee and the Mærse. That was where I had met Ingilmundr, at the fortress Æthelflaed had ordered built at Brunanburh to guard against Norse forays up the river Mærse. I remembered a striking-looking man, young, charming and about as trustworthy as an untrained hawk. Æthelstan, though, had trusted him. Had liked him.

'And Ingilmundr, I hear,' Domnall continued, 'has become a good Christian!'

'That will please Æthelstan,' I said drily.

'I hear that much about Ingilmundr pleases him,' Domnall said with a smile, 'especially his advice about Northumbria.'

'Which is?' I asked. Even to ask suggested my ignorance, but why else had Constantine sent Domnall, if not to surprise me?

'We're told Ingilmundr claims Northumbria is a wild, untamed land, that by right it belongs to Æthelstan, and that it needs a firm ruler, a Norseman perhaps? A Christian Norseman who will swear allegiance to Æthelstan and work tirelessly to convert the many heathens who infest the northern land.'

I stayed silent for a moment, testing the truth of what Domnall had said. I did not like it. 'And how, I wonder,' I said, 'does King Constantine know so much about the advice of a hunting companion?'

Domnall shrugged. 'You receive news from other countries, Lord Uhtred, and so do we. And King Owain, our new friend,' he nodded courteously at the grim Dyfnwal who was Owain's brother and chief warrior, 'is fortunate in having other friends, some of whom who serve Anlaf Guthfrithson.' He paused. 'In Ireland.'

I said nothing, but felt the shiver of cold again. Anlaf Guthfrithson was a cousin to Sigtryggr and Guthfrith, and he was renowned as a pitiless and brilliant warrior who had carved a savage reputation by defeating his Norse rivals in Ireland. I knew little else of him except that he was young, that he had made his warlike reputation quickly, and that he claimed the throne of Northumbria by kinship, a claim that did not keep me awake at nights because Ireland is a long way from Eoferwic and Bebbanburg.

'In Ireland,' Domnall repeated pointedly.

'Ireland is a long way off,' I observed shortly.

Dyfnwal spoke for the first time. 'A good ship can make the voyage between Strath Clota and Ireland in half a day.' His voice was toneless and harsh. 'Less,' he added.

'And what,' I asked Domnall, 'does Anlaf Guthfrithson have to do with Ingilmundr?'

'A year ago,' Dyfnwal answered instead, his voice still flat, 'Ingilmundr and Anlaf met on the island called Mön. They met as friends.'

'They're both Norsemen,' I said dismissively.

'Friends,' Domnall pointedly repeated Dyfnwal's last word.

I just looked at him, meeting his gaze. For a moment I did not know what to say. My first instinct was to challenge him, to deny that Æthelstan could possibly be so foolish as to trust Ingilmundr. I wanted to defend the king whom I had raised as a son, loved like a son, and helped to his throne, but I believed Domnall. 'Go on,' I said as tonelessly as Dyfnwal.

Domnall leaned back, relaxing, as if he understood that I had received the message he had brought me. 'There are two possibilities, Lord Uhtred,' he said. 'The first is that King Æthelstan is adding Northumbria to his realm. He is creating, what is it called? Englaland?' he said the word with scorn.

'And he will give its governance to a friend, to a man he can trust.'

'Ingilmundr,' I grunted.

Domnall held up a hand as if to tell me to wait before I spoke. 'And whoever rules in Northumbria,' he went on, 'whether it's Ingilmundr or another, Æthelstan will want to secure his northern frontier. He will build burhs, he will strengthen the existing burhs, and he will want those burhs held by men who are wholly loyal to him.'

He meant Bebbanburg, of course. 'King Æthelstan,' I said, 'has no reason to doubt my loyalty.'

'And he will want those men,' Domnall continued as if I had not spoken, 'to be Christians.'

I kept silent.

'The second possibility,' Domnall poured himself more ale, 'is that Ingilmundr works to be appointed as the governor of Northumbria and, once secure in Eoferwic and with Æthelstan far away in Wintanceaster, he invites Anlaf Guthfrithson to join him. The Norsemen need a kingdom, why not one called Northumbria?'

I shrugged. 'Ingilmundr and Anlaf will fight each other like polecats. Only one of them can be king, and neither will give way to the other.'

Domnall nodded as if he accepted my point. 'Except they'll share enemies, and shared enemies can make even polecats into unlikely friends.' He smiled and nodded at Dyfnwal in proof.

Dyfnwal did not smile. 'Anlaf Guthfrithson has a daughter,' he said, 'and she is not married. Nor is Ingilmundr.' He shrugged as if to suggest he had proven Domnall's argument.

Yet what was that argument? That Æthelstan wanted Northumbria? He always had. That Æthelstan had sworn not to invade Northumbria while I lived, but had broken the oath? That was true, but Æthelstan had yet to explain himself.

That Ingilmundr was an untrustworthy Norseman who had his own designs on Northumbria? So did Constantine. And one great thing stood in their way; Bebbanburg.

I do not claim that Bebbanburg is impregnable. My ancestor had captured the fort centuries before and I had captured it again, but any man, Saxon, Norse or Scot, would find Bebbanburg a challenge. I had strengthened an already formidable fortress, and the only sure way to seize it now was to place a fleet off Bebbanburg's shore and an army at its gates to stop supplies reaching us and so starve us into surrender. Either that or treachery. 'What do you want?' I asked Domnall, wanting this uncomfortable meeting to end.

'My king,' Domnall said carefully, 'is offering you an alliance.' He held up a hand to stop me speaking. 'He will swear never to attack you and, more, he will come to your aid if you are attacked.' He paused, expecting me to respond, but I stayed silent. 'And he will give you his eldest son as a hostage, Lord Uhtred.'

'I had his son as a hostage before,' I said.

'Prince Cellach sends you greetings. He speaks well of you.'

'And I of him,' I said. Cellach had been my hostage years before when Constantine had wanted a truce between Alba and Northumbria. The truce had been kept, and I had kept the young prince for a year and had grown to like him, but now, I thought, he must be middle-aged. 'And what,' I asked, 'does King Constantine want of me?'

'Cumbria,' Domnall answered.

I looked at Dyfnwal. 'Which will belong to Strath Clota?' I asked. Cumbria bordered the smaller kingdom and I could not imagine that King Owain would want Scottish warriors on his southern border. Neither man answered, so I looked back to Domnall. 'Just Cumbria?'

'King Constantine,' Domnall was speaking very carefully now, 'wants all the land north of the Tinan and the Hedene.'

49

I smiled. 'He wants me to be a Scot?'

'There are worse things to be,' Domnall smiled back.

Constantine had made the claim before, asserting that the great wall the Romans had built across Britain, a wall that stretched from the River Tinan in the east to the Hedene in the west, was the natural frontier between the Scots and the Saxons. It was an audacious claim and one I knew that Æthelstan would resist with all his power. It would make Bebbanburg into a Scottish fortress and, unspoken, but clear to me, it would demand that I swear allegiance to Constantine.

Northumbria, I thought, poor Northumbria! She was a small and ill-governed country with a greater nation on either frontier. To the north the Scots, to the south the Saxons, and both wanted her. The Norsemen of Cumbria, which was Northumbria's western region, would probably prefer the Scots, but the Saxons of eastern Northumbria had learned to fear the Scots, and their best defence was the power of Bebbanburg. 'And what of Bebbanburg?' I asked.

'The king swears it will belong to you and to your heirs for ever.'

'For ever is a long time.'

'And Bebbanburg is a fortress for all time,' Domnall said.

'And the Scottish Christians?' I asked. 'How long will they endure paganism?'

'King Owain,' Dyfnwal spoke again, 'respects the beliefs of the Norse in our country.'

That explained the hammer hanging next to the cross. 'He respects their beliefs,' I retorted sharply, 'for as long as he needs their swords.'

'I don't dispute that,' Domnall said. He glanced at my son who was sitting to my right. 'Yet I see your son is a Christian?' he asked gently. I nodded. 'Then in time, Lord Uhtred,' he continued, 'and may it be a very long time, Bebbanburg will belong to a Christian.'

I grunted at that, but said nothing. Was I tempted? Yes. But what Constantine had proposed was so bold, so drastic, that I had no response. Domnall seemed to understand that dilemma. 'We don't ask an answer now, Lord Uhtred,' he said, 'just that you think on these things. And give us an answer in three weeks.'

'Three weeks?'

'At Burgham,' he said.

'Burgham?' I asked, puzzled.

'You have not been summoned?' He sounded surprised.

'Where's Burgham?' I asked.

'A place in Cumbria,' Domnall said. 'King Æthelstan has summoned us all,' he spoke sourly, but almost spat his next words, 'for a Witan of all Britain.'

'I know nothing about it,' I said, wondering why Oda had not told me. 'And you'll be there?'

'We are summoned,' Domnall still spoke sourly, 'and when our master summons us, we must obey.' Meaning, I thought, that Æthelstan wanted to overawe the Scots with his army, and so persuade them to abandon any claims on Northumbria. And why, I wondered, would the Scots attend the meeting? Because Æthelstan was the strongest king in Britain and because behind the summons to talk was the threat of war, and it was a war Constantine did not yet want.

And Domnall had hinted that Æthelstan wanted more than just Northumbria, he wanted Bebbanburg too.

So once again my fortress was threatened, and this time I had no allies.

So I would go to Burgham.

51

THREE

Did Constantine really expect me to agree to his proposal? To swear loyalty to him and so deliver Bebbanburg and its wide lands to Scotland? He knew me too well to expect my agreement, but that was not what Domnall had been sent to secure. He had been sent to warn me that Æthelstan wanted Bebbanburg too. And that I did believe, because folk in Wessex had sent me word of what happened in Æthelstan's court and I did not like it. The great hall in Wintanceaster now had gilded beams, the throne had been lined with scarlet cloth, the king's bodyguard wore scarlet cloaks and had silver embellished helmets. Æthelstan would dazzle us with his magnificence, and about him were young, ambitious men who wanted land and silver and magnificence of their own.

And the King of all Britain summoned me to Burgham.

The summons was brought by a priest who was accompanied by forty horsemen whose shields displayed the dragon of Wessex with a lightning bolt grasped in one talon. 'The king sends you greetings, lord,' the priest said, then dismounted awkwardly and went on one knee to hand me a scroll that was tied with a red ribbon and sealed with the same dragon and lightning bolt pressed into the wax. It was Æthelstan's seal.

I was surly because Domnall had persuaded me to mistrust Æthelstan. I had permitted only a half dozen of the West Saxon horsemen to come through the Skull Gate and then denied them permission to go further than the stable yard where I reluctantly gave them weak ale and demanded that they leave my land before sunset. 'And you with them,' I told the priest, a young man with wispy hair, weak eyes, and a running nose.

'We're weary from travelling, lord,' the priest appealed to me.

'Then the sooner you're home the better,' I snarled, then tore the ribbon from the scrolled message.

'If you need help reading it, lord . . .' the priest began, then caught my eye and mumbled incoherently.

'Before sunset,' I insisted and walked away.

It was discourteous of me, but I was angry. 'They think I'm too old!' I complained to Benedetta after he left.

'Too old for what?'

'There was a time,' I said, ignoring her question, 'when I was useful to Æthelstan. He needed me! Now he thinks I don't matter, I'm too old to help him. I'm like the king in tæfl!'

'Tæfl?' she asked, stumbling over the unfamiliar word.

'You know. The game where you move pieces on a board. And he thinks I'm trapped because I'm old, that I can't move.'

'He is your friend!'

'He was my friend. Now he wants me gone. He wants Bebbanburg.'

Benedetta shivered. It had been a warm day, but by sunset the sea wind was moaning cold about the hall's high gables. 'Then what the Scottish man said? Yes? He will defend you?'

I gave a mirthless laugh. 'They don't want me, they want Bebbanburg too.'

53

'Then I will defend you,' she said fiercely. 'Tonight! We go to the chapel.'

I said nothing. If Benedetta wanted to pray for me then I would go with her, but I doubted her prayers were the equal to the ambition of kings. If my suspicions were correct then Æthelstan wanted Bebbanburg and so did Constantine because a kingdom needs strength. King Alfred had proved that great fortresses, whether burhs like Mameceaster or strongholds like Bebbanburg, were the most effective deterrents to invaders, and so Bebbanburg would either defend Æthelstan's northern frontier or Constantine's southern border, and its commander would not be named Uhtred, but would be a man of unquestioned loyalty to whichever king won.

Yet had I not been loyal? I had raised Æthelstan, taught him to fight, and given him his throne. But I was not a Christian, not handsome like Ingilmundr, and not a flatterer like those that rumour now said advised the King of Wessex.

The priest's message commanded me to meet Æthelstan at Burgham on the Feast of Zephyrinus, whoever he was, and I was to bring no more than thirty of my men and carry food enough to feed them for ten days. Thirty men! He might as well have asked me just to fall on my sword and please to leave the Skull Gate unbarred!

But I obeyed.

I took just thirty of my men.

But I also asked Egil Skallagrimmrson to keep me company with seventy-one of his Norsemen.

And so we rode to Burgham.

I had gone to Bebbanburg's chapel on the night before we left for Burgham. I did not go there often, nor did I usually go willingly, but Benedetta had pleaded and so I had led her into the cold night wind and thus to the small chapel which had been made next to the great hall.

I thought I must merely endure her prayers, but saw that she had planned this visit more carefully, because waiting in the chapel were a wide, shallow dish, a jug of water, and a small flask. The altar was bright with candles, which flickered as the wind gusted through the open door. Benedetta closed it, pulled the hood of her cloak over her dark hair, and knelt by the shallow dish. 'You have enemies,' she said bleakly.

'All men have enemies, otherwise they're not men.'

'I will protect you. Kneel.'

I was reluctant, but I obeyed. I am used to women and sorcery. Gisela would cast the sticks to tell the future, my daughter had used spells, while long ago, in a cave, I had been given dreams. Men are sorcerers too, of course, and we fear them, but a woman's sorcery is more subtle. 'What are you doing?' I asked.

'Hush,' she said, pouring water into the shallow dish. '*Il malocchio ti ha colpito*,' she went on quietly. I did not ask what the words meant because I sensed they were spoken to herself rather than to me. She pulled the cork from the small flask and then, very carefully, let three drops of oil fall into the water. 'Wait now,' she said.

The three drops of oil spread, glistened, and made shapes. The wind sighed at the chapel's roof and the door creaked. The waves beat at the shore. 'There is danger,' Benedetta said after staring at the pattern of the oil-stained water.

'There is always danger.'

'The dragon and the star,' she said. 'They came from the north?'

'They did.'

'Yet there is danger from the south,' she sounded puzzled. Her head was bent over the dish and the hood hid her face.

She was silent again and then she beckoned me. 'Come closer.'

I shuffled closer on my knees.

'I cannot come with you?' she asked plaintively.

'If there is danger? No.'

She accepted the answer, however unwillingly. She had pleaded to accompany me, but I had insisted none of my men could take their women so I could not make an exception for myself.

'And I do not know if this will work,' she said unhappily.

'This?'

'*Hai bisogno di farti fare l'affascinò*,' she said, looking up at me and frowning. 'I must protect you by,' she paused, looking for the word, 'a charm?'

'A spell?'

'But a woman,' she went on, still unhappy, 'may do this three times in her life. Only three!'

'And you,' I said carefully, 'have done it three times?'

'I made curses,' she said, 'on the slavers. Three curses.' She had been enslaved as a child, carried across Christendom and found herself in raw, cold Britain where she became a slave to King Edward's third wife. Now she was my companion. She made the sign of the cross. 'But God may give me one more spell because it is not a curse.'

'I hope not.'

'God is good,' she said. 'He gave me life again when I met you. He will not leave me alone now.' She put a forefinger into a ripple of oil. 'Come close.'

I leaned closer and she reached out and smeared her finger on my forehead. 'That is all,' she said, 'and when you feel danger is close? All you need do is spit.'

'Just spit?' I was amused.

'You spit!' she said, angry at my smile. 'You think God, the angels, and the demons need more than this? They know what I have done. It is enough. Your gods too, they know!'

'Thank you,' I said humbly.

56

'You come back to me, Uhtred of Bebbanburg!'

'I will come back,' I promised.

If I remembered to spit.

None of us knew where Burgham was, though the frightened priest who had brought the summons to Bebbanburg
assured me it was in Cumbria. 'I believe to the north of
Mameceaster, lord.'

'There's a lot of land to the north of Mameceaster,' I had
snarled.

'There's a monastery at Burgham,' he had said hopefully,
and when I didn't respond, just looked miserable. Then he
brightened. 'There was a battle nearby, lord, I think.'

'You think.'

'I think, lord, because I heard men talking of it. They said
it was your battle, lord!' he smiled as if expecting me to
smile too. 'They said you won a great victory there! In the
north, lord, near the great wall. They say you . . .' his voice
had tailed away.

The only battle that fitted his description was the fight at
Heahburh and so we followed the priest's vague directions
and rode westwards alongside the old Roman wall that
crossed Northumbria. The weather turned bad, bringing a
cold driving rain from the Scottish hills, and we made slow
progress across the high ground. We were forced to camp
one night in the stony remnants of a Roman fort, one of
the bastions of their wall, and I sat hunched in the lee of a
broken wall remembering the ghastly fight under the
ramparts of Heahburh's fort. Our fires fought the rain that
night and I doubt any of us slept much, but the dawn brought
clearing skies and a weak sunlight and, instead of pressing
on, we spent the morning drying our clothes and cleaning
our weapons. 'We're going to be late,' I told Finan, 'not that
I care. But isn't today the feast of saint whatever?'

'I think so. Not sure. Might be tomorrow?'

'Who was he?'

'Father Cuthbert said he was a pig-ignorant idiot who became pope. Zephyrinus the Idiot.'

I laughed at that, then watched a buzzard gliding through the midday sky. 'I suppose we should move.'

'Do we go to Heahburh?' Finan asked.

'Close,' I said. I had no desire to return to that place, but if the priest was right then Burgham lay somewhere to the south and so we followed rough tracks across the bare hills and spent that night in the valley of the Tinan, sheltered by deep trees. Next morning, in a small rain, we climbed out of the valley and I saw Heahburh on a distant hilltop. A shaft of sunlight moved across the old fort, shadowing the Roman ditches where so many of my men had died.

Egil rode beside me. He said nothing of the fight at Heahburh. 'So what do we expect at Burgham?' he asked me.

'Unhappiness.'

'Nothing new there, then,' he said grimly. He was a tall, good-looking Norseman with long fair hair and a prow of a nose. He was a wanderer who had found a home on my land and rewarded me with both friendship and loyalty. He said he owed me a life because I had rescued his younger brother Berg from a cruel death on a Welsh beach, but I considered that debt long paid. He stayed, I think, because he liked me and I liked him. 'You say Æthelstan has two thousand men?' he asked.

'That's what we were told.'

'If he takes a dislike to us,' he remarked mildly, 'we'll be a little outnumbered.'

'Just a little.'

'Will it come to that?'

I shook my head. 'He hasn't come to make war.'

'Then what is he doing here?'

'He's behaving like a dog,' I said. 'He's pissing on all his boundaries.' That was why he was in Cumbria, that wild and untamed western part of Northumbria. The Scots wanted it, the Irish Norse claimed it, we had fought for it, and now Æthelstan had come to place his banner on it.

'So he'll piss on us?' Egil asked.

'That's what I expect.'

Egil touched the hammer at his breast. 'But he doesn't like pagans.'

'So he'll piss harder on us.'

'He wants us gone. They call us strangers. Pagans and strangers.'

'You live here,' I said forcefully, 'you're a Northumbrian now. You fought for this land, so you have as much right to it as anyone.'

'But he wants us to be Ænglisc,' he said the unfamiliar word carefully, 'and he wants the Ænglisc to be Christians.'

'If he wants to swallow Northumbria,' I said savagely, 'then he'll have to swallow the gristle along with the flesh. Half of Cumbria is pagan! He needs them as enemies?'

Egil shrugged again. 'So he just pisses on us and we go home?'

'If that makes him happy,' I said, 'yes.' And I hoped I was right, though I really suspected I would have to fend off a demand for Bebbanburg.

Late that afternoon, as the road dropped into a wide, well-watered valley, we saw a veil of smoke to the south. Not a great dark pillar that might betray a hall or steading being burned, but a drifting mist of smoke hanging over the rich farmland in the river valley. It had to be where men were assembled and so we turned our horses southwards and, next day, came to Burgham.

Folk had been there before, the old people who used vast boulders to make strange circles. I touched my hammer when I saw the circles. The gods must know of those places, but what gods? Older gods than mine and much older than the nailed Christian god, and the Christians I had spoken with said such places were malevolent. The devil's play-grounds, they claimed, yet Æthelstan had chosen one such circle as the place of meeting.

The circles lay south of a river. I could see two of them, though later I discovered a third nearby. The largest circle lay to the west and that was where Æthelstan's banners flew amidst hundreds of men, hundreds of tents and hundreds of crude turf shelters, amongst which were campfires and tethered horses. There were banners by the score, a few of them triangular that belonged to Norse jarls, and most of those were to the south beside another river that ran fast and shallow across a stony bed. Closer to the largest circle was a mass of flags that were mostly familiar to me. They were the standards of Wessex; crosses and saints, dragons and rearing horses, the black stag of Defnascir, the crossed swords and the bull's head flags of Cent, all of which I had seen fly in battle, sometimes on my side of the shield wall and sometimes on the other. The leaping stag of Æthelhelm was there, too, though that house was no longer my enemy. I doubted it was my friend, but the long bloodfeud had died with the death of Æthelhelm the Younger. Mixed among the flags of Wessex were the banners of Mercia and of East Anglia, all now acknowledging the King of Wessex as their overlord. That, then, was the Saxon army come north, and judging by the number of banners, Æthelstan had brought at least a thousand men to Burgham.

To the west, in a smaller and separate encampment, there was a spread of unfamiliar banners, but I saw Domnall's red hand holding the cross, which suggested that was where the Scottish had pitched their tents or made turf shelters, while to the south, to my surprise, the red dragon banner of Hywel

60

of Dyfed rippled in the breeze. Closest to us, just beyond the river's ford, lay a dozen tents over which flew Guthfrith's three-sided flag of the viciously tusked boar. So he was here, and I saw that his small encampment was guarded by mailed warriors carrying Æthelstan's badge of the dragon and lightning bolt on their iron-rimmed shields. That same badge flew on Æthelstan's flag, which was carried by a monstrously tall pine trunk placed at the entrance to the largest stone circle, and next to it, on a pole just as high, there was a pale banner on which was blazoned a cross the colour of dried blood. 'What's that flag?' Finan asked, nodding at it.

'Who knows? Æthelstan's, I suppose.'

'And Hywel's here!' Finan said. 'I thought he was in Rome.'

'He's been and come back,' I said, 'or he's about to go. Who knows? The Welsh are here anyway.'

'And where's our banner?'

'At Bebbanburg,' I said, 'I forgot it.'

'I brought two of mine,' Egil said happily.

'Then fly one of them now,' I said. I wanted Æthelstan to see a three-sided flag showing the dark eagle of a pagan Norse chieftain coming to his encampment.

We splashed through the ford to be met by the West Saxons guarding Guthfrith's tents. 'Who are you?' A sour-looking warrior held up a hand to check us.

'Egil Skallagrimmrson.'

I had mischievously asked Egil to lead us across the river. On either side of him were his Norse warriors, while Finan and I hung back. We waited in the ford, the water rippling around our stallions' fetlocks.

'And where are you going?' the sour man demanded curtly.

'Wherever I want,' Egil said, 'this is my country.' He spoke Ænglisc well, most of it learned from the Saxon girls who

61

were willingly seduced, but now he was deliberately making his words awkward as though they were unfamiliar.

'You only come here if you're invited. And I don't think you are.' The surly man had been reinforced by a dozen West Saxon spearmen holding Æthelstan's shields. Some of Guthfrith's men had assembled behind them, eager for whatever entertainment seemed imminent, while more West Saxon men were hurrying towards the confrontation.

'I'm going there,' Egil pointed southwards.

'You're turning around and you're going back where you came from,' the sour-faced man said, 'all of you and all the way back. Back to your damned country across the sea.' His small force was growing by the minute and, in the way that rumours spread like smoke, still more men were coming from the Saxon encampment to swell his ranks. 'Turn around,' the man said slowly and insultingly, as if speaking to a stubborn child, 'and bugger off.'

'No,' I said, and pushed my horse between Egil and his standard-bearer.

'And who are you, grandpa?' the man asked belligerently, hefting his spear.

'Kill the old fool,' one of Guthfrith's men shouted, 'cut the old fool down!' His companions began jeering me, emboldened perhaps by the presence of Æthelstan's guards. The man who had shouted was young with long fair hair that he wore in a thick plait. He pushed his way through the West Saxons and stared insolently at me. 'I challenge you,' he snarled.

There are always fools who want reputation, and killing me was a swift route to warrior-fame. The young man was doubtless a good warrior, he looked strong, he evidently had courage, his forearms were bright with rings that he had taken in battle, and he yearned for the renown that would follow my death. More, he was emboldened by the press of

62

men behind him who were shouting at me to dismount and fight. 'Who are you?' I asked him.

'I am Kolfinn, son of Hæfnir,' he replied, 'and I serve Guthfrith of Northumbria.'

I suspected he had been with Guthfrith when I had barred the escape to Scotland and Kolfinn Hæfnirson now wanted to avenge that humiliation. He had challenged me and custom decreed I must answer the challenge. 'Kolfinn, son of Hæfnir,' I said, 'I have not heard of you, yet I know of all the warriors of Britain who have reputation. But what I do not know is why I should bother to kill you. What is your cause, Kolfinn, son of Hæfnir? What is our quarrel?'

He looked bemused for a heartbeat. He had a blunt face with a well-broken nose, and the gold and silver arm rings suggested he was a young warrior who had survived and won many fights, but what he did not have was a sword, or indeed any weapon. Only the West Saxons under the command of the sour-faced man carried spears or swords. 'Well,' I demanded, 'what is our quarrel?'

'You must not—' the sour-faced West Saxon began, but I cut him off with a gesture.

'What is our quarrel, Kolfinn, son of Hæfnir?' I demanded again.

'You are an enemy of my king,' he shouted.

'An enemy of your king? Then you would fight half of Britain!'

'You are a coward,' he spat at me, and stepped forward only to stop when Egil edged his stallion forward and drew his sword that he called Adder. Egil was smiling. The noisy crowd behind Kolfinn went silent and that did not surprise me. There is something about a smiling Norseman holding his beloved sword that will chill most warriors.

I pulled Egil back. 'You have no quarrel with me, Kolfinn son of Hæfnir,' I said, 'but I now have a quarrel with you.

And we shall settle the quarrel at a time and place of my choosing. That I promise you. Now make way for us.'

The West Saxon stepped forward, evidently feeling he should insist on his small authority. 'If you're not invited,' he said, 'you must leave.'

'But he is invited,' another man spoke. He had just joined the growing group of men barring our way and, like the man who had challenged us, had Æthelstan's cross and lightning bolt on his shield. 'And you, Cenwalh,' he went on, looking at the sour-faced man, 'are a slug-brained idiot unless, of course, you want to fight Lord Uhtred? I'm certain he will oblige you.'

Cenwalh, disgruntled, muttered something under his breath, but lowered his spear and backed away as the newcomer bowed to me. 'You're welcome, lord. I assume you are summoned?'

'I am. And you are?'

'Fraomar Ceddson, lord, but most folk call me Freckles.' I smiled at that because Fraomar Ceddson's face was a mass of freckles slashed by a white scar and ringed by flaming red hair. He looked up at Egil. 'I'd be grateful if you sheathed that sword,' he said mildly, 'the king has ordered that only guards may carry swords in the encampment.'

'He's guarding me,' I said.

'Please?' Fraomar said to Egil, ignoring me, and Egil obligingly sheathed Adder's long blade.

'Thank you,' Fraomar said. I reckoned he was in his mid thirties, a confident and competent-looking man, whose presence had dispelled the onlookers, though I saw how Guthfrith's men looked back at me with something close to hatred. 'We should find you somewhere to camp,' Fraomar went on.

I pointed south and west, to a space between the Saxon and Welsh encampments. 'That will do,' I said. I dismounted, threw the stallion's reins to Aldwyn, and walked with Fraomar ahead of my men. 'Are we the last to arrive?' I asked.

'Most folk came three days ago,' he said, then paused awkwardly. 'They took the oaths on Saint Bartholomew's day.'

'Not Saint . . .' I paused, unable to remember the name of the idiot pope. 'When was Bartholomew's day?'

'Two days ago, lord.'

'And what oaths?' I asked. 'What oaths?'

Another awkward pause. 'I wouldn't know, lord. I wasn't there. And I'm sorry about that idiot Cenwalh.'

'Why?' I really wanted to ask about the oaths, but it was plain Fraomar did not want to talk about them and I reckoned I would learn soon enough. I also wanted to know why the nervous priest had instructed us to come late, but reckoned Fraomar would have no answer to that. 'Is Cenwalh one of your men?'

'He's West Saxon,' Fraomar said. His own accent betrayed him as a Mercian.

'And the West Saxons are still resentful of Mercia?' I asked. Æthelstan was also a West Saxon, but the army he had led to take the throne of Wessex was largely Mercian.

Fraomar shook his head. 'There's not much trouble. The West Saxons know he was the best choice. Maybe a few still want to fight old battles, but not many.'

I grimaced. 'Only a fool wants a battle like Lundene again.'

'You mean the fight at the city gate, lord?'

'It was a horror,' I said, and so it had been. My men against the best of the West Saxon troops, a slaughter that still sometimes woke me at night with a feeling of doom.

'I saw it, lord,' Fraomar said, 'or the end of it.'

'You were with Æthelstan?'

'I rode with him, lord. Saw your men fighting.' He walked in silence for a few paces, then turned and glanced at Egil. 'He's really with you, lord?'

'He is,' I said. 'He's a Norseman, a poet, a warrior, and my friend. So yes, he's with me.'

'It just seems strange . . .' Fraomar's voice faltered.

'Being among so many pagans?'

'Pagans, yes, and the damned Scots. Welsh too.'

I thought how sensible it was of Æthelstan to order that no swords should be worn in the camp except, of course, for those men standing guard. 'You don't trust pagans, Scots or Welshmen?' I asked.

'Do you, lord?'

'I'm one of them, Fraomar. I'm a pagan.'

He looked embarrassed. He must have known I was not a Christian, the hammer at my chest told him that, if my reputation was not enough. 'Yet my father said you were the best friend King Alfred ever had, lord.'

I laughed at that. 'Alfred was never a friend,' I said. 'I admired him and he endured me.'

'And King Æthelstan must know what you did for him, lord,' he said, though to my ears he sounded dubious.

'I'm sure he appreciates what we all did for him.'

'It was a rare fight in Lundene!' Fraomar said, plainly relieved I seemed not to have noticed the tone of his previous remark.

'It was,' I said and then, as casually as I could, 'I haven't seen him since that day.'

The lure worked. 'He's changed, lord!' Fraomar hesitated, then realised he had to qualify that comment. 'He's become,' he paused again, 'very grand.'

'He's a king.'

'True.' He sounded rueful. 'I suppose I'd be grand if I was a king.'

'King Freckles?' I suggested, he laughed and the moment passed. 'Is he here?' I asked, gesturing at the huge tent erected in the large circle.

'He's lodging in the monastery at Dacore,' Fraomar said. 'It's not far away. You can camp here,' he had stopped in a wide swathe of meadow. 'Water from the river, firewood from the copse, you'll be comfortable enough. There's a church service at sundown, but I suppose . . .' his voice tailed off.

'You suppose right,' I said.

'Shall I tell the king you're here, lord?' Fraomar asked, and again there was a slight awkwardness in his voice.

I smiled. 'He'll know I'm here. But if it's your job to tell him? Do it.'

Fraomar left us and we set about making our shelters, though I took the precaution of sending Egil with a dozen men to scout our surroundings. I did not expect trouble, there were too many of Æthelstan's warriors for any Scotsman or Welshman to start a war, but I did not know this part of Cumbria and if trouble came I wanted to know how best to escape it. And so, while we made ourselves comfortable, Egil scouted.

I had brought no tents. Benedetta had wanted to fashion one from sailcloth, but I had assured her we were well used to making shelters and that our packhorses already had enough to carry with their heavy tubs of ale, barrels of bread, and sacks of smoked meat, cheese and fish. Instead of tents my men chopped down branches with war axes to make simple gable-shaped shelters lashed together by withies, cut turf with their knives to roof them, then lined the floors with bracken. They competed, of course, not to be the first finished, but for who could make the most elaborate shelter, and the winner, an impressive turf hut almost the size of a small hall, was given to me to share with Finan, Egil, and his brother Thorolf. Naturally we were expected to pay the builders with hacksilver, ale and praise, which we did, then watched as two men cut and stripped a towering larch trunk on which they hoisted Egil's eagle banner. By then the sun was setting and we lit our campfires. A dozen of my Christians wandered over to where hundreds of men were sitting listening to a sermon from a priest, while I sat with Finan, Egil and Thorolf and gazed moodily into the crackling fire.

I was thinking about oaths, about the tense atmosphere in the sprawling encampment where squads of heavily armed spearmen were needed to keep the peace, about the things Fraomar had not wanted to say, and about being instructed to arrive at Burgham days after other men had been summoned. I was thinking about Æthelstan. The last time I had seen him he had thanked me for giving him Lundene, he had praised me in the hall and roused the cheers of men, and with Lundene had come his emerald crown, but since that far-off day he had sent me no messages nor offered me any favours. I had given men hacksilver for building me a shelter, yet my reward for giving a man a kingdom was to be ignored.

Wyrd bið ful āræd.

Fate is inexorable.

The sermon had ended, the men were dispersing to their huts, while a band of monks, dark-robed and hooded, walked through the encampments chanting. The leading monk carried a lantern and a dozen men followed him, their voices low and haunting. 'Christian magic?' Thorolf asked sourly.

'They're just praying for a peaceful night,' Finan said, making the sign of the cross.

The monks did not come close to our shelters, but turned back towards the fires that had lit the evening sermon. Their voices grew fainter, then a peal of women's laughter sounded from the Welsh encampment. Egil sighed. 'Why didn't we bring our own women?'

'Because we didn't need to,' Finan said, 'every whore between Cair Ligualid and Mameceaster is here.'

68

'Ah!' Egil grinned. 'Then why am I sharing a shelter with you three?'

'You can use that spinney instead,' I said, nodding south towards a dark group of trees that lay between us and the Welsh encampment.

And saw the arrow.

It was a flicker in the night's flame-lit dark, a sudden spark as fire glittered quick from a steel head and from pale feathers, and it was coming towards us. I thrust left at Finan, right at Egil and threw myself flat, and the arrow seared across my left shoulder, catching my cloak. 'Move!' I shouted, and the four of us scrambled away from the fire, going towards shadows as a second arrow slashed through the darkness to bury itself in the turf. 'To me!' I yelled. I was safely behind a shelter now, hidden from the archer who had loosed his arrows from among the spinney's dark trees.

Egil, Thorolf and Finan ran to me. My men were leaving their shelters, coming to discover what had caused me to shout. 'Who has weapons?' I asked. A chorus of voices answered and, without waiting, I shouted at them to follow me.

I ran towards the spinney. I swerved to my left first, hoping not to be outlined against the bright fires, but knew I would be seen despite that small precaution. But there was, I thought, just one bowman, because if there had been two or more then we would have been attacked by a volley, not by a single arrow. I was also sure that whoever had loosed the arrow would already have fled. He must have seen a score of men coming, seen our swords reflecting the flame-light, and unless he was intent on dying he would be gone, but I still kept running. 'Bebbanburg!' I shouted, and my men took up the war cry.

We were still shouting as we crashed into the spinney's undergrowth, trampling brambles and saplings. No more arrows came and the noise slowly died. I stopped in the shadow of a thick trunk. 'What were we shouting about?' Berg asked.

'This,' Finan said, and tugged the arrow that was still caught in my cloak. He ripped it free and held it into the light. 'Christ, that's a long arrow!'

'Get into shadow,' I told him. 'All of you.'

'Bastard's long gone,' he growled, 'he can't see us.'

There was no moon, but our campfires and the flames from the Welsh encampment cast plenty of sullen red light among the trees. I started laughing. 'What?' Egil asked.

'We're not supposed to carry weapons,' I said, and gestured at the men in the trees, all of whom were carrying swords or axes, while still more of our men were streaming towards us from the shelters and all carrying their bright weapons.

Egil led some of his men to the southern edge of the trees, but went no further. The Norsemen just stood there, gazing into the night, searching for an archer who had been swallowed in the darkness. Finan hefted the missile. 'This isn't from a short bow,' he said dourly.

'No.'

'It's a hunting arrow.' He ran his fingers over the feather fletching. 'From one of those big bows that the Welsh use.'

'Some Saxons use them.'

'But rarely.' He flinched as he tested the arrowhead. 'Newly sharpened too. The earsling wanted you dead.'

I shivered as I remembered that flicker of light in the darkness, and that darkness was lessening because men, attracted by the noise, were running towards the spinney carrying flaming torches. The Welsh were closest and they came first, led by a huge man swathed in a fur cloak and carrying a mighty war axe. He barked an angry question in his own language and seemed unperturbed when my men raised swords to confront him, but before anyone could strike a blow a tall, bald-headed priest pushed the man aside.

70

The priest stared at me. 'Lord Uhtred,' he said, sounding amused. 'Does trouble follow you?'

'It finds me, Father Anwyn,' I said, 'and it's good to see you.'

'Bishop Anwyn now,' he responded, then spoke sharply to the huge man, who reluctantly lowered his formidable axe. Anwyn looked around the spinney, now crowded with my men and lit brightly by the torches the Welshmen carried. He smiled as he counted the hammer amulets. 'I see you still keep bad company, Lord Uhtred? And what were they shouting about? Didn't you know there was a service? Bishop Oswald was preaching!' He paused, looking at me, 'Bishop Oswald!'

'I'm supposed to know who that is?' I asked sourly. Anwyn's tone suggested that Bishop Oswald was famous, but why would I care? A long life had condemned me to hear too many Christian sermons. 'Why weren't you listening?' I asked Anwyn.

'Why would I need a bloody Saxon bishop to tell me how to behave?' Anwyn retorted, and his long bony face, usually so stern, broke into a smile. I had met him years before on a Welsh beach where my men and King Hywel's men had slaughtered Rognvald's Vikings. It was on that beach that Hywel had granted Berg his life. 'And what were you shouting about?' Anwyn asked. 'Were you frightened by a mouse?'

'By this,' I said, taking the arrow from Finan.

Anwyn took it from me, hefted it and frowned. He must have guessed what I was thinking because he shook his head. 'It wasn't one of our men. Come, talk to King Hywel.'

'He's not in Rome?'

'You think I'd ask you if he was in Rome?' Anwyn replied. 'The thought of keeping your company on that long journey gives me horrors, Lord Uhtred, but Hywel will want to meet you. For some strange reason he speaks well of you.'

But before we could move, still more men, carrying still more torches, appeared from the western side of the spinney.

Most carried shields that bore Æthelstan's dragon and light-ning bolt and they were led by a young man mounted on an impressive grey horse. He had to duck his head to get beneath the branches, then curbed the stallion close to me. 'You're carrying a sword,' he snarled at me, then looked around at all the other weapons. 'The king has commanded that only sentries carry weapons.'

'I'm a sentry,' I said.

That annoyed him, as it was meant to. He stared at me. He was young, maybe just twenty-one or -two, his boyish face clean-shaven. He had very blue eyes, bright blond hair, a long nose, and a haughty expression. In truth he was striking, a handsome man, made more striking by the quality of his mail and by the thick gold chain he wore about his neck. He carried a drawn sword and I could see that the heavy crosspiece was glinting with more gold. He still stared at me, his distaste for what he saw evident on his face. 'And who,' he asked, 'are you?'

One of his own men began to answer, but was hushed by Fraomar who had come with the young man. Fraomar was smiling. So was Anwyn. 'I'm a sentry,' I said again.

'You call me lord, old man,' the horseman said, then leaned from the saddle and lifted his gold-hilted sword so that the blade pointed at my hammer. 'You call me lord,' he said again, 'and you hide that idolatrous bauble around your neck. Now who are you?'

I smiled. 'I'm the man who will ram Serpent-Breath up your arsehole and slice off your tongue, you rat-faced piece of worm-shit.'

'God be praised,' Bishop Anwyn intervened hurriedly, 'that the Lord Uhtred still possesses the tongue of angels.'

The sword dropped. The young man looked startled. He also, to my satisfaction, looked scared. 'And you call me lord,' I growled.

He had nothing to say. His horse whinnied and stepped sideways as Bishop Anwyn took another step forward. 'There's no trouble here, Lord Ealdred. We just came because King Hywel is eager to see Lord Uhtred again.'

So this, I thought, was Ealdred, another of Æthelstan's favourite companions. He had made a fool of himself, thinking that his closeness to the king made him invulnerable, and he had suddenly become aware that he and his men were confronted and outnumbered by bitter Welshmen and hostile Northmen, both enemies of the Saxons. 'Weapons,' he said, but without any of his former arrogance, 'are not to be carried in the camp.'

'Were you talking to me?' I demanded harshly.

He hesitated. 'No, lord,' he said, almost choking on the last word, then turned his stallion with a brutal jerk of the reins and spurred away.

'Poor boy,' Anwyn said, plainly amused. 'But that poor boy will cause you trouble, lord.'

'Let him try,' I snarled.

'No, let King Hywel tell you. He'll be pleased you're here. Come, lord.'

So I took Finan, Egil and Berg, and went to meet a king.

I have met many kings. Some, like Guthfrith, were fools, some struggled because they never knew what to do, while a few, very few, were men who commanded loyalty. Alfred was one, Constantine of Alba another, and the third was Hywel of Dyfed. I knew Alfred best of the three and since his death many folk have asked me about him, and I invariably say that he was as honest as he was clever. Is that true? He was as capable of cunning as Constantine or Hywel, but for all three men that cunning was always used in the service of what they believed was the best for their people. I disagreed with Alfred frequently, but I trusted him because he was a man of his word. I hardly knew Constantine, but those who knew him well often compared him to Alfred. Alfred, Constantine and Hywel were the three greatest kings of my lifetime, and all three had wisdom and a natural authority, but of the three I liked Hywel the best. He had an ease that Alfred lacked and a humour as broad as his smile. 'My God,' he greeted me, 'but look what an ill wind has blown to my tent. I thought a pig had farted!'

I bowed to him. 'Lord King.'

'Sit down, man, sit down. Of course the King of the Sais has a great monastery as his lodging, but we poor Welshmen have to endure this,' he waved around the great tent, which was carpeted with thick woollen rugs, warmed by a brazier, furnished with benches and tables, and lit by a host of tall, thick candles, 'this hovel!' He turned and spoke in Welsh to a servant who hurried to bring me a drinking horn that he filled with wine. A dozen other men were in the tent, sitting on benches around the brazier and listening to a harpist who played in the shadows. Hywel waved the man to silence, then smiled at me. 'You're still living, Lord Uhtred! I am pleased.'

'You're gracious, lord King.'

'Ah, he butters me!' He spoke to the other men in the tent, most of whom I suspected did not speak the Saxon tongue, but they smiled anyway. 'I was gracious with His Holiness the Pope,' Hywel continued, 'who suffers from aches in his joints. I told the poor man to rub them with wool grease mixed with the urine of goats, but did he listen to me? He did not! Do you suffer from aches, Lord Uhtred?'

'Frequently, lord King.'

'Goat's piss! Rub it in, man, rub it in. It might even improve the way you smell!' He grinned. He looked as I remembered him, a sturdy man with a broad, wind-reddened face and eyes that readily creased with merriment. Age had whitened his clipped beard and his short hair over which he wore a simple gilt-bronze circlet. He looked to be about fifty years old, but he was still hale. He signalled to my companions. 'Sit, all of you, sit. I remember you.' He pointed at Finan. 'You're the Irishman?'

'I am, lord King.'

'Finan,' I supplied the name.

'And you fought like a demon, I remember that! You poor man, I'd think an Irishman had better sense than to fight for a Sais lord, eh? And you are?' He nodded at Egil.

'Egil Skallagrimmrson, lord King.' Egil bowed, then touched Berg's elbow, 'and this is my brother, Berg Skallagrimmrson, who has to thank you.'

'Me! Why would a Norseman thank me?'

'You spared my life, lord King,' Berg said, blushing as he bowed.

'I did?'

'On the beach,' I reminded him, 'where you killed Rognvald.'

Hywel's face darkened as he remembered that fight. He made the sign of the cross. 'Upon my word, but that was a wicked man. I take no pleasure in death, but that man's screams were like the balm of Gilead to my soul.' He looked at me. 'Is he honest?' He jerked his head at Berg. 'Is he a good man?'

'A very good man, lord King.'

'But not a Christian,' he said flatly.

'I swore to have him taught the faith,' I answered, 'because you demanded that as a condition for his life, and I did not break my word.'

'He chose otherwise?'

'He did, lord King.'

'The world is full of fools, is it not? And why, good bishop, are you holding an arrow? Do you plan to stab me?'

Anwyn explained what had happened in the darkness. He spoke in Welsh, but I did not need a translator to understand the tale. Hywel grunted when the bishop finished and took the arrow from him. 'You think, Lord Uhtred,' he asked, 'it was one of my men?'

'I don't know, lord King.'

'Did the arrow kill you?'

I smiled. 'No, lord King.'

'Then it wasn't one of my boys. My boys don't miss. And this isn't one of my arrows. We fletch them with goose feathers. These look like eagle feathers?' He tossed the arrow onto the brazier where the ashwood shaft flared up. 'And other men in Britain use the long hunting bow, do they not?' Hywel asked. 'I hear they have some small skill with it in Legeceasterscir?'

'It's a rare skill, lord King.'

'So it is, so it is. And wisdom is rare too, and you are going to need wisdom, Lord Uhtred.'

'I am?'

Hywel gestured to a man sitting next to him, a man whose face was hidden by the deep hood of his cloak. 'I have strange visitors this night, Lord Uhtred!' Hywel said cheerfully, 'you, your pagans, and now a new friend from a far place.'

The stink of the arrow's burning feathers soured the tent as the man pushed back his hood and I saw it was Cellach, eldest son of Constantine and Prince of Alba.

I bowed my head. 'Lord Prince,' I said, and knew that Hywel was right; I would need wisdom.

I was among Æthelstan's enemies.

76

FOUR

Cellach had been my hostage once, years ago, and for a year he had lived with me and I had become fond of him. Back then he had been a boy, now he was a man in his prime. He had his father's looks, the same short brown hair, blue eyes and serious face. He offered a wary smile as greeting, but said nothing.

'You would think, would you not,' Hywel said, 'that a meeting of the kings of Britain would be a matter for celebration?'

'Would I, lord King?'

Hywel heard my scepticism and smiled. 'Why would you say we were gathered, Lord Uhtred?'

I gave him the same answer I had given Egil as we journeyed to Burgham. 'He's like a hound,' I said, 'he's marking his boundaries.'

'So King Æthelstan is pissing on us?' Hywel suggested. I nodded, and Cellach grimaced. 'Or,' Hywel looked at the tent's roof, 'is he pissing beyond his frontiers? Enlarging his land?'

'Is he?' I asked.

Hywel shrugged. 'You should know, Lord Uhtred. You're his friend, are you not?'

'I thought I was.'

'You fought for him! Men still talk of your battle at the Lundene gate!'

'Battles get exaggerated, lord King. Twenty men squabble and in song it becomes a heroic bloodletting.'

'That's true,' Hywel said happily, 'but I do love my poets! They make my pitiful skirmishes sound like the slaughter of Badon!' He gave a sly smile as he turned to Cellach. 'Now that was a real battle, lord Prince! Armies in the thousands! And we Britons massacred the Sais that day! They fell to our spears like wheat before the reaping hook. I'm sure Lord Uhtred can tell you the tale.'

'It was three hundred years ago,' I said, 'or was it four? And even I'm not old enough to remember that story.'

Hywel chuckled. 'And now the King of the Sais comes to piss on us. You are right, Lord Uhtred. He has demanded of King Constantine much the same terms he inflicted on me a year ago. You know what those terms were?'

'I heard they were harsh.'

'Harsh!' Hywel was suddenly bitter. 'Your King Æthelstan demanded twenty-four pounds of gold, three hundred of silver, and ten thousand head of cattle a year. A year! Each year till the crack of doom! And we must give him hawks and hounds too! We are meant to send a hundred birds and two hundred hunting dogs to Gleawecestre each spring so he can choose the best.'

'And you pay?' I made it a question, though I knew the answer.

'What choice do I have? He has the armies of Wessex, of Mercia, and of East Anglia. He has fleets, and my country still has small kingdoms that itch me like fleas. I can fight Æthelstan! But to what end? If we don't pay the tribute he will come with a horde and the kings of the little kingdoms will join him and Dyfed will be harrowed hill and vale.'

'So you'll pay till the crack of doom?' I asked.

Hywel smiled grimly. 'The end of time is a long way off, Lord Uhtred, and the wheel of fortune turns, does it not?'

I looked at Cellach. 'He's demanding the same of your father, lord Prince?'

'More,' Cellach said abruptly.

'And,' Hywel continued, 'now he wants to add the army of Northumbria to his horde. He is pissing beyond his frontiers, Lord Uhtred. He is pissing on you.'

'Then he's only doing what you do,' I said flatly. 'What you do against all those lesser kings who itch you like fleas. Or what your father does,' I turned to Cellach, 'or what he'd like to do against Owain of Strath Clota or against the Kingdom of the Hebrides. Or,' I hesitated, then decided to confront him, 'what you'd like to do with my lands.'

Cellach just stared at me. He had to know of Domnall's visit to Bebbanburg, but he betrayed nothing, said nothing.

Hywel must have sensed the sudden discomfort between us, but he ignored it. 'King Æthelstan,' he said, 'claims to be making peace! A most Christian thing to do, yes?'

'Peace?' I asked, as if I had never heard of such a thing.

'And he makes peace by forcing us to come to this godforsaken place and acknowledge him as our,' he paused, 'how can I put it? As our High King?'

Monarchus Totius Brittaniae,' put in a sour voice from the tent's shadows and I saw a priest sitting on a bench. 'Monarch of all—' the priest began to translate.

'I know what it means,' I interrupted him.

'And the monarch of all Britain will tread us underfoot,' Hywel said softly.

'Piss on us,' Cellach added angrily.

'And to keep this most Christian peace,' Hywel went on, 'our High King would have strong garrisons on his borders.'

'Christian garrisons,' Cellach put in.

Again I said nothing. Hywel sighed. 'You know what we're saying, Lord Uhtred, and we know nothing more except this. Men made oaths to Æthelstan like obedient little boys! I swore to keep the peace, and Constantine did the same. Even Guthfrith knelt.'

'Guthfrith?'

Hywel looked disgusted. 'He grovelled like a toad, and swore to let Æthelstan keep troops in his country. And all those oaths were witnessed by churchmen, written on parchments and sealed with wax, and copies were given to us. But there was one oath taken in secret. And all my spies cannot tell me what that oath was, only that Ealdred knelt to the king.'

'And not for the first time,' Cellach added snidely.

I ignored that. 'Ealdred swore?' I asked Hywel.

'He swore an oath, but what oath? We don't know! And once the oath was sworn he was taken out of our sight and out of our hearing, we were only told that he's an ealdorman now! We must call him lord! But an ealdorman of what? Of where?'

Silence, except for a slight patter of rain on the tent's roof, a patter that came and went quickly. 'We don't know where?' I asked.

'Of Cumbria?' Hywel suggested. 'Of Northumbria?'

'Of Bebbanburg?' Cellach growled.

I turned my head and spat.

'You don't like my hospitality?' Hywel asked, amused.

I spat to keep faith with my promise to Benedetta, and because I did not want to believe what Cellach had suggested. 'I met Ealdred just now,' I told Hywel.

'Ah! I would spit too. I hope you called him "lord".'

'I think I called him a rat-faced turd. Something like that.'

Hywel laughed, then stood, which meant we all stood. He gestured me towards the tent's door. 'It's late,' he said, 'but let me walk with you, Lord Uhtred.'

A score of my men were waiting outside the tent and they accompanied us, as did twice as many of Hywel's warriors. 'I doubt your archer will try again,' Hywel said, 'but it's best to be sure, is it not?'

'He won't try, lord King.'

'It was not one of my men, I promise you. I have no quarrel with Bebbanburg.'

We walked slowly towards the campfires marking my shelters. For a few paces neither of us spoke, then Hywel stopped and touched my elbow. 'The wheel of fortune turns slowly, Lord Uhtred, but it does turn. It is not my time yet, but that time will come. But I doubt that Constantine will wait for the wheel's turning.'

'Yet he swore his oath to Æthelstan?'

'When a king has three thousand warriors on your frontier, what choice do you have?'

'Three thousand? I was told he only had two thousand.'

'Two thousand around Eoferwic and at least another thousand here. And King Constantine can count shields as well as any man. He was forced to promise not to interfere with Northumbria, and to pay tribute. He agreed.'

'So he's oath-sworn,' I said.

'And so were you and Æthelstan sworn together, but every man in Britain knows what happened to that oath. He promised not to invade your country, yet here he is. You and I follow the old ways, Lord Uhtred, we believe an oath binds us, but now there are those who say that an oath made under duress is no oath at all.'

I thought about that. 'Maybe they're right. What choice do you have if there's a sword at your throat?'

'The choice is not to swear, of course! Sign a treaty instead, maybe? But swear on the Lance of Charlemagne? On the very blade that pierced the side of our Lord?' He shuddered.

'But you swore?' I asked, knowing the question might annoy him.

It amused him instead. He chuckled, then touched my elbow again to signal we should walk on. 'I swore to keep the peace, no more. And as for the tribute? I agreed to it, but I did not swear to it. I said I could not bind my successors, and the boy understood me. He wasn't happy, Lord Uhtred, but he's no fool. He doesn't want trouble with the Welsh while his eyes are on the north country.'

'And what of Constantine,' I asked, 'will he keep his oath?'

'Not if he wants to keep his throne. His lords won't be happy to have their king accept this humiliation, and the Scots are a proud nation.' He walked a few paces in silence. 'Constantine is a good man, a good Christian and, I believe, a good king, but he can't afford to be humbled. So he buys himself a little time with this oath. And will he keep the oath? With Æthelstan? With a boy who breaks his promises? You want my thoughts, Lord Uhtred? I don't believe Constantine will wait for too long, and his kingdom is stronger than mine, much stronger!'

'You're saying he'll come south?'

'I'm saying that he can't let himself be bullied. I wish I could do the same, but for now I need peace with the Sais if I'm to make my country whole. But Constantine? He's made peace with Strath Clota, he'll do the same with Gibhleachán of the Hebrides, and with the beasts of Orkneyjar, and then he'll have no enemies in the north and an army fit to challenge Æthelstan's. If I was young Æthelstan I'd be worried.'

I thought of the dragon and the falling star, both coming from the north and both, if Hywel was right, prophesying war.

'I pray for peace,' Hywel went on, as if reading my thoughts, 'but I fear war is coming.' He lowered his voice. 'It will be a great war, and Bebbanburg, though I'm told it is formidable, is a small place to be trapped between two

82

great countries.' He stopped and put a hand on my shoulder. 'Choose your side well, Lord Uhtred, choose it well.' He sighed and looked up into the clouded night. 'There'll be rain tomorrow! But I wish you a restful sleep.'

I bowed to him. 'Thank you, lord King.'

'You may be a Sais,' Hywel called as he walked away, 'but it's always a pleasure to meet you!'

It was a pleasure to meet him too, or a pleasure of sorts. So Ealdred was an ealdorman, but of what? Of Northumbria? Of Cumbria?

Of Bebbanburg?

I slept badly.

Finan took the first guard duty that night, placing a dozen men around our shelters. I spoke to Egil for a while, then tried to sleep on the bracken bed. It was raining when I woke at dawn, a hard rain blowing from the east to dampen the fires and darken the skies. Egil had insisted that some of his men had stood guard with mine, but only one man had anything to report. 'I saw a snowy owl, lord,' a Norseman told me, 'flying low.'

'Flying where?'

'Northwards, lord.'

North towards Guthfrith's small encampment. It was an omen. An owl meant wisdom, but was it fleeing from me? Or pointing at me? 'Is Egil still here?' I asked the man.

'He left before dawn, lord.'

'Left where?' Finan had joined me, swathed against the rain in a sealhide cloak.

'He went hunting,' I said.

'Hunting! In this weather?'

'Last night he told me he'd seen some boar across the river,' I pointed south then turned back to the Norseman. 'How many men did he take?'

83

'Sixteen, lord.'

'Get warm,' I told the man, 'and get some rest. Finan and I want to exercise our horses.'

'We have servants for that,' Finan grumbled.

'Just you and me,' I insisted.

'What if Æthelstan sends for you?'

'He can wait,' I said and ordered Aldwyn, my servant, to saddle the horses. Then, as the wind gusted and the rain still pelted, Finan and I rode north. He, like me, was in battle-mail, the leather liners greasy, cold and damp. I wore my helmet and had Serpent-Breath at my hip. All around us was the wide spread of tents and shelters where the warriors of Britain were gathered uneasily at Æthelstan's command. 'Look at them,' I said as our horses picked their own path through the sodden grass, 'they're being told they're here to make peace, but every last man expects war.'

'You too?' Finan asked.

'It's coming, and what I should do is raise the ramparts of Bebbanburg and shut out the whole damned world.'

He grunted at that. 'And you think the world will leave us alone?'

'No.'

'Your land will be ravaged, your livestock killed, your steadings burned and your fields turned to waste,' he said, 'and what good will your ramparts be then?'

Instead of answering his question I asked one of my own. 'You think Æthelstan really gave Bebbanburg to Ealdred?' The question that had kept me awake.

'If he did,' Finan said, 'he's a fool. He needs you as an enemy?'

'He has thousands of men,' I said, 'and I have hundreds. What's to fear?'

'You,' Finan said, 'me. Us.'

I smiled, then turned eastwards. We were following the northern bank of the River Lauther which was in spate, fed by the storm, seething and churning over its stony bed. Guthfrith's encampment, crouched under the flail of wind-driven rain, lay to our left. There were few men visible there, most had to be sheltering from the weather, though a half dozen women were drawing water from the river with wooden buckets. They glanced at us nervously then carried their heavy pails towards the encampment where the camp-fires that had survived the night's rain smoked dully. I curbed my stallion and gazed at Guthfrith's shelters. 'I was ordered to bring only thirty men,' I said, 'but how many do you think Guthfrith has?'

Finan counted the shelters. 'At least a hundred.' He thought about that, then frowned. 'At least a hundred! So what are we doing here?' He waited for an answer, but I said nothing, just gazed at Guthfrith's camp. 'You're making yourself a target?' Finan asked.

'For an archer? No bow will shoot in this rain. The cord will be soaked. Besides, those men are watching.' I nodded towards a group of West Saxon horsemen who waited on the road that lay beyond Guthfrith's camp. That road forded the River Eamotum and then led north towards the Scottish lands, and I guessed that the men guarding the ford were the same men who had accosted us on our arrival, men who were charged with keeping the peace. 'Let's ride further east,' I said.

The rain's anger lessened as we rode, the wind became fitful and a low band of brighter cloud showed above the eastern hills. We followed the river past small patches of woodland and rough pasture. 'So Guthfrith swore loyalty to Æthelstan?' I said.

'But he'll still fight for Constantine,' Finan said.

'Probably.' I was thinking of Hywel's advice to choose my side well. My family had held Bebbanburg for almost four hundred years even though it was surrounded by a kingdom ruled by incomers, by Northmen, either Danes or Norse. Now Northumbria was the last kingdom in pagan hands and both Æthelstan and Constantine were eyeing it, wanting it. 'So why doesn't Æthelstan just kill Guthfrith?' I wondered aloud.

'Because of Anlaf, of course,' Finan answered confidently.

Anlaf. He was only a name to me, but a name that was becoming ever more familiar and ever heavier with threat. He was a young Norseman, the King of Dyflin in Ireland, who had made his reputation fast, and that reputation said he was a warrior to fear. He had conquered most of the other Norse kings of Ireland and reports from across the water claimed he had a fleet that could darken the sea. 'Guthfrith is family to Anlaf,' Finan went on, 'and if Guthfrith dies then Anlaf will claim the throne by inheritance. He'll bring his army over the water. He wants Northumbria.'

I swerved slightly northwards to the shelter of a copse and waited there, looking back the way we had come. A smudge of smoke hung in the sky from the myriad camp-fires of the men gathered by Æthelstan. Finan stood his horse beside mine. 'You think Guthfrith will follow us?' he asked.

'I suspect the archer last night was one of his men.'

'Likely as not.'

'And my death would be a gift to Æthelstan,' I added bitterly.

'Because he wants Bebbanburg?'

'He needs it. He needs fortresses all across the north and he knows I'll never surrender Bebbanburg. Never.'

Finan, rain dripping from his helmet's brow onto his grey beard, did not speak for a few heartbeats, then, 'He owes you everything.'

'He's risen above me. He's King of Britain and I'm old and irrelevant. He wants a new Britain dominated by Englaland and I'm a small pagan stone in his royal Christian shoe.'

'So what will you do?'

I shrugged. 'Wait till he summons me. I'll listen to him, then make up my mind.' I smiled wryly. 'If I live.' I nodded westwards. A dozen horsemen were following us, appearing between some low trees on the river bank. They were in mail, wore helmets and carried spears, swords, and shields blazoned with Guthfrith's boar. 'Let's keep going.'

We went on eastwards, faster now, the horses throwing up clods of damp earth from their heavy hooves. To our right the Lauther flowed to its junction with the River Eamotum that was hidden by thick trees to our left. Another belt of trees lay ahead and, once inside them, we lost sight of the horsemen who followed us. 'Go that way?' Finan suggested, pointing north to where the river was edged thick with trees. We stood a chance of losing the men behind us if we went into that larger patch of woodland, but I shook my head.

'We keep going,' I said.

'But . . .'

'Keep going!' I ducked under a low branch and spurred onto more wet pastureland. Ahead of us now I could see the two rivers getting ever nearer each other. 'Can we cross them?' Finan asked.

'We can cross the Lauther if we have to,' I said, pointing to the river to our right. I had sounded unenthusiastic because, though that smaller river was shallow, its water was piling and churning over a stony bed. 'I'd rather not try,' I added, 'because one stumble and those bastards will be on top of us. We'd do best to stay between the rivers.'

'They look as if they join!'

'They do.'

Finan gave me a curious look. We were riding towards the narrow point of land where the two rivers met and Guthfrith's horsemen were blocking our path back to the encampment, yet Finan heard the lack of concern in my voice. He glanced behind, frowned at the hurrying rivers, then looked at the thick woodland that still lay to our left. Then he gave a curt laugh. 'Boar hunting! You can be a sneaky bastard, lord.'

'Can be?'

He laughed again, suddenly glad he had ridden with me in the rain. We swerved northwards, heading for the trees, and behind us our pursuers came into sight. They were still a good distance away, but they must have reckoned we were trapped by the two fast-running and storm swollen rivers. I curbed the stallion, turned and faced them. If Egil was not where I suspected he was then we were indeed trapped, but I trusted the Norseman as much as I trusted Finan. 'I'm tempting Guthfrith,' I explained, 'because there's too much I don't understand.' Guthfrith's horsemen, I was not sure whether he would be with them, were spreading into a line that would drive us onto the narrow neck where the two rivers joined in a maelstrom of tumbling water. They were coming slowly, cautiously, but confident now that we could not escape them. 'I don't know what Guthfrith and Æthelstan promised each other,' I paused, watching the horsemen, 'and I want to know.' They were still two hundred paces away while we were perhaps fifty paces from the thick woodland. 'Any time now,' I said.

'You're sure Egil's here?'

'Does it matter? There's only twelve of them and two of us. What are you worried about?'

He laughed. 'And if Guthfrith is one of them?'

'We kill the bastard,' I said, 'but we question him first.'

And as I spoke so our pursuers drove their spurs back. They lowered their spears and hefted their shields as their big horses pounded the wet turf. We immediately spurred north towards the wood as if we sought the shelter of the trees and, as I urged my stallion into a gallop, I saw the flickers of light from spearheads among the leaves.

And Egil Skallagrimmrson came beneath his banner of the spread-winged eagle, his horses bursting from the wood in two groups, one charging straight at Guthfrith's men, the other aiming behind to cut off their retreat. Egil was screaming his war cry, standing in his stirrups, his sword Adder held high in the rain, and his brother Thorolf, a big man on a tall horse, rode beside him with his war axe ready to kill. They were Norsemen eager for a fight, and Finan and I slewed around to join their attack.

It took Guthfrith's men a horrified moment to realise the trap. The rain was driving into their faces, they thought us trapped, then a shout had alerted them. They, like us, turned their horses towards Egil, and one stallion slipped and fell. The rider shouted in pain, his leg crushed under the floundering horse, then Egil's spearmen slashed into them, throwing three men instantly from their saddles. Blood in the morning rain. Egil beat a spear aside with Adder and swung the blade back to crunch the edge into a man's face. The rest, trapped by Egil's second group of horsemen, were already throwing down swords and spears, shouting that they yielded. Only one man was trying to escape, bloodying his stallion's flanks as he spurred hard towards the Lauther.

'Mine!' Finan called, pursuing the fugitive.

'I want him alive!' I shouted. The man's scabbard flapped wildly as his horse pounded the sodden turf. For a moment I thought it might be Guthfrith himself, but the fugitive was too thin and had a long fair plait hanging beneath his helmet. 'Alive!' I shouted again, following Finan.

The man forced his horse down the steep bank into the Lauther's fast water. The stallion baulked, the spurs drew blood again, then one of the fore hooves must have trodden on a rock beneath the white-ravaged water because the horse fell sideways. The rider fell with him, somehow keeping hold of sword and shield. He managed to drag his leg from beneath the struggling horse, then tried to stand, but Finan, dismounted, was already standing over him with Soul-Stealer at his throat. I stopped at the top of the river bank. The fallen man's horse was trotting out of the water as the fallen man attempted to swing his sword at Finan, but then went very still as Soul-Stealer's point pricked the skin of his throat. 'You'll want to talk to this one,' Finan said, stooping to take the fallen man's sword and I saw that it was Kolfinn, the young man who had challenged me when we arrived at Burgham. Finan threw the sword onto the bank, then prodded Kolfinn to his feet. 'Up the bank, boy,' he said, 'and you won't need a shield.'

Kolfinn, streaming water, struggled up the muddy bank. He made a move towards his horse, but Finan rapped Soul-Stealer across his helmet. 'You don't need a horse either, boy. You walk.' Kolfinn scowled at me, looked as if he was about to say something, and then thought better of it. His long fair plait hung down his back, dripping, and his boots squelched as he was prodded towards the surviving men who were surrounded by Egil's spears.

'That was too easy,' Egil grumbled as I joined him.

We had eight prisoners, all of whom had been stripped of their mail, weapons and helmets. Their leader was a sullen man called Hobern and I took him aside as the others, under Norse spears, threw their dead companions into the Lauther. One of Egil's men was telling Kolfinn to take off his mail, but I stopped him. 'Let him be,' I said.

'Lord?'

'Let him be,' I repeated, then walked Hobern towards the river junction, followed by Thorolf, who carried his massive axe that he seemed eager to bury in Hobern's back.

So what, I asked Hobern, had been agreed between Æthelstan and Guthfrith?

'Agreed?' he asked sullenly.

'When Guthfrith swore his oath to Æthelstan,' I snarled, 'what was agreed?'

'Tribute, troops, and missionaries,' he said unhappily. He had been reluctant to talk, but Thorolf had thrust him onto his knees. Hobern had already lost his weapons, helmet and mail and he shivered in the chill rain. Now I was encouraging him to speak by holding a small knife close to his face.

'Missionaries?' I asked, amused.

'Guthfrith must be baptised,' he muttered.

I laughed at that. 'And the rest of you? You have to become Christians?'

'So he says, lord.'

I should not have been surprised. Æthelstan wanted to unite the Saxon peoples into one country, Englaland, but he also wanted every inhabitant of Englaland to be Christian, and Northumbria was still far from being a Christian country. It had been ruled by the Danes or the Norse for almost all my life, and more pagans were constantly coming by ship. Æthelstan could convert the country by slaughtering the pagans, but that would start a war that could invite the overseas Norse to intervene. It was better, far better, to convert the Northmen, and the fastest way to do that was to convert their leaders. It had worked in both East Anglia and Mercia so that the Danes who had settled in those lands were now kneeling to the nailed god, and some of them, like Bishop Oda, were rising in the church. I did not doubt that Æthelstan wanted Guthfrith dead, but killing him would only invite another member of his family to claim the throne and that would likely be Anlaf, the Norseman whose ships covered the sea and whose armies had conquered almost all his Irish rivals. It was better for Æthelstan to keep the weak Guthfrith on the throne, to force him to be baptised, to garrison his country with loyal Saxon troops, and to weaken his authority by demanding rich payments of tribute silver.

'And why,' I asked, 'did Guthfrith send you to follow me?'

Hobern hesitated, but I shifted the small knife so it hovered near his eyes. 'He hates you, lord.'

'So?'

Another hesitation, another shift of the blade. 'He wants you dead, lord.'

'Because I stopped him from reaching Constantine of Scotland?'

'Because he hates you, lord.'

'Does Æthelstan want me dead?'

He looked surprised at that question, then shrugged. 'He didn't say so, lord.'

'Guthfrith didn't say so?'

'He said that you were to pay him tribute, lord.'

'Me? Pay that turd tribute?'

Hobern shrugged as if to suggest he was not responsible for his answer. 'King Æthelstan said that Bebbanburg is in Guthfrith's realm and that you should swear loyalty to Guthfrith. He said your lands could make Guthfrith wealthy.'

'So Guthfrith must make war on me?'

'He must demand tribute, lord.'

And if I refused to pay, which I would, Guthfrith would take what he claimed I owed him in cattle. That would mean war between Eoferwic and Bebbanburg, a war that would weaken both of us and give Æthelstan the excuse to intervene as a peacemaker. 'Who was the archer last night?' I asked suddenly.

'Last night?' Hobern asked, then flinched as I pricked the skin beneath his left eye with the knife's point. 'Kolfinn, lord,' he muttered.

'Kolfinn!' I sounded surprised, but in truth I had half expected it would be the angry young man who had accused me of cowardice.

'He's Guthfrith's chief huntsman,' Hobern muttered.

'Did Guthfrith order my death?'

'I don't know, lord.' He flinched again. 'I don't know!'

I pulled the knife back an inch. 'Guthfrith received envoys from Constantine, didn't he?'

He nodded. 'Yes, lord.'

'And what did Constantine want? Guthfrith's alliance?'

Again he nodded. 'Yes, lord.'

'And Constantine would keep Guthfrith on the throne?'

Hobern hesitated, then saw the knife blade flicker. 'No, lord.'

'No?'

'He promised Guthfrith he could have Bebbanburg.'

'Bebbanburg,' I repeated flatly.

He nodded. 'Constantine promised him that.'

I stood, cursing the twinge in my knees. 'Then Guthfrith is a fool,' I said savagely. 'Constantine has wanted Bebbanburg for ever. You think he'd yield it to Guthfrith?' I sheathed the knife and walked a few paces away. Was I surprised? Constantine had sent Domnall to Bebbanburg with the offer of a generous treaty, but that offer simply hid the greater ambition to rule Northumbria, and as a generation of Northmen had discovered, to rule Northumbria you needed to possess its greatest fortress. If Guthfrith had allied himself to Constantine then he would have been dead in days and my great fortress would fly the flag of Alba.

'So what have you learned?' Finan had followed me.

'To trust no one.'

'Oh, that's useful,' he said caustically.

'They all want Bebbanburg. All of them.'

'So what do you want?'

'To settle a quarrel,' I said angrily. 'Did you bring that bastard's sword?'

'Kolfinn's sword? Here.' He held the sword out to me.

'Give it to him.'

'But . . .'

'Give it to him.' I stalked back towards the disconsolate prisoners. Kolfinn was the only one wearing mail, but he was soaked through, shivering in the gusting wind that was slashing rain from the east. 'You called me a coward,' I snarled at him, 'so take your sword.'

He looked nervously from me to Finan, then took the sword that the Irishman held out to him.

I drew Serpent-Breath. I was angry, not with Kolfinn, nor even with Guthfrith, but with myself for not recognising what was so damned obvious. There was Englaland, almost formed, there was Alba, with its ambition to rule still more territory, and between them was Northumbria, neither pagan nor Christian, neither Scottish nor Ænglisc, and soon it must be one or the other. Which meant I had to fight whether I wanted to or not.

But for now there was a lesser fight, and one, I thought, that would assuage the larger anger. 'You called me a coward,' I accused Kolfinn, 'and you challenged me. I accept your challenge.' I stepped fast towards him, then checked and took a pace backwards. He had retreated and I saw how his waterlogged boots had slowed him and so I went at him again, cutting Serpent-Breath in a wide, wild swing that he raised his blade to parry, but I had stepped away before the blades could meet and his parry faded. 'Is that the best you can do?' I taunted him. 'How did you get those arm rings? Fighting against children?'

'You're dead, old man,' he said and came for me. He was fast and he came for me as wildly as I'd seemed to go for him, he attacked so fast and so wildly that I was hard put to parry his first massive cut, but his sodden clothing made him clumsy. I was rain-soaked, but not as wet as Kolfinn, who grimaced as he swung again and I encouraged him by stepping back, pretending his savage assault was driving me away and I saw the joy come to his face as he anticipated being the man who had defeated Uhtred of Bebbanburg. He wanted the fight over quickly now, he gritted his teeth and stepped towards me and grunted as he swept his blade in a gut-slicing blow, and I stepped inside it and punched Serpent-Breath's hilt into his face. I hammered it into him, crushing one eye with the pommel and the sudden pain drained him of strength. He staggered back and I pushed him hard so that he fell. 'You called me a coward,' I said, then sliced Serpent-Breath to half sever his sword wrist. His fingers loosened their grip and I kicked the blade away into the wet grass.

'No!' he cried.

'I don't want to see your rotten face in Valhalla,' I told him, then used both hands to drive Serpent-Breath down into his chest, breaking through mail, leather and bone. He jerked, made a moaning sound that turned to a choking groan, then I tugged Serpent-Breath free and tossed her to Roric. 'Clean her,' I said, then stooped and pulled off Kolfinn's six arm rings, two of gold and four of silver, one of which was studded with garnets. 'Take his sword belt,' I told Roric.

We took everything of value from Guthfrith's men. Their horses, their coins, their mail, their helmets, their boots and their weapons. 'Tell Guthfrith he's welcome to weaken Bebbanburg,' I told Hobern, 'or welcome to try.'

We rode back to the encampment. Guthfrith must have seen us pass, and seen we were leading a dozen riderless horses, but he stayed hidden in his shelter.

And Fraomar was waiting for me. He bowed as I dismounted, and his freckled face looked dismayed when he saw the captured horses and saw Egil's men throwing down the captured weapons. He said nothing of what he saw, just bowed again. 'The king, Lord Uhtred, desires your presence.'

'He can wait,' I said. 'I need dry clothes.'

'He's waited a long time, lord.'

'Then he's well practised in waiting,' I said.

I did not change. The rain had washed Kolfinn's blood from my mail, but the stain was on my cloak, faded now to streaks of black, but still unmistakable. I made Fraomar wait for a while and then rode westwards with him to the monastery at Dacore. It lay in a small rainswept valley and was surrounded by patchwork fields and two well-tended orchards. There were more tents and shelters crammed into the fields, stands of bedraggled banners, and paddocks full of horses. More of Æthelstan's Saxon army was here, surrounding the timber-built monastery that sheltered their king.

I had to surrender Serpent-Breath at the monastery's gatehouse. Only the royal household warriors could wear weapons in a king's presence, though Hywel had made no fuss about Serpent-Breath the night before. I had brought Finan and Egil with me, and they laid Soul-Stealer and Adder on the table where another dozen swords lay. We added our seaxes, the short vicious broken-backed blades that could do such murderous work in the crush of a shield wall. My seax, Wasp-Sting, had bled the life from Waormund on the day I handed the crown to Æthelstan, and Waormund's death had begun the collapse of the army that had opposed Æthelstan. 'I should call that seax King-Maker,' I told the steward, who just looked dumbly at me.

Fraomar led us down a long passageway. 'There are only a few monks here,' he remarked as we passed doors that opened onto empty chambers. 'The king needed the space for his followers, so the brothers were sent south to another house. But the abbot was happy!'

'Happy?'

'We rebuilt his dining hall, and the king, of course, was more than generous. He gave the monastery the eye of Saint Lucy.'

'The what?'

'Saint Lucy was blinded before martyrdom,' Fraomar explained, 'and his holiness the Pope sent King Æthelstan one of her eyes. It's miraculous! It hasn't shrivelled and Lucy died seven hundred years ago! I'm sure the king will be pleased to show it to you.'

'I can't wait,' I growled, then paused as two guards, both in Æthelstan's scarlet cloaks, pushed open a pair of massive doors.

The chamber beyond must have been the newly built dining hall because it still smelled of raw timber. It was a long room, long and high, with great beams supporting a thatched roof. Six high windows were shuttered against the rain, so the hall was brightly lit by scores of thick candles burning on the long tables where fifty or sixty men sat. A dais was raised at the room's far end where the high table was set beneath a massive crucifix.

A raucous cheer welcomed me, which surprised and pleased me. Some men stood to greet me, men with whom I had stood shoulder to shoulder in shield walls. Merewalh, a good man who had led Æthelflaed's household troops, gripped my hand, and Brihtwulf, a rich young warrior who had led his men to fight beside me at the Crepelgate, embraced me, then stepped back as a sharp rapping noise from the high table demanded silence and order in the hall.

Æthelstan sat with six other men at the high table beneath the high crucifix. Bishop Oda, seated beside the king, had silenced the hall by hammering the table with the hilt of a knife. Æthelstan was at the table's centre where a thick stand of candles lit the gold circlet on his long dark hair, which,

I saw, glinted with the threads of gold he twisted into his ringlets. I assumed that Oda had demanded silence because my duty was to greet the king before I spoke to other men. He was right, of course, and I dutifully bowed. 'Lord King,' I said respectfully.

Æthelstan stood, which meant every other man in the hall also had to stand, the harsh scrape of the benches sounding loud in the silence. I bowed a second time.

The silence stretched. Æthelstan stared at me and I stared at him. He looked older, which naturally he was. The young man I remembered had become a handsome king with temples lightly touched by grey and with thin streaks of grey in his beard. His long face was stern. 'Lord King,' I said again, breaking the silence.

Then Æthelstan smiled. 'My friend,' he said warmly, 'my dear old friend! Come!' He beckoned me, then gestured to servants who stood in the shadows at the hall's edges. 'Benches for Lord Uhtred's companions,' he pointed at one of the lower tables, 'and bring them wine and food!' He smiled at me again. 'Come, lord, come! Join me here!'

I started forward, then stopped.

Four of the men who stood on the platform with Æthelstan were young warriors, their necks and arms bright with the gold of success. I recognised Ingilmundr who was smiling, and the sullen face of Ealdred, though the remaining two were strangers. And with the warriors were two priests, which was no surprise. Bishop Oda was in the place of honour at Æthelstan's right and he, like both the king and Ingilmundr, was smiling at me in welcome.

But the priest to Æthelstan's left was not smiling, he was scowling, and he was no friend of mine; indeed he hated me.

He was my eldest son.

* * *

98

I had stopped in astonishment when I recognised my son. Astonishment and disgust. I was tempted to turn and walk away. Instead I looked back to Æthelstan and saw his smile had faded to an expression that mingled challenge and amusement. He had wanted this confrontation, there must be purpose in it, and I was beginning to suspect that my eldest son's famous hostility towards pagans was a part of that purpose.

Æthelstan owed me. Back in Lundene, on the day when the road by the Crepelgate was soaked with West Saxon blood, he had acknowledged his debt to me. I had given him the city, and with the city came the crown of three kingdoms; Mercia, East Anglia, and Wessex. But in the years since he had ignored me. It made sense now. Æthelstan had his advisers; warriors like Ingilmundr and Ealdred, and he had his priests like Oda, and now he had another; Father Oswald. And Father Oswald hated me, and suddenly I remembered what the Welsh priest Anwyn had said the night before, that Bishop Oswald was preaching. My son was a bishop, and a close adviser to Æthelstan.

He had been named Uhtred at his birth. That is the tradition of our family. My elder brother was named Uhtred, but then a Dane took his head and threw it down in front of Bebbanburg's Skull Gate. My father had renamed me on that day and I have been Uhtred ever since.

I had also named my eldest son Uhtred, but he had ever been a disappointment. He had been a nervous and fussy child, frightened of the mail-clad warriors in my household, and unwilling to learn sword-skill. I confess I was a bad father, as my father had been too. I loved my children, but I was away at war and after Gisela died I had small time for them. Alfred had put the boys into a school at Wintanceaster where Uhtred had sucked greedily on Christian teats and I remembered my horror at seeing him dressed in white robes and singing in a choir. Both boys became Christians and only my beloved daughter followed my older gods.

My younger son, now called Uhtred, might be a Christian, but he took to the warrior's life. He learned the craft of the sword, of the spear, and of the shield, but my eldest followed a different road, a road that led to his becoming a Christian priest. I disowned him that day. I called him Father Judas, a name he embraced for a while before settling on Oswald as his new name. I forgot him, except on the few occasions he appeared in my life. He was with me on the day that my younger son killed Sigurd Ranulfson, and Sigurd's brother, Cnut, almost killed me. Father Oswald had stalked our shield wall that day, praying and encouraging us, but we did not reconcile. He hated pagans and I hated that he had rejected my family's fate.

Then Brida, that hell-bitch who hated Christians and who had once been my lover and had come to hate me in turn, had captured Father Oswald and gelded him. She died too, gutted by my daughter, and Father Oswald's grievous wound had healed. I had cared for him, saw him healed, but was still resentful that he had abandoned Bebbanburg. We had not spoken since those days, but sometimes in the dark of night, as the sea wind about Bebbanburg's roofs kept me awake, I would remember him, but never with affection. Only with regret and anger. He had betrayed the duty of our family, which was to hold Bebbanburg until the final chaos roils the earth, until the oceans boil and the gods fall in blood.

And here he was. A bishop too? He was staring at me hard-faced from the platform, standing next to his king in a place of honour. 'Come, lord!' Æthelstan said again, smiling again. 'Welcome! Come!'

Gratitude, my father had always said, is a disease of dogs. So I climbed the platform to discover if Æthelstan had any trace of the sickness left and whether my eldest son, who resented me, was working for the destruction of my life's ambition, which was to hold Bebbanburg for ever.

Wyrd bið ful āræd

Fate is inexorable.

FIVE

I ate little, drank less. Æthelstan sat me at the place of honour, to his right, moving Bishop Oda down the bench to make room for me. The king offered me wine, ham, cheeses, fresh bread, and almonds he said were a gift from the King of the Franks. He asked after my health and enquired of Benedetta. 'I heard she was living with you,' he said, 'and of course I remember her from my father's court.'

'Where she was a slave,' I snarled.

'And I remember her as a most beautiful woman,' he ignored my tone, 'and yes, a slave too. Is that why you haven't married her, lord?'

'Certainly not,' I said curtly, then decided some explanation was needed. 'She's superstitious about marriage.'

'As am I,' Æthelstan said with a smile.

'But you should marry, lord King,' I said. 'Your kingdoms need an heir.'

'They have one! My half-brother Edmund. You know him, surely?'

'I remember him as an irritating child.'

He laughed at that. 'You never liked children, did you? Even your own.'

There was a sting in those last three words. 'I loved my children,' I said, 'but I lost three.' I touched the hammer hanging at my neck.

'Three?' he asked.

'I had a son by my first marriage,' I explained. 'He died as a child.'

'I'm sorry. I didn't know.'

'Then Stiorra died.'

Æthelstan chose not to ask which child was the third, because he understood that I meant Bishop Oswald. And my eldest son was indeed a bishop, appointed to the diocese of Ceaster. He was still sitting to Æthelstan's left, but the two of us ignored each other. My son had bowed his head in a cold welcome as I climbed to the platform, but I had not responded, not even looked into his eyes. Then, at a moment when Æthelstan was distracted, I had turned to Bishop Oda. 'Why didn't you tell me?' I asked in a low voice.

Oda had not needed the question explained. He shrugged. 'The king wanted to surprise you, lord.' He had looked at me with his grave, clever eyes, his expression unreadable.

'You mean he wanted to shock me.'

'I mean he prays for a reconciliation. We all do. Your son is a good man, lord.'

'He's not my son.'

The anger and remorse were making me sullen. Æthelstan might have welcomed me profusely, but I still felt I was in a trap. Killing Kolfinn had been easy, but this welcome in a new-built hall was filling me with dread. 'Prince Edmund shows promise!' Æthelstan now said enthusiastically. 'He's become a good warrior, lord. He wanted to come north with us, but I left him to command in Wintanceaster.'

I grunted in response and stared down into the candle-lit hall where men looked back at me. I knew many of them, but to the younger men I was a stranger, a relic, a name from the past. They had heard of me, they had heard the stories of men killed and armies beaten, and they could see the bright rings on my arms, could see the scars of war on my cheeks, but they could also see the grey beard and the deep lines that marked my face. I was the past and they were the future. I no longer mattered.

Æthelstan glanced up at the shuttered windows. 'I do believe the sun is trying to shine,' he said. 'I hoped to take a ride,' he went on. 'You'll accompany me, lord?'

'I rode this morning, lord King,' I said ungraciously.

'In that rain?'

'There was a man I needed to kill,' I said. He just looked at me, his dark eyes sunk in his long face. His enemies had ridiculed him as 'pretty boy', but those enemies were dead now, and the pretty boy had outgrown his boyish looks to become a sternly handsome man, even an impressive man. 'He's dead now,' I finished.

I saw a trace of a smile. He knew I was provoking him, but he refused to take offence at my sullen manners. He might have forbidden men to quarrel, had given orders that weapons were not to be carried, yet I had just confessed to a killing and he simply let it pass. 'We'll ride,' he said firmly, 'and take some hawks, yes?' He clapped his hands, summoning the attention of everyone in the hall. 'The sun is out! Shall we hunt?' He pushed his seat back, prompting the whole hall to stand with him.

We would go hunting.

Neither Bishop Oda nor Bishop Oswald rode with us, which was something of a relief to me. Oda had told me that Æthelstan wanted a reconciliation and I had feared I would be thrust into my eldest son's company through the afternoon, but instead Æthelstan himself rode with me while most of the company trailed behind. A score of mail-clad warriors escorted us, grim men in scarlet cloaks carrying long spears and mounted on big stallions. 'You fear an enemy?' I asked Æthelstan as we left the monastery.

'I fear no enemies,' he said cheerfully, 'because I am well guarded.'

'So am I,' I retorted, 'but last night an archer tried to kill me.'

'So I heard! And you think they might try to skewer me too?'

'Perhaps.'

'And you thought it was one of Hywel's men?'

The question told me he knew I had been in Hywel's tent the night before. 'The Welsh use long hunting bows,' I said, 'but Hywel swears it was not one of his men.'

'I'm sure it wasn't! Hywel has no quarrel with you and he's made peace with me. I trust him.' He smiled. 'Have you ever tried to stretch a long hunting bow? I tried once! Dear God, but you have to be strong! I pulled the cord all the way back, but my right arm was trembling with the effort.' He turned to Ealdred who rode on his left. 'Have you ever tried to pull one, Lord Ealdred?'

'No, lord King,' Ealdred said. He was unhappy at being forced into my company and refused to look at me.

'You should try!' Æthelstan said cheerfully. He carried a hooded hawk, which moved its head sharply as we spoke. 'He's a tiercel,' Æthelstan said, lifting his wrist to show me the hawk. 'Lord Ealdred prefers to fly a female. She's bigger, of course, but I swear this little bastard is more vicious.'

'They're all vicious,' I said. I carried no bird. If I hunt I like to use a boar spear, but my son, my second son, was fond of flying hawks. I had left him in command of Bebbanburg and I hoped no vicious bastard was trying to take that fortress away from me while I was on the other side of Northumbria.

We had ridden back to the encampment and Æthelstan curbed his horse close to the big stone circle where his tent stood. He pointed to a great boulder that stood gaunt at the entrance. 'No one can explain those stones,' he said.

'The old people put them there,' I said.

'Yes, but why?'

'Because they knew no better, lord King,' Ealdred said.

Æthelstan frowned slightly as he gazed at the stone. Men had seen us and some wandered towards our horses, only to be shepherded away by the mounted guards. 'There are so many of them,' Æthelstan said, talking of the stones, 'all across the kingdom. Great circles of stone and we don't know why they were put here.'

'Pagan superstition,' Ealdred said dismissively.

'Your son,' Æthelstan was speaking to me and he meant my eldest son, 'would have us pull the stone circles down.'

'Why?'

'Because they're pagan, of course!'

'Those gods are dead,' I said, nodding at the stone, 'they can't trouble us.'

'They were never alive, Lord Uhtred, there is only one God!' Æthelstan waved at the man commanding his escort. 'Don't push them back! They mean no harm!' He was speaking of the men who had come to watch him pass and now he rode towards them, stopped close and spoke to them. I heard them laughing.

He had the gift, I thought. Men liked him. He looked like a king, of course, and that helped, but Æthelstan added his own elegance to the crown. Now, riding to hawk, he wore a simple gold circlet that glinted in the weak sunlight. His horse, a tall grey stallion, was caparisoned with soft leather embossed with golden badges, his spurs were gold, while his long black cloak was hemmed with golden thread. I looked at the men's faces and saw they were pleased their

106

king had stopped to talk with them. They grinned, they
smiled, they laughed at his words. They knew the rumours,
who did not? Rumours that said their king refused to marry
and preferred the company of young good-looking men,
but they did not mind because Æthelstan looked like a king,
because he had led them in battle and had proven that he
was as brave and as hard a fighter as any of his warriors,
and because he liked them. He trusted them. He was joking
with them now, and they cheered him.

'He's good.' Ealdred had edged his horse close to mine.

'He always was,' I said, still looking at Æthelstan.

There was an awkward pause, then Ealdred cleared his
throat. 'I should apologise to you, lord.'

'You should?'

'Last night, lord, I did not know who you were.'

'Now you do,' I said curtly, and spurred my horse
forward.

I was behaving badly. I knew that, but could not prevent
myself. There were too many secrets, too many ambitious men
who had their eyes on Northumbria, and I am a Northumbrian.
I am Jarl Uhtred of Northumbria, and my ancestors had taken
this land from the British and we had held it against them,
against the Danes and against the Norsemen. Now, I knew, I
must hold it again, but against whom?

I turned my horse, ignoring Ealdred, and saw that Egil
was deep in conversation with Ingilmundr, a fellow
Norseman, and Ingilmundr saw me looking towards them
and bowed his head. I did not respond, but noticed the big
golden cross hanging at his chest. Finan joined me. 'Learned
anything?' he asked quietly.

'Nothing.'

'I've learned,' he said quietly, 'that Ingilmundr has been
baptised.'

'I saw the cross.'

107

'You can't miss it! You could crucify a sheep on that cross. And he says he'll lead all the Norse of Wirhealum to Ceaster to be baptised too.'

'Ceaster,' I said bleakly.

'Because Bishop Oswald has convinced them of the truth,' Finan said tonelessly. He knew better than to say the bishop was my son. 'And perhaps he has?' Finan added sceptically. I grunted. Pagans did convert, of course, Bishop Oda was proof of that, but I trusted Ingilmundr about as much as I would trust a starving wolf in a sheepfold. 'Ingilmundr told me,' Finan went on, 'that we are all Ænglisc now.'

'We are?'

'I thought you'd be pleased.'

I laughed, though without much humour, and Æthelstan, coming back to us, heard me. 'You're cheerful, Lord Uhtred.'

'Always in your company, lord King,' I said sourly.

'And Finan, my old friend! How are you?' Æthelstan did not wait for an answer. 'Let's ride north! Lord Uhtred, you'll keep me company?'

We crossed the Eamotum's ford and pounded north on soggy turf beside the straight Roman road. Æthelstan, once away from the camp, had summoned a servant to take the hawk from his wrist. 'He doesn't like to fly in damp weather,' he explained to me, but I sensed he had not intended to hunt anyway. More mounted men had joined us, all in scarlet cloaks, all in mail, all helmeted and all carrying shields and heavy spears. Groups of them scattered in front of us, scouting the higher ground, making a wide cordon around the king who led me up a slight grassy rise to where ancient turf walls made a crude square. There were low masonry walls at one corner, the old stones thick with weeds and lichen. 'Probably a Roman camp,' Æthelstan explained as he dismounted. 'Walk with me!'

His scarlet-cloaked protectors surrounded the old camp, but only he and I walked the wet turf enclosed by the decayed walls. 'What did Hywel say last night?' he asked me without any small talk first.

I was surprised at the abruptness, but gave him a true answer that he was probably pleased to hear. 'That he'll keep his treaty with you.'

'So he will, so he will.' He paused and half frowned. 'At least I think he will.'

'But you were harsh with him, lord King.'

'Harsh?' He sounded surprised.

'He told me he pays twenty-four pounds of gold, three hundred of silver, and ten thousand head of cattle a year.'

'So he does.'

'Can't Christian kings make peace without a price?'

'It isn't a price,' he explained. 'We are an island under assault. The Norse flood into the Irish Sea, their fleets come with the north wind and their warriors seek our land. Wales is a small land, a vulnerable land, and their coasts have already been assailed. That money, Lord Uhtred, pays for the spears that will defend them.'

'Your spears?'

'Mine indeed! Didn't Hywel tell you? If his land is attacked then we will defend it. I am making a Christian peace, an alliance of Christian nations against the pagan north, and war costs money.'

'Yet your peace demands that the weak pay the strong. Shouldn't you be paying Hywel to keep his own army strong?'

Æthelstan appeared to ignore that question. He paced on, frowning. 'We are an island and an attack on one Christian kingdom is an attack on all. There has to be a leader, and God has decreed that we are the largest kingdom, the strongest, and so we will lead the defence against whatever pagans come to ravage the island.'

'So if the Norse land in northern Alba,' I suggested, 'you will march to fight them?'

'If Constantine cannot defeat them? Of course!'

'So Hywel and Constantine are paying for their own protection?'

'Why shouldn't they?'

'They didn't ask for it,' I said harshly, 'you imposed it on them.'

'Because they lack vision. This peace I'm forging is for their own good.' He had led me to the low masonry walls where he sat, inviting me to join him. 'In time they will understand that.' He paused as if expecting an answer, but when I said nothing, he became agitated. 'Why do you think I called this gathering in Burgham?'

'I've no idea.'

'This is Cumbria!' He waved a hand glinting with jewel-studded rings. 'This is Saxon land, our land, it was captured by our ancestors and for centuries it has been farmed by our people. There are churches and monasteries, roads and markets, yet in all Britain there isn't a more lawless place! How many Norse live here now? How many Danes! Owain of Strath Clota claims it as his own, Constantine has even dared name a man to rule it! Yet what country is it? It is Northumbria!' He stressed the last three words, slapping a stone as he said each one. 'And what has Northumbria done to drive out the invaders? Nothing! Nothing! Nothing!'

'I lost good men defeating Sköll Grimmarson at Heahburh,' I said fiercely, 'and there was no help from Mercia or Wessex then! Maybe because I hadn't paid them?'

'Lord, lord!' he said soothingly. 'No one doubts your courage. No one disputes the debt we owe you. Indeed I came to pay that debt.'

'By invading Northumbria?' I was still angry. 'Something you swore not to do in my lifetime!'

'And you swore to kill Æthelhelm the Elder,' he said quietly, 'and you didn't. Other men did.'

110

I just stared at him. What he had said was true, but it was also outrageous. Æthelhelm died because I had defeated his men, slaughtered his champion, and put his troops to flight. Æthelstan had helped, of course, but he could only join the fight because I had held and given him Lundene's Crepelgate.

'An oath is an oath,' he still spoke quietly, but with a firm authority. 'You swore to kill a man, you didn't, so the oath is invalid.' He held up a hand to still my protest, 'And it is decreed that an oath with a pagan has no force. Only oaths sworn on Christ and his saints can bind us.' Again he held up his hand. 'But I have still come to pay the debt I owe you.'

One man, even the Lord of Bebbanburg, cannot fight the army of three kingdoms. I felt betrayed, I was betrayed, but I managed to bite down on my anger. 'The debt,' I said.

'In a moment, lord, in a moment.' He stood and began pacing in the small space enclosed by the ruined walls. 'Cumbria is lawless, you agree?'

'It is.'

'Yet it is a part of Northumbria, is it not?'

'It is.'

'And Northumbria is an Ænglisc kingdom, yes?'

I was still getting used to that word, just as I was becoming accustomed to the name Englaland. There were some who preferred Saxonland, but the West Saxons, who were leading the efforts to unite all speakers of the Ænglisc tongue preferred Englaland. It encompassed not just the Saxons, but those who were Angles or Jutes. We would no longer be Saxons or Angles, but Ænglisc.

'Northumbria is Ænglisc,' I admitted.

'Yet now more men in Cumbria speak the northern tongues than speak our language!'

I hesitated, then shrugged. 'A good number do.'

111

'I went hawking three days ago, stopped to talk with a forester. Man spoke Norse! I could have been speaking Welsh for all he knew, and this in an Ænglisc country!'

'His children will speak our tongue,' I pointed out.

'Damn his children! They'll be raised pagan!'

I let that statement rest a moment, watching Æthelstan pace. He was mostly right. Northumbria had rarely exercised power over Cumbria, even though it was a part of the kingdom, and the Norse, seeing weakness, were landing on the coast and building steadings in the valleys. They paid no money to Eoferwic, and it was only the powerful burhs on the Mercian frontier that deterred them from raiding deep into Æthelstan's land. And it was not just the Norse who sensed the weakness of Cumbria. Strath Clota, that lay on Cumbria's northern border, dreamed of taking the land, as did Constantine.

As did Æthelstan. 'If you dislike the Norse,' I said, 'and want Cumbria to be Ænglisc, then why keep Guthfrith as king in Eoferwic?'

'You don't like him.'

'He's a foul man.'

Æthelstan nodded, then sat again to face me. 'My first duty, lord, is not to kill the Norse, though God knows I'll slaughter every last one if it is His will. My first duty is to convert them.' He paused, waiting for me to speak, but I said nothing. 'My grandfather,' he went on, 'taught me that those who are Christ's servants are neither Saxon nor Norse, neither Angle nor Dane, but live united in Christ. Look at Ingilmundr! Once a Norseman and a pagan, but now a Christian who renders service to me, his king.'

'And one who met Anlaf Guthfrithson on the island of Môn,' I put in harshly.

'On my orders,' Æthelstan retorted immediately, 'and why not? I sent Ingilmundr to deliver a warning to Anlaf, that

112

if his ambitions stretch to this island I will flay his skin and tan it to make myself a saddle. I trust the warning worked, because I know Anlaf is tempted by Cumbria.'

'Everyone is,' I said, 'including you, lord King.'

'But if the pagans of Cumbria can be converted,' he went on, 'then they will fight for their Christian king, not for some pagan adventurer from Ireland. Yes, Guthfrith is a foul man, but Christ's grace is working through him! He has agreed to be baptised. He has agreed to let me place burhs in Cumbria, garrisoned with my troops who will shelter the brave priests who will preach to the unconverted. He has agreed that two Saxon ealdormen will rule in Cumbria, Godric and Alfgar, and their troops will protect our priests. The pagans will listen to Guthfrith, he is one of them, he speaks their tongue. I have told him he must deliver a Christian Cumbria to me if he is to stay king. And think what would happen if Guthfrith were to die.'

'Women would be safer.'

Æthelstan ignored that. 'That family may rule in Ireland, but they believe their destiny is to rule both Dyflin and Eoferwic. If Guthfrith dies then Anlaf will try to take Northumbria. He will claim it as his birthright. Better to endure a drunken fool than fight a talented warrior.'

I frowned at him. 'Why not just kill Guthfrith and declare yourself king? Why not say Northumbria no longer exists, that it's all Englaland now?'

'Because I'm already the king here, because this,' he thumped a foot on the turf, 'is already Englaland! Guthfrith has sworn loyalty to me, I'm his overlord, but if I remove him then I risk revenge from his Irish family, and if the Irish Norse attack in the west I suspect Constantine will attack in the east. And then the Norse in Cumbria and the Danes of all Northumbria will be tempted to side with the invaders. Even the Welsh! Despite Hywel's promise. None of them like us! We're the *Sais* and they fear our power, they want to diminish us, and a war between us and all our enemies will be a more terrible war than any that even my grandfather fought. I don't want that to happen. I want to impose order on Northumbria. I don't want more chaos and bloodshed! And by keeping Guthfrith, and by keeping him on a tight rein, I will convert the northern pagans into law-abiding Christian folk and persuade our enemies that Northumbria is not an opportunity for ambitious men. I want a peaceful, prosperous, Christian island.'

'Ruled by Englaland,' I said grimly.

'Ruled by Almighty God! But if God decrees that Englaland is the most powerful kingdom in Britain then yes, Englaland must lead.'

'And to achieve that,' I still spoke sourly, 'you're relying on a drunken fool to convert us pagans?'

'And to keep Anlaf at bay, yes.'

'And you told the drunken fool to demand tribute from me.'

'You live in his land, why should you not contribute to his treasury? Why should you not swear an oath of loyalty to him? You live in Northumbria, do you not?' I was so shocked at his suggestion that I should swear loyalty to Guthfrith that I said nothing, though my indignation must have been stark on my face. 'Are you above the law, Lord Uhtred?' Æthelstan asked sternly.

'Guthfrith has no law,' I snapped. 'And pay him tribute? Why should I pay for his ale and his whores?'

'Lord Ealdred will keep a garrison in Eoferwic. He will ensure your silver is spent wisely. And as for the oath? It will be an example to others.'

'Damn the others,' I said angrily, then turned on him belligerently. 'I hear that Lord Ealdred,' I almost spat the name, 'was made an ealdorman.'

'He was.'

'Ealdorman of what?'

Æthelstan hesitated. 'Northumbria,' he finally said.

I had believed him till that moment. He had spoken urgently and passionately, driven by ambition, yes, but also by a genuine faith in his god, but that one-word answer was evasive and I challenged it harshly. 'I'm the Ealdorman of Northumbria.'

He smiled, recovering his equanimity. 'But a lawless country needs authority and authority flows from the king through his nobility. This king,' he touched the gold cross at his breast, 'has decided that Northumbria needs more than one ealdorman if it is to be tamed. Lords Godric and Alfgar in the west and two more, you and Lord Ealdred, in the east. But before you protest remember that I have come to pay you a debt.'

'The best payment is to leave me alone,' I growled. 'I'm old, I've fought since your grandfather's day. I have a good woman, a good home, and I need nothing more.'

'But suppose I was to give you all of Wiltunscir?' he asked. I just stared at him, astonished, and said nothing. He looked back at me and it seemed impossible that I had raised him, protected him, even loved him as a son. He had a confidence so far removed from the boy I remembered. He was a king now and his ambition embraced the whole island of Britain, maybe further. 'Wiltunscir,' he said again, 'is one of the richest shires in Englaland. You can have it, lord, and with it the greatest part of Æthelhelm's estates.' Again I said nothing. Æthelhelm the Younger, Ealdorman of Wiltunscir, had been my enemy and the man who had challenged Æthelstan's right to the throne of Wessex. Æthelhelm had lost, and had died losing, and his wealth had passed to the king. It was a vast wealth and Æthelstan had offered me most of it; the great estates spread across three kingdoms, the towering halls,

115

the forests full of game, the pastures and orchards, the towns with their prosperous merchants. And all of it, or most of it, had just been offered to me. 'After the king,' Æthelstan said, smiling, 'you will be the greatest lord in Englaland.'

'You'd give all that to a pagan?' I asked.

He smiled. 'Forgive me, lord, but you are old. You may enjoy the wealth for a season or two, and then your son will inherit, and your son is a Christian.'

'Which son?' I demanded sharply.

'The one you call Uhtred, of course. He's not here?'

'I left him in command at Bebbanburg.'

'I like him!' he said enthusiastically. 'I always liked him!'

'You grew up together.'

'We did, we did! I like both your boys.'

'I only have one son.'

Æthelstan ignored that. 'And I can't imagine your eldest wanting to inherit wealth. Bishop Oswald doesn't want worldly riches, just God's grace.'

'Then he's a most unusual churchman,' I snarled.

'He is, and he's a good man, lord.' He paused. 'I value his counsel.'

'He hates me.'

'And whose fault is that?'

I grunted. The less I talked of Bishop Oswald, the better. 'And what do you get in return for the wealth of Wiltunscir?' I asked instead.

He hesitated a heartbeat, then, 'You know what I want.'

'Bebbanburg.'

He held up both hands. 'Say nothing, lord! Say nothing now! But yes, I want Bebbanburg.'

I obeyed his command to say nothing, and was glad to obey because my immediate reaction was to refuse angrily. I am a Northumbrian and my life had been dedicated to regaining Bebbanburg, but in the wake of that impulse came other

116

thoughts. He was offering me so much wealth, Benedetta would have the comforts she deserved for ever, and my son would inherit a fortune. Æthelstan must have guessed my confusion because he had held up his hands to silence me. He did not want my impulsive answer, he wanted me to think.

He said as much. 'Think on it, lord. In two days we break camp. The kings will depart, the monks will return to Dacore, and I shall travel south to Wintanceaster. Tomorrow afternoon we give a great feast, and you must tell me your answer then.' He stood and stepped towards me, holding out a hand to help me stand. I let him pull me to my feet, and then he gripped my hand in both of his. 'I owe you much, lord, more perhaps than I can ever pay, and in the time you have left on this earth I would like you close to me, in Wessex, as my adviser, as my counsellor!' He smiled, unleashing his handsome charm on me. 'As you once looked after me,' he said softly, 'I shall look after you.'

'Tomorrow,' I said, and my voice sounded to me like a croak.

'Tomorrow afternoon, lord!' He slapped my shoulder. 'And bring Finan and your pet Norse brothers!' He strode towards our horses that were held by a servant beyond the old camp's low earthen wall. He turned suddenly. 'Make sure you bring your fellows! Finan and the Norsemen!' He had said nothing about Egil's men accompanying me despite his order that I should only bring thirty men. It appeared he did not mind. 'Bring all three!' he called back. 'And now, let's hunt!'

The Christians tell a story of how their devil took the nailed god to the crest of a mountain and showed him the kingdoms of the world. All could be his, the devil promised, if he just knelt and swore fealty. And like the nailed god I had been offered wealth and power. The nailed god refused, but I was no god and I was tempted.

* * *

Æthelstan, I realised, was like a man playing tæfl. He was moving his pieces about the squares to capture the tallest piece and so win the game, but by offering me Wiltunscir he was trying to remove me from the playing board altogether. And of course I was tempted. And as we had hunted he had tempted me further by casually saying that I would remain the Lord of Bebbanburg. 'The fortress and estate are yours forever, lord, so all I'm asking of you is to let me supply the commander and his garrison! And only until we're sure of peace with the Scots! Once those scoundrels have proved they mean to keep their oath then Bebbanburg will belong to your family for ever! All yours!' He had given me his dazzling smile, then spurred on.

So I was tempted. I would keep Bebbanburg, but live in Wiltunscir, where I would command land, men, and silver. I would die rich. And as I followed him, watching the hawks stoop on partridges and pigeons, I thought of that casual promise, that he would only hold Bebbanburg until there was peace with the Scots. It had sounded reassuring, but then I remembered that there had never been peace with the Scots and likely never would be. Even when the Scots spoke of peace they were readying for war, and when we spoke the same smooth words to them we were busy forging more spears and binding more shields. It was an enmity without end. Yet Wiltunscir? Rich, plump Wiltunscir? But what a king gave, a king could take away, and I thought of what Hywel had told me, how his successors might not feel bound by the agreement he had made with Æthelstan. And would Æthelstan's successors feel bound by any agreement he made with me? Would Æthelstan himself? For what need would Æthelstan have of me once he was in possession of Bebbanburg?

Yet he had gripped my hand, looked into my eyes and promised to look after me as I had once looked after him.

And I wanted to believe him. Better perhaps to spend my last years among Wiltunscir's lush pastures and heavy orchards, secure in the knowledge that my son, my second son, would be given his birthright when the Scots bent the knee.

'Will the Scots ever make peace?' I asked Finan that night.

'Will the wolf lie down with the lamb?'

'We're lambs?'

'We're the wolf pack of Bebbanburg,' he said proudly.

We were sitting with Egil and his brother, Thorolf, beside a fire. There was a bright half-moon that kept vanishing behind high, fast clouds, while the wind, briskly cold from the east, whirled the sparks of our fire high. I could hear my men singing as they sat around their fires, and sometimes they would bring us ale, though Æthelstan had sent me a small barrel of wine. Thorolf tasted it and spat. 'It's good for cleaning mail,' he said, 'but damn all else.'

'Vinegar,' Egil agreed.

'Æthelstan won't be pleased,' Finan put in.

'He didn't want the wine,' I said, 'why should he care?'

'He won't be pleased if you stay in Bebbanburg.'

'What can he do?' I asked.

'Besiege you?' Egil suggested uncertainly.

'He has enough men,' Thorolf growled.

'And ships,' his brother added. For the last two years we had been hearing how Æthelstan was building new and better ships. His grandfather, Alfred, had built a navy, but his ships had been heavy and slow, while Æthelstan, we had heard, was making ships that even a Norseman might admire.

Finan stared up at the sparks whirling in the wind. 'I can't believe he'd besiege you, lord. You gave him his throne!'

'He no longer needs me.'

'He owes you!'

'And he has Bishop Oswald spewing hatred into his ear,' I said.

'The best thing to do with bishops,' Thorold said savagely, 'is to gut them like summer salmon.'

No one spoke for a moment, then Finan poked the fire with a branch. 'So what will you do?'

'I don't know. Truly, I don't know.'

Egil sipped the wine again. 'I wouldn't clean my mail with this goat's piss,' he said with a grimace. 'Did you give an answer to King Constantine?' he asked. 'Didn't he expect to hear from you?'

'I've nothing to say to him,' I said curtly. Constantine might expect an answer, but I reckoned my silence would be answer enough.

'And Æthelstan didn't ask you about it?'

'Why should he?' I asked.

'Because he knows about it,' Egil said. 'He knows the Scots visited you at Bebbanburg.'

I stared at him through the flames. 'He knows?'

'Ingilmundr told me. He asked if you'd accepted Constantine's offer.'

There comes a moment in battle when you know you have it all wrong, that the enemy has out-thought you and is about to outfight you. It is a sinking feeling of horror and I felt it at that moment. I still stared at Egil, my mind trying to take in what he was telling me. 'I thought of saying something,' I admitted, 'but he didn't ask so I didn't speak.'

'Well, he knows!' Egil said grimly.

I cursed. I had thought of telling Æthelstan about the Scottish envoys, but had decided to keep silent. Better to say nothing, I had thought, than poke that sleeping polecat. 'And you said what to Ingilmundr?' I asked Egil.

'I said I knew nothing about it!'

I had been a fool. So Æthelstan, all the time he was offering me wealth, knew that Constantine had made me an offer and I had not mentioned it. I should have known that

120

Æthelstan's spies riddled Constantine's court, just as the Scottish king had his spies among Æthelstan's men. So what was Æthelstan thinking now? That I had deliberately deceived him? And if I was to tell him now that I would not surrender Bebbanburg to him then he would surely believe I was planning to give my allegiance to Constantine instead.

I heard the chanting of monks and saw the same small group as the previous night, again led by the man with the lantern who walked solemn and slow, around the encampment. 'I like that sound,' I said.

'You're a secret Christian,' Finan said with a grin.

'I was baptised,' I said, 'three times.'

'That's against church law. Once is enough.'

'None worked. I almost drowned the second time.'

'Pity you weren't!' Finan said, still grinning. 'You'd have gone straight to heaven! You'd be sitting on a cloud now, playing a harp.'

I said nothing because the chanting monks had turned south towards the Welsh encampment, but one of them had left the group furtively and was coming towards us. I held up a hand to silence my companions and nodded towards the hooded monk who seemed to be coming straight towards our fire.

He was. His hood was deep, so deep that I could not see his face as he paced towards us. His dark brown robe was belted with rope, a silver cross hung at his breast, and his hands were clasped in front of him as though he prayed. He did not greet us, did not ask if his company was welcome, but just sat opposite me between Finan and Egil. He had drawn the hood further forward so I still could not see his face. 'Please join us,' I said sarcastically.

The monk said nothing. The chanting faded away to the south and the wind blew sparks high.

'Wine, brother?' Finan asked. 'Or there's ale?'

He shook his head in answer. I caught a glimpse of fire-light reflected from his eyes, nothing more.

'Come to preach to us?' Thorolf asked sourly.

'I have come,' he said, 'to tell you to leave Burgham.'

I held my breath against the anger welling in me. This was no monk, our visitor was a bishop and I knew his voice. It was Bishop Oswald, my son. Finan recognised the voice too, because he glanced at me before turning back to Oswald. 'You don't like our company, bishop?' he asked mildly.

'All Christians are welcome here.'

'But not your pagan father?' I asked bitterly. 'Who put your friend and king on his throne?'

'I am loyal to my king,' he said very calmly, 'though my first duty is always to God.'

I was about to say something sharp, but Finan laid his hand on my knee in warning. 'You have a godly duty now?' the Irishman asked.

Oswald was silent for a few heartbeats. I still could not see his face, but sensed he was staring at me. 'Have you made an agreement with Constantine?' he finally asked.

'He has not,' Finan said firmly.

Oswald waited, wanting my answer. 'No,' I said, 'nor will I.'

'The king fears you have.'

'Then you can reassure him,' I said.

Again Oswald hesitated, then for the first time since he joined us, he sounded uncertain. 'He cannot know I am speaking to you.'

'Why not?' I asked belligerently.

'He would see it as a betrayal.'

I let that remark rest for a moment, then looked at my companions. 'He won't hear it from us,' I said, and Finan, Egil and Thorolf all nodded. 'A betrayal of what?' I asked, though in a more kindly tone.

'There are times,' Oswald said, his voice still hesitant, 'when a king's counsellor must do what he thinks is right, not what the king wants.'

'And that's betrayal?'

'In a small sense, yes, in the larger? No. It is loyalty.'

'And what does the king want?' Finan asked quietly.

'Bebbanburg.'

'He told me as much this afternoon,' I said dismissively, 'but if I don't want him to have it then he'll have to fight over my walls.'

'The king believes otherwise.'

'Otherwise?' I asked.

'Where force might fail,' Oswald said, 'guile might succeed.'

I thought how cleverly Æthelstan had captured Eoferwic, putting Guthfrith to panicked flight, and I felt a chill of fear. 'Go on,' I said.

'The king is persuaded you have an agreement with Constantine,' Oswald said, 'and he is determined to thwart that agreement. He has invited you to a feast tomorrow. While you are eating and drinking, Lord Ealdred will lead two hundred men across Northumbria.' He spoke flatly, as if reluctant. 'And Ealdred will carry a letter to my brother, a letter from the king. King Æthelstan and my brother are friends and my brother will believe the letter and welcome the king's men into the fortress, and Ealdred will then be the Lord of Bebbanburg.'

Finan swore quietly, then threw another length of firewood into the flames. Egil leaned forward. 'Why does the king believe a lie?' he asked.

'Because his advisers have convinced him that Constantine and my father are allied.'

'Advisers,' I growled, 'Ingilmundr and Ealdred?'

Oswald nodded. 'He was reluctant to believe them, but today you said nothing of meeting Constantine's men in Bebbanburg and that convinced him.'

123

'Because there was nothing to say!' I said angrily, and again thought what a fool I had been to say nothing. 'There was a meeting, but no agreement. There is no alliance. I sent his men away with a gift of goat's cheese. That's all.'

'The king believes otherwise.'

'Then the king . . .' I began and checked the insult. 'You say he's sending Ealdred?'

'Lord Ealdred and two hundred men.'

'And Ealdred,' I guessed, 'has been named Ealdorman of Bebbanburg?'

The dark cowl nodded. 'He has.'

'Even before I talked to the king?'

'The king was confident you would accept his offer. It was generous, was it not?'

'Very,' I admitted grudgingly.

'You could go to him tonight,' Oswald suggested, 'and accept?'

'And Ealdred becomes Lord of Bebbanburg?'

'Better him than Ingilmundr,' Oswald said.

'Better me than either!' I said angrily.

'I agree,' Oswald said, surprising me.

There was silence for a short moment, then Finan poked at the fire. 'Ingilmundr holds land in Wirhealum, yes?'

'He does.'

'Which is in your diocese, bishop, yes?'

'Yes.' Curtly.

'And?'

Oswald stood. 'I believe he is a deceiver. I pray to God I am wrong, but with all charity, I cannot trust him.'

'And the king does.'

'The king does,' he said flatly. 'You will know what to do, father,' he said, then turned abruptly and walked away.

'Thank you!' I called after him. There was no reply. 'Oswald!' Again no reply. I stood. 'Uhtred!' That had been

124

his name before I disowned him, and the sound of it made him turn. I walked to him. 'Why?' I asked.

To my surprise he pushed back the big dark cowl and in the firelight I saw his face was drawn and pale. Old too. His short hair and clipped beard were grey. I wanted to say something to acknowledge our past, to seek his forgiveness. But the words would not come. 'Why?' I asked again.

'The king,' he said, 'fears that the Scots will capture Northumbria.'

'Bebbanburg has always resisted them. Always will.'

'Always?' he asked. 'The only thing that lasts for ever is God's mercy. Our family once ruled all the land to the Foirthe, now the Scots claim all of it north of the Tuede. They want the rest.'

'And he thinks I won't fight them?' I protested. 'I took an oath to protect Æthelstan and I've kept that oath!'

'But he no longer needs your protection. He's the strongest king in Britain, and his advisers are poisoning him, telling him you can no longer be trusted. And he wants his flag on the ramparts of Bebbanburg.'

'And you don't want that?' I asked.

He paused, gathering his thoughts. 'Bebbanburg is ours,' he finally said, 'and though I deplore your religion I believe you will defend it more savagely than any troops Æthelstan posts on its walls. Besides, his troops will be wasted there.'

'Wasted?'

'The king believes that if his plan for peace doesn't work then the island of Britain will have to endure the most terrible war in its history and, if that happens, father, it won't be fought at Bebbanburg.'

'No?'

'The Scots can only defeat us if the pagans join them, and the strongest pagans are the Norsemen of Ireland. We know Constantine has sent gifts to Anlaf. He sent a stallion, a sword and a golden dish. Why? Because he seeks an alliance, and if the Irish Norse come with all their power they will take the shortest route. They'll land in the west.' He paused.

'You fought at Ethandun, father?'

'I did.'

'Where Guthrum led the Northmen?'

'Yes.'

'And Alfred the Christians?'

'I fought for him too,' I said.

He ignored that. 'So if Anlaf comes, father, it will be a war of grandsons. Guthrum's grandson against Alfred's grandson, and that war will be fought far from Bebbanburg.'

'You're saying I should go home and protect that home.'

'I'm saying you will know best what you should do.' He nodded abruptly and pulled the cowl over his head. 'Good night, father.'

'Uhtred!' I called as he turned away.

'My name is Oswald.' He kept walking and I let him go.

And for a moment I just stood in the lonely darkness, overwhelmed by feelings that I did not want. There was guilt about the son I had rejected and an anger for what he had revealed to me. For a moment I felt tears prick at my eyes, then I growled, turned and walked back to the fire where three faces looked up at me questioningly. There, venting my anger at last, I kicked over the barrel so that wine, or perhaps goat's piss, poured and hissed in the fire. 'We leave tonight,' I said.

'Tonight?' Thorolf asked.

'Tonight, and we go quietly, but we go!'

'Jesus,' Finan said.

'The king mustn't see us readying to leave,' I insisted, then turned to Finan. 'We go first, you, me and our men.' I turned to Egil and Thorolf, 'but you and your men will leave just before dawn.'

126

No one spoke for a few heartbeats. The wine still bubbled and hissed at the fire's edges. 'You really think Æthelstan plans to steal Bebbanburg?' Finan asked.

'I know he wants it! And he wants the four of us at his feast tomorrow, and while we're there he'll have men riding to Bebbanburg, and they'll be carrying a letter to my son, and my son and Æthelstan are old friends and my son will believe whatever the letter says. He'll open the Skull Gate and Æthelstan's men will ride in and they'll take Bebbanburg.'

'Then we'd better leave now,' Finan said, standing.

'We ride south,' I told Finan, 'because not far away there's a Roman track to Heahburh.'

'You know that?' he sounded surprised.

'I know there's a road south from Heahburh. It took the lead and silver to Lundene. We just have to find it, and Æthelstan won't expect us to use that road. He'll expect us to go north to Cair Ligualid and follow the wall east.'

'And that's the road we take?' Egil asked.

'Yes.' Egil had brought far more men to Burgham than I, and my hope was that Æthelstan would believe we had all taken the Roman road north and so send his pursuit that way while Finan and I rode like demons across the high country. 'Go before dawn,' I told Egil, 'and ride fast! He'll send men after you. And keep the fires burning here till you leave! Make them think we're still here.'

'What if Æthelstan's men try to stop us?' Thorolf asked.

'Don't attack them! Don't give them the excuse to start a war against Bebbanburg. They have to draw the first blood.'

'Then we can fight?' Thorolf asked.

'You're Norsemen, what else would you do?'

Thorolf grinned, but his brother looked worried. 'And when we get home,' he asked, 'what do we do?'

I did not know what to say. Æthelstan would surely interpret my flight as a hostile act, but would he think it signalled a Scottish alliance? I sat for a moment, riven by indecision. Better perhaps to accept his offer? But I was the Lord of Bebbanburg, I had spent most of my life trying to recapture the great fortress, and would I now meekly surrender it to Æthelstan's ambition to see his flag flaunted from my walls? 'If he attacks our land,' I told Egil and Thorold, 'make your best peace with him. Don't die for Bebbanburg. If he won't make peace, then take to your ships. Go viking!'

'We will . . .' Thorolf growled.

'. . . take ships to Bebbanburg,' Egil finished for his brother, who nodded.

I had fought so long and so hard for my home. It had been stolen from me when I was a child, and I had fought the length and breadth of Britain to regain it.

And now I must fight for Bebbanburg again. We would ride for home.

SIX

We rode through the moon-sifted darkness. When the clouds covered the moon we had to stop and wait till our path was visible again, and in the roughest places we led the horses, stumbling in the night, fleeing from a king who swore he was my friend.

It had taken time to saddle the horses, to cram bags with food, then to go south past the Welsh encampment and follow the Roman road that would eventually have led us all the way to Lundene. We were seen, of course, but no sentry challenged us, and my hope was that no one would think a group of horsemen travelling south were really intent on fleeing northwards. Behind us the fires in our abandoned camp flared high as Egil's men fed them.

The road forded a river, then ran straight through stone-walled pastureland to a small settlement where dogs barked behind palisades. I had only the haziest idea of this countryside, but knew we needed to turn north-eastwards and at the settlement's centre a road led that way. It looked like a cattle-track, deep trampled by hooves, but I saw broken stone edging the verges that suggested it had been made by the Romans. 'Is that a Roman road?' I asked Finan.

'God knows.'

'We need to go in that direction.'

'Then it's probably as good a road as any.'

I was following a star, just as we did at sea. We went slowly because both the road and its verges were rough, but before the stars were lost in encroaching clouds they told me the road was indeed taking us north-east towards the bare hills that slowly showed themselves in a grey dawn. I feared that the crude track was not the road I sought, and that it would end at the hills, but it climbed slowly towards even steeper hills, their summits shrouded in cloud. I looked behind to see a pall of smoke over distant Burgham. 'How long will it take us to get home, lord?' Aldwyn, my servant, asked anxiously.

'Four or five days if we're lucky. Maybe six?'

And we would be lucky if we did not lose a horse. I had chosen a route across the hills because it was the shortest way home, but in this part of Northumbria the slopes were steep, the streams fast, and the road uncertain. By now, I hoped, Egil was well on his way north towards Cair Ligualid and, I assumed, was being followed by Æthelstan's troops. As we climbed higher I constantly looked back to see if men were following us and saw none, but then the low clouds came even lower and I lost sight of the road behind. The small constant drizzle soaked us, the day grew colder and I told myself I was a fool. How could Æthelstan mean me harm? He knew what Bebbanburg meant to me, he knew me as a son knows a father. I had raised Æthelstan, protected him, even loved him, and finally I had guided him to his destiny of kingship.

But what is a king? My ancestors had been the kings of Bernicia, a kingdom that no longer exists, but which once stretched from the River Foirthe in what is now Alba to the River Tesa. Why were they kings? Because they were the wealthiest, nastiest and most brutal warriors in northern Britain. They had power and they made yet more power by conquering the neighbouring kingdom of Deira and calling their new country Northumbria, and they held that power until a still more powerful king unseated them. So was that all kingship demanded? Brute power? If that was all kingship required then I could have been a king in Northumbria, but I had never pursued that throne. I did not want the responsibility, the need to control ambitious men who would challenge me, and, in Northumbria, the duty to subdue the chaos that ruled in Cumbria. I had wanted to rule Bebbanburg, nothing more.

The road led on through the mist and drizzle. In places the track had almost disappeared, or else crossed slopes of shale. We still climbed through a wet, silent world. Finan rode beside me, his grey stallion jerking its head up with every other step. He said nothing, I said nothing.

And kingship, I thought, was not just brute power, though for some kings that was enough. Guthfrith relished the power of kingship and kept it by bribing his followers with silver and slaves, yet he was doomed. That was clear. He did not have enough power and if Constantine did not destroy him, then Æthelstan surely would. Or I would. I despised Guthfrith, knew him to be a bad king, but why was he king? For no other reason than family. His brother had been king and so Guthfrith, lacking nephews, had succeeded him and so custom had given Northumbria a bad king just when it most needed a good king.

And Wessex, I thought, had been more fortunate. At its lowest moment, when it seemed that Saxon rule was doomed and the Northmen would conquer all Britain, Alfred had succeeded his brother. Alfred! A man racked by sickness, bodily weak, and passionate about religion, law, and learning, and still the best king I had known. And what had made Alfred great? Not his prowess in war, nor his sallow appearance, but his confidence. He had been clever. He had possessed the authority of a man who saw things more clearly than the rest of us, who was confident that his decisions were the best for his country, and his country had come to trust him. There was more than that, much more. He believed his god had made him king, that he had been given the duty of kingship, and that duty carried with it a heavy responsibility. Once, talking with him in Wintanceaster, he had opened a great leather-bound gospel book, turned its creaking pages, and used a jewelled pointer to show me some crabbed lines written in black ink. 'You don't read Latin?'

'I can read it, lord, but I don't know what it means,' I had said, wondering what dull words he was about to read from his scripture.

He had pulled one of his precious candles closer to the book. 'Our Lord,' he had said, gazing at the book, 'tells us to give food to the hungry, water to the thirsty, shelter to the homeless, clothes to the naked, and care to the sick.' He had plainly recited from memory because, despite the pointer and the candle, his eyes had not moved. Then those sombre eyes had looked up at me. 'That describes my duty, Lord Uhtred, and it is a king's duty.'

'It doesn't say anything about slaughtering the Danes?' I had asked sourly, which made him sigh.

'I have to defend my people, yes.' He had put the jewel on the table and carefully closed the gospel book. 'That is my most important duty and, strangely, the easiest of all! I have mastiffs like you who are only too eager to inflict the necessary slaughter.' I had begun to protest, but he had abruptly waved me to silence. 'But God also demands that I care for his people, and that is a task that never ends and cannot be won by battle-slaughter. I have to give them

132

God's justice. I must feed them in times of scarcity. I have to care for them!' He had looked at me and I had almost felt sorry for him.

Now I did feel sorry for him. He had been a good man and a kind one, but his duty as king had forced him to be a savage man too. I remembered him ordering a massacre of Danish prisoners who had raped and plundered a village, I saw him condemn thieves to death, and I had followed him into battle often enough, but he did those necessities regretfully, resenting them because they interrupted his god's duty. He had been a reluctant king. Alfred would have been happiest as a monk or a priest, working with ancient manuscripts, teaching the young, and caring for the unfortunate.

Now his grandson, Æthelstan, was king, and Æthelstan was clever, he was kind enough, and he had proved himself to be a fearsome warrior, but he lacked his grandfather's humility. As I rode the mist-shrouded hills I thought of him and came to understand that Æthelstan had something his grandfather had never possessed; vanity. He was vain about his appearance, he wanted his palaces to be glorious, he dressed his men in matching cloaks to impress. And vanity made him want to be more than a king, he wanted to be the high king, a king of kings. He claimed he just wanted peace in the isle of Britain, but what he really wanted was to be admired as the *Monarchus Totius Brittaniae*, the glorious shining king on the highest throne. And the only way he could achieve that ambition was by the sword, because Hywel of Dyfed and Constantine of Alba would not bow the knee just because they were dazzled by Æthelstan. They were kings too. I knew that Hywel, like Alfred, cared desperately for his people. He had given them law, he wanted justice for them, and he wanted his people kept safe. He was a good man, maybe as great a man as Alfred had been, and he too wanted peace in Britain, but not at the price of submission.

133

Æthelstan, I thought, had let the emerald-studded crown change him. He was not a bad man, not vile like Guthfrith, but his desire to rule all Britain did not come from a care for Britain's people, but from his own ambition. And Bebbanburg appealed to that ambition. It was the greatest fortress of the north, a bastion against the Scots, and to own it would show all Britain that Æthelstan was indeed High King. There was no room for sentiment, not with glory and power and reputation at stake. He would be High King Æthelstan, and I would be a memory.

We stopped many times during the day to rest the horses, and all day we were shrouded in the low clouds. At dusk, as the road climbed a high valley, I was startled from my thoughts by a strange hollow knocking. I must have been half dozing, slumped in the high-backed saddle, because at first I thought the sound was a dream. Then I heard it again, the same hollow crack. 'What was that?'

'Dead enemies,' Finan said drily.

'What?'

'Skulls, lord!' he pointed down. We were riding beside the road where the turf was easier for the horses and I saw my stallion had kicked a skull that now rolled to the road's edge. I looked behind and saw a scatter of long bones, ribs, and still more skulls, some of them with deep clefts where an axe or sword had shattered the bone. 'They weren't buried deep enough,' Finan said.

'They?'

'We're beneath Heahburh, I think. So these must be Sköll's men. We buried ours up on the hill, remember? And my horse is lame.' His stallion was still jerking its head up every time it put its weight onto the right forefoot. The movement had become far more noticeable over the last mile or so.

'He'll not make it to Bebbanburg,' I said.

134

'Maybe a night's rest? It'll be dark soon enough, lord, we should stop.'

So we stopped beneath that place of death, Heahburh, and I was glad the mist still clung to the hills so I could not see the broken walls where so many had died. We watered the horses, made fires from what little wood we could scavenge, ate hard bread and cheese, wrapped ourselves in our cloaks, then tried to sleep.

I was fleeing from the boy I had raised to be king.

We took four days to reach Bebbanburg. Finan's horse had to be left behind with two men who had orders to bring it home when the lameness was cured. We lost two horseshoes, but we always carried old-fashioned iron-soled hoof-boots made of boiled leather and, once laced into place, they let the horses keep moving. We hurried slowly, meaning we could rarely travel above a walk, but pressed on into the evenings and started again as soon as dawn's grey light showed us the way. The weather had turned nasty, bringing slashing rain driven by cold east winds, and my only consolation was that if Æthelstan's men were pursuing Egil and Thorolf then they too would be struggling into the downpours.

Then, on the last day, as if to mock us, the sun came out, the wind turned south-west, and the wet fields around Bebbanburg seemed to steam in the rising heat. We rode the sandy neck leading to the Skull Gate and the sea roared to my right sending the endless waves seething onto the sand, their sound a longed-for welcome home.

And there was no enemy, or rather none of Æthelstan's men waiting for us. We had won the race. If it was a race? I wondered if I had panicked, if I was seeing enemies where there were none. Perhaps Æthelstan had been speaking the truth when he said I would remain Lord of Bebbanburg even if I lived in far-off Wiltunscir? Or perhaps the bishop

I had whelped had lied to me? He had no love for me. Had he panicked me into flight to make it look as though I was truly allied with Constantine? I worried that I had made the wrong choice, but then Benedetta came running through the inner gate, and my son behind her, and panic or no panic, I felt safe. I only had two of the most powerful kings in Britain wanting my fortress, and Guthfrith was being encouraged to harass me, but there was a solace in Bebbanburg's mighty defences. I slid from the tired stallion, patted his neck, then embraced Benedetta in sheer relief. The great gates of the Skull Gate slammed shut behind me and the locking bar thumped into its brackets. I was home.

'Æthelstan is really not your friend?' Benedetta asked me that night.

'The only friends we have are Egil and Thorolf,' I answered, 'and where they are I don't know.'

We were sitting on the bench just outside the hall. The first stars were showing above the sea that had calmed after the wind. There was enough light to show the sentries on the ramparts, while firelight spilt from the smithy and the dairy. Alaina was sitting with us, a distaff in her hands. She was a pretty girl who we had rescued in Lundene after her father and mother vanished in the chaos that followed King Edward's death. Her mother, we knew, had been a slave and, like Benedetta, came from Italy, while her father was a Mercian soldier. I had promised the child I would do my best to find either father or mother, but in truth I had made small effort to keep the promise. Now Alaina said something in Italian and though I spoke scarce ten words of that language I understood well enough that she had cursed. 'What is it?' I asked.

'She hates the distaff,' Benedetta said. 'So do I.'

'Woman's work,' I said unhelpfully.

'She is almost a woman now,' Benedetta said, 'she must think of a husband in a year or two.'

136

'Ha!' Alaina retorted.

'You don't want to marry?' I asked.

'I want to fight.'

'Get married then,' I said, 'it seems to work.'

'*Ouff*,' Benedetta said and punched me. 'Did you fight Gisela? Eadith?'

'Not often. And I always regretted it.'

'We'll find Alaina a good husband.'

'But I want to fight!' Alaina said earnestly.

I shook my head. 'You're a vicious little devil, aren't you?'

'I am Alaina the Vicious,' she said proudly, then grinned at me. I truly did hope to find her parents, though I had become fond of the girl, thinking of her almost as a daughter. She reminded me of my own daughter, now dead. She had the same raven-black hair as Stiorra, the same defiant character, the same mischievous smile.

'I can't think why any man would want to marry you,' I said, 'horrible little thing that you are.'

'Alaina the Horrible,' she said happily. 'Yesterday I disarmed Hauk!'

'Hauk?'

'Vidarr Leifson's son,' Benedetta explained.

'He must be fourteen?' I asked. 'Fifteen?'

'He cannot fight,' Alaina said scornfully.

'Why were you fighting him?'

'Just practice! With the wooden swords. The boys all do it, why shouldn't I?'

'Because you're a girl,' I said with mock sternness. 'You should be learning to spin, to make cheese, to cook, to embroider.'

'Hauk can learn to embroider,' Alaina said briskly, 'and I will fight.'

'I so hate to embroider too,' Benedetta said.

'Then you should fight with me,' Alaina declared firmly.

137

'Is there a name for a girl wolf?' she asked me. 'Like a vixen? Or a mare?'

I shrugged. 'She-wolf perhaps?'

'Then we will be the She-Wolves of Bebbanburg and the boys can wind wool.'

'You can't fight if you're tired,' I said, 'so the smallest she-wolf of Bebbanburg had better go to bed now.'

'I'm not tired!'

'*Vai a letto!*' Benedetta said sharply, and Alaina meekly obeyed. 'She's a dear one,' Benedetta said wistfully when the child had vanished into the hall.

'She is,' I said, and thought of my daughter dead, and Æthelflaed dead, and Gisela dead, and Eadith dead. So many dead. They were the ghosts of Bebbanburg, drifting through the smoke-sifted night to fill me with remorse. I held Benedetta with one arm and watched the moon-silvered waves sliding towards the shore.

'You think they are coming?' she asked, not needing to say who they were.

'Yes.'

She frowned in thought. 'Did you spit?' she asked abruptly.

'Spit?'

She touched my forehead where, in the chapel before I left for Burgham, she had smeared a patch of oil. 'Did you spit?'

'Yes.'

'Good! And I was right,' she said, 'the danger comes from the south.'

'You're always right,' I said lightly.

'*Ouff!* But will we be safe? If they come?'

'If we work hard, yes.' I expected a siege, and if my bishop son had spoken the truth then Ealdred was already close to Egil's steading and would doubtless come south to Bebbanburg, though I doubted he had enough men to seal the fortress by land, let alone the ships to close off the

138

harbour. I reckoned I would have to drive him away and then prepare the fortress for an ordeal which meant summoning my followers who held land from me, telling them to bring men, mail coats, weapons, and food. The harvest was still weeks away, but cheese, ham and fish would keep us alive. Herrings had to be smoked and meat salted. Forage had to be stored for the horses, shields had to be bound and weapons forged. In the spring I had purchased a whole cargo of Frisian ash staves and they must be cut to length and the smithy must hammer out new spear-blades. I had already sent scouts north and west to look for approaching horsemen, and to warn the closest settlements to be ready to flee to Bebbanburg for safety.

I expected Ealdred's men in the morning, though when I climbed to the fortress's highest point beside the great hall I saw no glow in the western or northern sky to betray men camping. I thought back to Domnall's visit and how he had said I had no allies and that, I thought, was true. I had friends all across Britain, but friendship is fragile when the ambition of kings was fanning the fires of war, and if Æthelstan's fears were right then it would be a more terrible war than any in Britain's history.

The next morning, at daybreak, I sent Gerbruht and forty men north in *Spearhafoc* to discover what they could of Egil's fate. There was a warm west wind that would drive the boat fast and bring it back just as fast unless the afternoon brought a summer calm. I sent a smaller ship to Lindisfarena where the mad bishop Ieremias presided over his followers. That ship brought back salt from the pans on the island's shore and promises from Ieremias that food would follow. He wanted silver, of course. Ieremias might have been mad and he was certainly no bishop, but he shared with most real bishops a love of shining coin. We needed his salt for the newly slaughtered meat, and the fortress's outer courtyard

139

ran with blood as cattle that should have lived till early winter were pole-axed and butchered.

And maybe I imagined the danger. Had my bishop son lied to me? He had subtly encouraged me to flee Burgham to forestall Ealdred's arrival, but what if Ealdred was not coming? Had Oswald merely wanted to persuade Æthelstan that I was truly allied with Constantine? My precipitate flight must look like betrayal to Æthelstan, and if Ealdred did not come then I could expect a much larger army led by Æthelstan himself, an army large enough to starve us into submission. A son's revenge, I thought, and touched the hammer at my breast and then, because a man can never be too careful with fate, I spat.

Then Ealdred came.

Oswi warned me of their approach. He had been posted well north of Bebbanburg, watching the road that led from Egil's land. Ealdred, I reckoned, would have followed Egil and now came south to Bebbanburg to fulfil Æthelstan's instructions. Even before Oswi reached the fortress I cupped my hands and shouted at my men. 'Get ready!'

I had planned a reception for Ealdred, and my men, eager to play their parts, ran to prepare themselves. They looked forward to the deception, unaware that I could be bringing the whole wrath of Saxon Britain down on Bebbanburg. Most concealed themselves in their living quarters, some filed up to the great hall to wait in the side chambers, but all donned mail, wore helmets, and carried weapons. Only a half dozen would be visible to Ealdred on the ramparts and those six had been ordered to look dishevelled and bored. Once Oswi had galloped across the sandy neck and was safe in the lower courtyard, the Skull Gate was closed and barred. 'Must be close to two hundred of them, lord,' he told me when he joined me on the rampart above the inner gate.

'Scarlet cloaks?'

'A good number of scarlet cloaks,' he said, 'maybe fifty?'

So Ealdred, who called himself Lord of Bebbanburg, had brought some of the king's own bodyguard, Æthelstan's finest troops. I smiled. 'Well done,' I told Oswi, then cupped my hands and called down to Berg, Egil's younger brother, who was one of my most loyal and capable men. 'You know what to do?'

He just grinned and waved as answer. I had given him five men who waited with him behind the Skull Gate. All were in mail, but I had deliberately given them old coats that had broken rings and were fouled with rust. Behind them the courtyard was thick with blood, buzzing with flies, and littered with slaughtered and half butchered beasts. I walked to the landward ramparts where I was hidden by deep shadow in a watch house where sentries could shelter on dirty nights and freezing days. Benedetta was with me, as was Alaina, who was over-excited. 'Are you going to kill him?'

'Not today.'

'Can I?'

'No.' I was going to say more, but just then the first scarlet-cloaked horsemen appeared. They came in a long line on tired horses and stopped in the village to stare at Bebbanburg across the harbour. What did they see? A massive whale-shaped rock rising from the coast and crowned by great timbers and approached only by the sandy neck to the south. They stood watching for some time as the stragglers caught up, and this, I guessed, was Ealdred's first view of the fortress and he was learning just how formidable it was. He would see my flag of the wolf's head flying at Bebbanburg's highest point and he could see too that the ramparts were thinly manned. I instinctively had stepped back into the deeper shadows, though there was no risk that

141

he could see me at that distance. 'That's them, father?' My son had joined us.

'That's them. You'll wait in the hall?'

'I know what to do.'

'Let's not kill them if we can help it.'

'*Ouff*,' Alaina said, disappointed.

'There are priests with them,' Benedetta said, 'two priests.'

'There are always priests,' I said sourly, 'if you want to steal something it's good to have your god with you.'

'They're coming,' my son said as the far horsemen spurred their mounts again and headed south towards the rough track that approached the Skull Gate.

I clapped my son on the shoulder. 'Enjoy yourself.'

'You too, father.'

'Go with him,' I told Benedetta.

Alaina followed her and for a moment I was tempted to call her back. She was too obviously enjoying herself, then I thought Ealdred probably deserved whatever scorn Alaina chose to give him. I turned back to the Skull Gate where Finan and a dozen men had just disappeared into the guard chamber. We were ready.

I moved to the ramparts by the inner gate, but stayed hidden. I was dressed in my war-glory; my brightest mail, the helmet with the silver wolf snarling at the crown, my arm rings glittering, high boots polished, a golden hammer at my breast, a silver-plated sword belt from which Serpent-Breath hung, and all half-covered with a lavish bearskin cloak I had taken from a dead enemy. A sentry on the fighting platform above the inner gate grinned at me and I put a finger to my lips in warning. 'Not a word, lord,' he said. The stench of blood was thick and would stay pungent till the rain cleaned the outer courtyard.

I heard voices calling from the Skull Gate's far side. Someone thumped on the gate itself, presumably with a spear butt. Berg slowly climbed to the rampart. I saw him yawn prodigiously before calling down, though again I could not hear what words were spoken, but nor did I need to. Ealdred was demanding entrance, explaining he had a letter from King Æthelstan addressed to my son, and Berg was insisting that only six horsemen could pass the gate. 'If young Lord Uhtred gives permission,' I had told him to say, 'then you're all welcome, but till then? Only six.'

The altercation lasted some minutes. Berg told me later that Ealdred had crowded his horsemen by the gate, plainly intending to force an entrance if the gates were opened to permit a mere six men. 'I told him to back the bastards way off, lord.'

'Did he?'

'Once he'd called me a damned pagan Norseman, lord, yes.'

The gates were finally pushed open, six men entered and the gates were dragged shut and the heavy bar dropped into place again. I saw a look of horror cross Ealdred's handsome face as his stallion picked a nervous way through the half-dismembered corpses and the puddles of congealed blood. He glanced scornfully at the dishevelled men. Finan, who had only been in place to close the gates forcefully if he was needed, stayed hidden. More words were exchanged, but again I could not hear them, though it was plain Ealdred was angry. He had expected my son to meet him in the outer courtyard, but instead Berg, following my careful orders, was inviting him and his companions to the great hall. Ealdred finally yielded and dismounted. One of his companions was a priest who plucked up the skirts of his robe as he tried to find a clean path through the blood and flies. I turned and hurried back along the ramparts, climbing to the rear of the great hall where I let myself in to the private chambers. Finan joined me there a few minutes later. 'Are they in the hall yet?'

'Just arrived.'

I was again hidden, this time by a curtain that hung over the door into the hall itself, where my son was flanked by his wife Ælswyth and by Benedetta. A dozen of my men, all as dishevelled as the warriors who had greeted Ealdred, lounged at the hall's edges. Finan and I watched through the small gaps between the curtain and the door jamb.

Berg escorted Ealdred into the hall, along with the four warriors and the priest who was a young man I did not recognise. My son, seated at the high table on the dais, waved a casual welcome and Berg, unable to suppress a grin, announced the visitor. 'He's called Ealdred, lord.'

Ealdred bridled at that. 'I am Lord Ealdred!' he insisted haughtily.

'And I am Uhtred, son of Uhtred,' my son said, 'and surely it is customary, Ealdred, to leave swords at the entrance of the hall, is it not?'

'My business,' Ealdred said, striding forward, 'is urgent.'

'So urgent that manners are left at the hall door instead of weapons?'

'I bring a letter from King Æthelstan,' Ealdred said stiffly, stopping some paces short of the dais.

'Ah, so you're a messenger!'

Ealdred managed to suppress a look of fury, but fearing an outburst, the young priest hurried to intervene. 'I can read you the letter, lord,' the priest offered to my son.

'I'll let you explain the longer words,' my son said, pouring himself ale, 'and though I realise you believe all Northumbrians are unlettered barbarians I think I can struggle through it without your help.' He gestured to Alaina who was standing behind Ealdred, her legs apart and head back in plain imitation of his arrogant stance. 'Bring it to me, Alaina, will you?'

144

Ealdred hesitated when Alaina approached him, but she said nothing, just held out her small hand and finally, seeing no other choice, he took the letter from his pouch and gave it to the child. 'It is customary, Lord Uhtred,' he said sharply, 'to offer guests refreshment, is it not?'

'It's certainly our custom,' my son said, 'but only to guests who leave their swords at the hall door. Thank you, my darling.' He took the letter from Alaina who returned to her post behind Ealdred. 'Let me read it, Ealdred,' my son said. He drew a candle closer and examined the seal. 'That's certainly King Æthelstan's seal, is it not?' He put the question to his wife, who peered at the wax stamp.

'It certainly looks like it.'

'You know the Lady Ælswyth, Ealdred?' my son asked. 'Sister of the late Ealdorman Æthelhelm?'

Ealdred was plainly getting more furious by the minute, but struggled to keep his voice level. 'I know Lord Æthelhelm was my king's enemy.'

'For a messenger,' my son remarked, 'you're remarkably well informed. Then you know who defeated Lord Æthelhelm in the battle at Lundene?' He paused. 'No? It was my father.' He held the letter, but made no attempt to open it. 'And what I find very odd, Ealdred, is that my father has gone to meet King Æthelstan, yet you bring me a letter. Wouldn't it have been easier just to give it to him in Cumbria?'

'The letter explains it,' Ealdred said, barely hiding his anger.

'Of course it does.' There was a pause as my son broke the seal and unfolded the big sheet, which, I could see, had two more seals at the lower edge. 'The king's seal again!' My son sounded surprised. 'And isn't that my father's seal next to it?'

'It is.'

'Is it?' My son peered at the second seal, which was certainly not mine, then handed the letter to Benedetta.

'What do you think, my lady? Oh, and Ealdred, do you know the Lady Benedetta? She is the Lady of Bebbanburg.'

'I do not.'

Benedetta gave him a scornful look, then pulled a second candle closer so she could examine the seal. 'The wolf,' she said, 'it is not right. The wolf of Lord Uhtred has four fangs, this has three and a . . .' she shrugged, unable to find the word she wanted.

'Three fangs and a smudge,' my son said. 'Perhaps my father's seal was damaged on your journey. You look uncomfortable, Ealdred, do pull up a bench while I struggle with the longer words.'

Ealdred said nothing, just linked his hands behind his back, a gesture Alaina immediately imitated, causing Ælswyth to giggle. Ealdred, who could not see the girl, looked infuriated.

My son began reading the letter. 'He sends me greetings, isn't that kind? And he says you are one of his most trusted advisers.'

'I am.'

'Then I'm doubly honoured, Ealdred,' my son beamed a smile.

'Lord Ealdred,' Ealdred said though gritted teeth.

'Oh! You're a lord! I forgot. Lord of what?' There was no answer and my son, still smiling, shrugged. 'No doubt you'll remember in time.' He went back to the letter, absentmindedly cutting a piece of cheese as he read. 'Oh dear,' he said after a while, 'this does seem strange. I am to house you here? You and two hundred men?'

'Such is the king's wish,' Ealdred said.

'So he says! And my father agrees!'

'Your father saw the wisdom of the king's wishes.'

'Did he, indeed? And what is that wisdom, Ealdred?'

'The king believes it imperative to hold this fortress against any attempt of the Scots to take it by force.'

'I can see my father would agree with that. And my father believes his own forces are incapable of doing that?'

'I have seen your forces,' Ealdred said defiantly, 'unkempt, ill-disciplined and filthy!'

'They are a disgrace,' my son said happily, 'but they can fight!'

'The king wishes Bebbanburg to be held securely,' Ealdred said.

'Oh Ealdred! How wise of the king!' My son leaned back in his chair and ate the scrap of cheese. 'It must be held securely, indeed it must! Is that why my father added his seal to the king's letter?'

'Of course,' Ealdred said stiffly.

'And you saw him do it?'

The slightest hesitation, then Ealdred nodded. 'I did.'

'And you're really a lord? Not a mere messenger?'

'I am a lord.'

'Then you're a lying toad of a lord,' my son said, smiling. 'A toad of no truth, a dishonest toad. No, worse, you're nothing but toad shit, lying toad shit. My father did not add his seal to this letter.'

'You're calling me a liar!'

'I just did!'

Ealdred, goaded to rage, put his hand on his sword's hilt and took a pace forward, but the sound of my guards drawing steel through the throats of scabbards checked him. 'I challenge you!' he snarled at my son.

'I challenge you!' Alaina imitated him, and Ealdred, suddenly realising the child was still behind him and, turning, seeing her imitate his movements, lashed out. He slapped her hard, making her cry out as she fell to the stone floor.

And I stepped through the curtain.

One of Ealdred's companions muttered a curse, but otherwise the only sounds in the hall were the sigh of the wind and my footsteps as I crossed the platform and went down the steps to the hall floor. I walked to Ealdred. 'So not only are you a liar,' I said, 'but you strike little girls.'

'I . . .' he began.

He got no further because I hit him. I too had been goaded to fury, but it was a cold fury, and the open-handed blow I struck was calculated, sudden and brutally hard. I might be old, but I have practised sword-craft every day of my life and that gives a man strength. My blow staggered him. He almost kept his feet, but I pushed him and he fell. Not one of his men moved, and no wonder, because forty of my men were now filing into the hall, their mail bright, their helmets gleaming, and their spears levelled.

I stooped and gave Alaina my hand. A brave girl, she was not crying. 'Do you have all your teeth?' I asked her.

She explored her mouth with her tongue, then nodded. 'I think so.'

'Tell me if any are missing and I'll take that toad's teeth to replace them.' I stood over Ealdred. 'You are not Lord of Bebbanburg,' I told him, 'I am. Now, before we discuss the king's letter, take off your swords. All of you!'

One by one they handed their swords to my son. Only Ealdred made no move, so my son simply dragged his blade from its scabbard. I had my men draw up tables and benches, then sat Ealdred and his men down. I called for wax and a candle and imprinted my seal on a scrap I tore from Æthelstan's letter, then showed it to the priest alongside the seal fixed to the letter. 'Are they the same seals?'

The priest stared at them, plainly unhappy to be asked, but finally shook his head. 'It doesn't appear so, lord,' he muttered.

'The church,' I said relentlessly, 'is adept at forgery. Usually to claim land. They produce a document apparently signed by some king who died two hundred years ago, add a copy of the poor man's seal, and claim he granted them so many

148

hides of valuable pasture. Is that what happened at Burgham? This seal was forged?'

'I wouldn't know, lord,' the priest still muttered.

'But the dishonest toad would know,' I said, gazing at Ealdred, who had nothing to say and who refused to meet my gaze. 'The brave warrior who hits small girls surely knows?' I goaded him and still he remained silent. 'You may tell the king,' I said, 'that I will hold Bebbanburg, that I have no alliance with the Scots and I never will.'

The priest glanced at Ealdred, but it was plain he would say nothing. 'What if there's war, lord?' the priest asked nervously.

'Look,' I said, pointing at the rafters of the hall where the ragged banners hung. 'Those flags,' I said, 'were all flown by the enemies of the Saxons. Some fought Alfred, some fought his son and some fought his daughter. And why do you think they hang there?' I did not give him time to answer. 'Because I fought them. Because I killed them.'

The priest looked up again. In truth the banners were so ragged and so discoloured by smoke he could hardly make them out, yet he recognised the triangular standards of the Northmen among the flags of Saxon warlords, and he could easily see how many there were. There were ravens, eagles, stags, axes, boars, wolves, and crosses, the badges of my enemies whose only reward for their enmity had been a few deeply dug feet of Saxon soil. 'When you came through the gate,' I said to the priest, 'you saw the skulls. You know whose skulls they are?'

'Your enemies, lord,' he whispered.

'My enemies,' I agreed, 'and I'm happy to add more skulls.' I stood, then waited. Just waited and let the silence stretch until at last Ealdred could not resist looking at me. 'There is only one Lord of Bebbanburg,' I told him, 'and you can go now. Your swords will be returned as you leave the fortress.'

They left in cowed silence and, as they passed beneath the gate where ravens waited, and as they picked their way past the blood and butchered cattle, they must have noticed that the guards were now in clean mail and carrying spears scoured of rust. Still none of them spoke, but mounted their horses in silence, took their swords in silence, and then spurred beneath the Skull Gate which slammed loud behind them.

'That's made trouble,' Finan said cheerfully. He walked towards the steps that led to the gate ramparts. 'You remember that question Domnall asked you?'

'Which one?'

'How many allies do you have?'

I climbed the steps with him, then watched as Ealdred and his men rode away. 'We have Egil,' I said bleakly, 'if he lives.'

'Of course he lives,' Finan said cheerfully, 'it'll take more than a little turd like Ealdred to kill Egil! So it's Egil and us against the rest of Britain?'

'It is,' I said, and Finan was right. We had no allies and an island of enemies. I had humiliated Ealdred and so made a dangerous enemy because he had the king's ear, and Æthelstan would see my defiance as both a provocation and an insult. The monarch of all Britain would see me as an enemy now. 'You think I should grovel?'

I could see Finan thinking about that question. He frowned. 'If you grovel, lord, they'll think you're weak.'

He rarely called me lord, and only when he wanted me to listen. 'So we defy them?'

'Wiltunscir doesn't tempt you?'

'I don't belong there,' I said. 'It's too soft, too plump, too easy. You want to live there?'

'No,' he admitted. 'I like Northumbria. It's almost as good as Ireland.'

I smiled at that. 'So what would you have me do?'

'What you always do, of course. What we always do. We fight.'

We watched until Ealdred and his horsemen were out of sight.

We were alone.

PART TWO

The Devil's Work

SEVEN

Not quite alone because Egil lived. He had ridden hard to stay ahead of his pursuers, reaching his home a full half day before Ealdred and his horsemen appeared. 'He came mid-afternoon,' Egil had told me, 'took one look at the two hundred warriors on the palisade and disappeared southwards.'

'Two hundred!' I said. 'You don't have two hundred warriors!'

'Give a woman a spear, lord, cover her tits with a mail coat, hide her hair with a helmet, and how can you tell? Besides, some of my women are more terrifying than my men.'

So Ealdred had gone from Egil's home to Bebbanburg, then south to Eoferwic where, we heard, he was living with over a hundred West Saxon warriors in Guthfrith's palace. More West Saxons had garrisoned Lindcolne, which meant Æthelstan was tightening his grip on Northumbria.

And this meant that he would surely squeeze Bebbanburg, though as the summer drew on we were left alone. It was a time for filling our storerooms, of strengthening ramparts that were already strong, and of relentless patrolling of our southern lands. 'When will they come?' Benedetta asked me.

'After the harvest, of course.'

155

'Maybe they won't come?'

'They will.'

And my friends in Eoferwic would surely give me warning if they could and I had plenty of friends in the city. There was Olla who owned a tavern and whose daughter Hanna had married Berg. Like all tavern-keepers he heard gossip, and his whores had secrets whispered into their ears. There was one-eyed Boldar Gunnarson who was still one of Guthfrith's household warriors, and there were priests who served Hrothweard, the archbishop. All those men, and a dozen others, found ways to send me news. Their messages were brought by travellers, by trading ships, and ever since I had humiliated Ealdred the messages said the same thing, that he wanted revenge. A letter arrived from Guthfrith, though the language betrayed it had been written by a West Saxon, demanding my allegiance and swearing that if I refused to kneel to him then he would ravage my lands to take what he claimed I owed him.

I burned that letter, sent a warning to Sihtric who commanded the garrison at Dunholm that secured my southern border, and more warnings to every village and settlement inside my lands, and still nothing happened. No warriors rode from Eoferwic, no steadings were burned, and no cattle or sheep were stolen. 'He does nothing!' Benedetta said scornfully. 'Maybe he is frightened of you?'

'He's waiting for Æthelstan's orders,' I explained. The king was far to the south in Wintanceaster and doubtless Ealdred was reluctant to move against me without Æthelstan's approval, and that approval must have been given because as the summer waned we heard that four West Saxon ships had come to Eoferwic with over a hundred more warriors and a great chest of silver. That money paid the smithies of Eoferwic to beat out spear-blades and to persuade priests to preach sermons that denounced Bebbanburg as a nest of pagans. Archbishop Hrothweard might have curbed that nonsense. He was a good man, and his liking for me and his dislike of Guthfrith had made him advise Ealdred against starting a war between Eoferwic and Bebbanburg, but Hrothweard had fallen gravely ill. The monk who brought me the news touched his forehead with a long finger, 'Poor old man doesn't know if it's today or Whitsun, lord.'

'He's moon-touched?' I asked.

The monk nodded. He and his three companions were carrying a gospel book to a monastery in Alba and had sought shelter for the night in Bebbanburg. 'He forgets to dress sometimes, lord, and he can hardly speak, let alone preach. And his hands shake so that they have to feed him his gruel. There are new priests in the city now, lord, priests from Wessex, and they're fierce!'

'You mean they don't like pagans?'

'They don't, lord.'

'Is Bishop Oswald one of them?'

He shook his tonsured head. 'No, lord, it's usually Father Ceolnoth who preaches in the cathedral.'

I laughed sourly. I had known Ceolnoth and his twin brother, Ceolberht, since boyhood and I disliked them as much as they disliked me. Ceolberht, at least, had reason to hate me because I had kicked out most of his teeth and that memory, at least, gave me a happy moment and such moments were scarce as the summer faded into autumn. The raids began.

They were small at first. There were cattle raids on my southern border, a barn was burned, fish traps destroyed and always the raiders were Norse or Dane, none of them carrying Guthfrith's symbol of a tusked boar on their shields and none of them West Saxons. I sent my son south with thirty men to help Sihtric of Dunholm, but my land was vast, the enemy cautious, and my men found nothing. Then

157

fishing boats were attacked, their nets and catch stolen and their ships dismasted. None of my folk was killed, not even wounded. 'It were two Saxon ships,' one of the fishermen told me when I took *Spearhafoc* down the coast.

'They had crosses on their prows?'

'They had nothing, lord, but they were Saxon. They had that belly look!' The ships built in the south had swollen bows, nothing like *Spearhafoc*'s sleeker lines. 'The bastards who boarded us spoke foreign, but they were Saxon boats.'

I sent *Spearhafoc* south every day, usually commanded by Gerbruht, while Egil's brother, Thorolf, brought *Banamaðr* to help, but again they found nothing. The cattle raids went on, while in Eoferwic the priests preached vituperous sermons claiming that any man who paid rent to a pagan lord was doomed to the eternal flames of hell.

Yet still no one was killed. Cattle were stolen, storehouses emptied, steadings burned and ships dismasted, but no one died. Ealdred was goading me and I suspected he wanted me to kill first because that would give him an excuse to declare an outright war on Bebbanburg. As winter approached the raids became larger, more farms were burned and Norsemen came across the western hills to attack my upland tenants. Still no one died, though the cost was high. Rents had to be forgone, timber cut for rebuilding, animals and seed corn replaced. A second letter came with Guthfrith's seal claiming I owed him fifteen pounds of gold and I burned that letter as I had burned the first, but it gave me an idea. 'Why don't we give him what he wants?' I suggested.

We were sitting in the hall, close to the great hearth where a fire of willow logs spat and crackled. It was an evening in early winter and a cold east wind gusted through the roof's smoke-hole. Benedetta stared at me as though I had gone as mad as poor Hrothweard. 'Give him Bebbanburg?' she asked, shocked.

No,' I said, standing, 'come.'

I led Benedetta, Finan and my son through the door that opened from the hall's dais. Beyond was our bedchamber, a heap of furs where Benedetta and I slept, and I kicked them aside to reveal the floor of thick wooden planks. I sent my son to fetch an ironbar and, when he brought it, told him to lift the heavy planks. He heaved on the crowbar, Finan helped him, and they lifted one floorboard clear. It was a huge piece of timber, a foot square and two paces long. 'Now the rest,' I said, 'there are seven of them.'

I was giving away no secrets. Benedetta knew what lay beneath our bed, and both Finan and my son had seen the gaping hole before, but even so they all gasped as the last timbers were dragged aside and the lanterns lit the hole beneath.

They saw gold. A dragon's hoard of gold. A lifetime of gold. Plunder. 'Jesus,' Finan said. He might have seen it before, but the sight was still awesome. 'How much is there?'

'More than enough to tempt Ealdred,' I said, 'and enough to distract Æthelstan.'

'Distract?' Benedetta stared down into the gleam and glitter of the hoard.

'Æthelstan,' I said, 'has made a kind of peace with all Britain, except for me. I need to give him another enemy.'

'Another enemy?' my son asked, puzzled.

'You'll see,' I said and climbed down into the hole that was a natural hollow in the rock on which Bebbanburg had been built. I lifted out the treasures. There was a golden dish wide enough to hold a haunch of beef. It had women and goat-legged men chasing each other around the rim. There were tall candlesticks, doubtless stolen from a church, that I had taken from Sköll, there were ingots, gold chains, beakers, jugs and cups. There was a leather bag filled with

159

jewellery, with sword decorations of intricate beauty, with brooches and clasps. There were rubies and emeralds, arm rings, and a crude golden circlet that Hæsten had worn. There were gold coins, a small Roman statuette of a woman wearing a crown of sun rays, and a wooden chest heaped with hacksilver. Some of the gold had been hoarded by my father, more by his brother, my treacherous uncle, but most was the treasure of my enemies, the hoard I kept for when hard times struck Bebbanburg.

I stooped and found a crude cup that I gave to Finan. The cup looked as though it had been beaten into shape with a stone hammer, it was rough and lumpy, but it was pure gold. 'Do you remember those graves to the west of Dunholm?' I asked him. 'The three graves?'

'In the hills?'

'In the high valley. There was a tall stone there.'

'The Devil's Valley!' he said, remembering. 'Three grave mounds!'

'The Devil's Valley?' Benedetta asked, making the sign of the cross.

Finan grinned. 'The old Archbishop of Eoferwic called it that. What was his name?'

'Wulfhere,' I said.

'Wulfhere!' Finan nodded. 'He was a gnarly old bastard. He preached that the graves hid demons and forbade anyone to go near them.'

'Then he sent his own men to dig into the mounds,' I took up the tale, 'and we ran them off.'

'And dug into the mounds yourself?' my son asked.

'Of course,' I grinned, then touched the crude cup, 'but that was all we found.'

'And some bones,' Finan added, 'but no demons.'

'But it's time,' I said, 'that the graves are filled with gold and haunted by demons.'

I would set a trap. I would offer Guthfrith gold, more gold than he had ever dreamed of, and I would give Ealdred what he wanted, a killing. Because I would kill first and I would kill ruthlessly, but for the trap to work it must be well laid and had to be kept secret.

It took much of the winter to prepare. The older, rougher pieces like the stone-beaten cup and a brutal-looking torque were left alone, as were the ingots, but some of the others, like the candlesticks and some Roman dishes, were hammered into shapeless lumps. Æthelstan had demanded twenty-four pounds of gold from Hywel as part of his tribute, and by the time our work was finished we had over a hundred pounds of gold stored in a stout wooden chest. We did that work in secret, only Finan and my son helping, so that no word about gold could leak from Bebbanburg.

Ealdred's goading never stopped, though it was sporadic. Horsemen would come at dawn to burn granaries or barns, and to drive away the livestock. Still they killed no one, nor took slaves, and their victims told us that the raiders were always Northmen. They spoke Danish or Norse, they wore hammers, they carried plain shields. The raids cost me silver, but did no great harm. Buildings could be replaced, grain was sent from Bebbanburg, as were cattle and sheep. We still sent men to ride our southern border, but I gave orders that none was to cross onto Guthfrith's land. It was war without death, even without fighting, and to my thinking it was pointless.

'Then why are they doing it?' Benedetta asked angrily.

'Because Æthelstan wants it,' was all I could say.

'You gave him the throne! It is unjust!'

I smiled at her indignation. 'Greed overcomes gratitude.'

'You are his friend!'

'No, I'm a power in his kingdom, and he must show that he's a greater power.'

'Write to him! Tell him you are loyal!'

'He wouldn't believe me. Besides, it's become a pissing contest.'

'*Ouff!* You men!'

'And he's king, he has to win.'

'Then piss on him! Do it properly!'

'I will,' I said grimly and, to make that happen, in the late winter when snow still lay in the shadowed hollows on the higher ground, I rode south with Finan, Egil and a dozen men. We took tracks through the hills rather than ride the Roman road, and we took shelter in taverns or small steadings. We claimed to be searching for land and maybe the folk believed us, maybe not, but we wore no finery, flaunted no gold, carried plain swords and took care to conceal our names. We paid for our shelter with hacksilver. It took us four days to reach the Devil's Valley and it was just as I remembered it.

The valley was high in the hills. Those hills climbed steeply to the east, west and north, but at the southern end was a lip that fell away to a deeper river valley where a Roman road ran straight from east to west. There were straggly pines in the high valley, and a stream that still had ice at its margins. The three burial mounds were in a straight line at the valley's centre, their grass white with frost. There were deep scars in the mounds showing where we had dug so many years before and where, doubtless, the villagers from the river valley had dug since. The tall stone that had stood at the southern end of the mounds had fallen and lay in the thin turf.

'Summer pasture,' Egil kicked at the grass as we walked towards the valley's lip. 'Not much good for anything else.'

'It's good as a place to find gold,' I said. We stopped at the valley's southern edge where a cold wind stirred our cloaks. The stream tumbled over the lip to join the river that glinted far beneath us in the winter sunlight. 'That must be the Tesa,' I pointed at the river. 'The border of my land.'

'So this valley is yours?'

'Mine. Everything to the river bank is mine.'

'And beyond?'

'Guthfrith's,' I said, 'or perhaps Ealdred's. Not mine, anyway.'

Egil gazed into the wider valley. From our high place we could clearly see the road, a village, and an earth track going from the settlement to the Tesa's northern bank, and another track leading away from the opposite bank, a clear sign that the Tesa could be forded. 'Where does the road go?' he asked.

I pointed east. 'It joins the Great Road somewhere over there, then down to Eoferwic.'

'How far?'

'Two days on horseback, three if you're not in a hurry.'

'Then this,' Egil said, 'would be a fine place for a fort.' He swept a hand around the ground where we stood. 'It has water, and from here you can see an enemy coming.'

'For a poet,' I said slowly, 'and a Norseman, you have a brilliant mind.'

He grinned, unsure of what I was saying. 'I'm a warrior too.'

'You are, my friend. A fort!' I looked down the slope and saw a sheep track that ran downhill at a steep angle. 'How long would it take to reach that village on horseback?' I pointed to the settlement by the river where smoke rose gently. 'Not long?'

'Not long.'

'Finan!' I called, and when he joined us I pointed to the village. 'Is that a church I see there?'

Finan, who had the best eyesight of any man I have ever known, glanced downhill. 'It has a cross on the gable. What else could it be?'

I had been wondering how we were to reveal the gold we would bury in the graves, but Egil's suggestion had given

163

me the answer. 'Come spring,' I said, 'we will build a fort here.' I pointed at the feeble pines. 'Start the palisade with those trunks. Buy more timber from the valley, buy ale there, buy food. You'll be in charge.'

'Me?' Finan said.

'You're a Christian! I'll give you forty men, maybe fifty, all Christians. And you'll ask the priest to come and bless the fort.'

'Which won't be finished,' Finan said.

'It will never be finished,' I said, 'because you'll show the priest the gold. You'll give him some gold!'

'And in a week,' Egil said slowly, 'every man in the Tesa valley will know of the gold.'

'Within a week,' I said, 'Guthfrith and Ealdred will know of the gold.' I turned to stare at the mounds. 'There's only one problem.'

'Which is?' Finan asked.

'We're a long way from Scotland.'

'That's a problem?' Egil asked.

'Maybe it doesn't matter.'

We would bait the trap, not for one king, but for three. Æthelstan had forecast that any new war in Britain would be the most terrible ever known, and claimed he did not want that war, yet he had started a war against Bebbanburg. True, it was a strange war with no deaths and small harm, but war it was and he had started it.

Now I would finish it.

Bishop Oda came as spring began to turn into summer. He arrived with a younger priest and six warriors who all showed Æthelstan's badge of the dragon and lightning bolt on their shields. The day had dawned unusually warm, but by the time Oda rode to the Skull Gate the first fret of the year had drifted in from the sea.

164

'I didn't even need a cloak this morning,' Oda complained as he greeted me, 'and now this fog!'

'A fret,' I said, 'what you Danes call a haar.' On hot summer days a thick North Sea fog would shroud the fortress. As often as not the sun would burn the fret away, but if an east wind blew from the sea the fret would be continually pushed ashore and might linger all day, sometimes dense enough to hide our seaward ramparts from the great hall.

'I bring you a gift,' Oda said as I ushered him into the hall.

'Ealdred's head?' I asked.

'A gift from the king,' he ignored my poor jest. He held out a hand to the young priest who gave him a leather-wrapped bundle which, in turn, was given to me.

The bundle was secured with string which I snapped. Inside the soft leather wrapping was a book. 'A book,' I said sourly.

'Indeed! But fear not! It isn't a gospel book. The king does not believe in casting pearls before swine. Dear lady!' He raised his hands in warm greeting of Benedetta who came towards us. 'You look more beautiful than ever.' Oda embraced her chastely. 'And I have brought you a gift from the king, a book!'

'A book,' I repeated, still sourly.

'We need books,' Benedetta said, then clapped her hands to summon servants. 'We have wine, bishop, and it is even good wine!'

'Your friends in Eoferwic, bishop,' I said bitterly, 'have tried to stop ships trading with us. Yet the ships still come, and they bring us wine.'

I took Oda to the dais, out of earshot of the six warriors who had dutifully surrendered their swords and had been shown to a table at the lower end of the hall where they were given bread, cheese, and ale. 'This is Father Edric, one

165

of my chaplains,' Oda introduced the young priest. 'He was eager to meet you, lord.'

'You're welcome, Father Edric,' I said unenthusiastically. He was a thin, pale-faced young man, scarce more than a boy, with a nervous expression. He kept glancing at the hammer I wore as if he had never seen such a thing before.

'Father Edric found the book for the king.' Oda touched the volume that I had placed unopened on the table. 'Tell Lord Uhtred about it, father.'

Edric opened and closed his mouth, swallowed, then tried again. 'It is *De Consolatione Philosophiae*, lord.' He stammered the title, then stopped abruptly, as if too scared to continue.

'And that is translated how?' Bishop Oda enquired gently of Edric.

'The consolation of philosophy,' Benedetta answered instead, 'by Boethius? An Italian.'

'A clever Italian,' Oda said, 'like you, dear lady.'

Benedetta had opened the book and her eyebrows rose in surprise. 'But this is in the Saxon tongue!'

'It was translated, dear lady, by King Alfred himself. And King Alfred was a friend to Lord Uhtred, was he not?' The question was directed at me.

'He never liked me,' I said, 'he just needed me.'

'He liked you,' Oda insisted, 'but disliked your religion. King Æthelstan, on the other hand, fears you.'

I stared at him. 'Fears me!'

'You are a warrior, lord, and you defy him. Men notice that, and if you can defy him so can others. How can Æthelstan be God's anointed king if his lords will not submit to him?'

'You say I defy him?' I snarled. 'I made him king!'

'And the king,' Oda said calmly, 'is convinced that God intended him to be the *Monarchus Totius Brittaniae*. He is persuaded that he is the child of God's destiny, fated to bring a time of peace and plenty to Britain.'

'So he encourages Ealdred to raid my lands.'

Oda ignored that. 'There is a hierarchy on earth as there is in heaven,' he continued, still calm, 'and just as Almighty God sits in power above all creatures of heaven and of earth, so must a king be exalted above all people who live in his lands. Constantine of Alba has submitted to Æthelstan, Hywel of Dyfed has kissed his hands, Owain of Strath Clota has bowed his head, Guthfrith of Northumbria is his servant, and only Uhtred of Bebbanburg has refused to take the oath.'

'Uhtred of Bebbanburg,' I said bitterly, 'swore an oath to protect Æthelstan. I protected him as a child, I taught him to fight, I gave him his throne, I have kept that oath and I need give him no other.'

'For the king's dignity,' Oda said, 'you must be seen to submit.'

'Dignity!' I laughed.

'He is a proud man,' Oda said gently.

'Then tell the proud man to call off his hounds, to publicly declare that I am Lord of Bebbanburg, not Ealdred, and to pay me gold for the damage his men have caused my land, and then, bishop, I will kneel to him.'

Oda sighed. 'The king was convinced you would accept his offer to be the Ealdorman of Wiltunscir! That was generous!'

'Bebbanburg is mine,' I said firmly.

'Read the book, lord,' Oda said, pushing the volume towards me. 'Boethius was a Christian, but his book does not try to persuade you to convert. It is a book of truths, that money and power are not the right ambitions of a virtuous man, but that justice, charity and humility will bring you contentment.'

'And the *Monarchus Totius Brittaniae*,' I stumbled over the unfamiliar Latin words, 'sends me that?'

'His fate is to be king. A man cannot escape his fate.'

'Wyrd bið ful āræd,' I answered harshly, which meant

that I, like Æthelstan, could not escape my fate, 'and my wyrd is to be Lord of Bebbanburg.'

Oda shook his head sadly. 'I was sent with a message, lord. The king requires Bebbanburg, he needs it to be a shield against the Scots.'

'It is already,' I said firmly, 'and you said Constantine had submitted to him. Why fear the Scots if they have submitted?'

'Because they lie,' Oda said. 'Constantine sends messages of peace to Æthelstan and he sends men and money into Cumbria. If it comes to war he wants the Norse of Cumbria on his side.'

I had heard the same, that Constantine was seducing the Norse in Cumbria with promises of land and wealth. 'If it comes to war,' I said sourly, 'Æthelstan will want me on his side.'

'He wants Bebbanburg,' Oda retorted.

'Or is it Ingilmundr and Ealdred who want Bebbanburg?'

Oda hesitated, then shrugged. 'I have told the king to trust you, and I have persuaded him to curb Ealdred.'

'I'm supposed to be grateful to you?'

'And the king has agreed,' Oda ignored the question, 'and he repeats his offer to you. Let the king garrison Bebbanburg and take Wiltunscir as your home.'

'And if I refuse?'

'Thus far, lord, the king has been merciful. He has declined to send his full power against this fortress. But if you defy him he will lead his army and his fleet here, and he will prove to you that he is indeed the *Monarchus Totius Brittaniae*.'

'But Uhtred is his friend!' Benedetta protested.

'A king does not have friends, dear lady, he has subjects. Lord Uhtred must offer submission.' He looked at me. 'And you must offer it by the Feast of Saint Oswald, lord.'

I stared at him for a heartbeat. I wanted to say a score of things, how I had raised Æthelstan, how I had protected him from vicious enemies and steered him towards the throne. Or to ask if Æthelstan was now so captive to the whisperings of Ingilmundr and Ealdred that he would kill me. Instead, almost in disbelief, I simply asked Oda if he was telling the truth. 'You say he'll declare war on me?'

'He will merely take what he believes is rightfully his, and so secure the northern frontier of his kingdom against the treachery of the Scots. And you, lord, if you submit before the Feast of Saint Oswald, can be Ealdorman of Wiltunscir. You have all summer, lord, all summer to think on it.' He paused, then sipped his wine and smiled. 'The wine is good! May we lodge here tonight?'

He and his men lodged that night and before Oda slept he walked with me on Bebbanburg's ramparts, just the two of us, looking out at the moon-shivered sea. 'Æthelstan is influenced by Ingilmundr and by Ealdred,' Oda confessed to me, 'and I regret that. Yet I dare say he listens to me too, which is perhaps why he's reluctant to force your obedience.'

'Then why—' I began.

'Because he is king,' Oda interrupted firmly, 'and as a great Christian king he cannot be seen to be indebted to a pagan lord.'

'Alfred was,' I said bitterly.

'Alfred never lacked confidence,' Oda said. 'Æthelstan claims that he was appointed king by Almighty God, but he constantly seeks confirmation of that. There are still men who whisper that his birth was illegitimate, that he is a bastard son of a common whore, and the king looks to prove that he is indeed God's anointed. Receiving the oaths at Burgham was one such proof, but men whisper that he tolerates paganism.' He looked at me. 'And how can he depend on a pagan? So he needs to show all Britain that he can command you, diminish you. And he believes, as I do, that you will accept his offer. It is a generous one!' He paused and touched my arm. 'What can I tell him?'

'Just that.'

'Just what?'

'That his offer is a generous one.'

'No more, lord?'

'That I will think about it,' I said grudgingly, and it was an honest answer even though I knew I would not accept it.

I would say nothing more and next morning, after saying prayers in Bebbanburg's chapel, Oda left. And on the following day Finan took forty-three warriors, all of them Christians, out of the Skull Gate and into the hills.

They were riding south. To the Devil's Valley.

'So Æthelstan comes in August?' Benedetta asked me.

I shook my head. 'It's too close to harvest time. He'll want his army to live off our land, so he'll wait till our granaries are full, then he'll come. But it won't happen.'

'No?'

'Æthelstan wants a war? I'll give him one.'

Ealdred's raids had ended, so an uneasy peace now existed between Eoferwic and Bebbanburg. I made sure that Guthfrith and Ealdred heard news of me. I went to Dunholm to talk with Sihtric and sailed *Spearhafoc* down the coast. The Devil's Valley was in the western part of my land and so I stayed in the east until, three weeks after Finan had left, I gave Gerbruht, the big Frisian, my mail coat, my wolf-crested helmet and a distinctive white cloak. Gerbruht even agreed to take off his cross and wear a hammer, though only after Father Cuthbert had assured him that he was not risking the fires of hell.

Gerbruht sailed the coast in *Spearhafoc*, pointedly buying fish from boats that had come from Guthfrith's land, while I rode into the hills with twenty men, two packhorses and a king's ransom in gold. I wore an old coat of mail, carried a plain helmet, but I did have Serpent-Breath at my side. We rode fast, reaching the high valley on the fourth afternoon beneath lowering skies.

Finan had made a palisade on the valley's lip. It was a crude wall of roughly trimmed pine logs and behind it were branch and turf shelters for his men. He had dug trenches as if preparing to make three more walls to complete a square fort that overlooked the Tesa's valley. 'They've noticed you?' I asked, nodding down at the nearest village.

'They've noticed us, right enough!' Finan sounded pleased. 'And I reckon Guthfrith has too.'

'You know that?' I asked, surprised.

'It took a week, only a week. Then horsemen came, three of them, all Danes. They rode up here and asked what we were doing. They were friendly.'

'And you told them?'

'I said we were building a fort for Lord Uhtred, of course.' Finan grinned. 'I asked if they lived on your land and they just laughed.'

'You let them look around?'

'They looked at the graves, laughed at the wall, and didn't see our swords. They saw men digging trenches and trimming logs. And they rode off that way.' He nodded east towards the road in the deeper valley, the road that led eventually to Eoferwic.

Guthfrith knew, I was sure of it. Little could be hidden in the countryside, and Finan had made sure some of his men drank in the village tavern. I suspected the three Danes had indeed come from Guthfrith, but even if not they would have spread the news that I was building a fort in the hills above the Tesa, and Guthfrith was probably laughing. He might have ceased his raiding, but would reckon that the new fort in the Devil's Valley would do me little good if he

171

started again. And it would do me no good at all if Æthelstan came with an army.

'You need to make pitch soon,' I told Finan.

'Easy enough, plenty of pine here. Why do I need it?'

I ignored the question. 'If anyone asks say you'll caulk the wall with it.'

Guthfrith knew, because we could not hide what we were doing, nor did we want to, but I desperately needed to hide the jaws of the trap we were making. I had sent word to Egil, asking him to be ready to send men, and had told Sihtric that I would need half his garrison, and ordered them to ride north first as though heading for the Scottish border before they turned west into the hills and then south to the Tesa. And I had to bring my own men from Bebbanburg, and all those men, travelling through the hills, would be noticed. They would assemble in a shallow dip of land west of the Devil's Valley, and it would be impossible that such an army could be hidden for long. Yet if Guthfrith and Ealdred were dazzled by the bait, and if they responded as quickly as greed could goad them, then there was a chance.

So early next morning Finan and I laid that bait. We dug into the northernmost mound, chopping through the stubborn earth with sharp spades. We had dug into the barrows years before and found only bones, antlers, flint arrowheads and the single gold cup, but that morning, as a half-moon paled in a cloudless sky, we hurled the treasure of Bebbanburg into the new hole we had made. We covered it roughly, then dug another ragged hole in the ground beside the mound, throwing the spoil onto the scar we had made in the mound. 'Tell your men this new hole is for pitch-making,' I suggested, 'then give it two days before you find the gold.'

'And three or four days for Guthfrith to hear about it?'

'That sounds right,' I said, hoping it was.

'A lord digging a hole?' Oswi, who had been standing guard, had wandered up with a big grin on his face. 'You'll be cooking for us next, lord!'

'This hole is for you,' I told him.

'Me, lord?'

'We need to make pitch.'

He grimaced at the thought of that foul job, then nodded at the scar in the mound. 'Did you dig there too, lord?'

'Years ago,' I said, 'we found a gold cup in this mound.'

'It's meant to be bad luck to disturb the mounds, lord. That's what they say in the village.'

I spat, then touched my hammer. 'We were lucky last time.'

'And this time, lord?' He laughed when I shook my head. 'You know the villagers are calling it the Devil's Fort now?'

'Then let's hope the devil protects us.'

Finan touched his cross, but Oswi, who had about as much religion as a chicken, just laughed again.

I left before midday. I sent two men to Dunholm with orders for Sihtric. He was to send his sixty men in three days, taking care that they went north before coming to the Devil's Fort. And, once home in Bebbanburg, I sent Vidarr Leifson to tell Egil that I would need his men at the Devil's Valley in five days. Vidarr had accompanied me to the Devil's Fort and was confident he could guide Egil's Norsemen back to the high valley. 'Five days from now,' I told him, 'not a day before or after.'

Then I had two days to ready my own men. I would leave just thirty to guard Bebbanburg under the command of Redbad, one of my son's warriors. He was a steady and reliable man, and thirty men were sufficient to man the ramparts when no attack was expected. I gave Gerbruht my helmet and cloak, then sent him down the coast again with orders to buy fish from Guthfrith's boats and to take *Spearhafoc* deep into the mouth of the Humbre so that trading ships would carry the news of my presence to Eoferwic.

Bebbanburg's big inner courtyard stank as pitch was burned out of pine, then smeared on shields. Weapons were sharpened, food crammed into bags, and Hanna, Berg's wife, brought me three new battle-standards she had sewn in secret.

And three days after I had returned to Bebbanburg I left again, this time riding my best stallion and leading fifty-three battle-hardened men into the hills.

Where we would do the Devil's work.

EIGHT

There was silence in the hills, not even the sound of a soft wind over thin grass. It was close to dawn and it seemed as if the starlit earth was holding its breath. A few high clouds drifted eastward where the horizon was just touched with a blade of grey.

I had been close to the Devil's Valley for two nights and a day, and no horsemen had come from Eoferwic. If none came on this new day then I would admit failure because it would be impossible to hide almost two hundred men and their horses for longer. True, we were in the hills, but we had already encountered one shepherd bringing his flock south. That man, his dogs and his sheep were under guard, but ever since Finan had revealed the gold, the villagers had been climbing to the Devil's Fort asking to see the hoard.

He had showed them the treasure, he had boasted of the new wealth and he had gone with half a dozen men to the village alehouse. He had worn the heavy golden torque and paid for their ale and food with a lump of gold. 'So Guthfrith has to come today,' Egil now told me. 'The bastard must know the gold's here.' The two of us were lying on the grass, watching the eastern horizon where the grey was slowly lightening.

I saw a horseman briefly outlined against the wolf-grey streak of dawn. That would be one of our men. I had given my son the responsibility of leading our scouts, who would watch the road from Eoferwic. They would watch from the hills, then retreat fast if they saw Guthfrith coming.

'Let's hope they both come,' I said vengefully. It still grated on me that Æthelstan had named Ealdred the Lord of Bebbanburg and, pleasant as it would be to slaughter Guthfrith, there would be even more pleasure in cutting Ealdred down.

I had expected Guthfrith the previous day, and every hour that he did not show gave me more anxiety. Finan had flaunted the gold, but the obvious question was why he had not immediately taken it north to Bebbanburg. He had told the villagers that he was waiting for me, that he needed another fifty warriors to ensure the gold's safe return to Bebbanburg, and that he wanted to search the other two mounds, but would Guthfrith believe that feeble story?

Sihtric of Dunholm climbed the slope behind us and dropped next to me with a grin and a curt nod of greeting. I had known him since he was a boy, the bastard child of Kjartan the Cruel who had been one of my worst enemies. Sihtric had none of his father's viciousness, but had grown to be one of my most trusted warriors. He had a gaunt face, a dark beard, a knife scar beneath one eye, and only four teeth when he grinned. 'I remember when you were good-looking,' I welcomed him.

'At least I was once,' he said, 'unlike some I can think of.' He nodded east into the glare of the rising sun that had just flared on the horizon. 'Smoke over there.'

'Where?'

Sihtric squinted. 'Long way off, lord. In the valley.'

'It could be mist,' Egil said. I could see the pale smear in the Tesa's shadowed valley, but could not be certain if it was mist or smoke.

'It's smoke and there's no village there,' Sihtric sounded certain. His men patrolled this part of my land and he knew it well.

'Charcoal burners?' Egil suggested.

'Wasn't there last night, lord,' Sihtric said, 'and they'd hardly build the pit overnight. No, that's Guthfrith's men. Bastards are camped there.'

'And are letting us know they're coming?' I asked dubiously.

'Folk have no sense, lord. And Guthfrith's a king and God only knows what the West Saxon boy thinks he is, but kings and lords don't abide being cold by night,' he grinned at the implied insult, 'and it's still dark down there, sun hasn't risen on the valley yet. You watch, that smoke will vanish in a few minutes.'

I watched, I waited, and Sihtric was right. The smoke or mist faded and disappeared as soon as the river valley's shadow shrank. I touched the hilt of Serpent-Breath and prayed that both Guthfrith and Ealdred were coming. I doubted that either would trust the other, which meant that both must come if they were to share the gold equally, but with how many men? I had assembled almost two hundred, but now, as the sun rose to burn the dew from the uplands, I began to worry that I did not have enough. I did indeed plan the devil's work that day, and to achieve it I needed to overwhelm whoever came to the Devil's Valley.

And I was sure they would come across the hills. Guthfrith would have heard that the view from the new fort dominated the valley of the Tesa so that if he rode the Roman road he would be seen long before he could hope to reach the high valley. So he must come through the hills, hoping to surprise and overwhelm Finan's men. Those men were still digging trenches, trimming pine logs, and excavating the mounds.

It was late morning when the first of my son's scouts came back to us. It was Oswi, who we saw intermittently as he made a wide detour to the north to ensure he did not appear on any skyline as he approached us. The day had warmed and his horse was white with sweat as he slipped from the saddle. 'A hundred and forty-three, lord,' he said, 'and coming over the hills just as you said they would.'

'How far?'

'An hour away? But they're canny, lord. They're coming slow and they have scouts too.'

'You weren't seen?'

He scoffed at that. 'We've watched them, lord, and they ain't seen a hair of us. Your son's taken the other lads north so they don't find him, but he's coming soon as he can. Doesn't want to be left out.'

We were on the western crest of the hills that enfolded the Devil's Valley. To my left, in the north, the ground rose higher and the slopes were steeper, while the eastern ridge, opposite us, offered an easy slope down to the mounds. I stared at that ridge, looking for any sign that an enemy scout was already there, but I saw nothing. Nor did I expect to. Any man there would be like us, lying low.

'Borrow a fresh horse,' I told Oswi, 'then ride down to warn Finan. Don't hurry! Just take it slowly.' If there was an enemy scout watching the valley then a horseman in a hurry would raise an alarm, while a man ambling into the valley would raise no suspicions.

The day grew warmer. I was in my mail coat, reluctant to put on the helmet in case it reflected sunlight to anyone on the far crest. I had brought one of my father's old helmets that had two big iron cheek-pieces which would leave only my eyes showing. My shield, waiting with Aldwyn in the lower ground behind me, was smeared with pitch. A black shield, such as Owain of Strath Clota's men carried, and Owain was now Constantine's ally. All our shields were black, while the three battle-flags showed a red hand holding a cross, the symbol of Domnall, Constantine's chief warrior. If Æthelstan knew I had killed Ealdred, let alone Guthfrith, he would have brought a mighty army to Bebbanburg long before the harvest. So someone else must take the blame.

'There's someone there,' Egil said.

I stared at the far ridge, my view blurred by the grass in which we lay. I saw nothing.

'Two of them,' Egil added.

'I see them,' Sihtric said.

Oswi had reached Finan, who only had thirty men now. I had brought the others up to join us. Finan, like his remaining men, wore no mail, had no helmet, and only wore a short seax instead of Soul-Stealer, his sword. His shield, mail coat, sword and spear were behind me, on the hill, as was the gold. Finan would pretend to flee when Guthfrith attacked, racing with his men up to our hilltop where they could retrieve their weapons and armour. Their shield, like mine, had been smeared with pitch so that when they joined the battle they would appear to be men from across the northern border.

'Over there!' Sihtric jerked his head northwards and I saw an enemy scout working his way around those higher hills. The man was on foot, going cautiously and staying back from the crest so he could not be seen from the valley. I swore. If he came another half mile he would see my men, but then he came to the gully where the stream poured from the hills and he paused. He stared towards us and I stayed motionless. The man waited a long time, then must have decided that he had no need to scramble across the steep gully with its fast-flowing stream because he turned back and I lost sight of him.

It was almost midday by now. High thin clouds hazed the sun. There was still no wind. Sheep bleated somewhere far to the west. Finan's men, some bare chested in the day's warmth, were saddling their horses, while two were carrying bundles from the shelters and putting them in the leather bags of two packhorses. They were carrying stones, but to the watching scouts it must have seemed that they were stowing the golden pieces. I wanted Guthfrith's men to think Finan was leaving, and that their best chance of capturing the treasure was to attack quickly. I pulled on my helmet, smelling the stink of old sweat in its leather liner. I pulled the heavy cheek-pieces closed and tied them together.

'They're there,' Sihtric breathed the words, though there was no chance of his being heard on the far ridge a half mile away. I stared, and thought I saw men lying on the crest, but the heat shimmered the skyline and I could not be certain. 'I saw a spearhead, lord,' Sihtric said.

'Two,' Egil confirmed.

I slithered backwards and turned to my horsemen. They were sweating in mail and close-fitting helmets. Flies buzzed around their horses. 'Soon!' I told them. They watched me anxiously. They were close to two hundred men mounted on heavy stallions, gripping baleful black shields and holding their long heavy spears. 'Remember,' I called, 'these are the men who raided our land! Kill them! But bring their leaders to me.'

'Lord!' Egil called urgently.

They were coming. I stood and ran back to the ridge top where I crouched. Guthfrith's men were spilling over the far crest in two groups, the smaller to my left. That group, maybe thirty or forty strong, was streaming down the far slope and I guessed their job was to circle around Finan's men to block their escape, but they were already too late. Finan and his men, feigning panic, were fleeing, apparently so panicked that they left the packhorses behind. I watched, careless that I could probably be seen, though I reckoned that the men hurrying their horses down the far slope were far too intent on their breakneck ride to notice me. I waited, beckoning Aldwyn forward with my stallion. Egil had gone back to mount his horse, as had Sihtric. I wanted the enemy to stop in the valley's centre, I wanted them to dismount and only then I would unleash my men. The smaller group, seeing Finan's men flee up the western slope were reining in their horses and turning towards the mounds where the large group who surrounded two standard-bearers were milling about. The flags, Guthfrith's boar and Æthelstan's dragon with its lightning bolt, hung lifeless in the still air. More men dismounted, and among them was Ealdred. I recognised his stallion, the big grey, and the gleam of his polished mail. He strode towards the packhorses as I heaved myself onto my stallion's back, took the shield and heavy spear from Aldwyn, then waved my men forward. 'Now kill them!'

I was angry, I was vengeful, and I was probably being rash. As my horse tipped over the crest I was reminded of the foolishness of men who played dice, who lost almost all their silver, but then put their faith and all that was left of their money on one last throw. If this worked I would give Æthelstan a new enemy, a new war, and that war would indeed be terrible. And if I lost then his vengefulness would have no limit.

The slope was steep. I leaned back against the saddle's high cantle, my shield banging against my left thigh, and I was tempted to curb the stallion. But on either side of me warriors were racing ahead and I spurred instead. I had warned my men not to use their usual war cry, not to shout Bebbanburg's name, though I heard someone call it aloud. 'Scotland!' I bellowed. 'Scotland!' We flew the flags Hanna had sewn, the flags showing Domnall's red hand gripping a heavy cross.

The slope lessened. The sound of hooves was like thunder. The enemy was staring astonished, then the dismounted men ran for their horses. Egil was slanting off to my left, his spear-points aiming for the smaller group who were turning to face him. Sihtric was galloping to the valley's lip to cut that line of escape. Our bright flags with their false badges were streaming. A horse fell behind Sihtric, the rider tumbling, spear turning end over end, the horse screaming, riders splitting around it, and then my stallion was threading the trunks where the pines had been felled.

I lowered the spear and let my stallion have his head.

And so we struck. It was ragged, that charge, but it hit like one of Thor's thunderbolts. The enemy was in panic, disorganised, some lucky men spurring desperately east-wards to safety, others turning their horses and blocking those who were screaming to escape, many just staring wide-eyed at Ealdred as if waiting for orders, while a few drew swords and came to meet us. One horseman readied his sword to swat my spear aside, but I raised it to threaten his frightened eyes, his sword came up to parry and I dropped the spear-blade to drive it deep into his lower chest, bending him back in the saddle. I let go of the haft and started to pull Serpent-Breath free, felt a blow on my shield, glimpsed a man with his mouth open turning his horse away from me as Berg slammed a spear into his pelvis. A scream, my horse swerving, more men with black shields on my right shouting incoherently as they speared into the hapless enemy. I saw Ealdred's grey horse ahead of me, he was flailing his sword to part men who obstructed him and I spurred my horse, left Serpent-Breath in her scabbard, came up behind him and, reaching out, seized the neck of his mail coat and dragged him backwards. He swung his sword wildly, I was turning my stallion, he came back over his horse's rump, shouted something and then fell with his left foot trapped in its stirrup. He was dragged along the ground for a few paces, then his horse was blocked by others. I threw down my shield and slid from the saddle. Ealdred struck at me with his sword, but he was half dazed, on his back, and the blow was feeble. The mail and the heavy rings on my forearm blocked the sword, then I dropped onto him, a knee in his belly, and pulled Wasp-Sting, my seax, free.

A seax, with its broken-backed shape and curved fore-blade, is a wicked weapon. I held its edge at Ealdred's throat. 'Drop the sword,' I ordered him, then pressed the short blade harder, saw the terror in his eyes, then the sword fell. My horsemen had swept past me, leaving enemy dead and dying. Many had escaped and I was content to let them go, knowing what tale they would tell in Eoferwic, the same story that would travel south to Æthelstan in Wessex. The Scots had broken their word.

Berg, always watchful of me in a fight, had dismounted too. I stood, kicked Ealdred's sword out of his reach, and told Berg to guard him. 'He's to stay on his back.'

'Yes, lord.'

'And where's Guthfrith?' I stared around the valley. Most of the enemy was fleeing up the eastern slope, a few were kneeling with outspread hands to show that they yielded. 'Where's Guthfrith?' I bellowed.

'I've got the bastard!' Sihtric shouted. He was driving Guthfrith ahead of his horse, using his sword to prod Northumbria's king towards me.

I did not need prisoners except for Guthfrith and Ealdred. I had Egil's men strip those who had surrendered of their mail, of their boots and of their weapons, then Thorolf, Egil's brother, ordered them to carry their wounded down the hill and across the Tesa's ford into Guthfrith's territory. 'And if you come back across the river,' he growled, 'we'll use your ribs to sharpen our swords.' His Norse-accented English

183

would sound foreign to the prisoners, most of whom would never have heard a Scottish voice. 'Now be on your way,' he finished, 'before we decide to eat you.'

That left Ealdred and Guthfrith. Both men had been stripped of their helmets and weapons, but were otherwise unharmed. 'Drag them here,' I snarled. I still wore the helmet with its heavy cheek-pieces, but as Ealdred and Guthfrith were pulled towards the packhorses, I loosened the leather lace. 'You wanted my gold?' I asked the two.

'Your gold?' Ealdred said belligerently. 'It's Northumbria's gold!' He must have been thinking that we really were a Scottish war-band.

I pushed the cheek-pieces aside and hauled the helmet off. I tossed it to Aldwyn. 'My gold, you rancid little turd.'

'Lord Uhtred,' Ealdred breathed the two words.

'It's yours,' I said, beckoning at the packhorses. 'Take it!' Neither man moved. Guthfrith, his broad face sour, took a pace backwards, bumping into one of the packhorses. I saw he wore a silver cross, the price of being allowed to stay on his throne, and he raised his hand to touch the amulet, then realised there was no hammer there and the hand went still. 'Take it!' I said again and half drew Serpent-Breath as a threat.

Ealdred did not move, just stared at me with a mixture of fear and loathing, but Guthfrith turned, lifted the bag's leather flap and found only stones. 'There is no gold,' I said, letting Serpent-Breath fall back into her scabbard.

Ealdred glanced around my warriors and saw nothing but mocking faces and bloodied swords. 'King Æthelstan will know of this,' he said.

'King Æthelstan will hear that you broke the truce and crossed the river onto my land, and that a Scottish raiding party found you.'

'He won't believe that,' Ealdred said.

184

'He's believed enough other nonsense!' I snapped. 'He believes I'm his enemy? He believes the Scots will endure his claim of kingship over all Britain? Your king has become a fool. He's allowed the crown to curdle his brains.' I drew Serpent-Breath, the long blade making a small sound as she slid through the fleece at the scabbard's throat.

'No,' Ealdred said. He understood what was about to happen. 'No!' he protested again.

'You call yourself the Lord of Bebbanburg,' I said, 'yet you have raided Bebbanburg's lands, burned its steadings, and stolen its cattle. You are Bebbanburg's enemy.'

'No, lord, no!' He was shaking.

'You want Bebbanburg?' I asked him. 'Then I will give your head a niche on the Skull Gate where my enemies will stare at the sea till the final chaos.'

'No—' he began, then stopped, because I had slammed Serpent-Breath forward, piercing his shining mail, scraping on a rib, and bursting his heart. He fell back against the packhorse and slid to the pale turf, jerking, making a choking noise, hands scrabbling feebly at his chest before one last spasm. Then he was still, except for his hands slowly curling.

Guthfrith had taken a step away from his companion. He watched Ealdred die, then as I put a boot on the dead man's chest and tugged Serpent-Breath free. His eyes went from her reddened blade to my face, then back to the blade. 'I'll tell Æthelstan it was the Scots!' he said.

'You take me for a fool?'

He stared at me. He was terrified, but he was brave enough at that moment. He tried to speak, failed, and cleared his throat. 'Lord,' he pleaded, 'a sword, please.'

'You made me kneel to you,' I said, 'so now you kneel.'

'A sword, please!' There were tears in his eyes. If he died without a sword he would never reach Valhalla.

185

'Kneel!' He knelt. I looked at my men. 'One of you give him a seax.'

Vidarr drew his short blade and handed it to Guthfrith who gripped the hilt with both hands. He rested the blade's tip on the grass and looked up at me with wet eyes. He wanted to say something, but could only shiver. Then I killed him. One day I will see him in Valhalla.

I had lied to Ealdred. I would not put his skull on Bebbanburg's gate, though Guthfrith's would have a place there. I had other plans for Ealdred.

But first we pulled down the wall that Finan had made and we heaped the bodies of our enemies, all but for Ealdred's corpse, onto the piled logs and burned them. The smoke drifted high into the windless air. We took off Ealdred's mail, his boots, his cross, anything of value, wrapped his corpse in cloaks and took it back to Bebbanburg where the body was placed in a coffin with a cross on its breast, and I sent it to Eoferwic, a city without a king now. And with the corpse I sent a letter, which regretted Ealdred's death at the hands of a Scottish war-band. I addressed the letter to Æthelstan, *Monarchus Totius Brittaniae*.

And waited to see what the monarch of all Britain would do next.

Constantine denied the attack on Ealdred and Guthfrith, but he also denied that he was fomenting trouble in Cumbria, which he was, and Æthelstan knew it. Constantine had even named one of his war chiefs, Eochaid, as the ruler of Cumbria. Some said Eochaid was Constantine's son, others that he was a nephew, but he was certainly a subtle and ruthless young man who by bribery, cunning and some slaughter had obtained the loyalty of Cumbria's Norsemen. Æthelstan had named Godric and Alfgar as his Cumbrian ealdormen, but neither dared ride the hills without at least a hundred

186

warriors, which meant that even Burgham, where Æthelstan had tried to impose his authority on all Britain, was now effectively ruled by Constantine.

So Constantine's protests that he had not launched the attack fell on sceptical ears in Wessex, but still there were rumours and Æthelstan was determined to discover the truth. He sent a priest all the way from Wintanceaster, a stern, raw-faced man named Father Swithun who was accompanied by three younger priests, all carrying satchels containing ink, quills, and parchment. Father Swithun was polite enough, asking permission to enter Bebbanburg and frankly admitting his purpose. 'I have been charged with discovering the truth of Lord Ealdred's death,' he told me. I think he half expected me to refuse him entrance, but instead I welcomed the priests, gave them housing, bedding, stabling, food and a promise to tell them whatever I knew.

'Yet, lord, you will not swear that truth on this?' Father Swithun asked when we met in the great hall. He had drawn a small, finely carved ivory box from his own satchel.

'And what is that?' I asked.

Swithun opened the small box reverently. 'It is the toenail of Lazarus, whom our Lord rose from the dead.'

'I'll swear it on your toenails,' I said, 'but you won't believe a pagan's oath so I wonder why you bothered coming at all?'

'Because I was instructed to come,' Swithun said primly. He was a dry, clever man and I knew his kind well. King Alfred had loved such churchmen, prizing their mastery of detail, their honesty and their dedication to truth. Such men had written Alfred's code of laws, but Father Swithun was now in Northumbria where the prevailing law was the sword. 'Did you kill Lord Ealdred?' he asked suddenly.

'No.'

Quills scratched on parchment.

'Yet it is known you disliked him?'

'No.'

Swithun frowned. The quills scratched. 'You're denying that dislike, lord?'

'I didn't dislike him,' I said, 'I hated him. He was a pompous, privileged, impertinent piece of shit.'

Scratch, scratch. One of the younger priests was smiling secretly.

'The Scots deny sending warriors, lord,' Swithun pressed on.

'Of course they do.'

'And point out that the death of Lord Ealdred occurred many miles from any Scottish lands. At least a three-day ride?'

'Probably five,' I said helpfully.

'And King Constantine remarks that he has never raided that far into King Æthelstan's kingdom.'

'How old are you?' I asked.

Swithun paused, slightly unsettled by the question, then shrugged. 'I am thirty-nine, lord.'

'You're too young! Constantine must have come to the throne when you were what? Eleven? Twelve? And the year after that he had three hundred Scottish warriors burning the barns around Snotengaham! There were other raids too. I watched his men from the walls of Ceaster, you remember that, Finan?'

'Like it was yesterday,' Finan said.

'And those places were far south of,' I paused, frowning, 'where was it that Ealdred died? The valley of the Tesa?'

'Indeed.'

'You should look in the chronicles, Father,' I said, 'and discover how often the Scots raid deep into Northumbria. Even northern Mercia!' I was lying through my teeth, as was Finan, and I very much doubted that Father Swithun would want to visit all the monasteries of Northumbria and

Mercia that might have monks keeping a chronicle, because if he did he would only have to plough through page after page of ill-informed nonsense. I shook my head sadly. 'Besides,' I said, as if the thought had only just struck me, 'I don't believe those men came from Constantine's land.'

'You don't?' Swithun sounded surprised.

'My belief is they came from Cumbria. Much closer. And the Scots are stirring up trouble there.'

'True,' Swithun said, 'but King Constantine has sent assurances that they were not his men.'

'Of course not! They were Strath Clotans. They're his ally now so he used them so he could deny that his own men came south.'

'He denied that too,' Swithun said primly.

'If you were a Northumbrian, father, you would know that the Scots can never be trusted.'

'And King Constantine has sworn the truth of his assertions on the girdle of Saint Andrew, lord.'

'Oh!' I looked convinced. 'Then he must be telling the truth!' The young priest smiled again.

Father Swithun frowned, then found a new page of the notes that he had on the table. 'I have been in Eoferwic, lord, and spoken with some of King Guthfrith's men who survived the fight. One of them was certain he recognised your horse.'

'No he did not,' I said firmly.

'No?' Swithun raised a delicate eyebrow.

'Because my horse was in the stables here. I was on board my ship.'

'We heard that too,' Swithun allowed, 'yet the man was quite certain. He says your horse,' he paused to look at his notes, 'displayed a stark white blaze.'

'And my stallion is the only horse in Britain that has a white blaze?' I laughed. 'Let's go to the stables, father. You'll find twenty horses like that!' He would also discover Ealdred's

189

fine white stallion that I had named Snawgebland, snow-storm, but I doubted Swithun wanted to explore our stables.

Nor did he, because he ignored the invitation. 'And the gold?' he asked.

I scoffed at that. 'There was no gold! No dragon either.'

'No dragon?' Swithun enquired delicately.

'Guarding the hoard of gold,' I explained. 'Do you believe in dragons, father?'

'They must exist,' he said cautiously, 'because they are mentioned in the scriptures.' He looked pained for a moment as he collected his notes. 'You do realise the consequences of King Guthfrith's death, lord?'

'Women are safer in Eoferwic.'

'And Anlaf of Dyflin will claim the throne of Northumbria. He's probably claiming it already! That is not a desirable consequence.' He looked at me almost accusingly.

'I thought Æthelstan claims Northumbria,' I answered.

'He does, but Anlaf might contest it.'

'Then Anlaf will have to be beaten,' I said, and that was probably the truest thing I spoke in that long meeting. I had lied happily, as had my men, even the Christians among them had sworn ignorance of Ealdred's death. It helped that they had been promised absolution by Father Cuthbert who, that evening at dinner, I introduced to Father Swithun.

'He was properly married, you know!' Father Cuthbert said as soon as I named Father Swithun.

'He was . . .' Swithun was totally confused.

'Married in church!' Cuthbert said happily, his empty eyes appearing to look past Swithun's right ear.

'Who was married in church?' Swithun, still astonished, asked.

'King Edward, of course! He was Prince Edward then, but I assure you he was properly married to King Æthelstan's mother! By me!' Father Cuthbert spoke proudly. 'And all those tales of his mother being a shepherd's daughter are simply nonsense! She was Bishop Swithwulf's daughter, Ecgwynn. I still had my sight then and she was a pretty little creature,' he sighed wistfully, 'so very pretty.'

'I never believed the king was born out of wedlock,' Swithun said stiffly.

'Enough folk did!' I said forcefully.

He frowned at that, but nodded reluctantly, and once the meal was served I regaled him with tales of Æthelstan's youth and how I had protected him from his many enemies who had wanted to keep him from the throne. I told him how I had rescued Father Cuthbert from the men who would have killed him to prevent him telling his story of Edward and Ecgwynn's marriage, and I let others tell of the fight at Lundene's Crepelgate that had finally defeated those enemies.

The priests left Bebbanburg next morning, their satchels filled with lies and their heads ringing with tales of how I had raised, protected and fought for the king they served.

'You think he believed you?' Benedetta asked me as we watched the priests take the road south.

'No,' I said.

'No?'

'That kind of man has a nose for truth. But he's confused. He thinks I lied, but he can't be sure.'

She put her arm through mine and leaned her head on my shoulder. 'So what will he tell Æthelstan?'

'That I probably killed Ealdred,' I shrugged, 'and that Northumbria is in chaos.'

Æthelstan claimed to be King of Northumbria, Constantine wanted to be King of Northumbria, and Anlaf believed he was King of Northumbria.

I strengthened Bebbanburg's ramparts.

* * *

There had been a grim satisfaction in Ealdred's death, but as the summer passed I began to suspect it was a mistake. The idea had been to throw all the blame onto the Scots, to divert Æthelstan's anger from me to Constantine, but reports from Wessex, sent by friends, suggested that Æthelstan had not been fooled. He sent me no messages, but men reported that he spoke angrily of me and of Bebbanburg. All I had really achieved was to throw Northumbria into chaos.

And Constantine took advantage of that chaos. He was a king, he wanted land because land was a gift he could give to his lords. Lords had tenants, and tenants carried spears, they tilled crops and raised livestock, and crops and livestock were money. And money paid for the spears. Cumbria was not the best land, but it had river valleys where grain grew tall, and hills where sheep could graze, and it was as fertile as most of Constantine's harsh kingdom. He wanted it.

And in the chaos that followed Guthfrith's death, when no king was crowned in Eoferwic to claim lordship of all the land, Constantine grew brazen. Eochaid, who had been named 'ruler' of Cumbria, held court in Cair Ligualid. Silver was given to the church there and the monks received a precious casket, studded with blood-red carnelians, that contained a chip of the boulder on which Saint Conval had sailed from Ireland to Scotland. The walls of Cair Ligualid were manned by Eochaid's men, most bearing a cross on their shields, though some carried Owain of Strath Clota's black shields. At least Anlaf, who claimed to be Guthfrith's successor, made no move to claim Northumbria. News said he was too distracted by his Norse enemies, that his armies were striking deep into Ireland.

But those Scottish shields meant that Constantine's troops were now deep inside Cumbria. They were south of the great wall the Romans had built, and Eochaid sent war-bands further south, into the land of the lakes, to demand rent or tribute from the Norse settlers. Most paid, those who refused had their steadings destroyed and their women and children taken as slaves. Constantine denied it, he even denied naming Eochaid as the ruler of Cumbria, claiming that the young man was acting on his own and was doing no more than the Norse did when they sailed from Ireland to take a patch of rough Cumbrian pasture as their own. If Æthelstan could not rule his own territory then what did he expect? Men would come and take what they wanted, and Eochaid was just another such settler.

The summer was waning when Egil came to Bebbanburg in his sleek ship *Banamaðr*. He brought news. 'A man named Troels Knudson came to me three days ago,' he said when he was seated in the hall with a pot of ale.

'A Norseman,' I grunted.

'A Norseman, yes,' he paused, 'from Eochaid.'

That surprised me, though there was no reason that it should. Half the men on the land Eochaid claimed to rule were Norse settlers and those who accepted him were treated well. There were no missionaries trying to persuade them to worship the nailed god, the rents were low, and if war came, which it must, then those Norsemen would likely fight in Eochaid's shield wall. 'If Eochaid sent him,' I said, 'he must have known you would tell me?'

Egil nodded. 'Troels said as much.'

'So whatever news he brought is for my ears too.'

'And comes from Constantine, probably,' Egil said. He paused to pull Alaina onto his lap. She was fond of him, as all women were. 'I made you a ship,' he told her.

'A real one?'

'A little one, carved from beechwood.' He pulled the model from his pouch. It was a beautiful thing, maybe the length of his hand. It had no mast, but there were tiny rowing

193

benches and a fine prow carved with a wolf's head. 'You can call it *Hunnulv*,' Egil said.

'*Hunnulv*?'

'A she-wolf. She will be the terror of the ocean!'

Alaina was delighted. 'I'll have a real ship one day,' she said, 'and it will be called *Hunnulv*.'

'And how are you going to buy a ship?' I asked her.

'I won't. You will.' She gave me her most impudent grin.

'I'm thinking of sending her to one of the hill farms,' I told Egil, 'one of the poorest ones where she'll have to work from daybreak to sundown.'

Alaina looked up at Egil. 'He won't!' she said confidently.

'I know he won't,' Egil said, smiling.

'So Troels Knudson?' I suggested.

'Sees war coming.'

I grunted again. 'We can all see that.'

'If there's a war,' Alaina asked, 'can I come?'

'No,' I said. 'You'll be too busy fetching water and washing sheep-shit from your clothes.'

'War is no place for small girls,' Egil said gently.

'So Eochaid sends a Norseman to tell us what we already know?' I asked.

'He tells us,' Egil went on, 'that the smithies of Wessex and Mercia are hammering out spear-blades, that Æthelstan has purchased three hundred horses from Frankia, and that the willows in Hamptonscir have been felled to make shields.'

'We knew that,' I said, though in truth I had not heard that Æthelstan had purchased horses.

'And almost all of those spears and shields,' Egil went on, 'are being sent to Lindcolne.'

I frowned, not sure I believed what Egil had said. 'I heard they were going to Mameceaster.'

'Some, yes. Most? Lindcolne.'

'How can they know that?'

Egil gave me a pitying look. 'If you were Constantine how much silver would you pay to get reliable news from Æthelstan's court?'

'More than I pay.'

'Æthelstan has sent spears to Mameceaster,' Egil said, 'and made sure folk saw the packhorses. But he's sent far more to Lindcolne, and they went by ship.'

'Up the rivers,' I said.

'And folk don't see what's in a cargo. Cover it with sail-cloth and it could be anything! Could be turnips! And those ships are waiting in the pool at Lindcolne. Twelve of them.'

'And Æthelstan is building a fleet,' I muttered.

'Two fleets,' Egil went on remorselessly, 'one in the Mærse, the other in the Temes. But Eochaid believes that his best shipwrights were sent to the Temes.'

'And Troels told you all this?'

'And more. Æthelstan sent troops to help Hugh of Frankia, and they've been summoned home.'

'So there will be war?' Alaina asked excitedly.

'But where?' I asked. Egil said nothing. 'And Troels's message?'

'That Eochaid would welcome an alliance.'

So here it was again, the same offer that Domnall had brought down from Scotland. I had never answered Constantine formally, but nor did I need to. Silence was refusal, but it seemed Constantine had not abandoned hope of bringing Bebbanburg onto his side. 'We fight for Eochaid?' I asked. 'And he fights for us?'

'Not just Eochaid. Constantine fights. Owain fights. It would be a northern alliance. Alba, Strath Clota, Cumbria, the Isles.' He counted off the nations by holding his fingers up one by one.

I raised my spread hand. 'And Bebbanburg.'

'And Bebbanburg,' Egil said.

I stared at him. He was a clever man and as good a friend as I ever had, yet there were times when he was a mystery to me. He was a Norseman, a pagan. So did he want me to join that northern alliance? Did I want to? I wanted Bebbanburg, I wanted to hand Bebbanburg to my son who was sitting beside me and listening anxiously.

'I can ride a horse,' Alaina said brightly. 'Finan's teaching me.'

'Hush, little one,' Egil said.

'You have an opinion?' I asked my son.

He shrugged. 'It depends whether Æthelstan plans to attack us or not.'

'And Eochaid insists you must make your decision before Æthelstan marches,' Egil added.

'If he marches,' my son said.

I ignored that. Æthelstan was going to war, I knew it, but against which enemy? Was I his enemy? And Constantine was readying for war and wanted the fortress of Bebbanburg on his side, but he was demanding that I declare that allegiance before Æthelstan marched. And why should he help me if I did not declare for him? If Æthelstan besieged Bebbanburg then Constantine would be free to make more mischief in Cumbria, or even to go further south into Mercia where he might expect allies from the smaller Welsh kingdoms.

'Whatever I decide,' I told Egil, 'you are free to make your own choice.'

He smiled at that. 'I'm your man, lord.'

'I'm freeing you from that oath.'

'The hound likes the leash,' he said with another smile.

'I do not understand,' Benedetta had been listening with a frown, 'what is so important about Lindcolne or Mameceaster?'

'Everything,' Egil said softly.

'There are two roads into Scotland,' I explained. 'On the western coast you go through Mameceaster then up through

Cumbria. On this coast you go from Lindcolne to Eoferwic, Eoferwic past this fortress, then on up into Constantine's land.'

'And if Æthelstan cares about the troubles in Cumbria,' Egil took up the explanation, 'he'll take the western road. He has a claim over Cumbria. He can drive Eochaid back into Scotland easily enough, but if he takes this road? The one past Bebbanburg? Who is he fighting? Not Eochaid.'

'He is your friend!' Benedetta protested.

'He was,' I said.

There was silence. I thought back to an evening when Æthelflaed, dear Æthelflaed, had asked me to swear an oath to protect her nephew. And I had protected him, while he had broken an oath by claiming I had not killed his enemy, which was true, except I had caused that enemy's death and lost good men in doing so. My honour was intact, but his? 'I won't break an oath,' I said.

'The hound loves the leash,' Egil murmured.

'No northern alliance?' my son asked, and I saw he thought that was the safest choice.

'I do not believe,' I said firmly, 'that Æthelstan means me harm. He owes me too much. If Constantine's spies tell him that weapons are being stored on the eastern road then he is being misled by Æthelstan. Æthelstan is clever! He's making Constantine believe he'll attack up this side of Britain, and he won't! He'll strike Cumbria like the lightning bolt on his shield.' I looked at Egil. 'Tell Troels I say no.'

'I will tell him,' Egil said quietly.

'Father . . .' my son began, then paused when I glared at him. He took a breath and went on. 'Æthelstan wants Bebbanburg, we know that! And yes, he wants to drive the Scots out of Cumbria, but he wants to control all of Northumbria! Where better to start than here?'

'Æthelstan will drive the damned Scots out of Cumbria,' I insisted firmly. 'He'll take the western road.'

Five weeks later Æthelstan marched. His fleet sailed up the coast and his army followed the Roman road north. And as my son had feared, he took the eastern road. At Lindcolne, which Æthelstan's troops had garrisoned after the meeting at Burgham, they were issued with new, bright-painted shields and long, steel-bladed spears. Then they kept marching.

To Bebbanburg.

NINE

The ships came first.

Six the first day. They were typical West Saxon ships with their heavy blunt bows, each containing between forty or fifty oarsmen. There was little wind, yet all had their sails hoisted and each sail bore Æthelstan's symbol of the dragon holding a lightning bolt. Each prow was topped with a cross.

The ships came inshore of the Farnea Islands, a wide channel, but treacherous unless a helmsman knew the waters. They came in single file and it was clear the leading ship did have such a helmsman because they avoided the dangers and rowed until they could gaze up at our high ramparts. The oarsmen backed water, men on the steering platforms shaded their eyes to stare at us, but none returned our waves. Then the rowers backed water and turned seawards, the late afternoon sun flashing reflected light from the rising and falling oar-blades. 'So they're not coming here,' Finan grunted, meaning that the ships were not coming into our harbour.

Instead they followed the lead ship into the southernmost group of the Farnea Islands and there spent the night. They were lucky, the winds stayed calm. They would have been safer in Lindisfarena's shallow anchorage, but there they would have been vulnerable to my men. 'So they're not friendly?' Benedetta asked me when, in the dawn, we saw the six masts showing above the islands.

'They don't seem to be,' I said, and later I sent a fishing boat to the islands with Oswi, dressed in a fish-stinking smock, pretending to be one of the crew.

'They're not friendly, lord,' he confirmed. 'Told us to go away.'

It was midday by then and shortly after, one of my tenants rode from the south to tell of an army marching towards us. 'Bloody thousands of them, lord,' he said, and it was shortly afterwards that we saw the first smoke rising in the south. We had all seen such smoke pillars before, rising into a summer sky to tell of a steading being burned. I counted six. I sent two horsemen north to warn Egil.

And by nightfall another twenty-three ships had arrived. Most were similar to the first six, blunt bowed and heavy, and all well crewed. A dozen were cargo ships, and all of them, including the six that had sheltered in the islands, worked their way over the bar and so into the tangle of channels and shallows inside Lindisfarena. There were too many men there now for my garrison to challenge. We could only watch and, as night fell, see the glow of campfires in the southern sky.

Daybreak brought the army. Horsemen first, over three hundred of them, and after them came men on foot, trudging in the day's warmth. There were packhorses and mules, women carrying burdens, more men, and more horses. I counted at least eleven hundred men and knew there were more strung out on the long road south. More horsemen went through the village to link up with the men on the fleet. The villagers had fled into the fortress, driving their livestock ahead of them, and soldiers moved into the houses, though, as far as we could see, they were doing little harm.

200

I had three ships, including *Spearhafoc*, moored in the harbour along with eight fishing boats. I had put no guards on the ships so they could easily have been captured and burned, but no one tried to swim out to them. Nor did any man come to the Skull Gate to talk to us, and I was not inclined to seek out a spokesman, even when, strangely, axemen cut down a grove of trees at the village's southern end, chopped the branches and piled them into a vast heap that they burned. The smoke boiled into the sky.

It was mid afternoon when Æthelstan arrived. Men lined the road long before he appeared, and I heard the sound of spear shafts and swords being beaten against shields as he came nearer. Men started to cheer, and I saw five standard-bearers come into view. They waved the flags from side to side so that they spread in the windless air. Two carried Æthelstan's personal flag, the dragon with the lightning bolt, two carried the dragon banner of Wessex, while the fifth had a great white flag with a scarlet cross.

Behind them were ranks of horsemen, all in mail and helmets, all carrying spears. They rode five abreast, most on grey horses and all wearing red cloaks despite the day's heat. I grimaced at the sight of the cloaks because they reminded me of Æthelhelm's men, though these cloaks were a richer red. Twenty ranks of horsemen appeared, then came two more standard-bearers with dragon banners, and just behind them, alone and on a big grey stallion, came Æthelstan.

Even at this distance he dazzled. His mail seemed to be made of polished silver, his helmet was burnished white and surrounded by a gold circlet. He rode straight-backed, proud, one gloved hand acknowledging the cheers of the men who lined the road's edges. His tall grey horse had a scarlet saddle cloth and a bridle glinting with gold. Æthelstan glanced at the great fire at the village's southern end which still spewed a thick pillar of smoke.

Behind Æthelstan were three black-robed priests mounted on black horses, then five more standard-bearers who led another one hundred red-cloaked horsemen. '*Monarchus Totius Brittaniae*,' Finan said drily.

'You learned Latin?'

'Three words too many. And how many men has he got?'

'Enough,' I said. I had long stopped trying to count them, but there were at least fifteen hundred, and still they came from the south, while offshore a dozen West Saxon warships rowed as close to Bebbanburg's shore as they dared. The message could not have been clearer. Bebbanburg had been surrounded by land and by sea, and we had just two hundred and eighty-three warriors inside the ramparts.

'I will call the devil onto him,' Benedetta said vengefully. She had joined us, holding Alaina by the hand.

'You can do that?' Finan asked.

'I am from Italy,' she said proudly, 'of course I can do that!'

I touched the hammer and thought how I needed Thor to send a great hammer blow down onto the men gathering at the end of the sandy neck leading to the Skull Gate. None had yet ventured onto the track, but then a dozen servants leading two packhorses came towards the gate. They stopped well out of bowshot and, as we watched, they unpacked a tent that they hurried to erect, suspending a gorgeous cloth of scarlet and gold from four tall poles. Pegs were driven deep into the sand, lines tightened, while three more servants carried rugs and chairs into the shadowed interior. Last of all two standard-bearers brought their flags, one the West Saxon dragon and the other Æthelstan's own banner, and they drove the poles deep into the sand either side of the tent's open doorway that faced the gate. Æthelstan, mounted on his big grey stallion, gazed out to sea as he waited for his servants to finish their task.

The servants walked away. A small wind stirred the flags and ruffled the sea, making the ships pull hurriedly away from the lee shore. Then Æthelstan dismounted and, accompanied by a single priest, walked to the tent. 'That's Bishop Oda,' Finan said.

Æthelstan paused at the tent's open doorway, turned and looked up to where I stood over the Skull Gate, and gave an ironic bow. Then he and Oda disappeared inside. 'Two of them,' I told Finan, 'so two of us.'

'Maybe he will kill you!' Benedetta sounded alarmed.

'Finan and me? Against a king and a bishop?' I kissed her. 'Pray for their souls, *amore*.'

'Call the devil!' Alaina urged excitedly.

'Pray we don't need him,' I grunted, then went down the steps to find my son. 'If men approach the tent,' I told him, 'send the same number out of the gate.' I nodded to Redbad. 'Open it up!'

The great bar was lifted, the bolts creaked back and the two heavy gates were pushed open.

And Finan and I went to meet the king.

I wore mail and had Serpent-Breath at my side. My boots were stained with dung from the outer courtyard where the villagers had driven their livestock. I was sweating. I must have stunk like a cornered marten. I grinned.

'What's funny?' Finan asked dourly.

'We're cornered, aren't we?'

'And that's funny?'

'Better to laugh than weep.'

Finan kicked a loose stone that skittered across the sand. 'We're not dead yet,' he sounded dubious.

'You'll like Wiltunscir,' I said. 'Plump orchards, pretty women, fat cows, rich pasture.'

'You're full of shit,' he said, 'and smell like it too.'

We fell silent as we approached the lavish tent. I ducked under the low doorway first and saw Æthelstan lounging long-legged in an ornate chair. He was sipping a glass of wine. It had to be Roman glass because it was so delicate. He smiled and waved a hand towards two empty chairs. 'Welcome, lord,' he said.

I bowed. 'Lord king,' I said politely, then nodded to Bishop Oda who sat straight-backed to Æthelstan's right. 'Lord bishop,' I greeted him and Oda inclined his head, but said nothing.

'Finan!' Æthelstan greeted the Irishman happily. 'Always a pleasure to see your ugly face.'

'It's a mutual pleasure, lord King,' Finan responded with a perfunctory bow. 'You want us to leave our swords outside?'

'Finan the Irishman without a sword? It wouldn't be natural. Sit, please. We have no servants with us so help yourself to the wine.' He waved at a table on which there was wine, more glass goblets, and a silver dish of almonds.

I sat, hearing the chair creak under my weight. Æthelstan sipped wine again. He wore a simple gold circlet over his long dark hair which, for once, had no golden wires twisted into his ringlets. His mail was polished, he wore long boots of soft black leather, his gloved fingers had rings of gold studded with emeralds and rubies. He gazed back at me, evidently amused, and I thought, as I always did when I met him, how handsome he had become as a man. A long face, wide-set blue eyes, a strong nose and a firm mouth, which seemed to hover on the brink of a grin. 'It is strange, is it not,' he broke the silence, 'how trouble always comes from the north?'

'Ours seems to come from the south,' I grumbled.

He ignored that. 'Cent? No trouble there, not for a long while. East Anglia? It's accepted I am its king. Mercia is loyal. Even Cornwalum is quiet! The Welsh probably dislike

204

us, but they make no trouble. Peace and prosperity wherever I look!' He paused to take an almond. 'Until I look north.'

'How many times have I told you that the Scots can't be trusted, lord King?'

That was rewarded with a wry smile. 'And can the Northumbrians be trusted?' Æthelstan asked.

'I seem to remember that Northumbrians fought for you.'

'Which doesn't answer the question. Can Northumbrians be trusted?'

I looked into his eyes. 'I have never broken an oath to you, lord King.'

He looked at me with what seemed amusement. If I a cornered marten, stinking and in peril, then he was the threat. He was the greater predator. 'Since Guthfrith died,' he broke the short silence, 'Northumbria has been in chaos.'

'It was in chaos before he died,' I said sharply. 'My steadings were being burned, and your friend Constantine was filling Cumbria with his troops.'

'My friend?'

'Didn't he swear you an oath?'

'Oaths are not what they were,' Æthelstan said carelessly.

'So you're teaching me, lord King,' I said harshly.

He did not like my tone and rewarded it with a bitter question. 'Why didn't you tell me Constantine sent emissaries to you?'

'I'm supposed to tell you every time I have visitors?'

'He offered you an alliance,' Æthelstan said, his tone still bitter.

'And offered it again last month.'

He nodded. 'A man called Troels Knudson, yes?'

'From Eochaid.'

'And what did you answer Troels Knudson, lord?'

'You already know,' I said harshly. I paused. 'You know, and yet, lord King, you are here.'

'With eighteen hundred men! And the crews of the ships. Will they be safe inside Lindisfarena?'

'Some will go aground at low tide,' I said, 'but they'll float off on the flood. They're safe enough. And why are you here?'

'To threaten you, of course!' He smiled. 'You haven't tasted the wine!'

Finan snorted. 'The last wine you gave us, lord King, tasted like goat's piss.'

'This isn't much better,' Æthelstan said, raising his glass. 'Do you feel threatened, lord?'

'Of course.'

'How many men do you have?'

'Fewer than you, lord King.'

He gazed at me again, and again he looked amused. 'Are you frightened, Lord Uhtred?'

'Of course I'm frightened!' I said. 'I've fought more battles than you have had birthdays, and before every one I was frightened. A man does not go into battle without fear. I pray I never see another battle. Ever!'

'Are you going to give me Bebbanburg?'

'No.'

'You would rather fight?'

'Bebbanburg is mine,' I said stubbornly. 'I only ask one favour of you.'

'Ask!'

'Look after my people. Benedetta, the women.'

'And you?'

'My ambition is to die in Bebbanburg.'

'I pray that happens,' Æthelstan said. He smiled again, a smile that was beginning to annoy me. He was toying with me as a cat played with its prey.

'Is there anything more to say, lord King?' I asked sourly.

'Oh, a lot!'

'Then say it.' I stood. 'I have work to do.'

'Sit down, lord.' He spoke with sudden anger and waited for me to obey him. 'Did you kill Ealdred?' he demanded, still angry.

'No,' I lied. He stared at me and I stared back.

I heard waves break on the nearby beach and neither of us spoke, just stared, and it was Æthelstan who broke the silence. 'Constantine denies it.'

'And so do I. You must decide which of us to believe.'

'Have you asked Owain, lord King?' Finan intervened.

'Owain? No.'

'I was there,' Finan said, 'I watched what happened, and the men who killed Ealdred carried black shields.'

'Owain is Constantine's puppy,' Æthelstan said savagely, 'and Constantine denies sending any men south.'

Finan shrugged. 'As Lord Uhtred said, you can't trust the Scots.'

'And who can I trust in the north?' He was still angry.

'Maybe you can trust the man who swore to protect you,' I said calmly. 'And who has kept that oath.'

He looked into my eyes and I saw the anger fade from his. He smiled again. 'You saw,' he said, 'that I burned some of your trees?'

'Better trees than houses.'

'And every pillar of fire you have seen, lord, came from trees. None from your people's settlements.' He paused, as if expecting me to react, but I just looked at him. 'You thought I burned your steadings?'

'I did.'

'And that is what the Scots are thinking.' He paused again. 'The Scots will be watching us. They expected me to march, and I've no doubt they've sent scouts into your land to spy on our progress.' He waved a hand westwards. 'They'll be lurking in those hills?'

I nodded cautiously. 'Probably, lord King.'

'They're good at that,' Finan said dourly.

'And after a week or two I've no doubt Constantine will realise that I have not come to battle him, but to crush the defiant Lord Uhtred. To capture his fortress. To show all Britain that there is no lord too powerful to resist me.' He paused, then turned to Bishop Oda who had not said a word since we had come to the tent. 'Why am I here, bishop?'

'To show that there is no lord in Britain capable of resisting you, lord King.'

'And which lord will learn that lesson?'

Oda paused, looked at me and gave a sly smile. 'Constantine, of course.'

'Constantine, indeed,' Æthelstan said.

Finan was quicker than me. I was still gaping at Æthelstan as the Irishman chuckled. 'You're invading Constantine's land!' Finan said.

'Only two people know that,' Æthelstan said, pleased at my astonished expression. 'Bishop Oda and myself. Every man in my army believes we're here to punish Bebbanburg. Many aren't happy! They regard you as a friend, Lord Uhtred, but they believe you have defied me. And what do you think Constantine's spies have heard?'

'What every man in your army believes.'

'And every man in my army, every man in my court, believes I'm here to starve you out. I said I was unwilling to lose men on your ramparts so we would let hunger do our work. And that would take me how long? Three months?'

'Longer,' I said sharply.

'And Constantine will believe that, because now only four men know what I plan. We four. I have to stay here for a week, maybe two, so that Constantine hears what he wants to hear. He'll have troops watching the frontier, no doubt, but once he's sure I'm intent on capturing Bebbanburg he'll send more men to make trouble in Cumbria.'

I was still trying to comprehend the deception he had planned, then wondered who was being deceived. The Scots? Who would think Æthelstan was besieging Bebbanburg. Or me? I just stared at him, and my silence seemed to amuse him. 'Let the Scots think I'm here to teach you a lesson, lord,' he said. 'And then?'

'And then?' I prompted him.

'And then, lord, I shall march north and lay Scotland to waste.' He spoke viciously.

'With just eighteen hundred men?' I asked dubiously.

'There are more coming. And there's the fleet.'

'Constantine wants Northumbria,' Bishop Oda spoke again, sounding almost bored. 'His lords have construed his presence at Burgham as a humiliation. To salvage his authority he needs to give them land, conquest, and victory. To which end he is stirring up trouble here, he denies it, and he needs to be reminded that Northumbria is a part of Englaland.'

'And I,' Æthelstan said, 'am the King of Englaland.' He stood and took a small leather bag from a pouch and filled it with the almonds. 'Take this as a present to your lady. Assure her she is in no danger.' He gave me the bag. 'Nor, lord, are you. Do you believe me?'

I hesitated a heartbeat too long, then nodded. 'Yes, lord King.'

He grimaced at my hesitation, then shrugged it off. 'For a week or two we must pretend. Then I shall strike north, and when I do, I shall expect your help. I want the Scots to see the banner of Bebbanburg among my forces.'

'Yes, lord King,' I said again.

We talked for a few more minutes, then were dismissed. Finan and I walked slowly back to the Skull Gate where

209

Guthfrith's head still had lank hair and scraps of raven-torn flesh. Our feet crunched in the sand as a wind from the sea stirred the thin dune grass. 'Do you believe him?' Finan asked.

'Who can you trust in the north?' I asked.

And all I knew was that Æthelstan was going to war. But against whom?

'It makes no sense,' Benedetta insisted that night.

'No?'

'He says Constantine was humiliated, yes? So Constantine makes trouble because he is humbled. But now Æthelstan will humiliate Constantine again? So there will just be more trouble!'

'Maybe.'

'Not maybe. I am right! The dragon did not lie. The evil comes from the north. Æthelstan is waking the dragon! You see if I am not right.'

'You're always right, *amore*,' I said, 'you're from Italy.'

She gave me a surprisingly sharp jab on the arm, then laughed. And, as I lay sleepless, I thought she was right. Did Æthelstan really hope to conquer Scotland? And how could he ever subdue their savage tribes? Or had he lied to me? Was he telling me that he would attack Scotland so that I was not ready for a sudden assault on Bebbanburg?

So we waited. By night the sky around Bebbanburg glowed with the fires of Æthelstan's army, and by day the smoke smeared into the gathering clouds. Where the gaudy tent had stood there was now a wooden fence, higher than a man and with a fighting step, ostensibly to stop us making a sally into the great encampment where, every day, more men arrived. Æthelstan's ships patrolled offshore, and six more warships joined them. It might not be a true siege, but it looked like one.

Then, some two weeks after Æthelstan had arrived, he went north. It took a whole day for his army to leave. Hundreds of men and horses, hundreds of packhorses, all filing north on the road that led to Scotland. He had not lied to me. The ships went too, spreading their dragon sails to a summer wind, and behind them came *Spearhafoc*.

I had promised Æthelstan that I would help, but I had no intention of stripping Bebbanburg of its garrison. I had pleaded age. 'A month or more on horseback, lord King? I'm too old for that. I'll send my son with a hundred horsemen, but with your permission I'll join your fleet instead.'

He gazed at me for a few heartbeats. 'I want the Scots to see your banner,' he said. 'Your son will carry it?'

'Of course, and the wolf's head is on my sail.'

He had nodded almost absently. 'Bring your ships then, and welcome.'

There would have been a time, I thought, when he would have pleaded for me to ride with him, to lead my men alongside his, but he was confident of his own strength now and, it was a bitter thought, he believed I was too old to be useful. He wanted me to go north, but only to show that he could command my loyalty.

And so, with a crew of forty-six, I took *Spearhafoc* out of the harbour to join his fleet that ghosted north in front of a small and fitful wind. Æthelstan might have told me to take my ships, but I took just *Spearhafoc*, leaving most of my men to garrison Bebbanburg under Finan's command. He hated the sea. I loved it.

It was a strange sea that day. It was calm. The southerly wind threw up no waves, but sighed across a long shining swell. Æthelstan's fleet was in no hurry, content to keep pace with his army that followed the northern road. Some of his ships even shortened sail so as not to outpace the plumper cargo ships that carried food for the army. It was a warm day for late summer, and we headed into a pearly haze, and *Spearhafoc*, good ship that she was, gradually slid through the fleet. She alone had a beast on her prow, the arrogant sparrowhawk, while the ships we overtook had crosses. The largest of them, a big pale-timbered ship called *Apostol*, was commanded by Ealdorman Coenwulf, the leader of Æthelstan's fleet, and as we drew near a man beckoned to us from the *Apostol*'s steering platform. Coenwulf stood beside the man, pointedly ignoring us. I steered *Spearhafoc* close enough to alarm the man who had beckoned. 'You're not to get ahead of the fleet!' he shouted.

'I can't hear you!'

Coenwulf, a pompous, red-faced man, very conscious of his noble birth, turned and frowned. 'Your place is in the rearguard!' he called abruptly.

'We're praying for more wind too!' I shouted back, waved cheerily and pushed the steering-oar over. 'Arrogant bastard,' I said to Gerbruht, who just grinned. Coenwulf shouted again, but that time I really did not hear him and I let *Spearhafoc* run until she was leading the fleet.

Coenwulf's ships sheltered in the Tuede that night and I went ashore to see Egil who I found on the fighting platform of his palisade and gazing upstream to where the sky was reddened by the fires of Æthelstan's camp. It was far off at the first ford crossing the Tuede. 'So he's really doing it?' Egil asked.

'Invading Constantine's land? Yes.'

'Poking the dragon, eh?'

'That's what Benedetta said.'

'She's a smart one,' Egil said.

'And I'm what?'

'The lucky one.' He grinned. 'So you're sailing north?'

'As a show of loyalty.'

'Then I'll come too. You might need me.'

212

'Me? Need you?'

He grinned again. 'There's a storm coming.'

'I've never seen the weather so settled!'

'But it's coming! Two days? Three?' Egil was bored, he loved the sea, and so he came to *Spearhafoc*, bringing his mail, helmet, weapons and enthusiasm, and leaving his brother Thorolf to guard his land. 'See if I'm not right,' he greeted me as he clambered aboard, 'there'll be a big blow soon!'

He was right. The storm came from the west and it came when the fleet was moored in the wide mouth of the Foirthe, which Egil called the Black River. Coenwulf had ordered his ships to anchor close to the southern shore. He would have preferred to beach the ships, but Æthelstan's army was still miles inland and would not return to the coast until they had crossed the Foirthe, and Coenwulf feared that his beached ships might be attacked by Constantine's men and so the anchor stones were hurled overboard. I doubted Constantine's army was anywhere close, but the ground beyond the southern shore rose gently to steep hills and I knew there was a settlement protected by a formidable fort on those heights.

'Dun Eidyn,' I said, pointing to the smoke showing over the hills. 'There was a time when my family ruled all the land up to Dun Eidyn.'

'Done what?' Egil asked.

'It's a fortress,' I said, 'and a sizeable settlement too.'

'And they'll be praying for a northern gale,' Egil said grimly, 'so they can plunder the wrecks. And they'll get it!'

I shook my head. The fleet was anchoring in a wide bay and the wind was blowing from the south-west, coming off the land. 'They're sheltered there.'

'Sheltered now,' Egil said, 'but this wind will turn. It'll blow from the north.' He looked up at the darkening clouds that raced towards the sea. 'And by dawn it will be a killer. And where are the fishing boats?'

'Hiding from us.'

'No, they've taken shelter. Fishermen know!'

I looked at his hawk-nosed, weather-beaten face. I reckoned myself a good seaman, but I knew Egil was better. 'Are you sure?'

'You can never be sure. It's the weather. But I wouldn't anchor there. Get yourself under the northern shore.' He saw my doubt. 'Lord,' he said earnestly, 'take shelter to the north!'

I trusted him and so we rowed *Spearhafoc* close to Coenwulf's ship, the *Apostol*, and hailed him to suggest that the fleet should cross the wide river mouth to shelter under the northern bank, but Coenwulf took the advice churlishly. He talked for a moment with another man, presumably the *Apostol*'s helmsman, then turned back to us and cupped his hands. 'The wind will stay in the south-west,' he bellowed, 'and you're to stay with us! And stay with the rearguard tomorrow!'

'Is he a good seaman?' Egil asked me.

'Wouldn't know a ship if it sailed up his arsehole,' I said. 'He only got the fleet because he's a rich friend of Æthelstan's.'

'And he's ordering you to stay here?'

'He's not my commander,' I growled, 'so we go there,' I nodded towards the distant coast, 'and we hope you're right.' We hoisted the sail and let *Spearhafoc* run north. We ran inshore of a rocky island and anchored close to the beach, a lone ship fretting in the freshening south-west breeze. The night fell and the wind rose, tugging at *Spearhafoc*. Waves broke on her cutwater, slinging spray down the deck. 'Still blowing south-west,' I said warningly. If the anchor rope broke we would be lucky to escape being driven ashore.

'It will turn,' Egil soothed me.

The wind did turn. It went to the west, blowing harder and bringing a stinging rain, and then it went north, just as

214

Egil had predicted, and now it howled through our rigging and, though I could see nothing in the night's darkness, I knew the wide river was being whipped into a welter of foam. We were in the lee of the land, but still *Spearhafoc* reared and shuddered, and I feared the anchor would drag. Lightning slashed the western sky. 'The gods are angry!' Egil called to me. He was sitting next to me on the steps of the steering platform, but had to shout to make himself heard.

'With Æthelstan?'

'Who knows? But Coenwulf is lucky.'

'Lucky!'

'It's almost low tide. If they're driven ashore they'll float off on the flood.'

It was a long, wet night, though blessedly the wind was not cold. There was shelter in the prow, but Egil and I stayed in the stern, facing the wind and rain, sometimes taking our turn to bail the ship of the rainwater that flooded from the bilge. And in the night the rain slowly stopped and the wind slowly dropped. Sometimes a gust would lurch *Spearhafoc* as she turned in the strong tidal current, but as the dawn edged the sea with grey the wind became mild and the clouds raggedly cleared as the last stars faded.

And as we sailed *Spearhafoc* south we saw there was chaos on the Foirthe's southern shore. Ships had been driven aground, including all the cargo ships. Most had been fortunate and were beached, but five had struck rocks and were now half sunk. Men struggled to remove the cargoes, while others dug under the hulls of the beached ships to help the flooding tide, and all of that work was being hampered by the Scots. There might have been a hundred men, some on horseback, who must have come from Dun Eidyn and who now jeered the stranded Saxons. They did more than jeer. Archers rained arrows on men struggling to free the ships, which made those men crouch behind shields or shelter behind the stranded vessels. Other

215

men would try to drive the Scottish archers away and the bowmen, unencumbered by mail, simply retreated, only to reappear further down the beach to start loosing arrows again. There were also some thirty horsemen and they threatened to charge the working parties, which forced Coenwulf to make shield walls. 'Do we help?' Egil asked.

'He's got close to a thousand men,' I said, 'what difference would we make?'

We lowered *Spearhafoc*'s wolf-head sail as we neared the ships that were still anchored offshore. *Apostol*, Coenwulf's ship, was one of them. We rowed close and I saw that most of his crewmen had been ordered ashore, leaving only a handful of men on board. 'We're going north!' I shouted to them. 'Tell Coenwulf we're looking to see if the bastards have a fleet coming!'

One of the men nodded, but did not answer, and we hauled the yard up the mast again, sheeted in the sail, brought the oars inboard and I heard the welcome sound of water running fast along *Spearhafoc*'s sleek flanks. 'You're really going north?' Egil asked.

'You have a better idea?'

He smiled. 'I'm a Norseman. When in doubt? Go north.'

'Constantine keeps ships on this coast,' I said, 'and someone should look for them.'

'We've nothing better to do,' Egil said, smiling. I suspect he knew that searching for Constantine's fleet was just an excuse to escape from Coenwulf and to let *Spearhafoc* have her head in the open sea.

The wind was south-west again, the perfect wind. The sun had risen and showed between the scattered clouds to reflect a myriad flashes of light from the sea. All across *Spearhafoc* men had laid cloaks and clothes to dry in the new sunlight. It was warm. 'A couple of women aboard,' Egil said, 'and life would be perfect.'

'Women on a ship?' I said, touching my hammer. 'That's asking for bad luck.'

'You refuse to take them?'

'I've had to,' I said, 'but never willingly.'

'In Snæland,' he said, 'there was a fishing boat crewed by women. Best sailors on the island!'

'What kind of man would use women as a crew?'

'Wasn't a man, it was a woman who owned the boat. Lovely creature if you could stand the smell of her.' He touched his hammer. 'Poor thing, she vanished one day. Never saw her or her boat again.'

I snorted, making Egil laugh. He had the steering-oar, plainly loving to helm a fast ship through a windswept sea. We left the Foirthe and turned north, but stayed near to the shore, steering close to the few harbours and river mouths to see if any of Constantine's ships were waiting for Coenwulf's fleet. We saw none. Fishing boats would see us coming and would beat for the coast, fearing us, but we ignored them and just sailed on.

As evening fell we turned eastwards, seeking the open sea rather than sail close to a strange coast in the darkness. We shortened the sail, and Gerbruht, Egil and I took turns at the steering-oar and once we were well clear of land we turned to follow the Scipsteorra, the ship star, that was bright in the north. As dawn edged the east we tightened the sheets and turned back towards the coast that was hidden beneath a great bank of cloud. *Spearhafoc* ran easily, bending to the steady south-west wind. We were in sunlight, but squalls obscured the coast, and it was out of those squalls that the four ships came.

Egil saw the sails first. They were dirty grey rectangles against the dark clouds, but within minutes we could see their hulls. 'They're not cargo ships,' Egil said, 'their sails are too big.'

The four ships were still far off and the one furthest west, closest to the land, vanished for a few moments as another dark squall swallowed her. We were sailing north-west and the four ships were running in front of the south-west wind, so I turned *Spearhafoc* northwards again and saw the four ships turn as well. 'The bastards are coming for us,' I grunted. They must have seen us outlined against the rising sun, and by now they would have seen the wolf's head glowing through the weave of our sail. They would know we were a pagan vessel, coming to plunder a coastal village or capture a cargo ship.

Egil thought the same. 'They can't think we're part of Coenwulf's fleet.'

'They don't know about it yet. The news won't have reached them.'

Spearhafoc quickened as she settled on her northern course. The steering-oar quivered in my hand and the water hissed along the hull. 'They'll not catch us,' I said.

'But they'll try,' Egil said.

And so they did. All morning they followed us, and though *Spearhafoc* was faster, they did not abandon the chase.

We were being pursued.

TEN

'God-damned Scottish Christians,' Egil grunted. The four pursuing boats all had crosses on their prows.

'And they're well crewed,' I said.

'You mean they outnumber us?'

'What do you think?'

'Four to one? Five?' Egil peered back at our pursuers. 'I almost feel sorry for them.'

I ignored his jest. I had deliberately slowed *Spearhafoc* by loosening her sheets and allowing the pursuers to come closer. I knew I could outrun them, but I was reluctant to keep sailing northwards so I had turned *Spearhafoc* eastwards towards the open sea again, but their response had been to follow, spreading into a line so that when and if I turned south at least one of their ships would be close enough to ram me. So now we were sailing north again and the four ships were steadily closing the distance. I could see they were all crammed with men and I let the two fastest ships come close enough that I could see bearded and helmeted faces watching us from the prows, then I sheeted in the sail hard and felt *Spearhafoc* respond. 'Maybe they'll give up,' I said as we bent to the wind and the water hissed faster down our hull.

We drew ahead, but the four were implacable. Two were longer than the others and those ships were faster, but even those two could not keep pace with *Spearhafoc*. Yet still they followed us even as the sun sank in the west and the sky darkened.

Night would offer small respite. The morning squalls had long gone and the sky was clear, lit by a three-quarter moon that rose from the sea. I turned east again, running in front of the gentling wind, and the four ships followed, though the two smaller ships were now nothing but dark shadows on the southern horizon. I thought of turning south, but the wind had slowed and to speed past the pursuers would mean rowing. They could row too, and their ships were better manned than mine. Besides, I was feeling the freedom of the sea, the desire neither to return to land nor to Coenwulf's testy leash, but to sail on to wherever fate would take me. Æthelstan did not need me. He had only asked me to sail as a token of loyalty, and I had provided that by giving him my son and his warriors, and so we followed the ship star northwards, on through the night, our wake glittering with the strange lights of the sea.

'Ran loves us,' Egil looked at the twinkling lights.

'She must love them too,' I said, nodding at the two nearest pursuers.

I wondered why they were so persistent. Had they recognised *Spearhafoc*? Her sail and the sparrowhawk on her prow were distinctive, but she rarely sailed this far north. Maybe it was simply that she was a pagan ship, lacking the cross that Christians displayed so prominently. Did they think we were a raider? Yet why pursue us so hopelessly? For a time the two larger ships had used their oars and they did close the distance, but some time in the night the wind freshened again and *Spearhafoc* slid away from them. 'We're doing Coenwulf a favour,' I told Egil when he woke from a brief sleep and took the steering-oar from me.

'A favour?'

'If those are the only ships Constantine has on this coast then we're drawing them away from Coenwulf. He should be grateful.'

'There must be more ships,' Egil said. We knew Constantine kept a fleet of around twenty ships on his east coast to protect his land from Norse raiders, and those ships, though not enough to defeat Coenwulf, could have caused him endless trouble. His fleet was supposed to sail up the coast, keeping in touch with Æthelstan's ground forces, ready to supply them with food, ale and weapons. I had escaped from Coenwulf's irritable command, but my only justification for that escape was the excuse to look for Constantine's fleet and it was more than possible we had passed their anchorage in the night. If that fleet heard about Coenwulf's ships they would surely sail south to confront him, and we should have been ahead of them to warn him of their coming, but the four ships were herding us ever northwards. I spat overboard. 'We should be going south,' I said, 'looking for his damned ships.'

'Not while those four are there,' Egil said, then turned and looked at the far moonlit ships. 'But they won't last long,' he said confidently, 'and nor will you unless you get some sleep. You look like you just crawled out of your grave.'

I slept, as did most of the crew. I thought I would wake after a couple of hours, but I woke to the rising sun and to hear Gerbruht bellowing from the steering platform. For a moment his words made no sense, then I realised he was shouting in his native Frisian. I stood, wincing at the stiffness in my legs. 'What is it?'

'A trader, lord!'

I saw that Gerbruht had slackened our sail and we were wallowing close to a wide-bellied cargo vessel. 'They all went north!' The helmsman, a stout, thick-bearded man, shouted.

221

The Frisian language was similar to our own, and I had little difficulty in understanding him. 'Fifteen of them!'

'*Dankewol!*' Gerbruht called back, and called to our crew to sheet in the sail again.

The wind was at our stern. *Spearhafoc* lurched as the sail bellied, and I staggered against the steps. 'We're still going north?'

'Still going north, lord,' Gerbruht confirmed cheerfully.

I climbed to the steering platform, looked south and saw no ships.

'They abandoned the chase,' Gerbruht said. 'I reckon they thought we were Viking and just chased us off!'

'So who went north?'

'Constantine's fleet, lord.' Gerbruht jerked his head towards the cargo ship that had settled on an eastern course. 'She was in a harbour and saw them leave three days ago. Fifteen big ships!'

'You trust them?'

'Yes, lord! They're Christians.'

I touched my hammer. Three dolphins were keeping pace with *Spearhafoc* and I took their appearance as an omen of good fortune. No land was in sight, though to the west a heap of white cloud showed above Constantine's realm. So his fleet had gone north? Why? I was sure the news of Æthelstan's invasion had not yet reached this far north or else those fifteen warships would be heading south to play havoc with Coenwulf's fleet. 'We should go south,' I said.

'Lord Egil told me we should look for their ships, lord.'

'Their damned ships went north! You just told me that.'

'But north to where, lord? Orkneyjar?'

'Why would they go there? Those islands are ruled by the Norse.'

'I don't know, lord, but last night Lord Egil said we should sail to Orkneyjar.' There was a plaintive tone to his voice.

Gerbruht was a Frisian and a fine seaman, never happier than when a steering-oar was quivering in his capable hands, and he plainly wanted to keep running with the wind rather than struggle south. 'Have you been to Orkneyjar, lord?' he asked.

'Once,' I said, 'but we can't go there now.'

'Lord Egil said we should visit.'

'Of course he did! He's a bloody Norseman and wants to drink with his cousins.'

'He says we'll get news there, lord.'

And that, I thought, was true. I doubted the fifteen ships had gone to the islands unless they were looking for a fight with the Norsemen who ruled there. More likely Constantine wanted his fleet on the western coast, hoping to make more trouble in Cumbria, and the fleet's commander was taking advantage of the stretch of fine weather to sail around Scotland's treacherous northern coast. And that meant that any news at Orkneyjar would likely be an absence of news. If the Scottish ships were not in the islands then they must have gone west. 'Where is Egil?'

'Sleeping, lord.'

I knew Æthelstan would want me to go south, but the lure of the wind checked me. Bebbanburg was safe with Finan in command, and I had no wish to tie myself to Coenwulf's fleet, which, if it had extricated itself from the Foirthe, would be sailing slowly up the coast. I could join them and appear to be a loyal supporter, or I could let Spearhafoc race on north to the wild islands of Orkneyjar and learn what news the Norsemen knew. In times of war, I persuaded myself, news was as precious as gold and so I shook my head. 'Just keep her running.'

'Yes, lord!' Gerbruht said happily.

I breakfasted on ale, hard bread, and cheese. The sea was empty, not a sail in sight, only the dolphins who seemed to

223

like running alongside *Spearhafoc*. The clouds stayed above the unseen land, but otherwise the sky was clear. Sometime after midday I saw cliffs far off in the west, and not long after we caught sight of the low islands that lie to the north of Constantine's land. 'You know anyone there?' I asked Egil, who had woken and come aft with his fair hair blowing loose in the ship-driving wind.

'Jarl Thorfinn. I first knew him in Snæland.'

'He'll welcome us?'

'He's called Skull-Splitter,' Egil added with a grin.

'Him!' I said. I had heard of Skull-Splitter, few men had not, but all I knew of him was that he was a renowned Norse leader who carried a long-hafted battleaxe named *Hausakljúfr*, which meant skull-splitter. 'He lives in Orkneyjar?'

'He and his two brothers rule the islands,' Egil said.

'Not much to rule,' I snorted.

'But rule they do. Skull-Splitter will growl at us, but he probably won't kill us. He likes me.'

'So he might kill me and welcome you?'

'That's what I'm hoping,' Egil said, grinning again, 'because then I get *Spearhafoc*. Unless Skull-Splitter wants her, of course.' He looked up at the ragged pennant at the mast's top that told where the wind was coming from. 'But you'll live. Jarl Thorfinn is the clever brother and he's too clever to make unnecessary enemies.'

Which reassurance carried us northwards. I knew that all the islands of Orkneyjar, like the other islands further north, had been settled by the Norse. They fished, and kept scrawny cattle and hardy sheep, but their main livelihood was to go viking down the coasts of Britain, Frisia, and Frankia. Constantine must hate their presence, but he had other Norsemen on his western coast, Æthelstan's Saxons to the south, and problems enough without enraging Thorfinn's savage men. 'They're not all clever,' Egil told me cheerfully, 'they're all *úlfhéðnar*, of course. Thorfinn especially. I saw him fight bare-bone naked once. He was awesome.'

I knew about the *úlfhéðnar*, I had even fought them at Heahburh. The name meant wolf-warriors and an *úlfheðinn* was a terrifying man to face in battle. They believed they were invulnerable, that they could fly, and that the spirit of Fenrir, the wolf of the gods, had possessed them. An *úlfheðinn* would attack in a frenzy, spitting and howling, driven by the henbane ointment they smeared on their skin. But frightening as they were, the *úlfhéðnar* could be defeated. A wolf-warrior was too savage, too unbridled, to stay in a shield wall. They believed they could win any battle on their own, and a lone man in a shield wall battle was vulnerable. The *úlfhéðnar* were terrifying, even wounded they would go on fighting like a cornered beast, but they could be killed.

'I have an *úlfheðinn*'s skull on Bebbanburg's gate,' I told Egil. 'I'll happily add another.'

He smiled at that. 'I'm told Thorfinn collects skulls too.'

We came to the islands in the late afternoon. Egil, who knew the waters, steered *Spearhafoc* and I noted how the small fishing boats did not flee from us. We had no cross on our prow, and they assumed we were Norse, and they knew no lone ship would dare enter the great harbour south of the biggest island unless they were friendly. We passed a point of land from where seals watched us, then shortened sail to glide across the huge anchorage. At least a score of boats were either moored or beached, their prows arrogant with serpent or dragon heads. 'Tide's flooding,' Egil said, 'shall we beach her?'

'We'll be safe?'

'Jarl Thorfinn won't attack us.' He sounded confident, and so we ran *Spearhafoc* up onto a shingle beach. Her keel grated, the hull shuddered, and we were still. A dozen turf-roofed hovels edged the beach, all with smoke drifting from their roof-holes. They had to be burning driftwood or peat because there were no trees on the low hills. More fires burned sullenly beneath wooden racks where seal meat and fish were being smoked. One or two folk came from the cottages, stared at us, and then, satisfied we were no threat, ducked back inside. A dog peed on our cutwater, then wandered to where a heap of cod heads were piled at the high tide line. Small fishing boats were on the beach, dwarfed by the dragon-headed ships. 'When I was a boy,' Egil said, 'my job was to cut the cheeks out of cod heads.'

'The best eating,' I said, then nodded at the cottages. 'Thorfinn lives here?' I asked, surprised by the settlement's small size.

'His hall is on the other side of the island,' Egil nodded north, 'but he'll soon know we're here. We just wait.'

It was almost dusk when two horsemen appeared from the north. They approached cautiously, hands on sword hilts, until they recognised Egil who they greeted enthusiastically. 'Where's your ship?' one of them asked. He meant *Banamaðr*, Egil's serpent-headed ship.

'Safe at home,' Egil said.

'We were told only one man can come to the hall.'

'Only one?'

'We have other visitors and not enough benches. Not enough ale either.'

'I shall bring my friend,' Egil said, indicating me.

The man shrugged. 'Bring him. The jarl won't mind two.'

I left Gerbruht in charge of *Spearhafoc* with strict instructions that there was to be no theft, no fights, and no trouble. 'We're guests here,' I told the crew, 'if you need food, which you don't because we have enough, you pay for it!' I gave Gerbruht a handful of hacksilver, then followed Egil over the side, splashed through the small waves and so up to the beach.

226

'You'll have to walk,' one of the horsemen said cheerfully, and we followed them north along a track that led past small fields of barley. Some had already been harvested and there were women and children gleaning in the dusk.

'How's the harvest?' Egil asked.

'Not enough! We'll need to take some from southern folk.'

'And even if it was enough,' Egil said, 'you'd still take it.'

'Aye, that's the truth.'

The journey was not far. We crossed a low spine of land and saw a larger settlement on the shore of a rocky bay where seven dragon-ships were anchored. A long, low hall lay at the centre of the village, and it was there that the horsemen led us. 'Do I give my sword to anyone?' I asked the horsemen, conscious that most jarls and all kings insisted that men did not carry weapons in the hall. Swords, axes and ale make for an unhappy night.

'Keep it!' the rider said happily. 'You're outnumbered!'

We went through the wide doorway into a hall lit by rushlights and two massive fires. There were at least a hundred men on the benches who fell silent as we entered, then a big man at the high table bellowed a greeting. 'Egil! Why didn't they tell me it was your ship?'

'I came in another, lord! How are you?'

'Bored!' He peered at me through the smoke. 'Is that your father?'

'A friend,' Egil said, stressing the word.

The big man, who I assumed was Thorfinn Skull-Splitter, frowned at me. 'Come closer,' he growled, and Egil and I obediently walked down the long hall's beaten earth floor, skirting the two hearths with their smoky peat fires, until we were in front of the low dais where a dozen men sat at the high table.

Thorfinn had heard the stress on the word friend, a stress that had warned him he might not appreciate my company.

He stared at me, seeing a grey-bearded man in a rich dark cloak with gold at my neck and a sword at my side. And I stared at him, seeing a thickly muscled Norseman with a prominent brow, a thick black beard, and very blue eyes. 'Friends have names, don't they?' he demanded. 'Mine is Thorfinn Hausakljúfr.'

'And mine,' I said, 'is Uhtredærwe.' That was an insult given me by Christians. It meant Uhtred the Wicked.

'He is the Lord Uhtred of Bebbanburg,' Egil added.

The reaction in the hall was flattering. The silence in which men had been listening to Thorfinn and Egil broke into murmuring. Some men stood to look at me. Thorfinn just stared and then, surprisingly, burst into laughter. 'Uhtred of Bebbanburg,' he said mockingly, holding up a hand to still the murmurs in the hall. 'You are old!'

'Yet many have tried to kill me,' I answered.

'And many have tried to kill me too!' Thorfinn said.

'Then I pray the gods give you old age too.'

'And what,' he demanded, 'is Uhtred of Bebbanburg doing in my hall?'

'I came to see Thorfinn Skull-Splitter,' I answered, 'and to see for myself whether he was as formidable as folk claim.'

'And is he?' Thorfinn spread his huge arms as if to display himself.

'No more formidable than Ubba the Horrible,' I said, 'and I killed him. Certainly no more than Cnut Longsword, and I slew him too. Men feared Svein of the White Horse, but he fought me and died, as did Sköll the *úlfheðinn*. And all their skulls now decorate the gate of my fortress.'

Thorfinn kept his eyes on me for a few heartbeats, then laughed loudly, and his laughter made the men in the hall beat on the tables and cheer. Norsemen love a warrior, they love the boasts of a warrior, and I had pleased them. All but for one man.

That man sat to Thorfinn's right, in the place of honour, and his face showed no amusement. He was a young man and I immediately thought he was the ugliest man I had ever seen, but also a man who seemed to exude power and menace. He had a high forehead that he had inked with a snarling dragon, wide-set eyes that were very pale, and a wide down-turned thin-lipped mouth. His hair was brown and woven into a dozen plaits, as was his beard. There was something animal-like in that face, though it was no animal I have ever seen, and no animal I would care to hunt. It was a brutal savage face, unblinking, gazing at me with the relish of a hunter. He was plainly of high rank because he wore an elaborately woven chain of gold around his neck and a simple circlet of gold about his plaited hair. He was holding a long thin-bladed knife, presumably for his food, but he pointed the sharp blade at me then spoke softly to Thorfinn who stooped to hear him, looked at me, then straightened.

'Lord Uhtred!' Thorfinn's face still showed pleasure. 'Meet your king.'

I was momentarily confused, but managed to find the right words. 'Which king?'

'You have more than one?' Thorfinn asked, amused.

'Constantine claims my land, as does Æthelstan,' I hesitated, then looked at the pale-eyed young man as I realised what Thorfinn had meant. Could it be true? Sudden anger drove my next words. 'And I'm told there's an impudent youth in Dyflin who claims it too.'

Thorfinn was no longer smiling. The hall was silent. 'Impudent?' Thorfinn asked in a dangerous voice.

'Is it not impudent to claim a throne you have never seen? Let alone tried to sit in? If claiming a throne is enough then why should I not claim the throne of Dyflin? To claim a throne is easy, to take it is hard.'

The young man drove the knife into the table, where it quivered. 'To take Saxon land,' he suggested, 'is easy.' He had a hard, gravelly voice. He gazed fixedly at me with those strangely pale eyes. Thorfinn might hope to be formidable, but this man truly was. He stood slowly, still looking at me. 'I am the King,' he said firmly, 'of Northumbria.' Men in the hall murmured their agreement.

'Guthrum tried to take a Saxon kingdom,' I said, silencing the murmurs. So this man was Anlaf, King of Dyflin, which meant he was Guthrum's grandson, 'and I was in the army that drove him to panicked flight and left a hillside sodden with the blood of his Northmen.'

'Do you deny that I am your king?' he asked.

'Constantine has troops in Cumbria,' I said, 'and Æthelstan occupies Jorvik. Where are your troops?' I paused, but he did not answer. 'And soon,' I went on, 'King Æthelstan's men will occupy Cumbria too.'

He sneered at that. 'Æthelstan is a whelp. He yelps like the bitch he is, but he will not dare go to war with Constantine.'

'Then you should know,' I said, 'that the whelp's army is already north of the River Foirthe, and his fleet is coming up the coast.'

Both Anlaf and Thorfinn just stared at me. The hall was silent. They had not known. How could they? News travels no faster than a horse or a ship can carry it, and I was the first ship to come to Orkneyjar since Æthelstan had invaded Constantine's land.

'He speaks the truth,' Egil put in drily.

'There is war?' Thorfinn recovered first.

'King Æthelstan,' I said, 'is tired of Scottish treachery. He is tired of Norsemen claiming kingship over his land, so yes, there is war.'

Anlaf sat. He said nothing. His claim to the throne of Northumbria was based on kinship, but to make that claim

230

true he had depended on chaos reigning in the north, and my news suggested that the chaos was being settled by Æthelstan's army. Now, if Anlaf was to make good on his claim to Northumbria's throne, he would have to fight Æthelstan and he knew it. I could see him thinking, and I could see he did not like his own thoughts.

Thorfinn frowned. 'You say the whelp's fleet is coming north?'

'We left it in the Foirthe, yes.'

'But Constantine's ships passed these islands three days ago. Going west.'

That, at least, confirmed what I had thought; that Constantine, unaware of Æthelstan's plans, had sent most of his ships to harry the Cumbrian coast. 'They had not heard the news,' I said.

'A bench,' Thorfinn said, then sat and slapped the table, 'for my guests,' pointing to the end of the high table.

Anlaf watched us as we sat and as ale was brought to us. 'Did you kill Guthfrith?' he demanded suddenly.

'Yes,' I said carelessly.

'He was my cousin!'

'And you didn't like him,' I said, 'and your claim to his throne, such as it is, depended on his death. You can thank me.'

There were chuckles from the hall, quickly stilled by Thorfinn's fierce gaze. Anlaf plucked the knife from the table. 'Why should I not kill you?'

'Because my death will achieve nothing, because I am a guest in Thorfinn's hall, and because I am not your enemy.'

'You are not?'

'All I care about, lord King,' I gave him that honorific because he was the King of Dyflin, 'is my home. Bebbanburg. The rest of the world can descend into chaos, but I will protect my home. I don't care who is king in Northumbria

231

so long as they leave me alone.' I drank some ale, then took a roasted leg of goose from a platter. 'Besides,' I went on cheerfully, 'I'm old! I'll be in Valhalla soon, meeting a lot of your other cousins who I put to death. Why would you want to send me there early?'

That provoked more amusement, though not from Anlaf who ignored me and instead talked quietly to Thorfinn, while a harpist played and maidservants brought more ale and food. The messenger who had summoned us to the hall had claimed a shortage of ale, but there seemed to be plenty and the noise in the hall grew raucous until Egil claimed the harp. That brought cheers till Egil struck the strings to demand quiet.

He gave them a song of his own making, a song full of battle, of blood-soaked ground, of ravens gorged with the flesh of enemies, but nowhere in the song did he say who fought, who won, or who lost. I had heard it before, Egil called it his slaughter-song. 'It warns them,' he had told me once, 'of their fate, and it reminds us that we are all fools. And, of course, the fools love it.'

They cheered him when the last chord of the harp had faded. There were more songs from Thorfinn's harpist, but already some men were falling asleep and others stumbling into the northern darkness to find their beds. 'Back to the ship?' Egil asked me quietly. 'We learned what we came to find out.'

We had learned that most of Constantine's ships had gone west and that would be good news for Æthelstan, and I supposed I should deliver it. I sighed. 'So we leave on the morning tide?'

'And hope the wind veers,' Egil said, because it would be a long hard slog if the wind stayed in the south-west.

Egil stood. He was about to thank Thorfinn for his hospitality, but the big man was already asleep, slumped on the table, so the two of us jumped down from the dais and walked to the door. 'Had you met Anlaf before?' I asked him as we went into the night's clear air.

'Never. He has a reputation though.'

'So I hear.'

'Savage, clever and ambitious.'

'A Norseman, then.'

Egil laughed. 'My only ambition is to write a song that will be sung till the world ends.'

'Then you should spend less time chasing women.'

'Ah, but the song will be about women! What else?'

We left Thorfinn's settlement, walking slowly between strips of seal meat drying on racks, then out to the barley fields. The moon was being chased by clouds. Behind us a woman screamed, there was men's laughter and a dog howling. The wind was light. We stopped when we came in sight of the southern water and I gazed at *Spearhafoc*. 'I shall miss her,' I said.

'You're selling her?' Egil sounded surprised.

'No one talks of ships in Valhalla,' I said softly.

'There'll be ships in Valhalla, my friend,' he said, 'and wide seas, strong winds, and islands of beautiful women.'

I smiled, then turned as I heard footsteps behind us. I had instinctively put my hand to Serpent-Breath's hilt, then saw it was Anlaf who followed us and who, seeing my hand on the sword, spread his own hands to show he meant no harm. He was alone. The moon was shining between clouds and reflected from his pale eyes, from the gold at his neck, and from the dull metal of his sword's hilt. No fancy decoration on that sword. It was a tool and men said he knew how to use it. 'Egil Skallagrimmrson,' he greeted us, 'you must come to Dyflin.'

'I must, lord King?'

'We like poets! Music! And you, Lord Uhtred, should come too.'

233

'I'm no poet and you don't want to hear me sing.'

He smiled thinly at that. 'I wanted to talk with you.' He gestured at a lump of rock beside the track. 'You'll sit with me?'

We sat. For a moment Anlaf said nothing, but looked towards *Spearhafoc*. 'Your ship?' he broke the silence.

'Mine, lord King.'

'She looks useful,' he said grudgingly. 'Frisian?'

'Frisian,' I confirmed.

'What is Æthelstan doing?' he asked abruptly.

'Punishing the Scots.'

'For what?'

'Being Scottish.'

He nodded. 'How many men?

'At least two thousand, probably more.'

'How many men can he raise?'

I shrugged because the question was probably unanswerable. 'Four thousand? More if he raises the fyrd.'

'More,' Egil said. 'He could lead five thousand warriors without the fyrd.'

'I agree,' Anlaf said. 'He put a thousand men into Ceaster and Mameceaster,' he said the unfamiliar names carefully, 'and has a fleet in the Mærse. That, I think, is why Constantine moved his ships. He expected an invasion of Cumbria.'

'And instead Æthelstan invaded in the east.'

'What will happen?' The pale eyes gazed into mine.

'Who knows, lord King?'

He nodded abruptly. 'Suppose Constantine survives? What then?'

'The Scots are a proud people,' I said, 'and savage. They'll want revenge.'

'Does Æthelstan wish to rule the Scots?'

I thought about that, then shook my head. 'He claims Northumbria, that's all, and he wants them to leave Cumbria.'

234

Anlaf frowned, thinking. 'Constantine won't fight now, not unless Æthelstan makes a bad mistake. He'll retreat into his hills. He'll take his punishment. There'll be skirmishes, of course, and men will die, but Constantine will wait. If Æthelstan follows him into the hills he'll find himself in bad country with too many enemies and not enough food, so he'll be forced to retreat. Then one day soon Constantine will lead an army into Æthelstan's lands, and that,' he paused and looked into my eyes, 'that will be the end of Englaland.'

'Maybe,' I said dubiously, 'but Æthelstan can always raise more warriors than Constantine.'

'Can he?' Anlaf paused, and when I gave no answer he offered his thin smile. 'Constantine wants something more than Cumbria,' he spoke quietly, 'he wants to destroy Saxon power, and to do that he will welcome allies.'

'The Norse,' I said flatly.

'The Norse, the Danes, the pagans. Us. Think about it, lord! Æthelstan hates the pagans, he wants them destroyed and gone from his land. But Constantine is shrewder. He knows our power and he needs power. He needs shields and swords and spears, and he's ready to pay for them with Saxon land. One king despises us, the other welcomes us, so who will we Northmen fight for?'

'Constantine,' I said bleakly, 'but you think he'd welcome you after he's won? He's a Christian too.'

Anlaf ignored my question. 'Æthelstan has one chance now, just one, and that is to slaughter every man north of Cair Ligualid, to scour the Scots off the face of the earth, but he won't do that because it can't be done, and even if it could, his feeble religion would tell him it's a sin. But he can't do it. He doesn't have enough men, so he talks of punishing the Scots, but punishment doesn't work, only destruction. He'll burn some villages, kill a few men, claim victory and retreat. And then the north will come down on him like a pack of hungry wolves.'

I thought of the dragon and the falling star and of Father Cuthbert's dire prophecy that the evil would come from the north. 'So you'll fight for Constantine?'

'He knows I want Northumbria. Eventually he'll offer it to me.'

'Why would Constantine want a pagan Norse king on his southern frontier?' I asked.

'Because such a king would be better than a Saxon who calls himself Lord of all Britain. And because Constantine recognises my claim to Northumbria. And I do have a claim,' he looked at me fiercely, 'an even better claim now that Guthfrith is dead.'

'Is that a thank you?' I asked, amused.

Anlaf stood. 'It is a warning,' he said coldly. 'When the northern wolves come, Lord Uhtred, choose your side carefully.' He nodded to Egil. 'You too, Egil Skallagrimmrson.' He looked up at the sky, judging the wind. 'You say Æthelstan's fleet is coming north?'

'They are.'

'This far?'

'As far as Æthelstan wants them to go.'

'Then I'd best sail home tomorrow. We'll meet again.' He said no more, but walked back towards Thorfinn's settlement.

I watched him go. I was thinking of King Hywel's words that Anlaf had just echoed; to choose my side well. 'Why is he here?' I asked.

'Recruiting,' Egil said. 'He's raising an army of the north and he'll offer it to Constantine.'

'And he wants you.'

'He wants you too, my friend. Are you tempted?'

Of course I was tempted. A pagan Northumbria was a beguiling prospect, a country where any man could worship

236

his gods without fear of a Christian sword at his neck, but a pagan Northumbria would still have Christians to the north and to the south, and neither Constantine nor Æthelstan would endure that for long. Nor did I trust Anlaf. Once he had seen Bebbanburg he would want it. 'All I want,' I told Egil, 'is to die in Bebbanburg.'

Anlaf's grandfather Guthrum had failed to defeat Alfred, and that failure had led to the spread of West Saxon power so that Alfred's dream of a united Saxon country, of Englaland, had almost come true. Now Alfred's grandson was trying to finish the dream's making, while in the north Guthrum's cold-eyed grandson was sharpening his sword.

The evil would come from the north.

The good weather continued, but an obstinate wind, more southerly than westerly, made us sail far into the North Sea before turning back towards the Scottish coast. It took us three days to discover Æthelstan's fleet that was further north than I had reckoned. Coenwulf had rescued almost all his ships from the Foirthe and most were now beached on a long wide stretch of sand, beyond which I could see plumes of smoke besmirching the western sky where Æthelstan's troops put settlements to the torch. Twelve of Coenwulf's warships patrolled the low coast, protecting the beached ships, and two of them raced towards us, but slowed and turned away when they were close enough to see the wolf's head on my sail.

'What do I do?' Gerbruht shouted from the steering platform.

We were coming from the south and I was standing in the prow, one hand on the carved sparrowhawk as I searched the low land beyond the long beach. There were tents and shelters in the fields, suggesting that much or all of Æthelstan's army was camped here, and the gaudy tent of rich scarlet and gold, that I had last seen outside Bebbanburg's Skull Gate, was pitched among them. 'What's the tide?' I called back.

Egil answered. 'Low! Still ebbing!'

'Then run her ashore, but gently.' I saw *Apostol*, Coenwulf's ship, and pointed to her. 'As close to *Apostol* as you can.'

As we coasted in through the low breaking waves I saw men carrying sacks to the beached ships. The harvest was being stolen. *Spearhafoc*'s keel grated, the ship shuddered to a stop and the sail was dropped. Egil joined me in the bows. 'We're going ashore?'

'You and I.' I pointed to the gaudy tent. 'I suspect Æthelstan's here.' I left Gerbruht in charge of the ship again. 'You can go ashore,' I told my men, 'but don't pick fights!' Most of my crew were Northmen, many wore Thor's hammer, but few had been on land during this voyage and they deserved a spell ashore. 'Don't fight!' I warned them again. 'And back on the ship by nightfall.'

'They'll fight,' Egil said as he and I walked up the beach.

'Of course they will. They're idiots.'

Æthelstan was not in the camp. He had ridden inland with over four hundred men and was doubtless responsible for the fires that smoked above the low hills. Two mailed men guarded his tents, but I growled at them and they reluctantly let us enter the gaudy tent where I growled again to summon ale from a servant. Then we waited.

Æthelstan returned in the late afternoon. He was in an ebullient mood and seemed pleased to see me. 'We laid them waste!' he boasted as he peeled off his mail coat. 'And do sit down again. Is that ale?'

'Good ale,' I said.

'We stole it from a settlement down the coast.' He sat and gazed at me. 'Coenwulf said you deserted the fleet.'

'Last time we saw the fleet, lord King, it was on a lee shore and being harried by Scotsmen. So while Coenwulf got out of his own mess we went looking for Constantine's ships.'

Æthelstan smiled, recognising my hostility to his fleet's commander. 'We heard that Constantine's ships went north. Fleeing us. Fifteen of them?'

'Fifteen, yes, but they weren't fleeing, lord King, they didn't even know you were here.'

'They'll know by now,' he said grimly. 'So what are they doing? Sheltering in the islands? Waiting for more ships before they attack us?'

'Is that what Coenwulf fears?'

'It's what he suspects.'

'Then he's wrong. They sailed west.'

'Probably gone to Cumbria,' Egil put in, 'you won't see them for a long time.'

Æthelstan gazed at us both for a few heartbeats. It was plain that this was news to him. 'You're sure?'

'I'm sure,' I answered. 'We think he left four ships on this coast, and they're probably staying in harbour now they've seen your fleet.'

'Then you bring me good news!' Æthelstan said happily. 'And your son has been useful!'

'Has he lost men?' I asked.

'Not one! The Scots won't fight.' He paused, then smiled as the tent flap was pushed aside and Ingilmundr appeared.

The tall Norseman stopped when he saw us, then forced a smile and gave me a perfunctory bow. 'Lord Uhtred.'

'Jarl Ingilmundr,' I responded coldly. I had disliked him from the first moment I had met him beside the Mærse. He was a young and strikingly handsome man with a straight blade of a nose and long hair that he wore tied in a leather lace so that it hung almost to his waist. When I had first encountered him he had worn a hammer about his neck, but now a bright cross hung from a golden chain. 'And this is Jarl Egil Skallagrimmrson.'

'I have heard of you,' Ingilmundr said.

239

'I would expect no less!' Egil answered happily.

'Ingilmundr brought two hundred warriors from Wirhealum,' Æthelstan interrupted enthusiastically, 'and very useful men they are too!'

'They're Norsemen,' Egil said mischievously.

'They are examples,' Æthelstan said.

'Examples?' I asked.

'That all men are welcome in Englaland so long as they are Christians.' Æthelstan patted the seat next to his, inviting Ingilmundr to sit. He also gave the hammer at my breast a rueful glance. 'And Lord Uhtred brings us good news,' he spoke to Ingilmundr, 'the Scottish fleet has gone, quite gone. Gone to the west coast!'

'They fled from you, lord King,' Ingilmundr said as he sat.

'It appears not. If Lord Uhtred is right they didn't even know we were here! But everyone else has fled.'

'Everyone else?' I asked.

'The bastards won't fight! Oh, they harry us. We can't send out small forage parties, but they won't confront our army. We know Constantine has men, at least fifteen hundred and that doesn't include his allies from Strath Clota, but they won't face us! They lurk in the hills.'

'They are frightened of you, lord King,' Ingilmundr said.

Æthelstan rewarded that with a warm smile. He loved the flattery, and Ingilmundr was adept at supplying it. He was oily, I thought, like the feel of raw seal flesh. 'He should be frightened of me,' Æthelstan said, 'and after this campaign I hope he'll be even more frightened!'

'Or angry,' I said.

'Of course he'll be angry,' Æthelstan showed a flash of annoyance. 'Angry, frightened, and chastened.'

'And vengeful,' I persisted.

Æthelstan gazed at me for a few heartbeats, then sighed. 'What can he do? I'm deep in his land and he refuses to

240

fight. You think he can do better in my land? If he takes one step beyond the frontier I'll crush him and he knows it. I have more spears, more swords, and more silver. He can be as vengeful as he likes, but he's also impotent. I will have peace in Britain, Lord Uhtred, and Constantine is learning the price he will pay for disturbing that peace.'

'Do you have more men, lord King?' Egil asked in a mild voice.

'I do,' Æthelstan said flatly.

'And if Constantine unites your enemies? The Norse of the islands, the Danish settlers, the men of Strath Clota, and the Irish kingdoms? You would still have more men?'

'That will not happen,' Ingilmundr responded to Egil.

'Why not?' Egil asked in a very polite voice.

'When did we Norse ever unite?'

That was a good question and Egil acknowledged it with a slight bow of his head. The Northmen, both Danes and Norse, were fearsome fighters, but notoriously quarrelsome.

'Besides,' Æthelstan went on, 'Constantine is a Christian. He told me once that his ambition is to retire to a monastery! No, lord, he won't rely on pagan swords. All he would achieve by asking Norse help is to invite more pagan enemies into his land and though he might be treacherous, he's no fool.' He frowned momentarily. 'And what would Constantine gain by allying himself with the Norse? They'll want a reward! What will he give them? Land?'

'Northumbria,' I said quietly.

'Nonsense,' Æthelstan said decisively. 'Constantine wants Northumbria for himself! Why in God's name would he put a Norse king on the throne in Eoferwic?'

'Because he wants something more than Northumbria,' I said.

'What?'

'The destruction of Saxon power, lord King. Your power.'

241

I think he knew I spoke the truth, but he dismissed it lightly. 'Then he'll just have to learn that Saxon power is indestructible,' he said carelessly, 'because I will settle his nonsense and I will have my peace.'

'And I will have Bebbanburg,' I said.

He ignored that, though Ingilmundr gave me a poisonous glance. 'We march tomorrow,' Æthelstan said, 'so we must rest tonight.' He stood, prompting all of us to stand.

That was our dismissal. I bowed, but Egil had one more question. 'March where, lord King?' he asked.

'Further north, of course!' Æthelstan answered, his good mood restored. 'To the far north! I will show Constantine that there is no part of his kingdom that I cannot reach. Tomorrow we go to the end of his realm, to the far northern end of Britain!'

So the *Monarchus Totius Brittaniae* was proving his title to be true. His spears would glint from the beaches of Wessex to the cliffs of the cold north, and Æthelstan believed that thereby he was stamping his authority on a sullen, rebellious land. But the Scots would not fight him, not yet, and so they had retreated into their mountains where they were watching, waiting, and dreaming of revenge.

And I remembered Anlaf's cold, pale eyes.

Choose your side carefully.

PART THREE

The Slaughter

PART THREE

The Slaughter

ELEVEN

Æthelstan's army reached the northern coast of Scotland where great waves shattered on towering cliffs, where the sea birds shrieked and eagles flew, and where the wind blew cold and fierce. There was no battle. Scottish scouts watched Æthelstan's army, but Constantine kept his troops far off to the west. It was a bleak, unfriendly land, and the unceasing wind brought the first hints of winter cold.

We stayed with the fleet, though to what end I could not tell because no ships challenged us. Æthelstan's army had marched and the fleet had sailed to the northern edge of Constantine's land and we had butchered cattle, burned fishing boats, stolen paltry stores of grain, and torn down pathetic turf-roofed hovels. And here, where the land ended in jagged cliffs, Æthelstan declared victory. I went ashore at the land's end and Æthelstan invited me to what he proclaimed was a feast, though in truth it was a score of men in a wind-lashed tent eating gristly beef and drinking sour ale. My son was among the guests. 'It's a miserable country,' he told me, 'cold, wet and poor.'

'They wouldn't fight you?'

'Skirmishes,' he said scornfully, 'but nothing more.'

Æthelstan overheard his comments. 'I offered them battle,' he called across the table, 'I planted the hazel rods.'

'I thought only the Northmen did that, lord King.'

'Constantine's scouts saw us do it. They know what it means! And Constantine didn't dare show his face.'

It was an old custom, brought to Britain by the men in dragon-ships. To plant the hazel rods was to choose a battle place and invite your enemy to come and fight. But Constantine, I thought, was too clever to accept the invitation. He knew Æthelstan's army outnumbered his and so he would give the Saxons their easy victory and hold his forces back for another day. And so the ground between the hazel rods stayed empty.

And we went south.

I let *Spearhafoc* run, leaving Æthelstan's fleet lumbering far behind, and then on a cold autumn day there was the blessed moment of rounding Lindisfarena's sands and slipping back into Bebbanburg's harbour. Benedetta waited for me, the great hall was warmed by a massive driftwood fire, and I was home.

Three weeks later Æthelstan's army marched past the fortress. There had been no battle, but he was still ebullient when I met him outside the Skull Gate. The Scots, he claimed, had been humiliated. 'They've pulled their forces back from Cumbria! That wretched man Eochaid is gone and Ealdorman Alfgar is back in Cair Ligualid.' Alfgar was one of the two ealdormen sent to pacify Cumbria.

'Good, lord King,' I said, because to say anything else would simply have annoyed him. Eochaid might well have gone back to Scotland, but I did not doubt that Cumbria's Norse settlers would still look north for protection, and while Alfgar and his garrison might be back in Cair Ligualid they were still surrounded by a sullen and hostile people. 'You'll dine with us tonight, lord King?'

'With pleasure, lord, with pleasure!'

He brought a score of men into the fortress. Ingilmundr was one, and he prowled about the ramparts, no doubt wondering how they could be assaulted. Bishop Oda was another, and he at least was welcome. I found a moment to talk alone with him, both of us sitting in the cold moonlight and gazing at the wind-fretted sea. 'I met Anlaf,' I told him.

'The king knows?'

'I didn't tell him. He has enough suspicions about me without learning that.'

'He will learn!'

'From you?'

'No, lord.'

'He'll doubtless hear a rumour,' I said, 'and I will deny it.'

'As you denied killing Guthfrith?'

'The world is a better place without Guthfrith,' I said harshly.

'I did notice a new skull at the gate,' Oda said slyly, and when I did not respond he just chuckled. 'So tell me, what does Anlaf want?'

'Northumbria.'

'No surprise there.'

'And he thinks Constantine will give it to him.'

Oda fingered the cross at his breast. 'Why would Constantine want a pagan Norse king on his southern border?'

'To humiliate Æthelstan, of course. And because he knows Æthelstan will never let the Scots rule in Eoferwic.'

'But why would Æthelstan allow Anlaf to rule there?'

'He won't,' I said, 'but if Anlaf has the Scots as allies? The Strath Clotans? The men of the Suðreyjar Islands? All the northern pagans?'

'All the northern pagans?' Oda asked pointedly, looking at my hammer.

247

I laughed sourly. 'Not me,' I said. 'I shall stay here and make my ramparts higher.'

Oda smiled. 'Because you're old? I seem to remember that Beowulf was as old as you when he fought the dragon, lord. And he killed the beast.'

And I had been sitting in this same place, just outside the hall, when I first heard of the great dragon flying southwards with its silver wings beating the sea into submission. 'Beowulf was a hero,' I retorted, 'and yes, he killed the dragon, but he died doing it.'

'He did his duty, my friend,' Oda said, then paused to listen to a gust of singing coming from the hall. Æthelstan had brought his own harpist who was playing the famous song of Ethandun, telling how Alfred had defeated Guthrum and his great army. Men beat their hands on the tables and roared the words, especially when the lines came that described how Uhtred the Northman had cut down the foemen. 'Mighty was his sword,' they bellowed, 'and eager its hunger. Many the Danish warrior rued the day.' Was I the last man alive who had fought on the hill of Ethandun?

'Is Steapa still alive?' I asked Oda.

'He is! As old as you, but still strong. He wanted to come with us to Scotland, but the king commanded him to stay at home.'

'Because he's old?'

'On the contrary! Because he wanted a strong warrior to defend the coast in case the Northmen landed ships.'

Steapa had been at Ethandun and he and I had to be among the few survivors of that great battle. He was a huge man, a fearsome warrior, and we had started as enemies, but had become close friends. Steapa had begun life as a slave, but had risen to command Alfred's household troops. He had once been given the ironic nickname Steapa Snotor, Steapa the Clever, because men reckoned him slow-witted,

248

but Steapa had proved himself to be a subtle and savage fighter. 'I should like to see him again,' I said wistfully.

'Then come south with us!'

I shook my head. 'I fear trouble in the north. I'll stay here.'

Oda smiled and touched my arm. 'You worry too much, my friend.'

'I do?'

'There will be no great war. Anlaf has Norse enemies in Ireland. If he brings his army across the sea those enemies will take his land, and if he brings just half his army that won't be enough to capture Northumbria, even with Constantine's help. Strath Clota says they're at peace, but now they've seen Constantine's weakness why shouldn't they attack him again? And do you really believe the pagan Norse will unite behind one man? They never have, so why should they now? No, my friend. There is much noise in the north because they are a noisy people, but the Scots have been beaten into submission, the Norse are more likely to fight each other than fight us, and I can assure you that there will be peace. Æthelstan will be crowned in Eoferwic, and, God be praised, Englaland will at last exist.'

'God be praised?' I asked sourly.

'One people, one nation, one god.'

Somehow that declaration made me feel doomed, perhaps because it spelt the end of Northumbria? I touched the hilt of the small knife I wore at my belt. In deference to Æthelstan's presence we had allowed no swords in the great hall, but the knife's hilt would be enough to ensure my passage to Valhalla. I had seen sudden death in the hall, men falling from the bench with a hand grasping at their chest, and though I felt well I knew that death had to be coming. And it had to be soon, I thought, and regret crossed my mind like a cloud shadow sliding across the sea. I might

249

never know what would happen, might never know whether Constantine sought revenge, or whether Anlaf would bring his fleet across the sea, or whether my son could hold Bebbanburg against all that the world could throw against it.

'Come inside, lord,' Oda stood, 'it's getting cold.'

'Does Æthelstan still want Bebbanburg?' I asked him abruptly.

'I think not, lord. That passion died with Ealdred.'

'Then I should thank whoever killed him.'

'Many of us agree, lord,' Oda said calmly, 'because he gave the king bad counsel.' For a moment I thought he would thank me, but he just smiled and turned away.

I let him go into the hall, but I stayed outside, still sitting, staring at the sea and at the moon-silvered clouds. I wanted to see the dragon. It did not come.

The dragon slept, but not in my dreams.

I had half forgotten the saga of Beowulf until Oda reminded me of the old tale. Beowulf was a Geat, one of the Norse tribes, who went to the land of the Danes to slaughter monsters. He slew Grendel, then Grendel's mother, and after fifty more winters had passed, he killed the dragon. The tale was sometimes chanted at feasts, to tables of warriors in the great halls of smoke and song.

And though this dragon of the north slept it still came to my dreams. Night after night I would wake sweating. Benedetta said I cried out in fear. She would hold me, comfort me, but still the dragon came. It did not fly on great wings that made the sea shudder, but slithered like a serpent through the underworld, through a pillared passage of stone-carved arches lit by the flames of its nostrils that gaped like caverns. It should have been sleeping, its vast slack body slumped on the heaped gold, on the piled helmets, on the goblets and plates, on the woven arm rings and on the cut gems of its hoard. But in every dream it was awake and crawling towards me.

I dreamed I was in a barrow-mound. I knew that, though how I knew I did not know. I knew the dragon had been burning steadings, spewing flame on my people's homes, and that it must be killed. I am the Lord of Bebbanburg, the guardian of my people, so it was my duty to go to its gold-hoard and kill the beast. I had armed myself with a great shield of iron, hammered by Deogol, Bebbanburg's black-smith. It was heavy, that shield, but a willow-board shield would have burst into flame at the dragon's first breath and so I carried the iron shield as the beast writhed towards me. It screamed, not in fear, but in rage, and its great head reared, I crouched, and the flame spewed about me with a roar like a thousand tempests. The fire wrapped me, seared and scorched me, it turned the shield red, and the very earth trembled as I forced my way forward and raised the sword.

It was never Serpent-Breath. It was an older sword, scarred and pitted, a sword battered by battle and I knew her name was Nægling, which meant the claw. A claw against a dragon, and as the beast reared again I attacked with Nægling, and it was a good strike! I lunged at the dragon's head, between the eyes, a killing blow into the killing place, and Nægling shattered. That was when I woke, night after night, sweating and terrified, as the flames spewed again and I staggered, fire-encircled, burning, and with the broken sword in my hand.

I feared to sleep, for to sleep was to dream, and to dream was to see my own death. It was a rare night when the dragon did not wriggle from his gold-lair and I did not wake in terror. Then as the long winter nights dragged on, the dream became more real. The dragon roared the fire a second time and I dropped the shield that was now glowing red, and threw away Nægling's useless hilt, and drew my seax. And on my right a companion came to share the fight. It was not Finan, but Sigtryggr, my dead son-in-law, whose wooden shield was burning, whose right arm stabbed with his long sword to pierce the dragon's head, and I stabbed too, with Bitter. Bitter? My seax was called Wasp-Sting, not Bitter, but Bitter proved a better blade than Nægling, for her bright edge sliced the dragon's throat and liquid fire poured to drench my arm with agony. There were two screams of pain, mine and the dragon's, and the great beast toppled, the fire died, and Sigtryggr was kneeling beside me and I knew that my length of days was over and that the joys of life were ending. Then I would wake.

'You had the dream again?' Benedetta asked.

'We killed the dragon, but I died.'

'You did not die,' she said stubbornly, 'you are here.'

'Sigtryggr helped me.'

'Sigtryggr! He was kin to Anlaf, yes?'

'And to Guthfrith.' I pushed the furs off my body. It was a cold winter's night, but I was hot. 'The dream is an omen,' I said, as I had said a hundred times before, but what did it mean? The dragon had to be Constantine and his allies, and by fighting them I would die, but my ally was a Norseman, Sigtryggr, and he was Anlaf's cousin, so was I meant to fight alongside Anlaf? Did Nægling break because I fought for the wrong side? I groped for Serpent-Breath's hilt. The sword was never far from me so that if death came in the dark I might have a chance to grip her.

'The dream means nothing,' Benedetta said sternly. 'It is an old story, that is all.'

'All dreams mean something. They are messages.'

'Then find an old woman who can tell you the meaning! Then find another, and she will tell you a different meaning. A dream is a dream.'

252

She was trying to reassure me. I knew she believed in dreams as messages, but she did not want to admit the truth of that dream where the dragon came from its hoard to gust its furnace heat. Yet by day the dream receded. Was the dragon Scotland? But it seemed Æthelstan was right and that the Scots had been cowed. There were few cattle raids, Eochaid stayed far from Cumbria where the Norse, though sullen, paid their land rents to Godric and Alfgar. Two years after Æthelstan's invasion the Scots even sent an embassy to Eoferwic where Æthelstan was holding court. They brought gifts; a precious gospel book and six cunningly carved walrus tusks. 'Our king,' their spokesman, a bishop, bowed to Æthelstan, 'will also send the tribute that we owe.' He seemed to bite the words as he said them.

'The tribute is late,' Æthelstan said sternly. The king, his long hair again bright with gold-threaded ringlets, sat tall in the throne that had belonged to Sigtryggr.

'It will come, lord King,' the bishop said.

'Soon.'

'Soon,' the bishop repeated.

I heard that the tribute was delivered to Cair Ligualid, though whether it was the full amount I did not hear. I had attended Æthelstan in Eoferwic and he had seemed pleased to see me, he teased me for my grey beard, was gracious to Benedetta, but otherwise ignored us. I left as soon as I could, returning to the sanctuary of Bebbanburg where the dream persisted, though not as frequently. I told Finan of the dream and he just laughed. 'If you fight a dragon, lord, I promise to be beside you. And pity the poor beast. We'll add its skull to the gate. That would be a fine thing to see, so it would.'

And in the next twelvemonth the dream faded. It still came, but rarely. There was a night at harvest time when Egil came to Bebbanburg and my warriors beat the tables and demanded a song and he gave them the story of

Beowulf. And even that did not revive the dream. I sat and listened to the tale's ending, how King Beowulf of the Geats, old and hoary, went to the deep barrow with his iron shield, and how he drew Nægling, his battle sword, and how the sword broke and how Beowulf, with one companion, then killed the beast with his seax, Bitter, and then was killed himself.

Warriors are sentimental. My men knew the story, yet they sat transfixed by its long telling, and there were tears when the end came. Egil struck deep chords on the harp, and his voice grew strong. 'Swa begnornodon Geata leode, hlafordes hryre.' I swear I saw men crying as Egil chanted the lines of mourning, how Beowulf's men lamented their dead lord, saying that of all the kings he was the best, the most generous, the kindest and the most deserving of honour. And when the last chord was struck Egil winked at me and the hall resounded with cheers and table-beating. I thought the dream must come again that night, but it stayed away, and in the morning I felt Serpent-Breath's hilt and was glad to be alive.

That was the dawn of a noise-day, an event my men always enjoyed. I had purchased horses in Eoferwic, thirty-five fine young stallions, and we took them to a stretch of sand just beyond the Skull Gate and there surrounded them. Many of the villagers came too, the women carrying pots and pans, the children overexcited, and then I gave the word and all of us began to make noise. And such a noise! Men beat swords together, clashed spear butts on shields, children shrieked, women beat pots together, all of us making a clangour fit to wake the dead in Bebbanburg's graveyard that lay not fifty yards away. Egil was still with us and I cupped my hands to shout into his ear. 'You should sing!'

'Me? Sing? Why?'

'The object is to frighten the horses!'

254

He laughed and bellowed insults instead. And we watched the animals. We ride horses into battle. Most times, of course, we make a shield wall and the horses are kept well back, but sometimes we ride them into the killing place and a frightened horse is a useless horse. Yet horses can be trained to survive the din, to ignore the shrieks, the clangour of blades and the piercing screams, and so we try to accustom them to the noise so that they will not fear the awful sound of battle.

And while we shouted and made our noise a horseman came from the west. Finan saw him first and touched my elbow. I turned and saw a weary horse, sweat-whitened, and a wide-eyed rider almost falling from the saddle with tiredness. He half collapsed when he dismounted, and only Finan's arm kept him upright. 'Lord,' he said, 'lord.' Then told me his message.

The dragon was coming south.

'The Scots, lord,' the messenger said, and he was so tired he could hardly speak and I checked his words with a raised hand and gave him a flask of ale.

'Drink,' I said, 'then talk.'

'The Scots, lord,' he said when he had drained the flask, 'they invaded.'

'Cumbria?' I guessed.

'Ealdorman Alfgar sent me, lord. He's going south.'

'Alfgar?'

'He's gone to join forces with Godric, lord.'

Men were crowding around to hear the news. I made them step back, and told Aldwyn to take the messenger's horse to the fortress. 'He needs water,' I told the boy, 'then walk him before you stable him.' I sat the messenger on a great bleached log of driftwood and made him tell his story slowly.

The Scots, he said, had crossed the River Hedene upstream of Cair Ligualid. 'Hundreds, lord! Thousands! We were lucky.'

'Lucky?'

'We had warning. Some men were hawking by the river at dawn, they rode to tell us.'

'You saw them?'

'The Scots, lord? Yes! And blackshields. The ealdorman sent me to tell you.'

'When was this?'

'A week ago, lord. I rode fast! But I had to avoid the Scots!'

I did not ask whether Alfgar had sent a messenger to Æthelstan because it was obvious that he would have done that before telling me, but nor did I necessarily believe the messenger. His name was Cenwalh and he was a West Saxon by his speech, but the thought occurred to me that he could still be a man in Constantine's service. There were plenty of Saxons in Scotland. Some were outlaws seeking sanctuary, others were men who had offended a great lord and fled north to escape punishment, and it was not past Scottish cunning to send such a man to persuade me to march away from Bebbanburg. If I stripped the fortress of most of its warriors and crossed Britain to face an enemy who did not exist then Constantine might well bring an army to assault my ramparts. 'Did you see any Norse warriors?' I asked Cenwalh.

'No, lord, but the Cumbrian Norse will fight for Constantine.'

'You think so?'

'They hate us, lord. They hate the cross . . .' his voice faltered as he saw my hammer.

'Back to the fortress,' I commanded my men.

I remember that day well, an autumn day of sunshine and small wind, of gentle seas and mild warmth. The harvest was

256

almost finished and I had planned a feast for the villagers, but now I had to plan for the chance that Cenwalh's tale was true. I asked Egil to hurry home and then send scouts north of the Tuede to search for any sign of a Scottish army gathering. Then I sent messages to those of my warriors who farmed my land, ordering them to Bebbanburg with their men, and I sent a man to Dunholm, to tell Sihtric that I might need his troops.

Then I waited. I was not idle. We sharpened spears, repaired mail, and bound willow-board shields with iron. 'You will go then?' Benedetta asked me.

'I swore an oath to protect Æthelstan.'

'And he needs an old man to protect him?'

'He needs the old man's warriors,' I said patiently.

'But he was your enemy!'

'Ealdred was my enemy. He misled Æthelstan.'

'*Ouff!*' she exclaimed. I was tempted to smile at that, but sensibly kept a straight face. 'Æthelstan has an army to protect him!' she went on. 'He has Wessex, he has East Anglia, he has Mercia! He has to have you too?'

'If he calls for me,' I said, 'I will go.'

'Perhaps he will not call.'

Or perhaps, I thought, Alfgar had panicked. Perhaps Constantine was raiding northern Cumbria and, once he had stolen the harvest and captured enough cattle, he would retreat into Scotland. Or perhaps Cenwalh's story was untrue? I did not know, though an instinct told me that the dragon and the falling star had come at last. It was war.

'If you go,' Benedetta said, 'I go too.'

'No,' I said firmly.

'I am not your slave! Not a slave any more! I am not your wife. I am a free woman, you said so yourself! I go where I want!'

It was like trying to argue with a tempest and I said nothing more. And I waited.

257

More news came, but it was unreliable, mere rumour. The Scots were south of the Ribbel and still advancing, they had gone back north, they were marching east towards Eoferwic, they had been joined by an army of Norsemen, that there had been a battle near Mameceaster and the Scots had won, next day it was the Saxons who had triumphed. Alfgar was dead, Alfgar was pursuing a beaten Scottish army north. Nothing was certain, but the news, mostly brought by traders, none of whom had seen an army or a battle, persuaded me to send war-bands to the west in search of some reliable report. I ordered them not to cross into Cumbria, but to seek out fugitives and it was one of those bands, led by my son, that brought troubling news. 'Olaf Einerson led sixteen men west,' my son told me. 'They took weapons, shields, and mail.' Olaf Einerson was a surly, troublesome tenant who had taken over his father's land and who was ever reluctant to pay me rent. 'His wife told me,' my son went on. 'She says he's gone to join the Scots.'

We heard other reports of Danes and Norsemen riding west over the hills with their men, and Berg, who took thirty men in search of news, came back to say that there were rumours of Scottish troops visiting Danish and Norse settlements offering silver and promises of more land. The only certainty I had was that Bebbanburg was not immediately threatened. Egil had led men deep into the north country, riding almost to the Foirthe, and found nothing. He brought that news to Bebbanburg and with him came his brother, Thorolf, and seventy-six mounted men. 'And we'll march together,' he said happily.

'I don't know that I'm marching yet,' I told him.

He looked around Bebbanburg's courtyard, crammed with the troops I had summoned from my estates. 'Of course you are,' he said.

'And if I march,' I warned him, 'I fight for Æthelstan not for the Norse.'

'Of course you do.'

'And the Norse will side with Constantine,' I said, and then, after a pause, 'and don't say of course they will.'

'But of course they will,' he said, smiling, 'and I will fight for you. You saved my brother's life, you gave me land, and you gave me friendship. Who else would I fight for?'

'Against the Norse?'

'Against your enemies, lord.' He paused. 'When do we march?'

I knew I had been delaying the decision, persuading myself that I waited for confirmation from a messenger I trusted. Was I reluctant? I had prayed never to stand in another shield wall, told myself that Æthelstan did not need my men, had listened to Benedetta's pleas, and had remembered the dragon coming from the gold-hoard with its burning nostrils. Of course I was reluctant. Only the young and fools go to war gladly. Yet I was prepared for war. My men were gathered and the spears were sharp.

'The Scots have ever been your enemies,' Egil went on quietly. I said nothing. 'And if you don't march,' he went on, 'Æthelstan will mistrust you more than ever.'

'He hasn't summoned me.'

Egil glanced at Finan who had joined us on the seaward rampart. A gust of wind lifted Finan's long grey hair, reminding me that we were old and that battle is a young man's game. 'We're waiting for a summons from Æthelstan,' Egil greeted the Irishman.

'God knows if any messenger can get through Northumbria these days,' Finan said.

'My tenants are loyal,' I said stubbornly.

'Mostly,' Finan said, 'yes.' But his dubious tone told me that not all my tenants were loyal to the Saxon cause. Olaf

259

Einerson had already gone to join the invaders and others would go too, and any messenger coming from the south would have to avoid the settlements of the Northmen.

'And what do you think is happening?' Egil asked me.

I hesitated, tempted to say I did not know and that I waited for real news, but these two men were my closest friends, companions of battle, and I told them the truth. 'I think the Scots are taking their revenge.'

'Then what are you waiting for?' Egil asked very quietly.

I answered just as quietly. 'Courage.' Neither man spoke. I stared at the water shattering white on the Farnea Islands. This was home, the place I loved, and I did not want to march across the whole width of Britain to stand in another shield wall. 'We march tomorrow,' I said reluctantly, 'at dawn.'

Because the dragon was flying south.

I rode unwillingly. It did not feel like my fight. To the south was Æthelstan, a king who had turned against me as he was dazzled by his own dreams of glory, while to the north was Constantine, who had ever wanted to take my land. I hated neither man, trusted neither, and wanted no part of their war. Except it was my war too. Whatever happened would decide the fate of Northumbria and I am a Northumbrian. My country is the hard high hills, the pounding sea coast, and the tough folk who make their living from the thin soil and the cold ocean. Beowulf rode to fight the dragon because he was the guardian of his people, and my people did not want to be ruled by their old enemy, the Scots. They were not enthusiastic about the southern Saxons either, regarding them as a soft, privileged people, but when swords are drawn and spear-blades glitter they will side with the Saxons. The Norse and the Danes of Northumbria might rally to Constantine, but only because they wanted to be left alone to worship the true gods. I would have liked that too, but history, like fate, is inexorable. Northumbria could not survive on its own and it must choose which king would rule, and I, as Northumbria's greatest lord, would choose the man I had once sworn to protect. We would ride to Æthelstan.

And so we travelled the familiar road to Eoferwic. Once there we would follow the Roman road through Scipton, across the hills and so down to Mameceaster. I was praying that Constantine's army would not have reached that far, because if he broke through the row of burhs that protected Mercia's northern frontier then he would be free to savage and plunder the rich Mercian fields. I led over three hundred warriors, including thirty-three from Dunholm and Egil's fearsome Norsemen. We were all mounted, and followed by over fifty servants leading packhorses that carried food, fodder, shields and spears. I had left just forty men to hold Bebbanburg under the command of Redbad, a reliable Frisian warrior, who would be helped by Egil's folk who I had encouraged to shelter behind the fortress's ramparts. There had been no sign of a Scottish invasion on the east coast, but Egil's men would sleep better knowing that their women and children were behind Bebbanburg's mighty walls. 'And if the Scots do come,' Egil told Redbad cheerfully, 'you put the women in helmets on the ramparts. They'll look like warriors! Enough to scare off the Scots.'

We still did not know what happened on Britain's western coast. Eoferwic was nervous, its garrison alert, but no men had marched eastwards. The city's leader, now that Guthfrith and Ealdred were dead, was the new archbishop, Wulfstan. He was a thin, irascible man who greeted me suspiciously. 'Why are you going?' he demanded.

'Why isn't the garrison sending men?' I retorted.

'Their task is to protect the city, not wander across Britain because of rumour.'

'And if Æthelstan is defeated?'

'I have good relations with the Northmen! The church will survive. Christ cannot be defeated, Lord Uhtred.'

I looked about the room where we met, a lavish chamber that had been built by the Romans and was warmed by a great fire and hung with woollen tapestries depicting Christ and his disciples. Beneath them, on long wooden tables, was a treasure trove of gold vessels, silver plates, and jewel-encrusted reliquaries. The room had never gleamed with so much wealth when Hrothweard had been arch-bishop, so was Wulfstan taking money? The Scots would bribe him, I was sure, and so would Anlaf. 'You have news?' I asked him.

'The Scots are said to be moving south,' he said dismiss-ively, 'but Alfgar and Godric will fight them before they reach Mameceaster.'

'Alfgar and Godric,' I said, 'can't have more than seven hundred men. If that. The Scots will have three times their number. And maybe the help of the Irish Norse?'

'They won't come!' he said too quickly, then looked at me indignantly. 'Anlaf is a minor chieftain, no more. He'll stay in his Irish bog.'

'Rumour says—' I began.

'A man of your experience should know better than to listen to rumour,' Wulfstan interrupted petulantly. 'You want my advice, lord? Leave this Scottish adventure to King Æthelstan.'

'You have news of him?'

'I assume he is gathering forces! He has no need of yours.'

'He might not agree,' I said calmly.

'Then the boy is a fool!' His anger broke through. 'A pathetic fool! Have you seen his hair? Golden ringlets! No wonder men call him "pretty boy"!'

'Have you seen the pretty boy fight?' I asked. He gave me no answer. 'I have,' I went on, 'and he's formidable.'

'Then he has no need of your forces nor of mine. I am not so irresponsible as to leave this city defenceless. And if I might advise you, lord, I would recommend you look to your own fortress. Our task is to keep the eastern parts of Northumbria peaceful.'

'So if Constantine wins,' I asked, 'we just wait to be attacked?'

He stared at me scornfully. 'And even if you do march,' he ignored my question, 'you'll be too late! The battle will be over. Stay home, lord, stay home.'

He was a fool, I thought. There would be no peace in Britain if Constantine won, and if Æthelstan gained a victory then he would note who had helped him and who had shrunk from the fight. I left Wulfstan in his rich home, spent a fitful night in Eoferwic's old Roman barracks, and led my men west in the morning. We travelled through the rich farmlands about the city, then slowly climbed into the hills. This was sheep country, and on the second day, as we neared Scipton, we met flock after flock being driven eastwards. They scattered off the Roman road as we approached, not just sheep and a few goats, but whole families. A shepherd was brought to me who spoke of Scottish raiders. 'You saw them?' I asked.

'Saw the smoke, lord.'

'Get off your knees, man,' I said irritably. Far ahead I could only see piled grey clouds on the western horizon. Was there smoke there? It was impossible to say. 'You say you saw smoke, what else?'

'Folk running, lord. They say there's a horde.'

But a horde of what? Other fugitives told the same confused story. A panic had spread on the western side of the hills and the only fact I could draw from the frightened folk was that they had come south to find the road that would lead them to the dubious safety of Eoferwic's walls.

That suggested Constantine's forces were still ravaging Cumbria well north of the Mercian border.

Finan agreed. 'Bastard should move faster. Can't be much opposing him?'

'Godric and Alfgar,' I pointed out.

'Who can't have enough men! Silly bastards should retreat.'

'Maybe Æthelstan has reinforced them?'

'The archbishop would have known, wouldn't he?'

'Wulfstan can't decide which side he's on,' I said.

'He won't be happy if Anlaf comes.'

'Constantine will protect him.'

'And maybe Constantine's retreating? He's smacked Æthelstan and reckons it's enough?'

'It doesn't smell that way,' I said. 'Constantine's no fool. He knows you don't smack an enemy, you tear his damned guts out and piss on them.'

We camped near Scipton, a small town with two churches, both of which were dilapidated. There were Danish steadings nearby and local folk said that most of those men had left, gone west. But to fight who? I suspected they were joining Constantine's forces, and many folk, hearing how many of my men spoke Norse or Danish, thought we were doing the same.

Next day we travelled on, heading south and west and still meeting fugitives who hurried out of our way. We talked to some and they told the same tale, that they had seen smoke and heard stories of a vast Scottish army that seemed to get larger with every report. One woman, who had two small children clinging to her skirts, claimed to have seen the foreign horsemen. 'Hundreds of them, lord! Hundreds.' There were still thick grey clouds to the north and west and I persuaded myself that some of the darker streaks were plumes of smoke. I hurried, haunted by Archbishop

Wulfstan's prediction that the battle would be fought by now. More and more of the fugitives were now travelling in the same direction as us, no longer trying to cross the hills, but heading south towards the stone ramparts of Mameceaster. I sent scouts ahead to clear the road that was left thick with sheep and cattle droppings.

We reached Mameceaster the next day. The garrison slammed the gates shut as we approached, doubtless fearing we were Constantine's men and it took a tedious argument to persuade them that I was Uhtred of Bebbanburg and no enemy. The commander of the garrison, a man named Eadwyn, had the first real news since Cenwalh had ridden to Bebbanburg. 'There's been a battle, lord,' he said gloomily.

'Where? What happened?'

'To the north, lord. Ealdorman Godric was killed. And Ealdorman Alfgar fled.'

'Where in the north?'

He waved a hand. 'North somewhere, lord.'

Fugitives from the defeated Saxon army had reached Mameceaster and Eadwyn summoned three of them. They told how Alfgar and Godric, the two men Æthelstan had appointed as ealdormen of Cumbria, had gathered their forces and marched north to face the Scots. 'It was on a stream, lord. We thought it would stop them.'

'And it didn't?'

'The Irish came round our left, lord. Howling savages!'

'The Irish!'

'Norsemen, lord. They had falcons on their shields.'

'Anlaf,' Egil said bluntly.

That was the first confirmation we had that Anlaf had crossed the sea and that we did not just face a Scottish army, but an alliance of Constantine's men and the Norse of Ireland, and if Anlaf had persuaded the lords of the islands then we would also face the *úlfheðnar* of the Suðreyjar and the Orkneyjar islands. The kings of the north had come to destroy us.

'There were hundreds of Norsemen!' one of the men said. 'Crazy like devils!' The three men were still shaken by their defeat. One of them had seen Godric cut down, then seen his body hacked into bloody ruin by Norse axes. Alfgar, they said, had fled the field before the battle ended, escaping on horseback as his surviving men were surrounded by Scots and Irish-Norse warriors. 'We ran too, lord,' one of the men confessed. 'I can still hear the screaming. Those poor men had no escape.'

'Where was the battle?'

They did not know, they only knew that Godric had marched them north for two days, had found the stream he thought would prove an obstacle to the invaders, and there had died. 'He left a widow,' Eadwyn said gloomily, 'poor lass.'

Eadwyn had heard no news of Æthelstan. He urged me to stay in Mameceaster and add my men to his garrison, because he had received an order to hold Mameceaster firm. Doubtless the same order had been sent to every burh on the northern Mercian border, but that told me nothing. We needed to know where Æthelstan was, and where Constantine and Anlaf were marching. Did they plan to strike east into the heartland of Mercia? Or keep marching south? 'South,' Egil said.

'Why?'

'If Anlaf's here . . .'

'And he is,' Finan said grimly.

'They'll stay close to the sea. Anlaf's fleet will have brought food.'

'There's plenty of food!' I said. 'The harvest was good.'

'And Anlaf will want a retreat if things go bad,' Egil said. 'He won't want to be too far from his ships.'

266

That made sense, though if Egil spoke the truth then what would Anlaf do when he reached Ceaster? The coast there swung sharply west into Wales and he would lose touch with his fleet if he went further south. 'Ceaster,' I said.

Egil looked at me, puzzled. 'Ceaster?'

'That's where they're going. Capture Ceaster and they have a fortress as a base, and a pathway into the heart of Mercia. They're going to Ceaster.'

Sometimes an idea seems to come from nowhere. Is it an instinct that comes from a lifetime of wearing mail and standing in shield walls? Or was it thinking what I would do if I were Anlaf or Constantine? We did not know where they were, we did not know what Æthelstan planned, I only knew that keeping my men behind Mameceaster's walls would achieve nothing. 'Send a messenger south,' I ordered Eadwyn, 'tell him to find Æthelstan, and to tell the king we're marching to Ceaster.'

'What if they're coming here?' Eadwyn asked nervously.

'They're not,' I said, 'they're going to Ceaster.'

Because Constantine and Anlaf wanted to humble Æthelstan. They wanted to rip the heart out of his ambitions for Englaland and piss on his corpse.

And they would try to do that, I was certain, at Ceaster.

TWELVE

The countryside north of the Mærse was deserted. Farms were abandoned, their granaries emptied and their livestock taken south, though we did encounter five herds of cattle being driven northwards. None of the herds was large, the smallest had seven cows and the largest fifteen. 'They're Norsemen,' Finan reported drily when he went to question the drovers of the first herd.

'They fear forage parties from Ceaster?' I suggested.

'They must do,' he said, 'but it's just as likely they want to sell milk and beef to Anlaf. You want us to take their cattle south?'

'Let them go.' I did not want to be slowed by cattle, and I did not care if Anlaf gained some beef because by now the army coming south must have taken plenty of livestock and would be eating well. I turned in my saddle and saw the drifts of smoke that marked Saxon steadings being burned. They were no closer. Undoubtedly there was an invading army to our north, but it seemed to have stopped at least a day's journey away from the Mærse.

I knew this country well from my time in Ceaster. It was an unruly stretch of hilly land, half settled by Saxons who lived uneasily with their Danish and Norse neighbours who, when I commanded the Ceaster garrison, had liked to cross into Mercia and steal livestock. We had returned the compliment, fighting a score of skirmishes, and I was thinking back on those vicious little fights when I saw trouble ahead.

The last and largest of the herds was coming north. The drovers had refused to clear their cattle from our path, and our vanguard, which was composed of a score of Egil's warriors, was being screamed at by a tall, stout woman. I spurred Snawgebland to find the woman haranguing and spitting at the Norsemen. She was a Dane and had evidently demanded to know where they were going and, on being told that we headed for Ceaster, had snarled that we were traitors. 'You should fight for the old gods! You're Norsemen! You think Thor will let you live? You're doomed!'

Some of Egil's men looked troubled and were relieved when Egil, riding beside me, told the woman she understood nothing. 'The enemy are Christians too, woman. You think Constantine wears the hammer?'

'Constantine fights alongside our people!'

'And we fight for our lord,' Egil retorted.

'A Christian lord?' she sneered. She was a raw-boned, heavy, red-faced woman, perhaps forty or fifty years old. I saw that her half-dozen drovers were either old men or young boys, which suggested her husband and his able-bodied men had all gone north to join Anlaf's forces. 'I spit on your lord,' she said, 'may he choke on his Christian blood.'

'He's a pagan lord,' Egil said, more amused than offended. He gestured at me. 'And a good man,' he added.

The woman stared at me and must have seen my hammer. She spat. 'You go to join the Saxons?'

'I am a Saxon,' I spoke Danish, her own tongue.

'Then I curse you,' she said, 'I curse you for being a traitor to the gods. I curse you by the sky, by the sea, by the earth that will be your grave.' Her voice was rising as she intoned the curse. 'I curse you by fire, I curse you by water, I curse you by the food you eat, by the ale you drink!' She was stabbing fingers at me with each phrase. 'I curse your children, may they die in agony, may the worms of the underworld gnaw their bones, may you scream in Hel for ever, may your guts be twisted in everlasting pain, may you—'

She got no further. Another scream sounded behind me and I saw a rider spurring from among the servants who were leading our packhorses. It was a woman's scream. The rider, cloaked and hooded in black, galloped to the woman and threw herself from the saddle, driving the much bigger woman down to the ground. The hooded woman was still screaming. I understood none of what she said, but the anger was unmistakable.

It was Benedetta. She had landed on top of the big woman and was now beating at her face with both fists and still screaming her anger. My men were cheering her. I touched Snawgebland with my heels, but Egil, who was laughing, reached out and checked me. 'Let her be,' he said.

The large woman had been winded and taken by surprise, but she was recovering. She was also much bigger than Benedetta. She heaved up, trying to throw the smaller woman off, but Benedetta managed to stay straddling her, still screaming and hammering her fists at the red face that was now spattered with blood from the woman's nose. The woman threw a punch at Benedetta that she fortuitously blocked with a forearm, but the strength of the blow silenced Benedetta who suddenly realised her danger. Again I started forward and again Egil stopped me. 'She'll win,' he said, though I could not see how.

But Benedetta was quicker than I was. She reached out, found a stone from the crumbling edge of the Roman road, and smashed it into the side of the woman's head.

'Ouch,' Finan said, grinning. My men, both Norse and Saxon, were laughing and cheering, and that cheering grew louder as the big woman sank back, evidently dazed, her mouth open as blood showed in her scrawny hair.

Benedetta snarled in Italian. I had learned a little of her language and thought I recognised the words for wash and mouth, then she stretched out her right arm and scooped a wet, messy handful of cow shit.

'Oh no,' Finan said, grinning.

'Oh yes!' Egil said happily.

'*Ti pulisco la bocca!*' Benedetta shrieked and slapped the handful of shit into the woman's open mouth. The woman spluttered, and Benedetta, not wanting to be spattered with the dung, stood. She bent and cleaned her hands on the woman's skirts, then turned to me. 'Her curses do not work,' she said. 'She speak shit? She eat shit. I have pushed the evil she spoke back into her mouth. It is done!' She turned, spat on the woman, and retrieved her horse. My men were still cheering her. Whatever damage the raw-boned woman might have caused to Egil's men had been undone by Benedetta. Warriors love a fight, admire a winner, and Benedetta had turned an evil omen into a good one. She rode her horse to me. 'See?' she said. 'You needed me. Who else can avert evil?'

'You shouldn't be here,' I said.

'I was a slave!' she said truculently. 'And all my life men tell me what to do. Now no man commands me, not even you! But I protect you!'

'I told my men they couldn't bring their women,' I said.

'Ha! There are many women with the servants! You men know nothing.'

Which was probably true and, if I was honest, I was comforted by her presence. 'But if there's a battle,' I insisted, 'you stay away!'

'And if I had stayed in Bebbanburg? Who would have protected you from that woman's curses? Tell me that!'

'You'll not win!' Egil called cheerfully.

I reached out and touched her cheek. 'Thank you.'

'Now we go,' she announced proudly.

We went.

If Benedetta's victory over the Danish woman was the first omen, the second was more ominous. We had ridden inland to the first ford where we could cross the Mærse and it was growing dark as, with the river behind us, we turned our horses westwards again and travelled the familiar road to Ceaster. The eastern sky was already black, while the west was a turmoil of dark cloud streaked with the dying fire of the disappearing sun. A chill wind blew from that sky of dark fire, lifting cloaks and horses' manes. 'There'll be rain,' Egil said.

'Pray God we reach Ceaster first,' Finan grunted.

And just then that red-black western sky was split by white lightning, not a small strike, but a jagged, horizon wide splintering of massive brilliance that momentarily threw the whole landscape into vivid black and white. A moment later the sound arrived, a bellow of Asgard's anger that rumbled overhead, crushing us with its noise.

Snawgebland bridled, jerked his head up, and I had to soothe him. I let him stand a moment, feeling him tremble, then nudged him forward.

'It's coming,' Egil said.

'What? The storm?'

'The battle.' He touched his hammer.

The lightning had struck over Wirhealum. What did that omen mean? That the danger came from the west? From Ireland where Anlaf had conquered his enemies and lusted after Northumbria? I spurred Snawgebland, wanting to reach

272

Ceaster's walls before the storm blew in from the sea. Another bolt of lightning slithered to earth, this one smaller, but much nearer, slashing down to the low hills and rich pastures of Wirhealum, the land between the rivers. Then the rain came. At first there were just a few scattered heavy drops, but then it began to fall in torrents, the noise so loud that I had to shout my warning to Egil. 'This is a graveyard! A Roman one! Stay on the road!'

My men were touching crosses or hammers, praying that the gods would not stir the dead from their long cold graves. Another sky-splintering shaft of lightning lit the walls of Ceaster ahead of us.

It took long wet minutes to persuade the guards on the high Roman ramparts that we were friendly, indeed it was not till my son, the bishop, was summoned to the fighting platform above the massive arch that the garrison reluctantly unbarred the huge gates. 'Who commands here?' I shouted at one of the guards as we spurred through the gate tunnel that was lit by two sputtering torches.

'Leof Edricson, lord!'

I had never heard of him. I was hoping the city would be commanded by a man I knew, alongside whom I had fought, and a man who would help us find shelter. That, I realised, would be hard because the city was crowded with refugees and their livestock. We pushed through cattle and I slid from Snawgebland's saddle in the familiar square that lay in front of Ceaster's great hall. I gave the reins to Aldwyn. 'You'll have to wait here till we find quarters. Finan! Egil, Thorolf, with me. You too!' I called to my son.

I took Benedetta as well. A guard at the outer door moved to block her, but a scowl from me made him step hurriedly back and I escorted her into the vast hall that the Romans had built and where an enormous fire blazed in the central hearth. There must have been a hundred men in the hall,

all of whom watched us sullenly. 'A woman!' one of them said indignantly. 'The warrior's hall is forbidden to women, except servants!' He was a tall, thin man with a straggling grey beard and worried eyes. He pointed at Benedetta. 'She must leave!'

'Who are you?' I demanded.

He looked even more indignant, as if I should have known his name. 'I would ask the same of you!' he said defiantly, and then heard my name being whispered among the men behind him and his demeanour changed abruptly. 'Lord,' he stammered, and looked for a moment as though he would drop to his knees.

'Leof Edricson?' I asked. He nodded. 'Mercian?' Again he nodded. 'And since when,' I demanded, 'has this hall been denied to women?'

'It is the warriors' hall, to be allowed in here is a privilege, lord.'

'She just beat ten types of shit into a Dane,' I said, 'so that makes her a warrior. And I have three hundred other warriors who are wet, hungry and tired.' I sat Benedetta on a bench close to the fierce fire. The rain beat on the high roof that was leaking in a dozen places, while far off to the west another burst of thunder rolled across the sky.

'Three hundred!' Leof Edricson said, then fell silent.

'You have quarters for them?'

'The city is full, lord.'

'Then they'll sleep in here, with their women.'

'Women?' he seemed shaken.

'Especially the women.' I turned to my son. 'Fetch them. The servants can hold the horses.'

He grinned, but just then the door to the hall opened and my eldest son, the bishop, entered, his priestly robe sopping wet. He looked at his brother, started to speak, then instead hurried towards me. 'Father!' he exclaimed. I said nothing. 'You came!' He sounded relieved. 'So Father Eadwyn reached you?'

'Who is Father Eadwyn?'

'I sent him a week ago!'

'You sent a Christian priest through Northumbria? Then you sent him to his death. Well done. What's happening?'

I had directed the last two words to Leof, but he seemed incapable of answering. It was my son the bishop who eventually replied, though neither he nor anyone else seemed to know much of what happened beyond Ceaster's walls except that Ingilmundr, Æthelstan's supposed friend, had ravaged all the land near the city. 'Ingilmundr!' I said bitterly.

'I never trusted him,' my son said.

'Nor did I.' But Æthelstan had trusted Ingilmundr, thinking that the handsome Norseman was proof that pagans could be converted into loyal Christians, but Ingilmundr must have been conspiring with Anlaf for months, and now he was stealing livestock and grain, burning farms and, worse, he had captured the small burh on the southern bank of the Mærse. 'He captured Brunanburh?' I asked, appalled.

'I ordered the garrison to leave,' Leof admitted. 'It was small, they couldn't have resisted an attack.'

'So you just gave him the burh? You didn't destroy the walls first?'

'We destroyed the palisade,' Leof said defensively, 'but the important thing is to hold Ceaster until the king comes.'

'And when will he come?' I asked. No one knew. 'You've heard nothing from Æthelstan?' Still no one answered. 'Does he know about Ingilmundr?' I asked.

'We sent messengers,' Leof said. 'Of course we did!'

'And have you sent men to confront Ingilmundr?'

'He has too many warriors,' Leof answered miserably. I looked at his men and saw some were ashamed, but most just looked as frightened as their commander who was frowning as my bedraggled troops, accompanied by a score of women, crowded into the hall.

'There was a time,' I said, 'when Mercians knew how to fight. Ingilmundr has joined the enemy, your job was to destroy him.'

'I don't have enough men,' Leof answered pathetically.

'Then you'd better hope I do,' I said.

'Maybe . . .' my son, the bishop, said tentatively, then faltered.

'Maybe what?'

'Leof is surely right, father, that the important task is to make certain Ceaster doesn't fall.'

'The important task,' I snarled, 'is to make sure your precious Englaland doesn't fall. Why do you think Ingilmundr rebelled?'

'He's a pagan,' my son said defiantly.

'And he's trapped on Wirhealum. Think about it! He has only two ways to escape if Æthelstan comes with an army. He can flee by boat, or he can march past Ceaster and try to retreat northwards.'

'Not if the king's army is here,' Leof insisted.

'And he knows that. And he doesn't have enough men to defeat Æthelstan, so why is he fighting? Because he knows he'll have an army at his back soon. He's no fool. He's rebelled because he knows an army is coming to support him, and you've let him collect the grain and meat he'll need to feed them.'

Nothing else made sense to me. An army was coming, an army of angry Scots seeking revenge, and a horde of pagan Norsemen wanting plunder. And in the morning I would ride to discover if I was right.

The storm had passed by daybreak, leaving a chill damp sky that slung short flurries of rain into our faces as we rode into Wirhealum. An old Roman road ran down the centre of the peninsula, going from Ceaster to the marsh-enclosed harbour at the north-western coast. Wirhealum, which I knew well, was a long stretch of land between the River Dee and the River Mærse, its coast edged with banks of mud and sand, its land cut with streams, but blessed with good pastures and low wooded hills. The northern half had been settled by Norsemen who had pretended to convert to Christianity, the southern half, nearer Ceaster, had been Saxon, but in the last few days they had been driven out, their homesteads burned, their granaries emptied, and their livestock stolen.

Now, as I led almost all of my three hundred men into the wind and rain, we avoided the Roman road. For much of its length it ran in a wide, shallow valley between pastures that, in turn, were edged by low thickly-wooded ridges. An enemy could watch the road from those trees, could gather men in their shelter and then ambush us. I suspected we had already been seen; Ingilmundr was no fool and surely had men watching Ceaster, but I chose concealment rather than make things easy for him to ambush us, and so led my men through the trees along the eastern ridge. We went slowly, threading the oaks and beeches as we followed Eadric, Oswi and Rolla, who scouted ahead on foot. Eadric was the oldest, almost as old as I was, and he took the ridge's centre. He was the best scout I had, with an uncanny ability to stay concealed and to spot enemies who were similarly hiding. Oswi, an orphan from Lundene, lacked Eadric's knowledge of the countryside, but he was cunning and intelligent, while Rolla, a Dane, was sharp-eyed and cautious till it came to a fight when he turned as vicious as a weasel. He was on the eastern flank of the ridge, and it was Rolla who alerted us to our first sight of the enemy. He beckoned urgently. I held up my hand to halt my men, dismounted, and, with Finan beside me, walked to join Rolla.

Finan was the first to respond. 'Dear God,' he breathed.

'There's a good few of them, eh?' Rolla said.

I was counting an enemy column that was following the track that edged the River Mærse. The rear of the column was still out of sight, but I reckoned we could see four hundred mounted men heading inland. To our left I could just see the remnants of Brunanburh, the fortress Æthelflaed had ordered built on the bank of the Mærse. Maybe Leof was right, I thought ruefully, and the garrison at Ceaster did not have enough men to face Ingilmundr's Norsemen.

'Are those bastards trying to get behind us?' Finan asked.

I shook my head. 'Even if we were seen leaving Ceaster they wouldn't have had enough time to assemble that force.'

'I hope you're right, lord,' Rolla grunted.

'Still more of them!' Finan said, watching a new group of spearmen appearing past the burh's ruins.

I sent my son with six men to warn Ceaster that some five hundred enemy horsemen were heading inland. 'Leof will do sweet nothing,' Finan grumbled.

'He can warn the nearest settlements,' I said.

The column slowly vanished. They had stayed on the coastal track, between the pasture land and the mudflats where dunlins, oystercatchers and curlews flocked. The tide was low. If they had wanted to trap us, I thought, they would have used the other ridge, hidden there by the trees and ready to cross the low wide valley to cut off our retreat. 'We go on,' I said.

'If he's sent five hundred men inland,' Egil asked when I rejoined the horsemen, 'how many does he have left?'

'Maybe not enough,' his brother Thorolf said wolfishly. Egil, the eldest of the three brothers, was thin, handsome, and amusing. He approached battle like a man playing tæfl, cautiously, thoughtfully, looking for an enemy's weakness before he struck with serpent speed. Thorolf, two years younger, was all warrior; big, black-bearded, grim-faced, and never happier than when he had his long-hafted war axe in his hand. He went into battle like an enraged bull, confident in his size and skill. Berg, the youngest, whose life I had saved, was more like Egil, but lacked his oldest brother's keen intelligence. He might have been the best sword-warrior of the three, all of whom were likeable, dependable, and skilled in battle.

The three brothers now rode with me as we went still deeper into Wirhealum. To our right was the wide Mærse, its mudbanks white with birds, while to our left the rich pastures of the vale had given way to heathland across which the Roman road ran spear-straight. We had passed the last of the destroyed steadings and ahead of us we could see other farms still standing, meaning we were crossing the invisible line between the Saxon part of the peninsula and the Norse settlements.

And for a time it seemed as if Wirhealum was at peace. We saw no more armed men.

There was a moment, a heartbeat, when that wide landscape was almost as still and silent as a grave. Rooks flew towards the Mærse, far off to our left a child drove three cows towards a palisaded steading, while flood waters glinted in the wide shallow valley. A kingfisher flashed across a stream that twisted sinuously between its deep muddy banks. The stream was high after the recent rain, its water turbid and turbulent. On the far ridge the trees grew thick, the oak leaves golden, the beeches a fiery red, the leaves all heavy and still in the windless air.

It was a strange moment. I felt as if the world held its breath. I was gazing at peace, at pasture, at the green good land that men wanted. The Welsh had owned this land once and they had seen the Romans come and the Romans go, and then the Saxons had come and they had bloodied the earth with sword and spear and the Welsh names had vanished because the Saxons took the land and gave it their own name. They called it Wirhealum which meant the pasture where the bog-myrtle grows, and I remembered Æthelstan, just a boy, killing a man beside a ditch thick with bog-myrtle, and how Æthelflaed, Alfred's daughter, had once asked me to collect leaves of bog-myrtle because it kept the fleas away. But nothing had kept the Norse away. They came on bended knee, begging to be given poor land, swearing peace, and both Æthelflaed and Æthelstan had granted them pasture and steadings, believing their oaths of peace, and believing that in time they would bend their knee to the nailed god. We saw none of them except for the small girl driving her cattle.

'Maybe they all went east,' Egil suggested.

'Five hundred men to invade Mercia?'

'They're Norsemen, remember,' he said lightly.

Eadric gestured us onwards. We were riding deeper and deeper into Norse land now, still hidden by the autumn trees, but betrayed by the birds that fled our approach. I was nervous. The enemy could outnumber us, surround us, trap us, but still there was no sign of that enemy. No birds flew in panic from the trees on the far ridge, no horsemen rode the Roman road or the track beside the Mærse. Then Rolla came back again. 'Lord? You'll want to see this.'

We followed him to the tree line, again looking out across the Mærse and further, out to sea, and there I saw the ships. 'Dear God,' Finan breathed again.

There were ships coming from the north, a fleet of ships. I counted forty-two, but there could have been more. There was scarce any wind so they were rowing, bringing men to the peninsula's end, and the leading ships were already within bowshot of land. 'Dingesmere,' I said. 'That's where they're going, Dingesmere.'

'Dingesmere?' Egil asked.

'A harbour,' I said, 'a big one.' It was a strange harbour at the seaward end of Wirhealum, a mostly shallow sea-lake edged with mud and rushes and approached by channels tangled with sandbanks, but Dingesmere was large enough and just deep enough at the lowest tides to hold a whole fleet of ships.

'Want me to look, lord?' Eadric asked.

We were still too far away to see the wide marshes at the peninsula's end, and I suspected that there were already hundreds of the enemy gathered there. I did not want to risk my men by leading them into a hornet's nest, but I needed to know if there was already an army somewhere close to Dingesmere. 'It might be too dangerous,' I told Eadric reluctantly, 'I suspect there's an army there.'

'There soon will be,' Egil said, watching the far ships.

'They'll not see me, lord,' Eadric said confidently. 'Plenty of ditches to hide in.'

I nodded. I almost told him to be careful, but that would have been a waste of words because Eadric was always cautious. He was also good. 'We'll wait for you back there,' I nodded down the ridge.

'It'll take a good time, lord!'

'We'll wait.'

'Maybe dusk,' he warned me.

'Go,' I said, smiling.

We waited, watching the far ships. 'They're not coming from Ireland,' Thorolf remarked, 'they're all coming from the north!'

He was right. The ships, which were still appearing, were coming down the coast. It was possible that the Irish Norse had crossed the sea and made landfall too far north, but Norsemen did not make that kind of error. 'It's Constantine's army,' I said, 'that's what's happening. It's the Scots.'

'In Norse ships?' Thorolf grunted. The far ships had beast-heads, not crosses, on their prows, and their hulls were leaner than the heavier Scottish ships.

'They're allies,' I said. 'Anlaf is bringing Constantine's army.'

'But why?' Egil asked. 'Why don't the Scots just keep marching?'

'Because of the burhs.' I explained how Æthelflaed had built a string of burhs on Mercia's northern frontier. 'How many men is Constantine bringing?'

'Fifteen hundred?' Finan guessed. 'Maybe more if the blackshields are with him.'

'And they'll march past those burhs in a great long line,' I said, 'and he's worried the garrisons will attack him.' I turned Snawgebland. 'We'll go a mile or so back.' If I was right, and if Anlaf's ships were ferrying Scottish troops to Wirhealum, then Anlaf's own army must already be ashore and we were too close to the peninsula's end for comfort. I could only wait for Eadric now, but would wait a little closer to Ceaster, and so we went back through the autumn trees and there, with sentries watching the north, we dismounted and let the time pass. The wind freshened and the far ships hoisted their sails. By mid afternoon we must have seen a hundred and fifty ships, while far to the east the smoke rose from steadings being burned by the horsemen we had seen earlier.

'He did say dusk,' Finan reminded me. He knew I was worrying about Eadric. 'And the old fellow is good! They'll not see him. He could sneak up on the devil himself.'

I was sitting in shadows at the edge of the trees, gazing down into the wide heathland scarred by the Roman road. Beneath me, at the foot of the slope, a stream flowed between steep muddy banks. 'No otters,' I said.

'Otters?' Finan sat beside me.

'A good place for otters.'

'They've been hunted out. Otter skin sells too well.'

'Kingfishers, though. I've seen two.'

'My grandmother said kingfishers bring good fortune.'

'Let's hope she's right.' I touched my hammer.

And just then Oswi came running back through the trees. 'Men coming, lord, on the road!' I looked northwards and saw nothing. 'They're a good way off, lord,' Oswi crouched beside me. 'Maybe thirty of them? All on horseback and carrying banners too.'

That was strange. We would flaunt our banners as we advanced to battle, but rarely flew them over small groups. 'They could be distracting us,' I suggested, 'and sending men through the trees?'

'Seen nothing in the woods, lord,' Oswi said.

'Go back, keep a sharp eye!'

'We'd better mount up,' Finan suggested, and by the time I was in Snawgebland's saddle the enemy horsemen were in sight. 'Thirty-four men,' Finan said.

'And two of them carrying branches,' Egil had joined us. We were standing our horses in the shadows.

'Branches!' Finan said. 'You're right.' I saw that two of the leading horsemen carried branches thick with brown leaves, a sign that the horsemen rode in truce.

'Maybe they're going to Ceaster?' I suggested.

'To demand the city's surrender?'

'What else?'

'We'd better get back first,' Finan said sourly, 'to make sure that bastard Leof doesn't say yes.' But then, before I could respond, half of the horsemen turned off the road and spread across the heath that lay between the road and the stream. They rode in small groups, stopping occasionally to gaze around, and looking for all the world like men judging whether to buy a stretch of land. The larger group stayed on the road, one of whom carried a bundle of spears, but the two men carrying the leafy branches cantered towards the ridge from where we watched. 'The bastards know we're here,' Finan said.

The two men gazed up into the trees, plainly looking for us and then waving their branches as if to make sure we had received their message. 'So much for stealth,' I said ruefully, 'but if they're offering a truce let's see who they are.'

Finan, Egil, Thorolf and Sihtric accompanied me down the ridge's slope. It was not steep, but at its foot the stream's bank was dangerously sheer and slippery with mud, while the stream itself, swollen by the recent rain, swirled high and fast, overflowing into the reed beds that grew thick at the gully's edge. One of the men with the branches trotted his horse to the opposite bank. 'The king asks that you do not cross.'

'Which king?'

'All of them. You observe our truce?'

'Till nightfall,' I called back.

He nodded, threw down the cumbersome branch and spurred his horse towards the larger group of men who had gone some distance towards Ceaster and there curbed their horses beside a wooden bridge that carried the road across the stream. They had turned there and were looking back up the road which here rose gently to a shallow crest where more of the horsemen waited. The crest, which was too low to be called a ridge, lay across the road. 'What are they doing?' Sihtric asked.

It was Egil who answered. 'Marking a battlefield.'

'A battlefield?' Finan asked.

'Those aren't spears,' Egil nodded towards the far horsemen carrying the long bundle, 'they're hazel rods.'

Finan spat towards the stream. 'Arrogant bastards. Æthelstan might have something to say about that.'

Egil had to be right. The enemy had chosen a battlefield and would now send a challenge to Æthelstan, wherever he was. It was a Norse tradition. Choose a place to fight, send the challenge and, once it was accepted, all raiding would stop. The enemy would wait here, would fight on their chosen ground, and the loser would cede whatever was demanded. 'What if Æthelstan doesn't accept?' Sihtric asked.

'Then they besiege Ceaster,' I said, 'and march on into central Mercia.' I glanced eastwards and saw the smoke from the fires that had been set by the raiders we had seen on the coastal track. 'And then they'll keep going south. They want to destroy Æthelstan and his kingdom.'

The men who had been waiting on the shallow crest now came towards us. 'Anlaf,' Finan said, nodding towards the falcon banner that a horseman carried. There were a dozen horsemen led by Anlaf himself who, though the day was now mild, wore an enormous bearskin cloak over his mail. Gold glinted at his neck and on his stallion's bridle. He was bare-headed except for a thin golden circlet. He was grinning as he approached the stream's bank. 'Lord Uhtred! We've been watching you all day. I could have killed you!'

'Many have tried, lord King,' I answered.

'But I am in a merciful mood today,' Anlaf said cheerfully, 'I even spared the life of your scout!' He turned in his saddle and waved to the men on the road. Three spurred towards us and, as they came closer, I saw Eadric, his hands bound behind him, was one. 'He's an old man,' Anlaf said, 'like you. You know my companions?'

I knew two of them. Cellach, Constantine's son and prince of Alba, nodded gravely to me, while next to him was Thorfinn Hausakljúfr, ruler of Orkneyjar and better known as Thorfinn Skull-Splitter. He carried his famous long-hafted axe and grinned wolfishly. 'Prince Cellach,' I greeted the Scotsman, 'I trust your father is well?'

'He is,' Cellach said stiffly.

'He's here?' I asked, and Cellach simply nodded. 'Then remember me to him,' I went on, 'and give him my hopes that he goes home soon.'

It was interesting, I thought, that Constantine had not come to help choose the battlefield, which suggested that Anlaf, the younger man, commanded the army, And Anlaf, I thought, was probably the more formidable enemy. He smiled at me with his unnaturally wide mouth. 'Have you come to join us, Lord Uhtred?' he asked.

'It seems you have enough men without me, lord King.'

'You'd fight for the Christians?'

'Prince Cellach is a Christian,' I pointed out.

'As is Owain of Strath Clota,' Anlaf pointed to a grey-haired man who scowled from the saddle of a tall stallion. 'But who knows? If the gods give us victory perhaps they'll convert?' He looked at the men who had brought Eadric to the stream. 'Let him stand,' he ordered, then turned back to me. 'You know Gibhleachán of Suðreyjar?'

Suðreyjar was the Norse name for the slew of stormy islands on Alba's wild western coast, and their king, Gibhleachán, was an enormous man, hunched and glowering in his saddle, with a black beard that fell almost to his waist where a massive sword hung. I nodded to him and he spat back.

'King Gibhleachán terrifies me,' Anlaf said cheerfully, 'and he claims his men are the fiercest warriors in Britain. They are *úlfhéðnar*, all of them! You know what the *úlfhéðnar* are?'

'I've killed enough of them,' I retorted, 'so yes, I know.'

He laughed at that. 'My men are *úlfhéðnar* too! And they win battles! We won a battle not long ago, against him.' Anlaf paused to point to a glum-looking man mounted on a big bay stallion. 'He is Anlaf Cenncairech. He was King of Hlymrekr until a few weeks ago when I ripped his fleet apart! Isn't that right, Scabbyhead?'

The glum man simply nodded. 'Scabbyhead?' I asked Egil softly.

'His last great Norse rival in Ireland,' Egil answered just as softly.

'Now Scabbyhead and his men fight for me!' Anlaf announced. 'And so should you, Lord Uhtred, I am your king.'

'King of Northumbria?' I asked, then laughed. 'An easy claim to make, hard to prove.'

'But we shall prove it here,' Anlaf said. 'You see the hazel rods? You will take a message to the pretty boy who calls himself King of all Britain. He can meet me here in a week's time. If we win, which we shall, there will be no more tribute paid from Alba. Northumbria will be mine. Wessex will pay me tribute of gold, much gold, and perhaps I'll take its throne too. I will be King of all Britain.'

'And if Æthelstan declines your invitation?' I asked.

'Then I will put the Saxons to the sword, I will burn your towns, destroy your cities, take your women as my playthings, and your children as slaves. You will send him that message?'

'I will, lord King.'

'You can cross the stream when we're gone,' Anlaf said carelessly, 'but remember we are in a truce.' He glanced down at Eadric. 'Throw him in,' he ordered.

'Untie him first,' I said.

'Are you a Christian, old man?' Anlaf demanded of Eadric, who looked thoroughly miserable. He did not understand the question, so looked at me.

'He wants to know if you're a Christian,' I translated for him.

'Yes, lord.'

'He is,' I told Anlaf.

'Then let his god prove his power. Throw the old man in.'

287

One of the horsemen who had brought Eadric dismounted. He was a big man, Eadric was small. The big man grinned, picked Eadric up and hurled him down into the turbulent stream. Eadric yelped as he fell, splashed into the brown water and vanished. Egil, the youngest of us, dismounted, but Eadric surfaced before he could jump in. Eadric spat water. 'It's not too deep, lord!'

'Seems his god does have power,' I said to Anlaf, who looked unhappy. This was a bad omen for him.

But though Eadric could hobble across the stream with his ankles bound and with the water up to his neck at one point, he had trouble keeping his footing and I knew he would never manage to scramble up the steep and slippery bank. I turned and shouted up at the ridge. 'Throw me a spear. Try not to hit me!'

A spear arched out of the leaves, fell and smacked into the turf a few paces away. Thorolf must have guessed what I planned because he dismounted before I could, took the spear and held its butt end to his brother. 'Down you go,' he said.

Egil slipped and slid down the bank, steadied by the spear his brother held, then pushed through the reeds, reached out and seized Eadric's collar. 'Come on!'

Both men slipped in the mud, but Eadric was hauled to safety where the hide-ropes binding his hands and feet were cut off. 'I'm sorry, lord,' he said when he reached me, 'I went too far and a bloody child saw me.'

'It's no matter, you're alive.'

'He has a tale to tell you!' Anlaf called, then turned his horse and spurred it savagely.

We stayed to watch as men thrust hazel rods into the earth. Anlaf directed them and finally left after giving us a derisive wave. 'You have a tale to tell?' I asked Eadric, who was now swathed in Sihtric's cloak.

'Hundreds of the bastards, lord! Couldn't count them! Swarming like bees. And the pool is full of ships, must be two hundred at least.'

'Which is why he didn't kill you,' I said, 'because he wants us to know.'

'And they're still arriving,' Egil said.

I sent Eadric to the ridge's top, then led my companions upstream till we found a place we could cross safely. The horses lurched down the bank, pushed through a boggy reed bed and splashed through the stream before clambering up onto Anlaf's chosen battlefield.

I went straight to where the bridge crossed the stream and looked north. If Æthelstan accepted the challenge then I reckoned we were about two hundred paces from where his forces would make their shield wall. From the wooded ridge the heathland had looked mostly flat with a gentle slope rising to where Anlaf would assemble his men, but from the road the slope looked steeper, especially to my left where the rough ground climbed towards the western ridge. A mass of men charging down that slope would hit Æthelstan's left wing like a blow from Thor's hammer. 'I've been praying never to stand in a shield wall again,' I said gloomily.

'Nor will you,' Finan said, 'you'll sit on your damned horse and tell us what to do.'

'Because I'm old?'

'Did I say that, lord?'

'Then you're too old too,' I said.

'I'm Irish. We die fighting.'

'And live talking too much,' I retorted.

We rode our horses up the road till we were on the low crest, then turned to look back at the field. This was the view Anlaf's forces would have and I tried to imagine the wide valley filled with a Saxon shield wall. 'It's obvious what he plans,' I said.

'A charge on his right?' Egil suggested.

'Down the steepest slope,' Thorolf added. 'Break Æthelstan's left wing then turn on the centre.'

'And it will be slaughter,' Sihtric added, 'because we'll be trapped by the streams.' He pointed to more reed beds that betrayed a smaller stream which would lie on Æthelstan's left flank. That smaller stream joined the larger, the gullies of the two streams easily distinguished by the tall reeds that grew at their edges. The streams slowly converged, their meeting place just to the west of the narrow bridge that carried the road towards Ceaster.

'Boggy ground,' Finan grunted.

'And if Æthelstan's army breaks,' Egil said, 'we'll be trapped by the streams. It will be a slaughter.'

'Which is why Anlaf chose this ground,' I said. I guessed that Æthelstan would have a shield wall some six hundred paces wide between the two streams. That was a long shield wall, needing about a thousand men in each rank, but the further back he went so that distance would diminish as the streams converged. The stream to our left, the one we had just crossed, was deeper and wider and I was gazing at that wider stream, thinking how I would fight the battle if I were Anlaf and thinking how confident I would be. He believed he could break Æthelstan's army with his famed wolf-warriors, turn the Saxon line and trap it against that deeper stream.

'Æthelstan should refuse the challenge,' Thorolf said.

'He'll lose Ceaster if he does,' I responded, 'Leof won't last two days.'

'Then Æthelstan fights him somewhere else, beats the bastard and takes Ceaster back.'

'No,' I said, 'if I were Æthelstan I'd accept the challenge.' No one spoke, they just gazed at the trap Anlaf had set. 'They'll attack all along Æthelstan's shield wall,' I went on, 'but Anlaf's best troops will be on his right. They have the highest ground so they'll charge downhill, try to break Æthelstan's left, then pin the rest of his army against the wider stream.'

'Where there will be slaughter,' Egil said.

'Oh it will be a slaughter,' I agreed, 'but who gets slaughtered? If I were Æthelstan I'd let Anlaf drive my left flank back.' My companions just looked at me, none spoke, but their faces betrayed doubt, all but for Finan, who looked amused.

Thorolf broke the uneasy silence. 'Will they outnumber us?'

'Probably,' I said.

'Certainly,' Egil said dourly.

'And Anlaf's no fool,' Thorolf went on, 'he'll have his best men, his *úlfhéðnar* on his right.'

'I would too,' I agreed, and silently hoped my men would not be on Æthelstan's left wing.

Thorolf frowned at me. 'They're vicious fighters, lord. No one has bested them in Ireland.'

'And they'll bend Æthelstan's line back against the stream,' I said, 'and our forces will be trapped there.'

'Trapped and slaughtered,' Thorolf said gloomily.

'But you think we can win,' Finan said to me, still amused. He looked at Thorolf. 'He usually does.'

'So tell us,' Egil put in.

'It's so obvious what Anlaf plans,' I explained, 'and it's so obvious that it's a winning plan, but I doubt he's thought beyond that. He expects to win this battle with one massive attack, one brutal assault by his best men on Æthelstan's left flank, but what happens if that goes wrong?'

'What does happen?' Egil asked.

'We win,' I said.

But winning depended on Æthelstan agreeing with me.

And whatever happened, Sihtric, Egil and Thorolf were right. It would be a slaughter.

THIRTEEN

'The arrogance of the man!' Æthelstan said angrily. 'He challenges me!'

It was two days later, days I had spent travelling south in search of the king whom I had found on the Roman road that led north along the frontiers of the Welsh kingdoms. His army had camped for the night and Æthelstan was in his gaudy tent at the centre of a vast spread of shelters and picketed horses. Bishop Oda was with him, as was his cousin Prince Edmund and half a dozen ealdormen, all of whom had peered gloomily at a scrap of linen on which I had used a piece of charcoal to draw a plan of Anlaf's chosen battlefield.

'Kings,' I said drily, 'are often arrogant.'

He gave me a sharp look, knowing I was referring to his attempts to take Bebbanburg. 'We don't have to accept his challenge,' he said irritably.

'Of course not, lord King.'

'And if we don't?'

'He'll besiege Ceaster,' I guessed, 'and ravage more of northern Mercia.'

'We're close enough to stop that,' he said irritably.

'So you'll fight him,' I said, 'where? Outside the walls of Ceaster? But to do that you must reach the city. The first thing he'll do is destroy the bridge over the Dee, and that will force you to make at least another two-day march inland, and give him more time.'

'Leof will hold the city.'

'Leof is pissing in his breeches already.'

Æthelstan frowned at me. He was wearing his hair plain, no gold-threaded curls, and was dressed in simple dark clothes. 'How many men does Anlaf have?' It was the third time he had asked me the question.

'I can only guess three thousand.' I suspected Anlaf's numbers were far greater than that, but this was not the time to add to Æthelstan's fears. 'A lot,' I went on, 'and the Scots are still joining him.'

'By ship! Why aren't our ships stopping that?' No one answered that because Æthelstan knew the answer perfectly well himself. His ships were still in the Sæfern and, besides, even if he could bring those ships north he would not have enough vessels to challenge Anlaf's huge fleet.

'At least three thousand,' I went on relentlessly, 'and doubtless more men will come from the islands, and from Ireland.'

'And I'll have more men if I wait.'

'You have enough, lord King,' I said softly.

'I have fewer than him!' he said angrily.

'And your grandfather was outnumbered at Ethandun,' I said, 'but he won.'

'So Steapa keeps reminding me.'

'Steapa! Is he with you?'

'He insisted on coming,' he said, frowning, 'but he's old! Like you!'

'Steapa,' I said forcefully, 'is one of the greatest warriors Wessex ever had.'

'So people tell me.'

'Then listen to him, lord King, use him!'

He shifted uncomfortably in his chair. 'And should I listen to you?'

'You're the king. You can do what you like.'

'And fight that arrogant bastard on a field of his choosing?'

'He's chosen a battlefield that gives him an advantage,' I said carefully, 'but it also gives us a good chance of beating him.'

No one else had spoken since I entered the tent, neither Æthelstan's men, nor Finan, who alone had accompanied me. I had travelled south with just six men, leaving Egil, Thorolf and Sihtric in Ceaster, and had chosen Finan because he wore the cross and because Æthelstan liked him. Finan now smiled. 'You're right, lord King,' the Irishman said softly, 'Anlaf is arrogant, and he's also savage, but he's not a subtle man.'

Æthelstan nodded. 'Go on.'

'He's won his wars in Ireland by massive attacks, lord King, by using bigger armies than his enemies. He's famous for mounting terrifying assaults with his *úlfhéðnar* and inflicting dreadful slaughter. Men are frightened of him, and he relies on that, because a terrified man is already half beaten. He wants you to accept his battle site because he sees a way to beat you.' Finan pointed to the scrap of linen with its crude charcoal lines, 'He thinks he can destroy the left wing of your army, then surround the rest and turn the stream to blood.'

'So why give him that chance?' Æthelstan asked.

'Because he hasn't thought beyond that,' Finan said, still talking quietly and soberly. 'He knows his plan will work, so he doesn't need to think of another. He's drinking ale in some hall on Wirhealum tonight and praying you will give him what he wants, because then he won't be King of Northumbria, but King of all Britain. That's all he sees. All he wants.'

There was silence, except for the sound of singing somewhere in Æthelstan's camp. Prince Edmund, who, until Æthelstan married and had a son, was the next king, broke it. 'But if we refuse his choice of battleground,' he said, 'we can choose our own. Maybe a place that gives us an advantage?'

'Where, lord Prince?' Finan asked. I was letting Finan do the talking now because I sensed that Æthelstan was irritated by me. 'If we don't arrive at Ceaster in the next five days,' Finan went on, 'the bridge over the Dee will be gone. Leof will surrender the city because Anlaf will offer him terms. Then their army will march into Mercia. We'll pursue, and he'll still choose a battlefield, only one that gives him an even bigger advantage.'

'Or we trap him somewhere,' Æthelstan said.

'You might, lord King,' Finan said very patiently, 'or he might trap you? But I assure you that you have a good chance of destroying him on Wirhealum.'

'Ha!' Coenwulf, who was sitting with his fellow ealdormen, snarled. He had been scowling at me. I smiled at him, which succeeded in annoying him even more.

Æthelstan ignored Coenwulf. 'You say Anlaf commands them? Not Constantine?'

'Anlaf chose the battlefield,' I said.

'And Constantine allowed that?'

'So it seems, lord King.'

'Why?' He asked the question indignantly, as though he was offended by Constantine accepting a lesser role.

Finan still answered for me. 'Anlaf has the reputation of a warrior, lord King. He has never lost a battle and he's fought many. Constantine, though a wise king, does not have the same renown.'

'Never lost a battle!' Æthelstan repeated. 'And you think we can beat him at a place of his choosing?'

Finan smiled. 'We can destroy him, lord King, because we know what he will do. And we will be ready for it, prepared for it.'

'You make it sound easy,' Coenwulf put in angrily, 'yet Anlaf has the numbers, and he's chosen the field. It's madness to accept the challenge!'

'We have to fight him somewhere,' Finan said patiently, 'and at least we know what he'll do at Wirhealum.'

'You think you know!'

'And those *úlfheðnar*,' Æthelwyn, another of the ealdormen, spoke for the first time, 'I worry about them.' I saw how the others nodded agreement.

'You've not fought them,' I said, 'but I have. And they're killed easily.'

'Easily!' Coenwulf bridled at my claim.

'They believe they're invulnerable,' I said, 'and they attack like madmen. They're frightening, but catch their first wild blow on your shield then slice a seax into their belly and they go down like any other man. I've killed enough of them.'

Æthelstan grimaced at that boast. 'Whether we fight Anlaf at Wirhealum or somewhere else, we still have to face the *úlfheðnar*,' he said, dismissing Æthelwyn's objection. He looked into my eyes. 'Why are you so sure we can win at Wirhealum?' he asked.

I hesitated, tempted to invent a fantasy that might persuade them. The fantasy would be about the second king called Anlaf, the ruler of Hlymrekr who Anlaf derided as Scabbyhead and who had been forced to bring his men to fight for his conqueror. I wanted to suggest that his men would fight less forcefully, that if we broke them we would break Anlaf's line, but I did not believe that. The men of Hlymrekr would fight for their lives as fiercely as any other, so instead I looked into Æthelstan's eyes. 'Because we'll break their shield wall, lord King.'

'How?' Coenwulf demanded indignantly.

'The same way I've broken other men's shield walls,' I retorted derisively.

There was an awkward silence. I had sounded arrogant, but it was an arrogance no man wanted to challenge. I had broken shield walls and they knew it, just as they knew I had fought more battles than any of them. None of them spoke, only looked at Æthelstan, who was frowning at me. I think he suspected that my answer was an evasion. 'And if we are to fight at Wirhealum,' he said slowly, 'I need to make a decision tonight?'

'If you want to reach Ceaster in time, yes,' I said.

Æthelstan still looked into my eyes, simply looked. He said nothing, nor did anyone else. I stared back. The decision was his, and he knew that his throne depended on it, just as he knew that Finan had spoken for me earlier, and our confidence intrigued him. 'Stay, Lord Uhtred,' he finally spoke. 'The rest of you get some sleep.'

'But—' Æthelwyn began.

'Go!' Æthelstan snarled. 'All of you, go!'

He waited until the others were gone, then poured two beakers of wine. He handed one to me. 'You met Anlaf,' he said flatly.

'I did.'

'Did he ask you to fight for him?'

'Of course.'

'How do I know you didn't say yes?'

'Because I took an oath to protect you. I've never broken it.'

I was sitting, sipping the wine, which tasted sour to me, while Æthelstan paced up and down the thick rugs. 'Æthelwyn says I can't trust you.'

Æthelwyn was one of the newer ealdormen, a man I did not know and who had never stood near me in a shield wall. 'Ealdred said the same,' I said brutally, 'so did Ingilmundr.'

He flinched at that, went on pacing. 'I wanted to be king,' he said softly.

'I made you king.'

He ignored that. 'I wanted to be a good king, like my grandfather. What made him a good king?'

'He thought of others before himself,' I said, 'and he was clever. So are you.'

He stopped and turned on me. 'You killed Ealdred.' It was a statement, not a question.

I hesitated for a heartbeat, then decided this was a time for honesty. 'I did.'

He grimaced. 'Why?'

'To protect you.' I did not add that I was protecting him from bad advice. He knew that.

He frowned at me, thinking. 'So you caused this war. I assume you killed Guthfrith too?'

'I did,' I said, 'and this war was coming whether Ealdred or Guthfrith lived or died.'

He nodded. 'I suppose it was,' he said quietly, then looked at me accusingly. 'You have frost now.'

'Frost?' I asked.

'The stallion. I gave him to Lord Ealdred.'

'A generous gift,' I said. 'I renamed him Snawgebland. Do you want him back?'

He shook his head. He seemed remarkably unmoved by my confession, but I suppose he had always suspected that I was Ealdred's killer and, besides, he had far greater problems to face. 'I always feared that if Guthfrith died you would take Northumbria's throne.'

'Me!' I laughed. 'Why would I want that trouble?'

He paced the rugs, sometimes glancing at the scrap of linen. He finally stopped to stare down at the linen. 'My fear,' he said, 'is that God will punish me.'

'For what?'

298

'My sins,' he said quietly.

'God let you become king,' I said forcefully, 'he let you make peace with Hywel, he let you invade Scotland, and he's let you finish what your grandfather began.'

'Almost finish. And I could lose it all in one day. Maybe that will be God's punishment?'

'Why would your god favour Anlaf over you?'

'To punish me for pride.'

'Anlaf is proud too,' I said.

'He is the devil's creature.'

'Then your god should fight him, destroy him.'

He started pacing again. 'Constantine is a good Christian.'

'Then why is he allied to a pagan?'

He stopped and gave me a wry smile. 'It seems I am too.'

'Pagans,' I said, 'me and Egil Skallagrimmrson.'

'He'll fight for us?'

'He will.'

'Small mercies,' Æthelstan said softly.

'How many men do you have?' I asked.

'Just over a thousand West Saxons,' he said, 'and sixteen hundred Mercians. Your men too, of course, and more are arriving every day.'

'The fyrd?' I asked. The fyrd was the army raised from the country, an army of ploughmen, foresters, and peasants.

'A thousand,' he said, 'but God knows what use they'll be against Anlaf's men.'

'Even with the fyrd,' I said, 'you're probably going to have fewer men than Anlaf, but you can still win.'

'How?' he demanded sharply. 'Simply by fighting more savagely than they do?'

'By fighting more cleverly than they do,' I said, and picked up the lump of charcoal and sketched some new lines on the linen, explaining as I went. 'That,' I finished, 'is how you can win.'

He gazed at the crude drawing. 'So why didn't you show that to Æthelwyn and the others?'

'Because if a dozen men know what you plan before the battle then they will tell another dozen men, and they will then tell others. How long before Anlaf also knows?'

He nodded acceptance of that, still staring at the linen. 'And if I lose?' he asked quietly.

'There will be no Englaland.'

He still looked down at the changes I had made on the map. 'Archbishop Wulfhelm tells me that God wanted me to be king,' he said quietly. 'I forget that sometimes.'

'Trust your god,' I said, 'and trust your troops. They're fighting for their homes, for their wives, for their children.'

'But fighting in a place Anlaf chooses?'

'And if you beat him in a place of his choosing then you humiliate him, you will prove to be what you say you are, *Monarchus Totius Brittaniae*.'

He gave a brief smile. 'You appeal to my pride, lord?'

'Pride is good in a warrior,' I said.

He looked up at me and for a heartbeat I saw the child I had raised, a child constantly in fear of his life, but a child with courage. 'You really think we can win?' he asked.

I dared not let my doubts show. I tapped the linen map. 'Do what I advise you, lord King, and by month's end you will be the monarch of all Britain and the streams of Wirhealum will run thick with the blood of your enemies.'

He paused, then nodded. 'Ride for Ceaster at dawn, lord. I will give you my decision before you leave.'

I went into the night, but before I dropped the tent's flap behind me I saw he had fallen to his knees and was praying.

It started to rain.

Steapa rode with us next day. He looked old. He was still a huge man with a frightening face and the air of a warrior who would resort to violence at the smallest slight. I had been scared of him when we first met, but had learned that beneath his grim exterior was a kind soul. His hair and beard were white now, and his skull-face was deeply creased, but he still mounted his horse easily, and still carried a great sword that had begun its life slaughtering Alfred's enemies. 'It should have killed you too,' he growled when I greeted him.

'You were never good enough,' I said. 'You were too slow. You moved like a haystack.'

'I was just giving you a chance.'

'Funny, I was giving you one too.' We had fought all those years ago on Alfred's command. The fight was supposed to establish my guilt or innocence, but it had been interrupted by Guthrum's invading forces. The fight had never finished, though I had never forgotten my fear of facing Steapa, even after we became friends. 'Maybe we'd better finish the fight,' I suggested. 'You'd be easy to beat now. Slow and old.'

'Old! Me? Have you seen yourself? You look like something the dog chewed and spat out.'

He was riding with us because Æthelstan had been beset with doubts through the night and had sent Steapa to look at Anlaf's chosen battlefield. 'If Steapa agrees with you,' the king had told me at dawn, 'then tell Anlaf we'll meet him there.' I had not argued. The decision, in the end, belonged only to Æthelstan, and I was only surprised he had chosen Steapa to accompany us. I would have expected one of the younger ealdormen, but Æthelstan had chosen Steapa for good reasons. 'He's fought more battles than any of us,' Æthelstan had told me in the dawn, 'he's fought as many as you! And he knows how to use ground, and he won't let you persuade him if he disagrees.'

'And if you disagree?' I asked Steapa as we rode northwards.

'We beat the bastard somewhere else. But I'm glad to be out of that lot,' he jerked his grizzled head to indicate

Æthelstan's army. 'Too many bloody churchmen and young lordlings who think they shit lavender instead of turds.'

Æthelstan would be marching north behind us, but he would not cross the Dee unless Steapa assured him the battlefield was a good choice. If Steapa disliked the land between the streams on Wirhealum then Æthelstan would destroy the Roman bridge across the Dee, leave Ceaster to its fate and move eastwards to find another place to confront the invaders.

'It'll be a bloody business wherever we fight the bastards,' Steapa said.

'It will.'

'I never liked fighting Norsemen. Mad buggers.'

'I don't suppose they like fighting you either,' I said.

'And the Irish Norse use arrows, I'm told.'

'They do,' Finan said curtly.

'So do we,' I put in.

'But Anlaf will have more archers,' Finan said. 'They use bows a lot. They stand the archers behind the shield wall and make the sky rain arrows. So heads down, shields up.'

'Jesus,' Steapa grumbled.

I knew what he was thinking. He no more wanted to stand in another shield wall than I did. For all our long lives we had been fighting; fighting the Welsh, fighting other Saxons, fighting the Scots, fighting the Danes, fighting the Norse, and now fighting an alliance of Scots, Danes and Norsemen. It would be grim.

The Christians tell us we must have peace, that we should melt our swords to make ploughshares, yet I have yet to see a Christian king light the furnace to melt the battle-steel. When we fought Anlaf, whether it was on Wirhealum or deeper inside Mercia, we would also face Constantin's men and Owain of Strath Clota's warriors, and almost all of them were Christians. The priests on both sides would wail to

302

their nailed god, calling down his help, screaming for vengeance and victory, and none of it made sense to me. Æthelstan could kneel to his god, but Constantin would be kneeling too, as would Owain. Did their nailed god really care who ruled Britain? I brooded on that as we hurried north, following the Roman road through intermittent showers that blew chill from the Welsh hills. And what of the Welsh? I was sure Anlaf had sent emissaries to Hywel and to the lesser Welsh kings, and they had reason enough to dislike Æthelstan who had forced them to bow the knee and pay tribute. Yet I suspected Hywel would do nothing. He might not like the Saxons, but he knew what horrors would descend on his country if Æthelstan released his army into the hills. Hywel would let the Norse and the Scots fight his old enemy, and if they won then he would seize what land he could, and if Æthelstan won, Hywel would smile across the frontier and quietly build up his strength.

'You're thinking, lord,' Finan said accusingly. 'I know that face.'

'Best not to think,' Steapa said, 'it only leads to trouble.'

'I was wondering why we're fighting,' I said.

'Because the filthy bastards want our country,' Steapa retorted. 'So we have to kill them.'

'Did they all fight before we Saxons came?' I asked.

'Of course they did,' Steapa insisted, 'stupid bastards fought each other, then fought the Romans and once they'd gone, they fought us. And if they ever beat us, which they won't, they'll fight each other again.'

'So it never ends.'

'Christ,' Finan said, 'you're gloomy!'

I was thinking of the shield wall, that place of pure terror. As a child, listening to the songs in the hall, we only want to grow up to be warriors, to wear the helmet and the mail, to have a sword men fear, to wear the rings thick on our

303

forearms, to hear the poets sing of our prowess. But the truth was horror, blood, shit, men screaming, weeping, and dying. The songs don't tell of that, they make it sound glorious. I had stood in too many shield walls and now rode to determine whether I would stand in one more, the biggest yet and, I feared, the worst.

Wyrd bið ful āræd.

We reached Ceaster late the following afternoon. Leof was relieved to see us, then aghast when I told him the battle might yet be fought on Wirhealum. 'It can't be!' he said.

'Why not?'

'What if he wins?'

'We die,' I said brutally. 'But the decision isn't made yet.'

'What if the king chooses to fight elsewhere?'

'Then you have to hold Ceaster against a siege till we relieve you.'

'But—' he began.

'You have family here?' Steapa demanded curtly.

'A wife, three children.'

'You want them raped? Enslaved?'

'No!'

'Then you hold the city.'

Next morning, still in a persistent drizzle, we rode north towards Anlaf's chosen field. Steapa was still angry at Leof. 'Yellow-bellied fool,' he grumbled.

'He can be replaced.'

'He'd better be.' He rode in silence for a while, then grinned at me. 'Was good to see Benedetta!' He had met Benedetta in Ceaster's great hall.

'You remember her?'

'Of course I remember her! You can't forget a woman like that. I always felt sorry for her. She shouldn't have been a slave.'

'She isn't now.'

'But you're not married to her?'

'Italian superstition,' I said.

He laughed. 'So long as she shares your bed, who cares?'

'And you?' I asked. I knew his wife had died.

'I don't sleep alone, lord,' he said, then nodded ahead to the bridge that crossed the larger stream, close to where the smaller joined it. 'That's the stream?' he asked.

'You can see the hazel rods just beyond it.'

'So the bridge would be behind us?'

'Yes.'

He spurred to the bridge, which was little more than trimmed oak trunks laid between the high banks and only wide enough to take a small farm cart. He curbed his horse on the bridge and looked along the larger stream, seeing its deep gully and the reeds on either bank. He grunted, but said nothing, just turned to stare at the first hazel rods that were planted a hundred paces north, beyond which the heathland gradually rose towards the low crest. At first sight it was an unpromising battlefield that yielded the higher ground to the enemy and suggested we would be trapped on the boggy ground at the edge of the streams' gullies.

Steapa urged his horse on, reaching the hazel rods. We were accompanied by Finan, Egil, Thorold, Sihtric and a dozen warriors, two of whom held damp branches with their dripping autumn leaves. 'I suppose the earslings are watching us?' Steapa nodded towards the trees on the western ridge.

'They will be.'

'What's that?' He pointed west to where we could see a broken palisade on the ridge's summit.

'Brynstæþ, a farmstead.'

'Anlaf's men are there?'

'They were,' Egil answered, 'but they left two days ago.'

305

'Probably there now,' Steapa said unhappily. He rode on, leading us to the low crest marked by the hazel rods where Anlaf hoped to make his shield wall. 'He'll think we're fools if we agree to this place,' he said.

'He already thinks Æthelstan is a frivolous idiot.'

He snorted at that, then walked his horse west to the highest point of the crest. 'So you think he'll attack down this slope?' he asked, looking back towards the bridge.

'I would.'

'Me too,' he said after a moment's thought.

'But he'll attack all along the line as well.'

Steapa nodded. 'But this will be his heaviest attack, right here.'

'Straight down the slope,' I said.

Steapa gazed down the gentle slope. 'That's what I'd do,' he said. He frowned, and I knew he was thinking of what else Anlaf might do, but ever since I had first seen this place I could not imagine another plan. Attacking from his right would pin Æthelstan's army against the deeper stream. Some men would escape across the gully, but in the panic many would drown, most would be slaughtered, and the fugitives could be pursued and killed by Anlaf's horsemen, most of whom would be Ingilmundr's men, the same ones we had seen setting off eastwards to ravage Mercia beyond Ceaster. I doubted that either Anlaf or Constantine had brought many horses, they were difficult and awkward to ship, which meant only those horses already on Wirhealum would make the pursuit. But if my charcoal-sketched plans came true then the pursuit would be the other way, with Anlaf fleeing and our men following.

'Suppose his main attack is from his left?' Steapa suggested.

'He'll force us back onto the smaller stream and it's easier to cross.'

'And he loses the advantage of the slope,' Finan put in.

Steapa frowned. He knew what I had suggested to Æthelstan, but he also knew that the enemy had ideas of their own. 'How clever is Anlaf?'

'He's no fool.'

'He'll think we're fools to accept.'

'Let's hope he does think that. Let him think we're arrogant, that we're confident we can shatter his shield wall. We treat him with derision.'

'You'll have a chance to do that right now,' Thorolf growled and we turned to see a score of horsemen coming from the north. Like us they displayed the branches of truce.

'I need a moment,' Steapa said, then spurred his horse down the slope where we believed Anlaf would launch his most brutal attack. He galloped to the lower land where Æthelstan's left flank would make its shield wall, then curved around so he could follow the stream's bank. I could see him looking into the smaller stream, then he spurred again and came back to join us. By then I could see that Anlaf was among the approaching horsemen and with him were Constantine and Ingilmundr. We waited.

'The bastard,' Steapa growled as he saw the approaching horsemen.

'Ingilmundr?'

'Treacherous bastard,' Steapa spat.

'He knows Æthelstan is no fool.'

'Except he fooled the king for long enough, didn't he?'

We fell silent as the horsemen came closer. They reined in a dozen paces away and Anlaf grinned. 'Lord Uhtred! You return. You bring your king's answer?'

'I was exercising my horse,' I said, 'and showing Lord Steapa the countryside.'

'Lord Steapa,' Anlaf said the name. He would have heard of Steapa, but only as a man from his grandfather's time. 'Another old man?'

307

'He says you're an old man,' I told Steapa.

'Tell him he's an earsling, and that I'll gut him from his balls to his gullet.'

I had no need to translate, Ingilmundr did that and Anlaf laughed. I ignored him, looking at Constantine instead. I had met him often enough and I respected him. I bowed my head briefly. 'Lord King, I am sorry to see you here.'

'I had no wish to be here,' he said, 'but your king is insufferable. Monarch of all Britain!'

'He's the most powerful monarch in Britain,' I suggested.

'That, Lord Uhtred, is what we are here to decide.' He spoke stiffly, but I sensed some regret in his voice. He was old too, maybe a handful of years younger than me, and his stern, handsome face was lined and his beard white. He wore, as he always did, a cloak of rich blue.

'If you abandon your claim in Cumbria,' I told him, 'and march your men back to Alba, then we have nothing to decide.'

'Except who rules Northumbria,' Constantine said.

'You would let a pagan rule there?' I asked, nodding at Anlaf, who was listening to Ingilmundr's translation as we spoke.

'Better a pagan ally than an arrogant whelp who treats us like dogs.'

'He believes you are a good Christian, lord King,' I said, 'and that all the Christians of Britain should live in peace.'

'Under his rule?' Constantine snarled.

'Under his protection.'

'I don't need Saxons to protect me. I want to teach them that Scotland will not be humiliated.'

'Then leave this land,' I said, 'because King Æthelstan is bringing his army, an undefeated army, and your humiliation will be greater.'

'Bring the army,' Ingilmundr said in the Saxon tongue, 'because our spears are hungry.'

'As for you,' I said, 'you treacherous piece of shit, I'll feed your corpse to Saxon pigs.'

'Enough,' Steapa growled. 'You want to fight my king here?'

'If he dares come,' Ingilmundr translated Anlaf's answer.

'Then keep the truce for one more week,' Steapa said.

There was silence after Ingilmundr translated that. Anlaf looked surprised, then suspicious. 'You accept this battle-field?' he finally asked.

'Tell him we accept,' Steapa said, 'we will beat you here. It's as good a place as any, and the army we bring cannot be beaten!'

'And you want another week?' Anlaf asked. 'So you can assemble more men to be slaughtered?'

'We need a week to bring our army here,' Steapa said.

Anlaf did not look at Constantine, which surprised me, he just nodded. 'One week from today,' he agreed.

'And until then,' Steapa demanded, 'you stay north of these hazel rods, and we stay south of those.' He pointed at the line of rods north of the bridge.

'Agreed,' Constantine said hurriedly, perhaps to show that he was Anlaf's equal.

'Then we shall meet again,' Steapa said, turned his horse and, without another word, spurred towards the bridge.

Ingilmundr watched Steapa ride down the shallow slope. 'Æthelstan gave him the authority to make the decision?' he asked.

'He did,' I said.

'And they call him Steapa Snotor!' Ingilmundr sneered, then translated the old insult to Anlaf.

Anlaf laughed. 'Steapa the stupid! We shall meet one week from today, Lord Uhtred.'

I said nothing, just turned Snawgebland and spurred to follow Steapa. I caught up with him as we approached the bridge. 'So you agree with me?' I said.

'If we don't fight him here,' Steapa said, 'we lose Ceaster and he marches into northern Mercia. We'll fight him eventually, but he'll choose a higher hill than this one, a steeper slope, and the fight will be twice as hard. This isn't the best place to fight, but you're right. There's a good chance we can win here.' The hooves of our horses clattered loud on the bridge. 'He's got the advantage,' Steapa went on, 'and it won't be easy.'

'It never is.'

'But if God is on our side? We can win.' He made the sign of the cross.

Next day he rode south to meet Æthelstan who was bringing his army north. The decision was made. We would fight at Wirhealum.

Steapa had insisted on a week's truce to give Æthelstan's army time to arrive in Ceaster, though that only took three days. On the evening of the third day there was a service in the church Æthelflaed had built, and Æthelstan insisted all his commanders attended and brought men with them. I took fifty of my Christians. Monks chanted, men bowed, knelt and stood, and finally my son, the bishop, stood before the altar and preached.

I had not wanted to attend, but Æthelstan had ordered me to be present, and so I stood at the back, among the shadows cast by the tall candles, and braced myself for whatever my son would say. He was known for his hatred of pagans and I expected a rant, ostensibly aimed at Anlaf, but doubtless meant for me too.

But he surprised me. He spoke of the land we protected; a land, he said, of farms and coppiced woodlands, of lakes and high pastures. He spoke of families, of wives and children. He spoke well, not loudly, but his voice reached us clearly enough. 'God,' he said, 'is on our side! It is our land

310

that has been invaded, how can God not support us?' I listened to that and supposed that Constantine's bishops had claimed the same when Æthelstan invaded his land. 'We will claim all the land that is rightfully ours,' my son went on, 'because Northumbria is a part of Englaland, and we fight for Englaland. And yes, I know that Northumbria is rife with pagans!' I groaned inwardly. 'But Englaland has its pagans too. Bishop Oda was born a pagan! I was raised as a Northumbrian pagan! Yet we are both Ænglisc!' His voice was rising. 'We are both Christians! Both bishops! How many in this church had pagan parents?' That question took everyone by surprise, but gradually the hands went up, including my son's hand. I was astonished by how many raised an arm, but of course the majority of Æthelstan's troops were from Mercia, and the northern part of that country had been ruled and settled by the Danes for a long time. My son lowered his hand. 'But now we are not Danes or Saxons,' he went on strongly, 'neither pagans nor Christians, but Ænglisc! And God will be with us!'

It was a good sermon. We were all nervous. Every man in Æthelstan's army knew we were fighting on land the enemy had chosen, and a rumour had hurried through the army that Æthelstan himself had disapproved of Steapa's acceptance. 'It's nonsense,' Æthelstan told me irritably. 'It's not perfect ground, but probably as good as we can expect.'

It was the day after my son's sermon and there were twelve of us exploring the wooded ridge that would lie on the left of Æthelstan's battle line. I had sent Eadric and Oswi to scout the ridge as far as the ruined palisade of Brynstæþ, and they had assured us there was no enemy among the trees beyond the settlement. Meanwhile fifty other horsemen were riding the chosen battlefield, going as far north as the truce allowed, and one of them wore Æthelstan's distinctive cloak and his helmet with its gold ring like a coronet. The enemy would be watching them, but so far Anlaf's men had not been seen coming further south than they had agreed, and I was confident that Æthelstan's exploration of the ridge was hidden from enemy scouts.

Æthelstan wore a drab mail coat and a battered helmet, looking like any other soldier who would have to stand in the shield wall. He was mostly silent, staring down from the ridge at the battlefield, then going as far as Brynstæþ's ruined palisade. 'What was here?'

'A Saxon family,' I said. 'They owned most of the land around here. They sold timber and kept some sheep.'

He grunted. 'It will do,' he said, then turned to look again at the valley where the road ran straight towards the distant sea. 'Egil's Norsemen will fight?'

'They're Norsemen, lord King, of course they'll fight.'

'I'll put you on the right,' he said, 'hard against that stream.' He meant the deeper stream. 'Your job will be to push their left back, make them think that's our plan.'

I felt an unworthy relief that I was not being posted on Æthelstan's left where we expected the assault of Anlaf's fiercest warriors. 'We'll push,' I said, 'but not too far.'

'Not too far,' he agreed, 'maybe not far at all. Just hold them still, that will be enough.' We would have fewer men than the enemy and if we pushed too far forward we would have to thin our ranks to fill the growing space between the streams. 'There's something else you can do for me, lord,' he went on.

'Tell me, lord King.'

'We have to win this battle,' he said, 'and afterwards we have to occupy Cumbria. We have to hit them hard! They've rebelled!' He meant the Danes and Norse who had settled in that restless region and who had flocked to join Constantine's army as it marched south.

'It can be done, lord King,' I said, 'but you'll need a lot of men to do it.'

'You'll need a lot more men,' he corrected me, then paused, still looking down into the valley. 'Ealdorman Godric left no heir.' Godric had been the man Æthelstan had appointed as ealdorman of northern Cumbria, and who had died trying to stop Constantine's advance. He had been young, wealthy and, reports said, brave. He had been over-whelmed by the Scottish attack, his shield wall broken, and he had been cut down trying to rally his men. 'Some two hundred of his men escaped the battle,' Æthelstan said, 'and others are probably still alive, hiding in the hills.'

'I hope so.'

'So I want you to take over his land and his men.'

I said nothing for a moment. Godric had been given vast tracts of northern Cumbria, and if I became their owner, then Bebbanburg's land would stretch from sea to sea across Britain. I would have to garrison Cair Ligualid and a dozen other places. I would become the Saxon shield against the Scots, and that, I thought, was good. Yet for that silent moment I also felt confusion. 'Not three months ago, lord King, you were trying to take Bebbanburg from me. Now you're doubling my lands?'

He flinched at that. 'I need a strong man on the Scottish frontier.'

'An old man?'

'Your son will inherit.'

'He will, lord King.'

I saw a buzzard circle high over the battlefield. It tipped its wings to the small wind, then soared northwards. I touched my hammer, thanking Thor for sending a good omen.

'There is one problem,' Æthelstan went on.

'There always is.'

'Ealdorman Godric left no heir, so the owner of his land is his widow, Eldrida. I can compensate her for the loss of the land, of course, but silver is short. War consumes it.'

'It does,' I answered warily.

'So marry her.'

I looked at him, aghast. 'I have a woman!'

'You're not married.'

'As good as, lord King.'

'Are you married? You've gone through some pagan ceremony?'

I hesitated, then told the truth. 'No, lord King.'

'Then marry Eldrida.'

I did not know what to say. Eldrida, whoever she was, would plainly be young enough to be my granddaughter. Marry her? 'I am . . .' I began, then found I had nothing to say.

'I'm not asking you to bed her,' Æthelstan said irritably, 'except once, to make it legal, then you just put the girl away somewhere and stay with your Benedetta.'

'I plan to stay with her,' I said harshly.

'It's a formality,' he said. 'Marry the child, take her land and fortune, and defend the north. It's a gift, Lord Uhtred!'

'Not for her,' I said.

'Who cares? She's a woman with property, she will do as she's told.'

'And if we lose this battle?' I asked.

'We won't,' he said curtly, 'we mustn't. But if we do she'll be swived by a horde of Scotsmen and Norsemen. So will every other woman in Englaland. Take the gift, lord.'

I nodded, which was as much confirmation as I could give him, then looked back to the valley where, in two days, we would fight.

For Englaland.

FOURTEEN

Next day Æthelstan moved his army out of Ceaster and onto the heathland between the ridges. We camped either side of the road just short of the narrow bridge that would take us onto the chosen battlefield. There were tents for the ealdormen, but most of us made shelters from branches we chopped from the trees on the eastern ridge. It had taken most of the day for the men on foot to reach the encampment and to cut wood for shelters and fires, and Æthelstan sent orders that the army was to rest, though I doubt many men slept. Wagons brought food and bundles of extra spears. The only men who did not march with us were five hundred West Saxon horsemen who left Ceaster late in the afternoon and camped some way behind the rest of the army. Steapa commanded them. 'I had a dream last night,' he told me before we left the city.

'A good one, I hope.'

'It was Alfred.' He paused. 'I never understood him.'

'Not many of us did.'

'He was trying to put on his mail coat and it wouldn't go over his head.' He sounded puzzled.

'That means we're going to win tomorrow,' I said confidently.

'It does?'

'Because his mail coat wasn't needed.' I hoped I was right.

'I never thought of that!' Steapa said, reassured. He hesitated. I was about to mount Snawgebland and he took a pace towards me. I thought he was about to cup his hands to help me into the saddle, but instead he gave me a shy and crude embrace. 'God be with you, lord.'

'We'll meet tomorrow evening,' I said, 'on a field of dead enemies.'

'I pray so.'

I had said my farewell to Benedetta and made sure she had a good horse and a rich purse of coins. 'If we lose,' I had told her, 'you get out of the city, cross the bridge over the Dee, and go south!'

'You will not lose,' she said fiercely, 'I cannot lose you!' She had wanted to come to the battlefield, but I had forbidden it and she had reluctantly accepted my insistence, though at a price. She had unlooped the heavy gold cross from about her neck and pushed it into my hands. 'Wear it for me,' she said, 'it will keep you safe.'

I hesitated. I did not want to offend my gods, and I knew that the cross was valuable, a gift to Benedetta from Queen Eadgifu. 'Wear it!' she said sharply. 'It will keep you safe, I know it!' I hung the cross about my neck, along with the silver hammer. 'And don't take it off!' she warned me.

'I won't. And I will see you after we've won.'

'Make sure you do!' I left Eadric with her, telling him he was too old to fight and to keep her safe and to take her far southwards if the battle was lost. She and I had kissed, then I left her with tears in her eyes.

I had not told her of Æthelstan's offer of a bride. That offer had appalled me as much as I suspected it would enrage Benedetta, and that morning I had glimpsed Eldrida as she went to church in the company of six nuns. She looked like a nun herself, dressed in drab grey robes and with a heavy silver cross at her breast. She was a small, plump girl with a face that reminded me of an indignant piglet, but the piglet was worth a fortune.

We were camped south of the bridge, ready to move to the battlefield at dawn. We had bread, cold beef, cheese, and ale. Showers blew through after nightfall and we saw the northern land beyond the small crest of the battlefield glow with the campfires of our enemies. They had marched south from Dingesmere where their ships were moored in the sea-pool, and there was not a man in our force who did not gaze at that great glow and wonder how many men were grouped around those fires. Æthelstan had brought over three thousand men to his encampment, not counting the fyrd who could contribute little against Anlaf's trained warriors. Æthelstan also had Steapa's five hundred men who were camped some two miles behind us, but I reckoned Anlaf and Constantine must have had closer to five thousand. Some insisted they had six or even seven thousand, but no one truly knew.

I ate with my son, Finan, Egil and Thorolf. We said little and ate less. Sihtric joined us, but only to drink ale. 'When does the truce end?' he asked.

'Midnight.'

'But they won't fight till daylight,' Egil said.

'Late morning,' I said. It would take time to array the armies, and then for the fools to flaunt themselves between the lines to offer single combat.

Rain pattered on the sailcloth we had rigged between poles as a crude shelter. 'The ground will be wet,' Finan said gloomily, 'slippery.'

No one answered. 'We should sleep,' I said, but knew sleep would be difficult. It would be difficult for the enemy too, just as the ground would be as slippery for them as it was for us. The rain hardened and I prayed that it would last through the next day because the Irish Norse liked to use archers and rain would slacken the cords of their bows.

I walked around my men's campfires. I said the usual things, reminded them that they had trained for this, that the hours and days and months and years spent practising would keep them alive next day, but I knew many must die despite their skill. The shield wall is unforgiving. A priest was praying with some of my Christians, and I did not disturb him, just told the rest to eat, to sleep if they could, and to be confident. 'We're the wolves of Bebbanburg,' I told them, 'and we have never been defeated.'

A burst of harder rain made me move towards the brighter fires at the encampment's centre. I expected no fighting till late morning, but I was wearing mail, mostly for the warmth that the leather liner gave me. There was candlelight showing in the king's gaudy tent and I wandered towards it. Two guards at the entrance recognised me and, because I wore no sword or seax, let me pass. 'He's not here, lord,' one of them said.

I went inside anyway, just to escape the rain. The tent was empty except for a priest in his embroidered robes who was kneeling on a cushion in front of a makeshift altar that held a silver crucifix. He turned when he heard me and I saw it was my son, the bishop. I stopped, tempted to leave the tent, but my son stood, looking as awkward as I felt. 'Father,' he said uncertainly, 'the king has gone to talk to his men.'

'I was doing the same.' I decided I would stay. The rain would surely drive Æthelstan back to his tent. I had no real reason to talk to the king, other than to share our fears and hopes of the next day. I crossed to a table and saw a clay jug of wine that did not smell like vinegar so I poured some into a beaker. 'I don't suppose he'll mind me stealing his wine.' I saw my son had noticed the heavy gold cross hanging at my neck. I shrugged. 'Benedetta insists I wear it. She says it will protect me.'

'It will, father.' He hesitated, his right hand touching his own cross. 'Can we win?'

I looked into his pale face. Men said he resembled me, though I could not see it. He looked nervous. 'We can win,' I said as I sat on a stool.

'But they outnumber us!'

'I've fought many battles when I was outnumbered,' I said. 'It isn't numbers, it's fate.'

'God is on our side,' he said, though he did not sound certain.

'That's good.' I had sounded sarcastic and regretted it. 'I liked your sermon.'

'I was aware you were in the church,' he frowned, as if unsure that he had preached the truth. He sat on a bench, still frowning. 'If they win tomorrow . . .'

'It will be a slaughter,' I said. 'Our men will be trapped against the streams. Some will escape over the bridge, but it's narrow, and some will scramble through the gully, but most will die.'

'So why fight here?'

'Because Anlaf and Constantine believe we can't win. They're confident. So we use that confidence to defeat them.' I paused. 'It won't be easy.'

'You're not frightened?'

'Terrified.' I smiled. 'Only a fool is not frightened before a battle. But we've trained our men, we've survived other fights, we know what to do.'

'So do the enemy.'

'Of course.' I sipped the wine. It was sour. 'You weren't born when I fought at Ethandun. Anlaf's grandfather fought Æthelstan's grandfather there, and we were outnumbered. The Danes were confident, we were desperate.'

'God won that battle for us.'

'So Alfred said. Me? I think we knew we would lose our homes and our land if we lost, so we fought with a desperate ferocity. And we won.'

'And tomorrow will be the same? I pray so.' He really was frightened and I wondered whether it was better that he had become a priest because he might never have made a warrior. 'I must have faith,' he said plaintively.

'Have faith in our men,' I said. I heard some singing in the encampment, which surprised me. The men I had spoken with had been brooding on what the next day would bring, too sombre to sing. We had heard no singing from the enemy camp either, but suddenly there was a small group of men making a raucous noise. 'They're in good spirits,' I said.

'It's the ale, I suppose?' he said.

An awkward silence followed. The ragged singing came closer, a dog barked, and the rain made its seething noise on the tent's roof. 'I never thanked you,' I said, 'for your warning at Burgham. I'd have lost Bebbanburg if you hadn't spoken.'

For a heartbeat he seemed flustered, not sure what to say. 'It was Ealdred,' he finally found his tongue. 'He wanted to be Lord of the North. He was not a good man.'

'And I am?' I asked, smiling.

He did not answer that. He frowned at the singing, which was getting louder, then made the sign of the cross. 'The king said you told him how we could win the battle?' he asked, his nervousness plain again.

'I suggested something.'

'What?'

'Something we're not telling anyone. Suppose Anlaf sends men tonight to take a prisoner? And the prisoner knew?' I smiled. 'That would make your god's job a lot harder if he means us to win.'

'He does,' he said, trying to sound firm, 'tomorrow the Lord will work wonders for us!'

'Tell that to our troops,' I said, standing, 'tell them your god is on our side. Tell them to do their best and be sure that their god will help.' I poured the wine onto the rugs. Æthelstan, I reckoned, had taken shelter elsewhere and I would return to my men.

My son stood too. 'Father,' he said uncertainly, then looked at me with tears in his eyes. 'I'm sorry, but I never could be the son you wanted.'

I was struck by his misery, embarrassed by the raw feeling of regret that we both felt. 'But you are!' I said. 'You are a lord of the church! I'm proud of you!'

'You are?' he asked, astonished.

'Uhtred,' I said, using the name I had taken from him in anger, 'I'm sorry too.' I held out my arms and we embraced. I had never thought to embrace my eldest son again, but I held him close, so close that my hands were scratched by the gold and silver wire embroidered into his robes. I felt tears in my eyes. 'Be brave,' I said, still holding him, 'and when we've won you must visit us at Bebbanburg. You can say mass in our chapel.'

'I'd like that.'

'Be brave and have faith,' I said, 'and we can win.'

I left him, cuffing my eyes as I walked away from the tent that glowed from all the candle lanterns inside. I passed campfires where men squatted in the rain, heard the voices of women from inside the shelters. Every whore in northern Mercia had followed the army and for all I knew from Wessex too. The raucous singing was far behind me now. They were drunk, I decided, and I had almost reached the fires of my own men when that singing turned to angry shouting. A scream cut the night. There was the distinctive sound of blades clashing. More shouts. I had no weapon other than a small

321

knife, but I turned and ran towards the commotion. Other men were running with me towards a sudden flare of lurid light. The king's tent was on fire, the wax-smeared linen blazing bright. The shouting was all around me now. Men were carrying swords, their eyes wide with fear. I saw the guards who had stood at the tent door were dead, their bodies lit by the fierce flames of the burning linen. Æthelstan's bodyguard, distinctive in their scarlet cloaks, were making a cordon around the tent, others were hauling the burning fabric down and away. 'They've gone!' someone bellowed. 'They've gone!'

A group of Anlaf's men had somehow crept into the encampment. It had been those men who had been singing, pretending to be drunk. Their hope had been to kill Æthelstan and so tear the heart from our army on the eve of battle, but Æthelstan had been nowhere near his tent. They had found a bishop instead.

Æthelstan came to the charred ruin of his tent. 'Were there no sentries?' he was asking angrily of one of his companions, then saw me. 'Lord Uhtred. I am sorry.'

My eldest son was dead. Cut by swords, his blood reddening his lavish robes. His heavy pectoral cross had been stolen. His body had been dragged from the burning tent, but too late. Now I knelt by him and touched his face that was unmarked and oddly peaceful. 'I'm sorry,' Æthelstan said again.

For a moment I could not speak. 'We had made our peace, lord King.'

'Then tomorrow we will make war,' Æthelstan said harshly, 'terrible war, and we will avenge his death.'

Tomorrow the lord would work wonders for us? Except my eldest son was dead and the flames of the campfires blurred as I went back to my men.

*   *   *

Dawn. Birds singing in the high woods as though this was just another day. The rain had eased in the night, but a shower blew through as I left my shelter. My joints ached, reminding me that I was old. Immar Hergildson, the young Dane I had saved from a hanging, vomited beside the charred remains of a campfire. 'Drunk last night?' I asked him, kicking away a dog that came to eat the vomit.

He just shook his head. He was pale, frightened. 'You've stood in a shield wall,' I told him, 'you know what to do.'

'Yes, lord.'

'And they're frightened too,' I said, nodding north to where the enemy was camped beyond the low crest.

'Yes, lord,' he said uncertainly.

'Just watch for the low spear thrust,' I told him, 'and don't lower your shield.' He had been prone to doing so in practice. A man in the enemy's second rank would thrust a spear at an ankle or calf and Immar's natural reaction was to lower the shield and so open himself to a sword thrust into the throat or chest. 'You'll be fine,' I told him.

Aldwyn, my servant, brought me a cup of ale. 'There's bread, lord, and bacon.'

'You eat,' I told him. I had no appetite.

My son, my only son now, came to me. He was pale too. 'It was Ingilmundr,' he told me.

I knew he meant that it had been Ingilmundr who had infiltrated our camp and killed my eldest son. 'You know that?'

'He was recognised, lord.'

That made sense. Ingilmundr, the tall handsome Norseman who had sworn his oath to Æthelstan, who had pretended to be a Christian, who had been given land on Wirhealum, and who had made his secret alliance with Anlaf, had led a group of men through the darkness. He knew Æthelstan's army, he spoke our language, and in the rainswept night he had come to kill the king, hoping to

323

leave us leaderless and afraid. Instead he had killed my son and, in the night's blazing chaos, had escaped into the dark. 'It's a bad omen,' I said.

'A good omen, father.'

'Why good?'

'If he had struck a few minutes earlier you would have died.'

I had lain awake, thinking just that. 'Your brother and I made our peace,' I told him, 'before he died.' I remembered the embrace, and my awareness that he had sobbed silently on my shoulder. 'I was a bad father,' I said softly.

'No!'

'Too late now,' I said harshly. 'And today we kill Ingilmundr. And we make it hurt.'

I was wearing leggings and a tunic, but Aldwyn brought me my best coat of Frisian mail, the links heavy, backed with leather, and edged at the neck and skirt hems with gold and silver rings. I pulled on my rich bracelets, the glittering trophies of victories past that would betray to the enemy that I was a warlord. I pulled on the heavy boots that were lined with iron strips and heeled with golden spurs. I buckled the smaller sword belt, sewn with silver squares, that held Wasp-Sting at my right side, then the heavier belt, blazoned with gold wolf heads that held Serpent-Breath at my left hip. Around my neck I wrapped a scarf of rare white silk, a gift from Benedetta, and over it I hung a thick gold chain, with the silver hammer hanging over my heart and next to it the gold cross that Benedetta swore would protect me. I fastened a night-black cloak about my shoulders, then pulled on my finest war-helm that was crested with a silver wolf. I stamped my feet then walked a few paces to settle the heavy armour. Aldwyn, an orphan from Lundene, stared at me wide-eyed. I was a warlord, the warlord of Bebbanburg, a warlord of Britain, and Aldwyn saw glory and power, ignorant of the fear that made my stomach sour, that mocked me, that made my voice harsh. 'Is Snawgebland saddled?'

'Yes, lord.'

'Bring him. And Aldwyn?'

'Lord?'

'You stay behind the wall, well behind. There'll be arrows flying, so stay out of range. If I need you, I'll call you. Now fetch the horse.'

We would be the first of Æthelstan's men to cross the bridge onto the battlefield. He had asked me to hold the right flank, hard against the deeper stream. We expected the hardest fight to be on the left flank where Anlaf would unleash his wild Norse warriors, but the right flank would be hit hard too, because whoever faced us would be eager to break our shield wall and so pour men behind Æthelstan's battle line.

I placed Egil and his men next to the stream, then arrayed the men of Bebbanburg in four ranks, and to their left Sihtric formed his warriors. Beyond them, in the long centre of his line, Æthelstan placed the men of Mercia, while his left wing, which we suspected would face Anlaf's own Norsemen, was trusted to five hundred of his West Saxon warriors.

A shower gusted from the west, lasted two or three minutes, and blew over. I advanced my line fifteen paces. No enemy was visible yet and I suspected Anlaf was assembling his army beyond the low crest that spanned the valley, ready to reveal them in one frightening advance, but as we waited I had the men in my rearmost rank use their seaxes to dig holes and to cut swathes of the long wet grass. Each hole was about the breadth of two hands and three hands' breadth deep, and all were filled with the cut grass. The enemy would be watching us even if we could not see them, but I doubted they would understand what we were doing, and even if they did the men attacking us would be concentrating only on our shields and blades. When the holes were dug and well hidden we retreated the fifteen paces.

I was behind the line, mounted on Snawgebland. Egil and Sihtric were also on horseback, and both had kept a dozen men well back from the shield wall to serve as reinforcements. I had Finan with twenty men behind. Those were perilously small numbers to throw into a broken shield wall, but all of Æthelstan's army was stretched thin. I also had two dozen archers with their hunting bows. I was reluctant to deploy more. The arrows would force the enemy to lower their heads and raise their shields, but in a clash of shield walls it was the blades in men's hands that did the killing.

Æthelstan himself was riding along the front of the line, accompanied by Bishop Oda and six mounted warriors. Æthelstan looked glorious. His horse was caparisoned with a scarlet saddle cloth, his spurs were gold, his horse's bridle was trimmed with gold, and his helmet was ringed with a golden crown. He wore a scarlet cloak over shining mail, had a gold cross on his breast, while his sword scabbard was all gold, a gift that had been given to his father by Alfred. He was talking to his troops, and I remembered his grandfather doing the same at Ethandun. Alfred had seemed more nervous of making that speech than he was of the battle itself and I could still see him, a slender man in a worn blue cloak, talking in a high-pitched voice and slowly finding the right words. Æthelstan had more confidence, the words came easily to him, and I rode to join him as he came to our troops. I steered Snawgebland carefully to avoid the scatter of holes, then bowed my head to the king. 'Lord King,' I said, 'welcome.'

He smiled. 'I see you're wearing a cross, Lord Uhtred,' he said loudly, nodding towards Benedetta's gold ornament, 'and that pagan bauble too?'

'This bauble, lord King,' I said just as loudly, 'has seen me through more battles than I can count. And we won them all.'

My men cheered that and Æthelstan let them cheer, then told them they fought for their homes, for their wives, for their children. 'Above all,' he finished, 'we fight for peace! We fight to drive Anlaf and his followers away from our land, to teach the Scots that to trespass on our land is to gain nothing but graves.' I noted how he did not appeal to the Christians, but was aware that here, on his right wing, he had Norsemen and Danes fighting for him. 'Say your prayers,' he said, 'and fight as you know how to fight, and your god will keep you, he will preserve you, and he will reward you. As will I.'

They cheered him, and Æthelstan gave me a quizzical look as if asking how he had done. I smiled. 'Thank you, lord King,' I said.

He led me a few paces away from my men. 'Your Norsemen will stay true?' he asked in a low voice.

'That worries you?'

'It worries some of my men. Yes, it worries me.'

'They will stay true, lord King,' I said, 'and if I'm wrong then Bebbanburg is yours.'

'If you're wrong,' he said, 'then we're all dead.'

'They will stay true. I swear it.'

He glanced down at my chest. 'The cross?'

'Woman's sorcery, lord. It belongs to Benedetta.'

'Then I pray the sorcery protects you. All of us. Steapa is ready, so all we must do is hold the enemy firm.'

'And win, lord King.'

'That too,' he said, 'that too,' then turned to ride back along the line.

And just then the enemy came.

* * *

327

We heard them first.

There was a dull hammer blow that seemed to shudder across the heath. It was the sound of a drum, a huge war drum, and it was beaten three times and the third stroke was the signal for the enemy to start clashing blades on shields. They shouted, and all the time that great drum beat like the heart of a monstrous unseen beast. Most of my men had been sitting, but now they stood, brought their shields up and stared at where the road vanished over the low crest.

The noise was massive, yet still the enemy was hidden. The first we saw of them was their standards appearing above the crest, a long line of flags showing eagles, falcons, wolves, axes, ravens, swords, and crosses. 'We have the Scots,' Finan said to me. Their blue flags were on the enemy's left and meant that Constantine's men would assault my shield wall. Anlaf's soaring falcon was on the enemy's right and confirmed what we had expected, that his main assault would be against our left.

'Fate has been good to us!' I called to my men. 'It's sent us the Scots! How many times have we beaten them? And they'll see we're the wolves of Bebbanburg and they'll be scared!'

We talk nonsense before battles, necessary nonsense. We tell our men what they want to hear, but the gods decide what will happen.

'Fewer archers, perhaps?' Finan muttered. The Scots did use archers, but not many. I looked up at the sky and saw that the clouds were thickening to the west. Perhaps it would rain again? A downpour would weaken the threat of archers. 'And are you sure you want your son in the front rank?' Finan asked.

I had placed my son, my only son I realised with a pang, at the centre of my men. 'He has to be there,' I said. He had to be there because he would be the next Lord of

Bebbanburg and he must be seen to take the same risks as the men he would lead. There was a time when I would have been there, at the head and centre of my men's shield wall, but age and sense had kept me behind the line. 'He has to be there,' I said again, then added, 'but I've put good men beside him.' Then I forgot my son's peril because the enemy appeared across the skyline.

Horsemen came first, a long scattered line of perhaps a hundred men, some carrying the triangular standards of the Norse, and behind them came the shield wall. A vast wall, stretching across the valley with shields of every colour, the blackshields of Strath Clota next to Constantine's Scots, and above the wall the weak sun reflected from a forest of spearheads. The enemy stopped at the top of the crest, beating their shields, roaring defiance, and I knew every one of my men was trying to count their numbers. It was impossible, of course, they were packed too tight, but I reckoned there had to be at least five thousand men facing us.

Five thousand! Perhaps it was fear that made the enemy look more numerous, and I did feel fear as I watched that horde of men beat their shields and shout their insults. I reminded myself that Guthrum had brought almost as many men to Ethandun and we had beaten them. And his men, like Owain of Strath Clota's troops, had carried black shields. Was that an omen? I remembered after the battle how the blood had not shown on the fallen black shields. 'Looks like six ranks,' Finan said, 'maybe seven?'

We had three, with just a few men making the scanty fourth. And the enemy's ranks would grow as the line advanced and was forced to shrink by the converging streams. It was never enough to kill the front rank of a shield wall, to break it we had to pierce all six ranks, or all seven, or however many faced us. My throat felt dry, my stomach sour, and a muscle in my right leg was twitching. I touched the silver hammer, searched the sky for an omen, saw none, and gripped the hilt of Serpent-Breath.

The enemy was resting the lower rims of their round shields on the ground. Shields are heavy and a shield arm tires long before the sword arm. They were still beating swords and spear-hafts on the shields. 'They're not moving,' Finan said, and I realised he was talking because he was nervous. We were all nervous. 'They think we'll attack them?' he asked.

'They hope we will,' I grunted. Of course they hoped we would attack, trudging up the shallow slope of wet heath-land, but though Anlaf doubtless thought Æthelstan was a fool to have accepted this battlefield he must have known we would stay on the lower ground. I could see their leaders riding up and down in front of the grounded shields, pausing to harangue the men. I knew what they would be saying. Look at your enemy, look how few they are! See how weak they are! See how easily we will shatter them! And think of the plunder that waits for you! The women, the slaves, the silver, the cattle, the land! I heard the bursts of cheering.

'Lot of spears in the Scottish line,' Finan said. I ignored him. I was thinking of Skuld, the Norn who waited at the foot of Yggdrasil, the giant ash tree that supports our world, and I knew Skuld's shears would be sharp. She cuts the threads of our lives. Some men believed Skuld left Yggdrasil during a battle to fly above the fighting, deciding who will live and who will die, and again I looked up as if expecting to see an ash-grey woman, massively winged, with shears bright as the sun, but all I saw were grey clouds spreading. 'Sweet Jesus,' Finan muttered and I looked back to see horsemen cantering down the gentle slope towards us.

'Ignore them!' I called to my men. The approaching horsemen were the fools who craved single combat. They came to taunt us and to seek fame. 'Leave your shields resting,' I shouted, 'and ignore them!'

Ingilmundr was among the men who came to challenge us. In his right hand he carried Bone-Carver, his sword, its blade shining. He saw me and swerved towards my men. 'You've come to die, Lord Uhtred?' he called. His horse, a black stallion, came close to the hidden holes we had dug, but he turned away at the last moment to ride along the line of my troops. He looked magnificent, his mail polished, his cloak white, his bridle glinting with gold, his helmet crowned with the wing of a raven. He was smiling. He pointed Bone-Carver towards me. 'Come and fight, Lord Uhtred!' I turned to look across the stream, pointedly ignoring him. 'You lack courage? So you should! Today is the day of your death. All of you! You are sheep, ripe for slaughter.' He saw Egil's triangular banner with its eagle. 'And you Norsemen,' he was speaking in Norse now, 'you think the gods will love you today? They will reward you with pain, with agony, with death!'

Someone in Egil's ranks let out a resounding fart, which provoked raucous laughter. Then the men began beating their shields, and Ingilmundr, failing to goad anyone to face him, turned his horse and cantered towards the Mercian troops to our left. None of those men would be goaded either. They stood silent, shields resting, watching the enemy who taunted them. A horseman carrying the black shield of Owain's men came to look at us. He said nothing, spat towards our line, then turned away. 'He was counting us,' Finan said.

'He didn't need many fingers,' I said.

How long did we stand there? It seemed an age, but for the life of me I cannot remember whether it was a few minutes or an hour. None of us rode out to accept the enemy's challenges, Æthelstan had ordered us to ignore them, and so the young fools mocked us, rode their stallions proudly, and we just waited. The sky clouded over and a

331

spatter of rain swept in from the sea. Some of my men sat. They shared flasks of ale. A Mercian priest came to my ranks and some of the men knelt to him as he touched their foreheads and muttered a prayer.

Anlaf plainly hoped we would advance on him, but he must have known that we were not such fools. If we attacked his line we would have to extend ours to fill the widening gap between the streams, and our ranks would thin still further. And we would have to advance uphill, which meant that the battle was his to begin, but he also waited, hoping we would become ever more frightened, ever more overawed by the number of warriors he had brought to the field.

'Bastards are rearranging themselves,' Finan said, and I saw that the Scots on the extreme left of the enemy line were moving men. Some who had been in the centre of the front rank were being ordered to the edges, while others took their places. 'Eager, aren't they?' I asked, then called to Egil. 'Svinfylkjas, Egil!'

'I see it!'

A svinfylkjas was what we called a swine-wedge because it was shaped like the tusk of a boar. The enemy, instead of crashing their shield wall into ours, were putting their strongest men and best fighters into three groups and, as they neared us, those groups would make wedges that would try to burst through our shield wall like boar tusks ripping through wattle fencing. If it worked it would be quick and savage, tearing bloody gaps in our shield wall that the Scots would widen and so get behind Æthelstan's line. Constantine no doubt knew that Anlaf's plan was to break our left, but he wanted his share of the glory and so was forming his most formidable warriors into swine-wedges that he would hurl onto my men in the hope of breaking our right before the Norsemen shattered the left.

'Trust in God!' a voice called and I saw Bishop Oda riding from the Mercians to call to my men. 'If God is with us, none can prevail against us!'

'Half of these men are pagans,' I told him as he came close.

'Odin will protect you!' he called, now in his native Danish. 'And Thor will send a mighty thunderbolt to destroy that rabble!' He curbed his horse close to mine and smiled. 'Is that better, lord?'

'I approve, lord Bishop.'

'I am sorry,' he spoke very low, 'about your son.'

'Me too,' I said bleakly.

'He was a brave man, lord.'

'Brave?' I asked, remembering my son's fear.

'He defied you. That takes bravery.'

I did not want to talk about my son. 'When the fighting starts, lord Bishop,' I said, 'stay well back. The Norse like to use arrows, and you're a tempting target.' He wore his bishop's robes, embroidered with crosses, though I could see there was a mail coat showing at his neckline.

He smiled. 'When the fighting starts, lord, I shall stay with the king.'

'Then make sure he doesn't go into the front line.'

'Nothing I can say will stop him. He's ordered Prince Edmund to stay back.' Edmund, Æthelstan's half-brother, was the heir.

'Edmund should fight,' I said. 'Æthelstan has nothing to prove, Edmund does.'

'He's a brave young man,' Oda said. I grunted at that. I was not fond of Edmund, but in truth I had only known him as a petulant child and men now spoke well of him. 'You saw the Scots rearrange themselves?' Oda asked.

'Did Æthelstan send you to ask me that?'

He smiled. 'He did.'

'They're making three *svinfylkja*s, lord Bishop,' I did not need to explain the word to Oda, a Dane, 'and we're going to slaughter them.'

'You sound confident, lord.' He wanted reassurance.

'I'm frightened, lord Bishop. I always am.'

He flinched at those words. 'But we will win!' he insisted, though without much conviction. 'Your son is in heaven now, lord, and though God already knew what is at stake here today, your son will have told him more. We cannot lose! Heaven is on our side.'

'You believe that?' I asked him. 'Aren't there priests telling the Scots the same thing?'

He ignored those questions. His hands were fidgeting on his reins. 'Why are they waiting?'

'To give us plenty of time to count them. To scare us.'

'It works,' he said very quietly.

'Tell the king he has nothing to worry about on his right flank.' I touched the hammer, hoping I was right, 'And as for the rest? Pray.'

'Unceasingly, lord,' he said, then reached out and I gripped his hand. 'God be with you, lord.'

'And you, lord Bishop.'

He rode back towards Æthelstan who was standing his horse at the centre of our line, surrounded there by a dozen of his household warriors. He was staring intently towards the enemy and I saw him suddenly jerk his reins so that his horse took a backwards step before he reached out and patted its neck. I turned to see what had startled him.

The enemy had lifted their shields and lowered their spears.

And were coming at last.

The enemy came slowly, still beating blades against their shields. They came slowly because they wanted to keep their shield wall solid, their line as straight as possible. Yet they

334

were nervous too. Even when you outnumber an enemy, when you hold the high ground, when victory is almost certain, the fear still grips you. The sudden lunge of a spear, the fall of an axe, the edge of a blade can kill even at the moment of triumph.

My men stood and shuffled together. Shields clattered as they touched. The front rank was all men with either a sword or an axe as their chosen weapon. The spears were in the second rank. The third rank was ready to hurl spears before drawing a sword or hefting an axe. The fourth rank was spaced out because there were not enough men to fill it.

I loosened Serpent-Breath in her fleece-lined scabbard, though if I dismounted and joined the shield wall I would use Wasp-Sting, my seax. I drew her, saw the light reflect from her blade that was not much longer than my forearm. Her tip was honed to a savage point, her foreblade was sharp enough to serve as a razor, while her broken-shaped back blade was thick and stout. I thought of Serpent-Breath as a noble weapon, a sword fit for a warlord, while Wasp-Sting was the cunning killer. I remembered the exultation I had felt at Lundene's Crepelgate as I had pierced Wasp-Sting into Waormund's belly, how he had gasped, then staggered as the life blood oozed past her blade. That victory had given Æthelstan his throne. I looked to my left and saw the king was standing his horse close behind his Mercian troops, a target for archers and spearmen. Bishop Oda was close by Æthelstan, next to his standard-bearer.

Aldwyn was holding my standard with its wolf-head badge. He was waving it from side to side to let the approaching Scots know that they faced the wolf-warriors of Bebbanburg. Egil had his eagle flag flying. Thorolf, his brother, was in the centre of the front rank, tall and black-bearded, a war axe in his right hand. The enemy was three hundred paces away now and I could see Constantine's blue cross on a flag and Domnall's red hand holding another cross, while just to their left was the black banner of Owain. 'Six ranks,' Finan said, 'and bloody archers too.'

'We'll send our horses back,' I said, 'and close up.'

I turned and beckoned Ræt, Aldwyn's younger brother. 'Bring my shield!'

Beyond Ræt, on the far side of the bridge, I could see people who had come from Ceaster to watch the battle. They were fools, I thought, and Æthelstan had forbidden them to come, but such orders were pointless. The guards on the city gates were supposed to stop them, but those guards were old or wounded men, too easily overwhelmed by an anxious crowd. Some of the women had even brought their children, and if our army was broken, if we began to flee in panicked chaos, those women and children would have no chance of reaching the safety of the city. There were priests there too, their hands raised in supplication to the nailed god.

Ræt stumbled under the weight of the heavy shield. I dismounted, took the shield from him and gave him Snawgebland's reins. 'Take him back to the bridge,' I told him, 'but watch for my signal! I'm going to need him again.'

'Yes, lord. Can I ride him, lord?'

'Go!' I said. He scrambled into the saddle, grinned at me, and kicked his heels. His legs were too short to reach the stirrups. I slapped the stallion's rump and then joined the fourth rank.

And waited again. I could hear the enemy's shouts, see the faces above the shield rims, and see the glitter of the blades meant to kill us. They had not formed a swine-wedge yet, they wanted to surprise us, but I could see how the man commanding the company nearest the stream had placed his largest men in the middle of the front rank. Three huge brutes carrying axes were at the very centre

336

and they would form the point of the wedge. All three were shouting, their mouths open, their eyes glaring from beneath their helmet rims. They would clash with Egil's men. Two hundred paces.

I looked to my left and saw that Anlaf's Norsemen were trailing the rest of the advancing line. Was that to convince us that their strongest effort would be here on their left? Already, as the enemy advanced into the ground between the converging streams, their line was shortening, their ranks thickening. I could see Anlaf on horseback behind his men. His helmet gleamed silver. His banner was black with a great white falcon soaring. Ingilmundr was in the centre, displaying a banner of a flying raven. The blades hammered on shields, the shouts were louder, the great war drum beat its death rhythm, but still they did not hurry. They wanted to frighten us, they wanted us to see death coming, they wanted our land, our women, our silver.

One hundred paces and the first arrows flickered from behind the enemy line. 'Shields!' I called, though it was unnecessary because the front rank had already crouched behind their shields, the second rank put their shields just above the first and the third completed the wall. The arrows struck with distinct thumps. A few slid through the gaps. I heard a curse from someone who had been struck, but no man fell. Two arrows struck my shield and a third glanced off the iron rim. I was tilting the shield above my helmet and could see under its lower rim that the enemy was quickening pace. The *svinfylkjas* was forming to my right, the men in the front rank hurrying to get ahead and then I saw another was forming in front of me, aiming straight at my son. A fourth arrow struck my shield's lower rim, glanced off and missed my helmet by an inch.

I had never stood in the rear rank of a shield wall since I had become an ealdorman, but my men expected me to stay behind on this day. I was old and they wanted to protect me, and that was a problem, because already men were glancing behind to make certain I had not been struck by the arrows that were falling all along Æthelstan's line. In the centre of the line, where the Norse from the islands would assault the Mercians, a horse bolted, its rump bloodied by arrows. I hated being behind the wall. A man should lead from the front, and I had a sudden certainty that Skuld, the Norn who was soaring above the field to choose her victims, would punish me if I stayed at the back.

I had sheathed Wasp-Sting again, thinking I would not need her, but now I dragged her from her scabbard. 'Out of the way,' I shouted. I would be damned before I let my men fight a *svinfylkjas* without me. I pushed between the files, bellowing at men to make way, then thrust my way between my son and Wibrund, a tall Frisian armed with a lead-weighted axe. I crouched, shield in front, and drew Wasp-Sting.

'You shouldn't be here, father,' my son said.

'If I fall,' I said, 'look after Benedetta.'

'Of course.'

A cheer had gone up from the enemy when they saw me join the front rank. There was reputation to be made in the death of a warlord. I looked past the shield's rim and saw the anger, fear and determination on bearded faces. They wanted my death. They wanted renown. They wanted the song of Uhtred's death to be sung in Scottish halls, and then the spears were flung, the swine-wedge screamed their war cry.

And the battle began.

FIFTEEN

The spears were flung from the rear ranks of the Scots and thumped into our shields. I was lucky, a spear hit the top half of the shield hard enough for the tip to show through the willow, but the weight of the haft pulled it free and the spear fell at my feet as I stood to meet the swine-wedge's charge. They came for us in a screaming rush, mouths and eyes wide, axes lifted, heavy spears ready to lunge, and then they reached the holes we had dug.

At the tip of the swine-wedge was an enormous brute, his beard spread across his mailed chest, his half-toothless mouth open in a snarl, his eyes fixed on my face, his scarred helmet decorated with a silver cross, his shield showing the red hand of Domnall, and his axe's edge glinting. He raised the axe, plainly intending to hook my shield down to uncover me before he lunged with the spike that tipped the axe-head, but then his right foot slammed into one of the holes. I saw his eyes widen as he tripped, he slammed down onto his shield, slid forward on the damp ground, and Wibrund, to my right, struck down with his lead-weighted axe to split the man's helmet and skull. First blood splashed bright. The rest of the swine-wedge was in chaos. At least three men had fallen and now others tripped on them, stumbled, and their shields flew wide as they flailed for balance, and my men stepped forward, lunged or hacked, and the swine-wedge became a mess of blood, corpses, and writhing men. The ranks behind pushed forward, thrusting the leading men into the chaos where more were tripped. One youngster, his beard little more than red fuzz, kept his footing and suddenly found himself facing me and he screamed in rage, looked terrified and swung his sword right-handed in a wild hack that I caught on my shield. He had forgotten his training because he turned his whole body to the left with the violence of his swing and his shield went with him and it was easy to slide Wasp-Sting into his belly. His mail was old and rusty, with rents lashed with twine, and I remember thinking it was perhaps a coat discarded by his father. I supported him on my shield as I ripped the blade up, as I twisted it and tugged it free. He fell at my feet, half whimpering and half gasping, and my son thrust his seax down to end his noise.

An axe blade struck my shield so hard that the willow boards split. I could see the blade's newly sharpened edge showing in the gap and reckoned the weapon was trapped there. I tugged the shield back, dragging the man towards me, and again Wasp-Sting stabbed upwards. This was unthinking work, just a lifetime of practice that was made easy by the enemy's disarray. The man tugged at his axe as he tried to escape the agony in his guts, and I wrenched the shield, the axe came free and I slammed the iron shield-boss into his face, then rammed Wasp-Sting into his groin. All that happened in the time it takes to draw two or three breaths, and already the Scottish attackers were in chaos. The bodies of dead and wounded men tripped those still on their feet and any man who tripped joined that grim obstacle. The men behind the fallen had learned of the grass-filled holes, could see the bloody mess in front of them and so

340

came cautiously. They no longer shouted insults, but tried to step around the dead, and their shields no longer touched, which made them more cautious still. Caution makes a man nervous, and our enemy had lost the one advantage an attacker has in a shield wall, the sheer impetus of fear-driven rage. 'Spears!' I shouted, wanting more spearmen in our front rank. The Scots could not charge us now, only come carefully past the grass-filled holes and past their dead and dying comrades, and that made them vulnerable to lunges from our ash-hafted spears.

That first charge had been stopped and the Scottish front rank had suffered grievously, most of them now a blood-soaked barrier to the men behind, and those men were content to wait rather than stumble over the dead and dying and so come to my unbroken shield wall. They shouted insults and beat blades against shields, but few tried to assault us, and those few retreated when spears reached for them. I saw Domnall, his face furious, dragging men to make a new front rank, and then a hand suddenly grabbed the collar of my mail coat and hauled me backwards. It was Finan. 'You old fool,' he growled as he pulled me clear of the last rank, 'you want to die?'

'They're beaten,' I said.

'They're Scots, they're never beaten till they're dead. They'll come again. The bastards always come again. Let the youngsters deal with them.' He had dragged me to the back of the shield wall where arrows were still falling, but to little effect because the archers behind the enemy shield wall were shooting long to avoid their own men. I looked left to see that Æthelstan's shield wall was holding firm all along the line, though Anlaf's right wing, which we suspected was his main attack, still hung back. 'Where's Æthelstan?' I asked. I could see his riderless horse with its distinctive saddle cloth, but there was no sign of the king.

'He's a fool like you,' Finan said, 'he went into the Mercian wall.'

'He'll live,' I said, 'he's got a bodyguard, and he's good.' I stooped, tore out a handful of coarse grass and used it to clean Wasp-Sting's blade. I saw one of my archers dipping his arrowhead in a cow pat, then he stood, notched the arrow and sent it over our shield wall. 'Save your arrows,' I told him, 'till the bastards come again.'

'They're not very eager, are they?' Finan said, sounding almost disapproving of the enemy.

And it was true. The Scottish troops had made a savage effort to break my shield wall, but had been thwarted by the holes we had dug, then shocked by their own losses. Their best and fiercest warriors had been put in the swine-wedges, now most of those men were corpses and the rest of Constantine's troops were wary, content to threaten, but in no hurry to try again to break us. My men, heartened by their success, were jeering the enemy, inviting them to come and be killed. I could see Constantine in their rear, mounted on a grey horse, his blue cloak bright. He was watching us, but making no effort to throw his men forward, and I guessed he had wanted to smash through my line and so show Anlaf that his troops could win the battle without the help of the savage Norsemen from Ireland, but that effort had failed and his men had suffered horribly.

But if the Scots were showing caution, so was the rest of Anlaf's line. They had failed to break my men nor had they pierced the much larger contingent of Mercian troops, and now the enemy was staying out of range of any spear thrust. They were shouting, and occasionally men would move forward, only to retreat when the Mercian troops beat them off. The arrow showers had diminished, and only a few spears were being thrown. The first assault had been as fierce as I expected, but its repulse seemed to have taken the rage from the enemy, and so the battle, scarcely begun, had paused all along the opposing shield walls, and that struck me as strange. The first collision of shield walls is usually the fiercest moment of battle, a sustained savagery of blades and rage as men try to prise open the enemy and carve through his ranks. That opening fight is fierce, as men, keyed up by fear, try to end the battle fast. Then, if that first vicious clash does not break the wall, men do step back to catch their breath and try to work out how best to break the enemy, and they come again. But in this battle the enemy had hit us, failed to break us, and stepped back quickly to wait beyond the reach of our spear lunges. They still threatened, still snarled insults, but they were not eager to make a second assault. Then I saw how men in the enemy army were constantly looking to their right, glancing up the shallow slope to where Anlaf's fearsome Norsemen still hung back. 'He's made a mistake,' I said.

'Constantine?'

'Anlaf. He told his army what he planned, and they don't want to die.'

'Who does?' Finan said drily, but still looked puzzled.

'All these men,' I swept my seax to indicate the enemy's stalled shield wall, 'know that Anlaf plans to win the battle with the Norsemen on his right. So why die waiting for that attack? They want that attack to panic us and break us, then they'll fight again. They want his Norsemen to win the battle for them.'

I was certain I was right. The enemy had been told that Anlaf's fearsome *úlfhéðnar*, the Norsemen of Dyflin who had won battle after battle, would splinter Æthelstan's left wing and so destroy our army. Now they waited for that to happen, reluctant to die before the men of Dyflin gave them victory. The heathland was still noisy. Thousands of men were shouting, the great war drum was still thumping, but the real sounds of battle, the screams, the clash of blades on blades, was lacking. Æthelstan had ordered us not to attack, to defend, to stay on our ground and hold the enemy until he broke their wall, and so far his army had done his bidding. There were still some clashes along the length of the shield walls as men summoned the courage to attack and there would be a brief fight, but Æthelstan's shield wall was holding. If it was to be broken then Anlaf's own men must do the breaking and the rest of his army was waiting for that ferocious attack, but Anlaf's wild Norsemen were still a hundred paces from Æthelstan's left wing. Anlaf was probably holding them back in the hope that Æthelstan would weaken that unengaged wing to strengthen his centre, but that would not happen unless there was a disaster among the Mercian troops. And Anlaf, I thought, must send his *úlfhéðnar* soon, and when they came the battle would start again.

Then Thorolf decided he could win it.

Egil, like me, was behind his troops, leaving his brother to stand as the shield wall's leader. They had broken one of the swine-wedges, leaving a heap of bloodied corpses in their front, and now the Scots who opposed them were content to shout insults, but were reluctant to add their bodies to the corpse pile. Their shield wall had shrunk, not just from the men who had died in their first screaming assault, but because all shield walls have a tendency to move to their right. Men close with the enemy and, as the axes, swords and spears try to find gaps between the shields, men instinctively shuffle to their right to gain the protection of their neighbour's shield. The Scots had done that, opening a small gap at the very end of their line, a gap between the shields and the stream's deep gully. It was only two or three paces wide, but Thorolf was tempted by it. He had defeated the best that Constantine could hurl against him, now he

344

saw a chance to turn the enemy's flank. If he could lead men through the gap, turn on Constantine's flank and so widen the gap, we could get behind the Scottish shield wall, panic it, and start a collapse that would spread up the enemy's line.

Thorolf did not ask Egil, nor me, he just moved some of his best men to the right of the line, then stalked in front of the shield wall, taunting the Scots, daring any of them to come and fight him. None did. He was a daunting man, tall and broad-shouldered, with a heavy-browed face beneath his shining helmet that was crowned with an eagle's wing. He carried a shield with his family's eagle emblem, and in his right hand was his favourite weapon, a heavy, long-hafted war axe that he called Blood-Drinker. He wore gold at his neck, his thick forearms were bright with arm rings, he looked what he was, a Norse warrior of renown.

And suddenly, as he paced the line, he turned and ran for the gap, bellowing at his men to follow. They did. Thorolf put down the first man by slashing Blood-Drinker in a blow so powerful that it beat down the shield and buried itself in the man's neck, cleaving down to his heart. Thorolf was bellowing, driving on, but his axe was lodged in the mangled ribs of his first victim, and a spear took him in the side. He shouted in anger, his voice rising to a scream as he stumbled and more Scotsmen came. They were part of Constantine's reserve and the king sent them fast and the spears stabbed, the swords lunged and Thorolf Skallagrimmrson died at the stream's edge, his mail slashed and pierced, his blood draining to reeds beside the swirling water. The Scotsman who had first speared Thorolf wrenched Blood-Drinker free and swung it at the next Norseman, clouting his shield so hard that he was hurled down into the stream's gully. The Scots hurled spears at him and he rolled into the water, reddening it as his mail-weighted body sank.

The men who had followed Thorolf retreated fast and it was the turn of the Scots to jeer and taunt. The spearman who had killed Thorolf flaunted Blood-Drinker, calling on us to come and be killed. 'That man is mine,' Egil said. I had gone to join him.

'I'm sorry,' I said.

'He was a good man.' Egil had tears in his eyes, then drew his sword, Adder, and pointed it at the Scotsman who was flourishing Thorolf's axe, 'and that man is mine.'

Then the great drum, hidden somewhere behind Anlaf's men, thumped the air in a new and faster rhythm, a huge cheer sounded, and Anlaf's Norsemen started down the slope.

Those Norsemen bellowed their challenge and came in an undisciplined rush. Many were *úlfheðnar* and thought themselves invincible, believing that sheer rage and violence would shatter the large West Saxon contingent on Æthelstan's left. I did not know it, but Æthelstan himself had moved to that flank to take command of his West Saxons, and the moment he saw the Norse begin their charge he ordered a retreat.

That was one of the most difficult things any commander has to achieve. To keep the shield wall tight while walking backwards needed rigid discipline, the men had to keep their shields touching as they stepped back, and all the time seeing a shrieking horde racing towards them, but the West Saxons were amongst the best of our warriors and I heard a voice calling out the steps as they steadily backed away. The men beside the smaller stream were being constricted by the gully and I saw files breaking off to form another rank behind the three who steadily moved back, bending Æthelstan's battle line into the shape of a bow. Then, after about twenty backward paces, they stopped, the shields clattered as they were aligned, and the Norsemen struck. Their charge was ragged, the bravest men reaching the West Saxons first and leaping at the shields as if they could hurtle through Æthelstan's ranks by sheer speed, but the spears met them, the shields crashed together, and the West Saxons held firm. The charge of the Norsemen roused the rest of Anlaf's line that surged forward and the battle seemed to wake up, the din of swords beating on blades and shields rose, and the screaming began again. The black-shields of Strath Clota were clawing at my men, the Scots were trying to clear the dead out of their path to reach us, with the man holding Thorolf's axe leading them. 'The bastard,' Egil said.

'No—' I began, but Egil was gone, screaming at his men to get out of his way. The Scotsman saw him coming, and I saw a fleeting look of alarm on his face, but then he roared his own challenge, hefted his blue-painted shield and swung the axe as Egil burst through his own front rank.

The Scotsman was a fool. He had been trained with sword and spear, the axe was an unfamiliar weapon and he swung it wildly, thinking that brute force would smash Egil's shield aside, but Egil checked his rush, swayed back, the axe went on swinging and he lunged with Adder as the Scotsman desperately tried to check the axe's weight. Adder slid into the man's belly, he folded over the pain, Egil hammered his eagle-painted shield into the man's face, twisted the sword, ripped it up and dragged it out to spill the man's guts onto Thorolf's corpse. The axe flew into the stream as Egil struck with Adder again and again, slashing the dying man's head and shoulders until one of his men pulled him back as the Scots came to avenge the bloodied man.

'I feel useless,' I snarled at Finan.

'Leave it to the youngsters,' Finan told me patiently, 'you taught them.'

'We need to fight!'

'If they need old men,' Finan said, 'then things will be desperate.' He turned to watch Æthelstan's West Saxons. 'They're doing well.'

The West Saxons were still retreating, but steadily, bending the line back and drawing the Mercians in the centre back with them. Anlaf, I reckoned, must think this battle won. His larger force had not broken Æthelstan's shield wall, but he was forcing it back and soon he would have us trapped against the larger stream. I could see Anlaf now, galloping on a great black horse, bellowing at his men to attack all along the line. His sword was drawn and he pointed it towards us and his ugly face was distorted by fury. He knew he had won this battle, his plan had worked, but he still had to break us and he was impatient. He neared Constantine and shouted something I could not hear over the battle-rage, but Constantine spurred his horse forward and yelled at his men.

Who came again. It was pride now. Who could be first to break us? The Norse were hammering at Æthelstan's left and centre, and now the Scots came to prove they were the equal of Anlaf's wild warriors. I saw Domnall bully his way to the front rank, an axe in his hand, and he led a charge against Egil while Prince Cellach came against my men. Cellach's men screamed as they charged, and again some tripped in the holes, and others were pushed from behind and stumbled on corpses, but they came with levelled spears and bright axes, and I glanced once at the ridge to the west, saw nothing, and went to join my men who were being pushed back by the Scots. Berg, who commanded my left wing, was shouting at men to keep their shields firm, but there was an anger in the Scots that made them terrible. I saw Rolla go down, his helmet split by an axe, saw Cellach move into the gap and kill Edric, who had once been my servant, and more men were following Cellach. The prince's sword was bloodied and he now faced Oswi who blocked a lunge with his shield and rammed his seax forward, only to have it knocked aside by Cellach's shield. Cellach was in a battle-rage. He slammed Oswi with his shield, throwing him backwards, then bellowed a challenge at the men in the third rank. One swung an axe, Cellach knocked it aside with his sword, lunged at Beornoth who managed to parry the blade with his seax, and Cellach thrust the shield again. Oswi somehow wriggled free, his right leg mangled by a spear thrust, and Cellach drew his sword back for another lunge. His furious attack had served as a makeshift swine-wedge, and it had gored through my two front ranks. Cellach only had to break through Beornoth and he would be through our line, followed by a mass of men. Our shield wall would be pierced, the battle lost, and Cellach knew it.

'To me!' I called to Finan's men we had kept in reserve, and I ran to the shield wall where Cellach was screaming victory as he hammered Beornoth with his iron-bossed shield. I pushed Beornoth aside and rammed my own shield forward, throwing Cellach back. I was bigger than the Scottish prince, taller, heavier, and just as savage, and my shield hurled him back two paces. He recognised me, he knew me, he even liked me, but he would kill me. He had been my hostage as a child and I had begun his education, teaching him shield-craft and sword-skill, and I had come to like him, but now I would kill him. Finan was beside me, his men behind us, as we pushed forward to fill the gap Cellach had opened. Cellach was fighting with his long-sword, I had Wasp-Sting. 'Go back, boy,' I snarled at him, though he was no longer a boy, he was a grown warrior, heir to Scotland's crown, and he would win this battle for his father and for Anlaf, but a long-sword is no weapon for a shield wall. He stabbed it at me, my shield caught it and I kept the shield going forward, driving his blade back, and that turned him and I rammed the heavy shield

349

further forward and Finan, now on my right, saw the opening and lunged his seax to pierce Cellach's mail at his waist. Cellach instinctively rammed his shield down to knock away Finan's seax and so opened his fate to Wasp-Sting. He knew it. He looked at me, he knew he had made a mistake, and there was almost a look of pleading on his face as I slid Wasp-Sting over his shield's rim to slice his gullet. The blood sprayed into my face, momentarily blinding me, but I felt Cellach drag down Wasp-Sting's blade as he fell.

'So much for old men,' Finan said, then slashed his seax at a bearded, blood-soaked man trying to avenge Cellach. He cut through the man's wrist, then sliced his blade up to slash his cheek open. The man staggered back and Finan let him go. Someone dragged Cellach's body back out of our shield wall. A prince would have valuable mail, gold-studded scabbards, silver on his belts, and gold about his neck, and my men knew I shared the plunder of battle with them.

Finan's men had repaired our shield wall, but the Scots were enraged by their prince's death. They had retreated beyond the gory line of corpses, but would come again, and Domnall would lead them. He came from my right, shouting at his men to avenge Cellach. He was a tall man, reputed to be a beast in a fight, and he wanted a fight now. He wanted to savage his way through our shield wall and he wanted my death as payment for Cellach, and he leaped the corpses, bellowing rage, and Finan went to meet him.

It was a huge angry Scot with a long-sword fighting a small Irishman armed with a seax, but Finan was the fastest swordsman I had ever seen. The Scots had started forward, but paused to watch Domnall. He was their king's war-leader, an indomitable man with a reputation, but he was also enraged, and though rage can win battles it can also blind a man. He swung his huge sword at Finan who took a step back, Domnall thrust his shield forward to knock Finan off balance, but Finan sidestepped and whipped his seax forward to pierce the mail just above the wrist of Domnall's sword arm. He stepped back again as the iron-bound shield came in a massive swing intended to batter Finan to the ground, but the Irishman went to his right with snake speed and the seax swept up to slice into Domnall's shield arm, and Finan, still moving to his right, now moved into his opponent and rammed the seax through Domnall's mail, through the leather beneath, and into the ribs beneath the armpit. Domnall staggered back, wounded but not beaten, and the rage had gone to be replaced by a cold determination.

The Scots were chanting at Domnall, urging him on, just as my men were shouting for Finan. Domnall was hurt, but he was a huge man who could absorb a lot of hurt and keep fighting. He had learned of Finan's speed, but reckoned he could counter it with sheer strength and so he swept the sword again in a blow that would have felled an ox. Finan caught the blow on his shield, and it was strong enough to jar him off balance and Domnall's shield slammed into the smaller man and Finan was thrown backwards. Domnall followed, but hesitated when Finan recovered fast, and instead the big Scotsman covered himself with his scarred shield and held the sword level, inviting Finan to attack. He wanted to keep the Irishman at sword's length so the much shorter seax could do no more damage. 'Come, you bastard,' he growled, and Finan accepted the invitation, moving to his right, away from Domnall's sword, but his foot appeared to tread on a wounded man and he staggered. His sword arm flailed and Domnall saw the opening and lunged the sword, but Finan had only pretended to stumble. He pushed himself off with his right foot, moving fast to his left, lowering his shield to deflect the lunge across his body, and the seax sliced with wicked speed to chop into Domnall's neck. Domnall's bright helmet had a mail skirt to protect his neck, but the seax drove through it, the blood was sudden, and Finan, teeth-gritted, was sawing the blade back as Domnall fell. And the Scots roared in anger, clambering over the dead and dying to avenge their leader, and Finan dodged back into the shield wall as the enemy came. I shouted our wall forward to meet them where the dead made an obstacle and there was the hard clash of shield on shield. We shoved against the enemy as they pushed against us. The man pressing on my shield was screaming at me, his spittle flying over our shields' rims. I could smell the ale on his breath, feel the blows on my shield as he tried to thrust a seax into my belly. He managed to use the boss of his shield to lurch mine to the left and I felt his seax slide by my waist, then he gave a choking cry as Vidarr Leifson cut his shoulder with an axe, just as an axe from the Scottish second rank slammed down onto my battered shield. The blow split the iron binding and splintered the willow and I pushed it to the left to open my assailant's body, and Immar Hergildson, who had been so terrified at dawn, thrust his spear from our second rank and the man went down.

We held them. They had attacked with an extraordinary savagery, but we were defended by the ridge of bodies. It is impossible to hold a shield wall tight when stepping on corpses and wounded men, and Scottish bravery was not enough. Our shield wall was tight, theirs was ragged, and again they retreated, unwilling to die on our blades. Vidarr Leifson hooked Domnall's corpse with his axe and dragged it with its rich plunder back into our ranks. The Scots jeered, but did not come again.

I left my son in command of the shield wall and went back with Finan. 'I thought you were too old to fight,' I growled at him.

'Domnall was old too. He should have known better.'

'Did he touch you?'

'Bruised, nothing more. I'll live. What happened to your knife?'

I looked down and saw that my small knife had gone. The sheath, that hung from one of my sword belts, had been cut away, presumably by the spitting Scot who had managed one lunge with his seax. He had been left-handed and if his seax had been an inch closer he would have sliced my waist. 'It wasn't valuable,' I said. 'Only used it for eating.' And if that was the worst that happened to me in this battle I would be fortunate.

We went to the ground behind the wall where our wounded lay. Hauk, Vidarr's son, was there, being bandaged by a priest I did not know. It had been his first battle and the mangled mail and blood at his right shoulder suggested it would be his last. Roric was piling plunder that included Cellach's rich helmet that was inlaid with gold tracery and crowned with eagle feathers. If we survived there would be many such rich pickings from this battle. 'Get back in the line,' I told Roric.

The deaths of Cellach and Domnall had prompted another pause. The Scots had attacked, they had so nearly broken us, but we had held and there were now more bodies between us, some crying, most dead. The stench of blood and shit was too familiar. I looked left and saw the Mercians were also holding, but our line, even though it had shrunk its width, was perilously thin. The Mercians appeared to have no reserve at all, and too many wounded men were on the ground behind their wall. Anlaf had gone back to his right wing that had pushed Æthelstan's West Saxons to the road, meaning the northern end of the bridge was now in Norse hands. The road to Ceaster was open, guarded only by a small group of West Saxons who had made a shield wall at the bridge's southern end, but Anlaf did not care. Ceaster could wait; all he wanted now was to slaughter us beside the stream and he was shrieking at his Norsemen to kill Æthelstan's West Saxons. A horseman came from that fight, galloping along the rear of our shield wall, and I saw it was Bishop Oda. 'For God's sake, lord,' he shouted, 'the king needs help!'

We all needed help. The enemy was scenting victory and pressing hard on our left and centre. The West Saxons had tried and failed to regain the northern end of the bridge and, like the Mercians, were now being pushed hard. Anlaf was summoning reinforcements to face the West Saxons. He had reserves, we had almost none, though Steapa and his horsemen were still hidden. 'Lord!' Oda shouted at me. 'Even a few men!'

I took a dozen, reckoning I could not spare more. The Mercians were closer to Æthelstan, but their shield wall dared not be thinned. Our whole shield wall was now half the length it had been when we started and it was dangerously thin, but the battle was fiercest where Æthelstan's bright banner flew. Oda trotted his horse beside me. 'The king insists on fighting! He shouldn't be in the front rank!'

'He's a king,' I said, 'he has to lead!'

'Where's Steapa?' Oda asked, and there was pure panic in his voice.

'He's coming!' I shouted, hoping I was right.

Then we reached the wounded men pulled from Æthelstan's West Saxons and I led my few men into the ranks, pushing men aside, bellowing at them to make way. Folcbald, the huge Frisian, and his cousin Wibrund were both with me, and they forced a passage to where Æthelstan was fighting. He was magnificent! His fine mail was covered in Norse blood, his shield was broken open in at least three places, and his sword was red to the hilt, yet still he fought, inviting the enemy to come to his blade. That enemy had to step over bodies, and even the *úlfheðnar* among them were reluctant. They wanted Æthelstan dead, knew that his slaughter would be the beginning of his army's utter defeat, but to kill him they had to face his quick sword. To the left and to the right of the king there were scarlet-cloaked men pushing forward, shields crashing against Norse shields, spears slicing forward and axes splitting willow-boards, but there was a space around Æthelstan. He was the king of battle, he dominated them, he taunted them, and then a tall, black-bearded Norseman with bright blue eyes beneath a scarred helmet, and with a long-hafted battleaxe stepped into the space. It was Thorfinn Hausakljúfr, Jarl of Orkneyjar, who looked half-crazed, and I suspected he had smeared his skin with the henbane ointment. He was no longer just a Norse chieftain, he had become an *úlfheðinn*, a wolf-warrior, and he howled at Æthelstan and hefted his vast battleaxe. 'Time to die, pretty boy!' he shouted, though I doubted Æthelstan understood the Norse, but he understood Thorfinn's intent, and he let the big man come. Thorfinn was fighting without a shield, just carrying *Hausakljúfr*, his famous axe. Like Æthelstan he was blood-soaked, but I could see no wound. The blood was Saxon blood and Skull-Splitter wanted more.

He swung the axe one-handed, Æthelstan met it with his shield and I saw the blade split the willow-boards. Æthelstan swung the shield to his left, hoping to take the axe with it and so open Thorfinn's body to a lunge from his sword, but Thorfinn was fast. He stepped back, wrenched his axe free and slammed it down, aiming for Æthelstan's sword arm. The blow should have severed the king's arm, but Æthelstan was just as fast, pulling the sword back, and the great axe crashed onto the blade close to the hilt. There was an ominous-sounding crack and I saw that the king's sword had broken and Æthelstan now held a blade no longer than a man's hand. Thorfinn shouted in triumph and swept the axe back. Æthelstan met it with his battered shield, stepped back, the axe swept again and again beat into the shield that was now ragged with holes, and Thorfinn raised his axe to bring it hard down onto Æthelstan's gold-ringed helmet.

And Bishop Oda was beside me, off his horse, screaming in his native Danish for the king to hold fast, and Oda pulled Serpent-Breath from my scabbard. Æthelstan raised his shield, caught the downward blow that split the shield almost in two, then Oda, screaming the king's name, threw Serpent-Breath hilt first. Æthelstan had been driven to his knees by the force of the shield-splitting blow, but heard Oda, he turned and snatched Serpent-Breath out of the air, swept it hard to cut into Thorfinn's left thigh, dragged it back, then stood and rammed the splintered shield into Thorfinn's face. The big Norseman stepped back to give *Hausakljúfr* the space for a killing blow and Æthelstan, fast as the lightning on his flag, rammed Serpent-Breath forward, kept ramming, driving the blade deep into Thorfinn's belly, then wrenching it up and down, side to side, and Skull-Splitter fell, Thorfinn fell with his axe, and Æthelstan had a bloodied boot on his enemy's chest as he ripped Serpent-Breath free.

And Steapa came.

We did not know of Steapa's coming at first. Folcbald and Wibrund were at my side, and we were fighting off a surge of furious Norsemen who came to avenge Thorfinn's death. Gerbruht, who was one of my most loyal men, was on my right, trying to protect me with his shield and I had to snarl at him to move it aside to give me room to lunge Wasp-Sting. My shield was hard against a Norse shield, the man was trying to skewer me with his sword, and I shouldered Gerbruht aside, let the Norseman slide his blade between our shields, and I met it with Wasp-Sting's razor-sharp edge, letting the man slide his forearm against the seax until the

356

pain made him draw back. His tendons and flesh were cut to the bone and it was easy to thrust Wasp-Sting up into his ribs. All he could do now was batter me with his shield, his sword arm was useless, he could not step back because of the press of men behind him, and I was content to let his body shield me while the blood drained from his sliced wrist. And then, over the shouts and the clangour of the blades, I heard the hoofbeats.

Steapa had been hidden on the western hill among the autumn trees just behind the broken palisade of Brynstæþ. He had been ordered to wait until the battle had turned, until Æthelstan's left wing had been forced back against the streams and the enemy would be fighting with their backs to the western ridge.

And now he came, leading five hundred mail-bright horsemen on big stallions. Anlaf had thought to use the slight slope to assault Æthelstan's left, and now Steapa was using the steeper slope of the ridge to launch a thunderbolt at Anlaf's rear. And Anlaf's men knew it. The pressure on our line lessened as Norsemen shouted warnings of the attack coming from their rear, an attack that came down the ridge's slope like a flood of doom. 'Now!' Æthelstan shouted. 'Forward!' Men who had thought themselves doomed saw rescue, and the whole West Saxon line went forward in a howling rush.

The horsemen hurled the stallions at the lesser stream. Most leaped the gully, some scrambled through, and I saw at least two horses fall, but the charge came on, the noise of the hooves a rising thunder over which I could hear the shouts of the riders. Almost all Steapa's men carried spears, the points lowered as they neared the back of Anlaf's shield wall.

Where there was chaos. The back of a shield wall is where the wounded are dragged, where servants hold horses, where a scatter of archers loose their bows, and those men, at least those who could move, ran to take shelter in the shield wall's rearmost rank. That rank had turned, was desperately trying to make a wall, their shields touching, but the panicked men pushed them aside, screaming for help, and then the horsemen struck.

Horses will shy away from a shield wall, but the men seeking shelter had opened the wall to leave gaps and the horses kept coming. They struck with the fury of the *úlfhéðnar*, they pierced the wall wherever there was an opening and the spears shattered mail and ribs, the horses reared, they flailed hooves and snapped at terrified men, and the shield wall broke in terror. Men just ran. West Saxon horsemen discarded spears and drew swords. I saw Steapa, terrible in his anger, slash his great sword down to cut a man deep into his chest. The man was dragged along by the blade as Steapa turned northwards to pursue the fleeing enemy. And we went forward into the chaos. The shield wall in front of us, till now an impenetrable barrier, broke apart and we began killing in a frenzy. I picked up a dead Norseman's sword because now, with the enemy scattering, was no time for the close work of a seax. This was the slaughter time. The fleeing enemy had their backs to us and they died fast. Some turned to fight, but were overwhelmed by vengeful pursuers. The luckiest of the enemy had horses and spurred away northwards, most following the Roman road towards Dingesmere. Steapa's men followed, while Æthelstan shouted for his horse to be fetched. His bodyguard, all in their distinctive scarlet cloaks, were mounting their stallions. I saw Æthelstan, still with Serpent-Breath in his hand, climb into his saddle and spur towards the pursuit.

The Scots, being furthest from the place where Steapa's horsemen had shattered the shield wall, were the last to break. It took them a few moments to even realise the disaster, but seeing their pagan allies broken they too turned and fled. I was looking for Ræt and my horse, then realised he must have crossed the bridge before Æthelstan's men retreated past it. I looked towards the encampment and bellowed his name, but could not see him. Then Wibrund brought me a bay stallion. 'He probably belongs to one of the king's bodyguard, lord,' he said, 'and that man's probably dead.'

'Help me up!'

I spurred northwards, shouting for Egil as I neared my men. He turned and looked at me. 'Don't pursue!' I called to him. 'Stay here!'

'Why?'

'You're Norsemen. You think Æthelstan's men will know the difference?' I called for Berg, Egil's youngest brother, and told him to keep twenty Christians to guard Egil's troops, then I spurred on. Finan and my son wanted to come with me, but had no horses. 'Catch up with me!' I shouted at them.

My borrowed stallion picked his way through the piles of corpses that marked where the shield walls had met. Some of the dead were my men. I recognised Roric, his throat slashed open, his face drenched in blood, and I suspected I had sent him to his death when I ordered him to leave the plunder. Beornoth, a good fighter who had met a better one, now lay on his back, a look of surprise on his face where flies crawled across his open eyes and mouth. I could not see what had killed him. Oswi, his face pale, lay with his mangled leg tightly bandaged and he tried to smile. Blood seeped through the bandages. 'You'll live,' I told him, 'I've seen others worse.' There would be others, too many others, just as there would be widows and orphans in Constantine's land. Once past the stinking ridge of bodies I put spurs to the horse.

It was late afternoon, the shadows were lengthening, and I was surprised by that. The battle had seemed short to me, short and terrifying, yet it must have lasted much longer than I realised. The clouds were clearing and the sun threw shadows from the corpses of men who had been killed as they tried to run away. Men were plundering the bodies, stripping mail, searching for coins. The crows and ravens would come soon to enjoy the battle feast. The heathland was littered with swords, spears, axes, bows, helmets, and countless shields, all thrown away by men desperate to escape our pursuit. I could see Steapa's horsemen ahead. They were riding just fast enough to overtake the fugitives who they would cripple with a spear or a slash of a sword, then leave them to be killed by the men who followed on foot. I could see Æthelstan's banner, the victorious dragon with its lightning bolt, on the Roman road and I spurred towards it. I came to the low rise of ground where Anlaf's army had assembled and checked the stallion because the view was so startling. The wide shallow valley was filled with fleeing men, and behind them and among them were our merciless troops. They were wolves among sheep. I saw men try to yield, saw them cut down, and knew that Æthelstan's men, freed from the almost certain doom of imminent defeat, were releasing their relief in an orgy of slaughter.

I stayed on the higher ground, watching in amazement. I felt relief too, and a strange detachment as if this was not my battle. This was Æthelstan's victory. I touched my chest, feeling for the hammer amulet I had hidden beneath my mail, fearing to be mistaken for an enemy pagan. I had not expected to survive, despite the sorcery of Benedetta's cross. When the enemy had come in sight, that great horde of shields and blades, I had sensed a doom. Yet here I was, watching a gleeful slaughter. A man staggered past, miraculously drunk, carrying an ornate helmet and an empty scabbard decorated with silver plaques. 'We beat them, lord!' he called.

'We beat them,' I agreed, and thought of Alfred. This was how his dream was coming true. His dream of a godly country, one country for all the Saxons, and I knew Northumbria was no more. My country was gone. This was now Englaland, born in a welter of killing in a valley of blood.

'The Lord has wrought a great thing!' a voice called to me, and I turned to see Bishop Oda riding from behind. He was smiling. 'God has given us the victory!' He held out his hand and I grasped it with my left hand, my right still holding the borrowed sword. 'And you wear the cross, lord!' he said with delight.

'Benedetta gave it to me.'

'To protect you?'

'So she said.'

'And it has! Come, lord!' He spurred his horse and I followed, thinking how women's sorcery had protected me through the years.

There was one last fight before that day ended. The Scottish and Norse chieftains were mounted on swift horses and they outpaced the pursuit, galloping desperately towards the safety of the ships, but some men stayed to delay us. They formed a shield wall on a low rise and among them I saw Ingilmundr and realised that these must be the men who lived in Wirhealum. They had been granted the land, they had pretended to be Christians, their women and children still lived in the steadings of Wirhealum and now they would fight for their homes. There were no more than three hundred men in two ranks, their shields touching. They surely knew they must die, or perhaps they believed mercy would be given. Æthelstan's men faced them in a ragged crowd over a thousand strong and growing larger every minute. Steapa's men on tired horses were there, as was Æthelstan's mounted bodyguard.

Ingilmundr walked out of the shield wall, going towards Æthelstan who still held Serpent-Breath. I saw him talk to the king, but could not hear what he said, nor what Æthelstan answered, but after a moment Ingilmundr knelt in submission. He laid his sword on the ground, which surely meant that Æthelstan was letting him live, for no pagan would die without a sword in his hand. Oda thought the same. 'The king is too merciful,' he said disapprovingly.

Æthelstan urged his horse forward till he was close to Ingilmundr. He leaned from the saddle and said something and I saw Ingilmundr smile and nod. Then Æthelstan struck, Serpent-Breath slicing down in a sudden savage stroke, and the blood spurted from Ingilmundr's neck, and Æthelstan struck again, and again, and his men cheered and swarmed forward to overwhelm the Norsemen. There was the hammering of shields again, the clash of blades, the screams, but it was over so quickly and the pursuit went on leaving a rill of dead and dying men on the small rise.

By dusk we had reached Dingesmere and could see the escaping ships rowing into the Mærse. Almost all were gone, but most of those fleeing ships were empty, the crews left to guard them had taken them to sea to escape pursuit and so abandoned hundreds of enemy who were slaughtered in the shallow waters of the marsh. Some begged for mercy, but Æthelstan's men had none and the water between the rushes turned red.

Finan and my son had found me and watched with me. 'It's over, then,' Finan said in a tone of disbelief.

'It's over,' I agreed. 'We can go home.' And I suddenly longed for Bebbanburg, for the clean sea and the long beach and the wind from the water.

Æthelstan found me. He looked stern. His mail, cloak, horse, and saddle cloth were stained dark with blood. 'Well done, lord King,' I said.

'God gave us the victory.' He sounded tired, and no wonder, for I doubted that any man had fought harder in the shield wall that day. He looked down at Serpent-Breath and gave me a wry smile. 'She served me well, lord.'

'She's a great sword, lord King.'

He held her out to me, hilt first. 'You will dine with me tonight, Lord Uhtred.'

'As you command,' I said and took the sword gratefully. I could not put her in the scabbard till she was cleaned, so I tossed away my borrowed sword and held Serpent-Breath as we rode back down the long road in the gathering dark. Women were searching the dead, using long knives to kill those close to death before plundering the bodies. The first fires pricked the early dark.

It was over.

EPILOGUE

I am Uhtred, son of Uhtred, who was the son of Uhtred, and his father was also called Uhtred, and they were all lords of Bebbanburg. I am that too, though these days folk call me the Lord of the North. My lands stretch from the wind-beaten North Sea to the shores facing Ireland and, though I am old, my task is to stop the Scots coming south into the land we have learned to call Englaland.

I have imposed peace on Cumbria. I did it by sending my son and Egil to punish those who would cause trouble. They hanged some, burned steadings, and gave land to men who had fought on the heath at Wirhealum. Much of Cumbria is still occupied by Danes and Norsemen, but they live in peace with the Saxons, and their children have learned to speak the Saxon tongue and some now worship the nailed god of the Christians. We are proud to be Northumbrians, yet we are all Ænglisc now and Æthelstan is called the King of Englaland. His shattered sword hangs in his great hall at Wintanceaster, though I have not travelled south to see it. He was generous to me, rewarding me with gold and silver taken at the field on Wirhealum where so many men lie buried.

There was a feast three days after the battle. Æthelstan had wanted it on the night of the battle, but men were too tired, there were too many injured who needed care, and so he waited until he could gather his leaders in Ceaster. There was more ale than food, and what food there was did not taste good. There was bread, some hams, and a stew that I suspected was horse-flesh. Maybe a hundred and twenty men gathered in Ceaster's great hall after Bishop Oda held a service in the church. A harpist played but did not sing, because no song could match the slaughter we had endured. It was called a victory feast, and I suppose it was, but until the ale had loosened men's tongues, it felt like a funeral. Æthelstan gave a speech in which he lamented the loss of two ealdormen, Ælfine and Æthelwyn, but then spread praise among the men listening from the benches. He raised a cheer when he singled out Steapa, who had taken a spear thrust in his shield arm when his horsemen had shattered Anlaf's shield wall. He named me too, calling me the warlord of Englaland. Men cheered.

Englaland! I remember first hearing that name and finding it strange. King Alfred had dreamed of an Englaland and I had been with him when he marched from the marshes of Sumersæte to assault the great army led by Anlaf's grand-father. 'We were supposed to die at Ethandun,' Alfred had once said to me, 'but God was on our side. There will always be an Englaland.' I had not believed him, yet over the long years I had fought for that dream, not always willingly, and now Alfred's grandson had conquered the northern alliance and Englaland stretched from the Scottish hills to the southern sea. 'God gave us this country,' Æthelstan declaimed in Ceaster's hall, 'and God will keep it.'

Yet Æthelstan's god allowed both Anlaf and Constantine to escape the slaughter of Wirhealum. Anlaf is in Dyflin, muttering that he will return, and perhaps he will because he is young, ambitious, and bitter. I am told that the king of the Scots has relinquished his throne and gone to live in a monastery and that his realm is now ruled by Indulf, his second son. There are still cattle raids across my northern border, but fewer, because when we find the raiders we kill them and nail their heads to trees to warn others what awaits them.

The dragon and the star did not lie. The danger came from the north, and the dragon died on the heath of Wirhealum. Domnall and Cellach died there. So did Anlaf Cenncairech who was known as Scabbyhead. He was King of Hlymrekr in Ireland, forced to fight at Wirhealum by his conqueror whose name he shared. Owain of Strath Clota fell too, cut down by Sihtric's men amidst his blackshields. Gibhleachán, King of the Suðreyjar islands, was speared from behind as he tried to flee. The poets say seven kings died, and perhaps they did, but some were mere chieftains who just called themselves kings. I rule more land than some kings, but call myself the Lord of Bebbanburg and that is the only title I have ever wanted, and it will belong to my son and to his son. I sometimes sit on the terrace outside the great hall and look at the men and women who serve me, and then I gaze at the endless sea, at the clouds building over the inland hills, at the walls I have made higher, and I murmur thanks to the gods who have looked after me for so long.

Benedetta sits with me, her head on my shoulder, and sometimes she looks towards the hall I built at the fortress's northern end and she smiles. My wife lives there. Æthelstan insisted on the marriage, sometimes I think to mock me, and so Eldrida the piglet became my wife. I had thought Benedetta would be enraged, but she was amused. 'Poor child,' she said, and has ignored her ever since. Eldrida is scared of me and even more scared of Benedetta, but she delivered me her lands in Cumbria, and that was her purpose. I try to be kind to her, but all she wants is to pray. I built her a private chapel and she brought two priests to Bebbanburg and I hear their prayers whenever I go near the Sea Gate. She tells me she prays for me, and perhaps that is why I still live.

Finan also lives, but he is slower now. So am I. We must both die soon. Finan asks that his body be taken to Ireland to sleep with his ancestors, and Egil, who has a Norseman's endless desire to be at sea, has promised he will fulfil that wish. My only request is to die with a sword in my hand, and so Benedetta and I share our bed with Serpent-Breath. Bury her with me, I tell my son, and he has promised that my sword will go to Valhalla with me. And in that great hall of the gods I will meet so many men that I once fought, who I killed, and we shall feast together and watch the middle-earth beneath us and see men fight as we once fought, and so the world will go on till Ragnarok's chaos engulfs it.

And until the day when I shall go to the hall of the gods I shall stay in Bebbanburg. I fought for Bebbanburg. It was stolen from me, I recaptured it, and I have held it against all my enemies, and whenever I sit on the terrace I wonder if, a thousand years from now, the fortress will still stand, still unconquered, still brooding over the sea and the land. I think it will remain until Ragnarok comes, when the seas will boil, the land shatter and the skies turn to fire, and there the story will end.

Wyrd bið ful āræd.

Never before in this island was there such slaughter.
Anglo-Saxon Chronicle, AD 938,
on the Battle of Brunanburh

HISTORICAL NOTE

The Battle of Brunanburh was fought in the autumn of AD 937. Æthelstan, monarch of the kingdoms of Wessex, Mercia and East Anglia, defeated an army led by Anlaf Guthfrithson, King of Dyflin in Ireland, and by Constantine of Scotland. They were joined by the men of Strath Clota, by the Norse warriors of what are now the Orkneys and the Hebrides, and by sympathetic Northmen from Northumbria. They were defeated. The *Anglo-Saxon Chronicle* broke into verse to celebrate the victory, noting 'never was there such slaughter in our islands'. For years afterwards it was simply known as 'the great battle'.

It was undoubtedly a great battle and a terrible slaughter, and it was also one of the most important battles ever to have been fought on British soil. Michael Livingston, who is surely the greatest expert on Brunanburh, notes in his book, *The Battle of Brunanburh: A Casebook*, that 'the men who fought and died on that field forged a political map of the future that remains with us today, arguably making the Battle of Brunanburh one of the most significant battles in the long history not just of England, but of the whole of the British Isles . . . in one day, on one field, the fate of a nation was determined'.

That nation was England, and Brunanburh is its founding moment. When Uhtred's story began, there were four Saxon kingdoms, Wessex, Mercia, East Anglia, and Northumbria, and King Alfred had a dream to unite them into one. To do that he needed to repel the invading Danes who had conquered Northumbria, East Anglia, and northern Mercia. Alfred's son Edward and his daughter Æthelflaed reconquered East Anglia and Mercia, but Northumbria remained stubbornly independent and ruled by Norsemen. Scotland lay to its north, Æthelstan's Saxon kingdom to the south, and both had an interest in its fate. Æthelstan wanted to fulfil his grandfather's dream of a united England, Constantine feared and resented the growing power of the Saxons, which could only grow more powerful if Northumbria became a part of England.

That growing power was demonstrated in AD 927 at Eamont Bridge in Cumbria when Æthelstan demanded the presence of Constantine and the rulers of Northumbria to swear loyalty to him. He had already demanded the same oath from Hywel of Dyfed. Æthelstan was now calling himself the *Monarchus Totius Brittaniae*, yet he was content to leave Guthfrith on Northumbria's throne. Guthfrith's death meant that his cousin, Anlaf of Dyflin, now had a claim to Northumbria's throne and it also led to unrest as Constantine increased his influence in Northumbria, especially in the western part, Cumbria. That unrest led to Æthelstan's invasion of Scotland in AD 934. His army and fleet reached the northernmost part of Constantine's kingdom, but it seems the Scots avoided any major battles, leaving Æthelstan free to pillage their land.

So the 'northern problem' became soured with hatred and humiliation. Constantine had been humiliated twice, first at Eamont Bridge, then by his inability to stop Æthelstan's invasion. He was intent on destroying, or at the least severely diminishing, the growing power of the Saxons, and so allied himself with Anlaf. Their intent, when they invaded Æthelstan's land in 937, was to take revenge on the Saxons and put Anlaf on Northumbria's throne where he would rule a buffer-state between Constantine and his most dangerous enemies. That attempt failed at Brunanburh and the Saxons incorporated Northumbria into their own country, and so the Kings of Wessex became the Kings of England. It is fair to say that before the battle there was no England. As dusk fell on that bloody field, there was.

By any measure that makes Brunanburh a significant battle, yet curiously it has been forgotten. Not only is it forgotten, but for centuries no one even knew where the battle had been fought. Many claims for the site of the battle have been put forward over the years, ranging from southern Scotland to County Durham or Yorkshire, and ingenious theories were advanced, mostly depending on the place name and on clues that could be drawn from ancient chronicles, but no certainty emerged. There were two major contenders. One insisted that the battle had to be fought close to the River Humber on England's east coast, the other favoured the Wirral on the west coast. In the twelfth century a monk called John of Worcester wrote a history in which he said that Anlaf and Constantine brought a fleet into the River Humber, and that assertion has bedeviled the argument ever since. Anlaf did indeed bring a strong fleet from Ireland, but it is fanciful to believe that he would sail that fleet halfway around the British coast to reach the Humber, when the crossing from Dublin to the English west coast is so direct and so short. What was lacking in the argument was any archaeological evidence, but in the last few years that evidence has at last been found by Wirral Archaeology who have discovered artefacts and grave pits that would place the Battle of Brunanburh firmly on the Wirral. The quickest way to locate the battle site is to say that if you are driving north on the M53 then the slaughter took place just to the north and west of Exit 4.

The various accounts of the battle, most written years or even centuries after the event, do record the death of a bishop during the preceding night. The unnamed bishop's death is attributed to Anlaf himself, who, in a feat similarly ascribed to King Alfred, infiltrated Æthelstan's camp in an attempt to assassinate Æthelstan, but instead discovered a bishop. There was no bishopric of Chester in 937, so my version is entirely fictional, as is Bishop Oda's snatching of Uhtred's sword at the height of the fighting. That story also comes from the chronicles, which claim that the bishop performed a miracle by supplying Æthelstan with a sword when the king's blade was shattered. Bishop Oda, son of Danish invaders, eventually became the Archbishop of Canterbury.

Was the battlefield decided in advance and marked by hazel rods? We have a fragment of a document called *Egil's Saga*, in which Egil Skallagrimmrson (a Norseman who apparently fought for Æthelstan) describes how the field was marked with hazel rods and mutually agreed as the place the armies would meet. It seems an extraordinary idea, but it was a convention of the period and I adopted it. Other sources claim that Æthelstan reacted late to the invasion, which poses the question why Constantine and Anlaf did not push further inland once they had concentrated their armies on the Wirral, and using an agreed battle site offers an explanation.

The Battle of Brunanburh was the founding event of England, though the Norse did not abandon their ambitions. Æthelstan died in 940, just three years after his great victory, and Anlaf returned to England and successfully took Northumbria's throne and then captured a swathe of northern Mercia. Æthelstan's successor, King Edmund, finally drove him out, re-establishing the kingdom of England that Æthelstan had won at Brunanburh.

The story of England's making is not well known, which strikes me as strange. I received a good education, but it passed swiftly over the Anglo-Saxon period, pausing to mention King Alfred, and then began a more detailed account at 1066. Yet William the Conqueror, himself the grandson of a Viking raider, captured a country which, at Alfred's death, did not even exist. Alfred undoubtedly dreamed of making one country, but it was his son, his daughter, and his grandson who made the dream come true. In AD 899, the year Alfred died, the Danes still ruled in Northumbria, East Anglia, and northern Mercia. There were still four kingdoms, and it was a miracle that Wessex had survived the onslaught. In AD 878 Alfred had been driven as a fugitive to the Somerset marshes, and it must have seemed as though Wessex would fall to the Danes. Instead, at the battle of Ethandun, Alfred defeated Guthrum and began the expansion of his territory that fifty-nine years later would see the slaughter at Brunanburh and the unification of the four Saxon kingdoms. It truly is an extraordinary tale.

AUTHOR NOTE

I am enormously grateful to Howard Mortimer of Wirral Archaeology who showed me many of the artefacts discovered at the battle site and generously gave me a tour of the Wirral. His colleague, Dave Capener, provided me with his written assessment of the battle, which I have largely copied in this fictional version. Cat Jarman, an archaeologist at the University of Bristol, was helpful with many queries, and it was Dr Jarman who identified the small knife discovered on the battlefield, which Wirral Archaeology so generously gave me. I am grateful to all the members of Wirral Archaeology who offered help and advice, and ask their forgiveness if I have somewhat simplified the battlefield to make it more understandable. I am also grateful to Michael Livingston who generously shared his thoughts with me, and am especially grateful that he reminded me of Beowulf's great age when he killed the dragon!

War Lord is dedicated to Alexander Dreymon, the actor who has brought Uhtred to life in the television series, and he must stand for all the extraordinary actors, producers, directors, writers, and technicians who have flattered these novels with their talents. I should also thank the wonderful people at my publishers, HarperCollins, who have been so supportive, as has my agent, Anthony Goff. Above all I owe thanks to my wife, Judy, who has endured fourteen years of shield walls and slaughter with her customary grace and patience. To all of them, thank you!

Also by Bernard Cornwell

The LAST KINGDOM Series
(formerly The WARRIOR Chronicles)
The Last Kingdom
The Pale Horseman
The Lords of the North
Sword Song
The Burning Land
Death of Kings
The Pagan Lord
The Empty Throne
Warriors of the Storm
The Flame Bearer
War of the Wolf
Sword of Kings
War Lord

Azincourt

The GRAIL QUEST Series
Harlequin
Vagabond
Heretic

1356

Stonehenge

The Fort

The STARBUCK Chronicles
Rebel
Copperhead
Battle Flag
The Bloody Ground

The WARLORD Chronicles
The Winter King
The Enemy of God
Excalibur

Fools and Mortals

Gallows Thief

A Crowning Mercy
Fallen Angels
(Originally published under the name Susannah Kells,
the pseudonym of Bernard Cornwell and his wife, Judy.)

Non-Fiction

Waterloo: The History of Four Days,
Three Armies and Three Battles

The SHARPE series
(in chronological order)

Sharpe's Tiger (1799)
Sharpe's Triumph (1803)
Sharpe's Fortress (1803)
Sharpe's Trafalgar (1805)
Sharpe's Prey (1807)
Sharpe's Rifles (1809)
Sharpe's Havoc (1809)
Sharpe's Eagle (1809)
Sharpe's Gold (1810)
Sharpe's Escape (1811)
Sharpe's Fury (1811)
Sharpe's Battle (1811)
Sharpe's Company (1812)
Sharpe's Sword (1812)
Sharpe's Enemy (1812)
Sharpe's Honour (1813)
Sharpe's Regiment (1813)
Sharpe's Siege (1814)
Sharpe's Revenge (1814)
Sharpe's Waterloo (1815)
Sharpe's Devil (1820-1821)

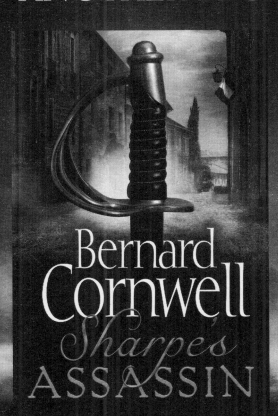

ONE STORY ENDS
ND ANOTHER BEGINS...

Bernard
Cornwell
Sharpe's
ASSASSIN

UHTRED'S WAR IS OVER, BUT
RICHARD SHARPE RETURNS...

Discover the iconic hero in the new novel
from Bernard Cornwell

COMING AUTUMN 2021